# UNDER A HAMMOCK MOON

and you can practically feel the heat of the sun of your face, the breeze in your hair and the scent of the hibiscus on the wind"

– John Grigsby, Lexington, Virginia, USA.

"I really enjoyed this book. Laughed my head off. Really hits home with life on the island"

– Tracy Rigby, Nevis, West Indies.

"A glorious Caribbean yarn. As a frequent visitor to the Caribbean I can attest to the accurate setting of this ripping yarn. With a mixture of humour, intrigue, sex, and drama, this book has it all"

– Ed Nealon, Perth, Australia.

"A book with a comfortable fast pace and very funny throughout. The Caribbean was merely on my list for a holiday, but now has moved to first place!"

– GAN.

"At one level it is a glorious romp through expatriate high life, at another it is a fun thriller for deckchair reading. However, more than that it is a hugely affectionate tribute to the islanders themselves and the challenges of everyday life and politics under the hot tropical sun. Enjoy"

– Stella Nokes, Banff, Canada.

# BOOKS BY GRAHAM LORD

## NOVELS

*Marshmallow Pie*
*A Roof Under Your Feet*
*The Spider and the Fly*
*God and All His Angels*
*The Nostradamus Horoscope*
*Time Out of Mind*
*A Party to Die For*
*Sorry, We're Going to Have to Let You Go*
*Under a Hammock Moon*

## AUTOBIOGRAPHY

*Ghosts of King Solomon's Mines*
*Lord's Ladies and Gentlemen: 100 Legends of the 20$^{th}$ Century*

## BIOGRAPHY

*Just the One: The Wives and Times of Jeffrey Bernard*
*James Herriot: The Life of a Country Vet*
*Dick Francis: A Racing Life*
*Arthur Lowe*
*Niv: The Authorised Biography of David Niven*
*John Mortimer: The Devil's Advocate*
*Joan Collins: The Biography of an Icon*

These books by Graham Lord can be ordered from
www.fernhillbooks.co.uk

# UNDER A HAMMOCK MOON

## BY

## GRAHAM LORD

Potbake Productions
Trincity, Trinidad and Tobago

First published in 2012 by
FERN HILL BOOKS

P. O. Box 902
Charlestown
Nevis
St Kitts and Nevis

Books may be ordered by contacting:

Potbake Productions
#3, 3rd Street West
Beaulieu Avenue
Trincity
Trinidad
www.potbake.com

ISBN: 978-976-95236-7-8

Graham Lord is a British author who has written nine novels, seven biographies, two autobiographies and several short stories. His books, which are all described on his website, www.graham-lord.com, have been translated into French, Italian, Portuguese, Dutch, German, Russian and Chinese.

He was born and educated in Southern Rhodesia (now Zimbabwe), raised in Mozambique, took an honours degree in History at Cambridge, and spent twenty-three years as Literary Editor of the *Sunday Express* in London, where he wrote a weekly column about books and met almost every major English language author of the 1960s to the 1990s, from P. G. Wodehouse and Graham Greene to Muriel Spark and Ruth Rendell.

After leaving the *Sunday Express* in 1992 to become a full-time author he wrote regularly for *The Daily Telegraph*, *The Times* and the *Daily Mail* and from 1994 to 1996 he edited the short story magazine *Raconteur*.

He has two daughters and lives in the West Indies and the South of France with the English artist, Juliet Lewis, who designed the cover of this book. He is about to publish a memoir of all the famous writers, actors and politicians he met during his forty years in Fleet Street. He has just published a memoir, *Lord's Ladies and Gentlemen: 100 Legends of the 20th Century*, and is now working on a new novel.

For Juliet

# CONTENTS

# CHAPTER 1

## WELCOME BY WE PARADISE

I flew from Barbados into the sunset and the island of Innocent in a cramped little nineteen-seater Carib Airlines Twin Otter with four vast white Americans and eleven massive black Innocentians jammed against each other in the tiny seats, their giant thighs packed together like supermarket chicken. How do these people get so *big*? They must eat six meals a day. There was also a pale, anorexic, middle-aged white English couple – probably vegetarians – and a rangy young Rastafarian who was wearing a garish tee-shirt depicting his 'Living God' (the very dead Emperor Haile Selassie of Ethiopia) and on his head a thicket of dreadlocks and what looked like a multi-coloured tea cosy. The airless little cabin stank of old sweat and new perfume.

You've never heard of Innocent? I'm not surprised. It's an insignificant speck of volcanic rock in the Caribbean between Barbados and St Vincent, just seven miles long and five miles wide. Columbus spotted it on the horizon in June 1502 as he passed by on his way to Hispaniola. He didn't bother to stop – why would you? – but he named it Inocente, saying that from a distance it looked like Paradise, a sinless Garden of Eden, and it looked pretty good from the sky, as well, as we came in to land. It's an old volcano, dormant but not extinct, 3,050ft high, with a peak like a wizard's pointed hat, a plump waist of mountainous jungle, a mini-skirt of dry lowland, and a narrow hem of white beach. It has about

1

nine thousand black inhabitants, most of them the descendants of British slaves, plus a few hundred Indian immigrants from Guyana and a couple of hundred British, American and Canadian expats on the run from snow, ice, drizzle and income tax. For them the island really is a paradise because it has no taxes, none at all: no income tax, wealth tax, capital gains tax or death duties. The government is funded by hundreds of dubious offshore financial institutions that pay it handsomely to shelter them from the laws and demands of the tax authorities in their own countries, so the place is anything *but* innocent, crawling as it is with tax dodgers, questionable banks, bogus investment companies, financial advisers, crooks, fraudsters and criminals on the run. On the surface, though, it's just a sleepy tropical island where nothing at all has happened since 1787, when a bored young English naval captain, Horatio Nelson, sailed by in search of French warships, took one look at the volcano through his telescope, decided not to stop, and sailed on north to the island of Nevis, where he married an unfortunate young widow, Fanny Nisbet, carted her off to England, and dumped her cruelly in a cold, damp, draughty vicarage in Norfolk while he cavorted all around Europe with a fat English tart called Emma Hamilton.

The Twin Otter bounced twice on the runway, staggering under its hefty load, and wheezed towards a smart modern terminal that bade us WELCOME TO THE HONOURABLE EUSTACE Q. PONSONBY INTERNATIONAL AIRPORT. When did airports suddenly turn into people? JFK, Charles de Gaulle, Leonardo da Vinci, John Lennon – they'll be calling Heathrow 'David Beckham' next. Not a bad idea, actually, considering the amount of kicking, hacking, tackling, pushing and jostling that you have to do if you're going to catch your flight.

My leg was numb after twenty minutes' intimacy with a plump haunch on the narrow seat beside me. She flashed me a blaze of white teeth and purple lipstick. 'Welcome by we paradise, maan,' she beamed. 'You ain' never gunna wanna leave.'

Led by the anorexics, we clambered down a rickety little metal ladder and straggled across the tarmac towards the gleaming arrivals hall, where we were greeted by three posters showing a flirty young girl with a flower behind her ear and the slogan WELCOME TO PARADISE. We filled in endlessly long immigration and customs forms – 'are you intending to foment an armed uprising in Innocent or otherwith to disturb the peace?'; 'have you ever had sexual relations with a four-legged animal?' – and then we joined one of the two queues in front of a glassy cubicle under signs that read BELONGERS and UNBELONGERS. Despite this segregation both queues headed towards just one immigration officer, a chirpy young man in a crisp white uniform with blue and gold epaulettes, who dealt first with the passenger at the head of the BELONGERS queue and then the passenger at the head of the UNBELONGERS queue.

'Good night, ladies and gentlemen,' he said in a precise Oxford accent. 'Welcome to paradise.'

'I *live* 'ere!' squawked the anorexic English woman.

'Then welcome *back* to paradise, madam,' he grinned.

'I bin livin' 'ere *free* years,' she said indignantly.

'Forgive me, madam,' he chuckled. 'You white people all look the same to me.'

He stamped my passport with permission to stay for a month and gave me another big smile. 'Have a nice stay, Mr Barron,' he said. 'Thank you,' I said. 'Tell me, why do you have two separate queues when you're the only immigration officer on duty?'

He smiled. 'It makes each queue look shorter than it really is. It prevents the passengers becoming restless.'

'Ingenious. And why do we have to fill out such a long immigration form?'

'Innocent is a very small island, Mr Barron. Not everyone takes us seriously. By asking you to fill out a long immigration form we are hoping that you will take us seriously.'

'And do all the answers get logged on some computer?'

He laughed heartily. 'Good Lord, no! We just throw them away.'

'Thank you.'

'No problem. Don't worry. Be happy.'

I swung my suitcase off the luggage belt and wheeled it towards the exit, which was flanked by two posters depicting an idyllic palm-fringed beach above the greeting WELCOME TO PARADISE. The toffee-coloured customs officer was young, slim and stunningly beautiful, with green eyes and long, dark hair. She smelled of something flowery. I was mesmerised.

'Is this really paradise?' I stammered. I've *never* stammered.

She smiled. I'll remember that smile until the day I die. 'For sure,' she said, 'but we don't have any snakes in this Garden of Eden. There's nothing poisonous here.' She grinned. 'Except my mother-in-law. And we don't have any apples, either, just paw-paw and ganja.'

'Ganja?'

'Marijuana.'

She ticked my two suitcases with a piece of white chalk, smiled again, and said 'OK, Mr Barron, away you go.' But I couldn't just leave her, just like that, not without saying something else, anything else. She really was gorgeous.

'So you must be Eve,' I blurted.

All right, all *right*, it was pathetically corny, but she really was very pretty.

'Eve? Not me. I like clothes too much.' She winked. 'Enjoy,' she said.

Through the exit doors beyond the customs checkpoint, on the right of the airy entrance hall, a huge photograph of the Honourable Eustace Q. Ponsonby, MP, CBE, GPI, MA, gazed benignly across the concourse: a slim, handsome, middle-aged man with a naughty smile. A computer screen above my head announced that our flight from Barbados was about to arrive ten days ago and that a LIAT flight had just left for Trinidad in three months' time. A group of young local guys with surprisingly shrill voices were loafing about the hall, joshing each other and twittering like birds.

Parked at the kerb outside were some battered old minibus taxis. I climbed into the first, a scratched and dented yellow Mitsubishi with GLADIATOR painted in red across the front. The ancient driver grinned toothlessly.

'Good night,' he said.

'Hello,' I said. 'Would you take me to Hummingbird House, please? At Nelson's Rest. Do you know it?'

'Me knows *ebery*where,' he said with dignity.

My seat belt was slack and frayed. 'Is it compulsory to wear seat belts here?' I asked.

'Only if you am so desirous,' he said.

We drove into the setting sun as it flirted with the shimmering sea. They say in Innocent that if you watch the horizon very closely just as the sun dips out of sight you will glimpse for a second the legendary Green Flash, the last of all the rainbow colours to say goodnight. I'd made several trips to the tropics but I'd never seen the Green Flash and I didn't see it now. Perhaps it was just a hoax to tease gullible tourists, or perhaps you have to believe in it before you can see it, like God.

We turned south along the west coast, the exhaust belching black smoke, bouncing and rattling across dozens of potholes, some as deep as coconuts. On the right the turquoise Caribbean was melting gently into gold, on the left the volcano towered above us, darkening in the dusk. Beyond the rustling palms and the pale pink beach, pelicans were plummeting vertically into the sea in search of supper, as fast and true as arrows, as prehistoric as pterodactyls. A gaggle of moth-eaten goats ambled across the road

5

and three cows wandered absent-mindedly ahead of us, unimpressed by the angry hooting of motorists. Hurtling wildly towards us came convoys of jeeps, low-slung sports cars with spoilers and darkened windows, and manically speeding minibuses painted in garish colours and emblazoned with names in fancy lettering: **CASANOVA**, CHEEKY LADY, AX ME BOUT JESUS. Pedestrians waved at us, adults as well as children. We passed small, brightly painted wooden houses with colourful little gardens of purple bougainvillaea, yellow hibiscus, pink and white oleander, red poinsettia. A platoon of cheeky little vervet monkeys loped across the road. We rattled through villages called Mosquito Bay, Cotton Beach, Hopetown and eventually the island's ramshackle little 18th Century capital, Columbus, which throbbed with raucous music thundering from every wooden balcony and open doorway. The main street was clogged with rush-hour traffic and jay-walkers, the pavements jammed with noisy pedestrians shouting, laughing and high-fiving each other. Geriatric chickens pecked with hopeless optimism in the gutter and a family of mangy dogs lay panting and dribbling in the dusk, grateful for the end of another sweltering day.

As the tropical night fell like a curtain and wrapped us in sudden darkness the taxi farted out of town and up into the hills past an old stone plantation inn and a ruined sugar mill. A donkey shambled by like a bored grey ghost and the road twisted higher up the side of the volcano until we turned off the main island road and jolted up a rough, rutted track, dodging large boulders and sharp stones. For ten minutes we bounced along the track, springs squeaking, as I clung to the strap beside the passenger seat and the driver hung grimly onto the steering wheel and muttered.

'They really ought to do something about this road,' I said.

He snorted. 'Dis guv'ment dey no gib a damn about dis road. Dis road ain't got no guv'ment voters, see, 'cos in de last election all de parsons up here done vote for de upposition party, so de guv'ment done said "fuck'em, if dey don't vote for we, dey don't not get no road".'

Hummingbird House was a yellow wooden bungalow with lights blazing from every room. A massive woman with a strong resemblance to the ferocious heavyweight boxer Mike Tyson emerged onto the verandah and lumbered towards us, her bosoms as enormous as any opera singer, limbs like a Sumo wrestler, and a loose floral dress that could have doubled as the cover for a four-seater sofa. Her huge feet were clad in a hefty pair of hiker's boots.

'Good night!' she bellowed, hauling me out of the minibus, enfolding me in a vast embrace, and kissing me noisily on both cheeks. She smelled overpoweringly of carbolic soap.

'You is de Baron David,' she roared. '*Lard* David. Me's honoured, You Lardship.'

She tried to curtsy, sinking towards the ground and almost falling over.

'Er – I'm David Barron, actually,' I said, 'not *Lord* David. Just Mr Barron. How do you do?'

She glared at the taxi driver, who took a nervous step back. 'Snowflake!' she growled, 'you should be a*shame* o' youself, drivin' 'is noble Lardship in dat stinky ol' heap o' rust.' She kicked the minibus. It winced.

'I'm not a Lord,' I said. 'I'm just David Barron. *Mr* Barron.'

She ignored me. 'Me's you arse-keeper,' she said.

'I'm sorry?'

'Me cleans de arse and does de larndry, me Lard. Miz Quaintance, dat's me: Miz *Gossamer* Quaintance – an' me be very pleased to make *you* 'quaintance!' She cackled, scooped up my two suitcases as if they were filled with feathers, and whisked them towards the house. 'Follow me, You 'ighness!' she bellowed. 'Dis way for de gormy chicken supper!'

The taxi driver shook his head as she went inside. 'Dat Miz

7

Quaintance,' he quavered, 'she gib me de colly-wobbles.'

'Do people here usually kiss strangers?' I said.

'Well, one time Miz Quaintance done marry a Franchman,' he said, 'from Martinikwy.'

'From where?'

'Martinikwy. Is a Franch island up to de nort'.'

'Martinique?'

'Dat de one! You got it. Dey's Franch up dere. De Franch be kissin' each udder *ebery*where. Dey call it de Franch kissin'.'

'She's married? Miz Quaintance?'

'Not no more. De Franchman 'e done gib her a baby an' den 'e drop dead.'

I could well believe it.

'Now she just got one regular sweetman what sees to her bedtime needs.'

'He runs a sweet shop? Confectionery?'

'No, no, he her sweetman, her fancy man: Belly-Up Robinson.'

He pressed a business card into my hand. MR MARGARET MORGAN ESQ, it said, MAJIK CARPIT TAXI.

'*Margaret*?' I said.

He nodded lugubriously. 'Me mammy done wanted a girl.'

'But Miz Quaintance called you Snowflake?'

'Dat me street name.' He chortled. 'Dey all calls me Snowflake 'cos I's so black.'

I paid him and the minibus belched, rattled and squeaked away into the night, trailing a less than magic carpet of carbon monoxide.

The yellow house sparkled in the balmy night. Light streamed out of every door and window. The air was soft, warm and fragrant with tropical scents, the verandah heady with lush flowers tumbling from hanging baskets. Beyond the living room I could glimpse the still, gleaming surface of a deep blue swimming pool. In London it would be cold, grey, and raining.

'Lard David!' yelled Miz Quaintance from somewhere inside the house. I found her on the kitchen floor, lying face down in front of the cooker and tugging at the handle of a small aperture at the bottom of the cooker, under the oven.

'You supper be ready, You Lardship. Gormy chicken. Go in de little boys' room an' do you business, an' remember you wash you 'ands.'

'What on earth are you doing on the floor?' I said.

'Dis damn American grill!'

'The grill's right down there? On the ground?'

'Yus. De Americans always put dey grills at de bottom of dey cookers.'

'That's ridiculous. So you have to lie on the ground to light the grill?'

'Dat's right. Dey done send lots o' mens to de moon but dey cain't not make a proper grill. An' anudder t'ing also: dis damn cooker am Jewish.'

'A *kosher* cooker?'

'It don't not work on Friday night an' Saturday. On Friday night an' Saturday de cooker lock itself 'cos dat be de Jewish religion: no cookin' at de weekend.'

'You're joking!'

'Not so. Dat de troof. De owner of dis 'ouse, 'e done bought de cooker from a Jew-man over by Musk-Eater Bay, an' de Jewish cookers all lock demselfs for de weekend. You cain't cook nuttin' on dis damn cooker till Sunday marnin'.'

I didn't believe her at first but three days later, on the Saturday, I tried to turn the cooker on and nothing happened. An electronic message flashed across the little screen on the front of the cooker: SHABBAT MELAKHA, it said sternly. IGNITING A FIRE IS FORBIDDEN TODAY.

In the lavatory I found a hand-written notice taped to the wall above the bowl:

9

**<u>PLEASE CONSERVE WATER.</u>**

IF IT'S YELLOW LET IT MELLOW.

IF IT'S BROWN FLUSH IT DOWN.

I laughed aloud for the first time in months.

# CHAPTER 2

## CRICKET, COURT AND CHRISTIANITY

I slept for hours, knackered by the long journey from London, but I woke long before dawn with my body clock still three or four time zones behind me somewhere high above the Atlantic. The night was a riot of chattering insects. A regiment of randy cicadas chirped with demented lust and a battalion of tree-frogs whistled and beeped like electronic gadgets. I ducked out from under my mosquito net, opened the hurricane shutters and wandered onto the pool deck. It was gloriously cool and still. The moon loitered behind scattered cloud but the pool shimmered with pale reflections of the universe. The air was fresh and clean after wafting across three thousand miles of ocean, the old slave route from Africa to Innocent. A faint breeze fingered the tamarind tree beyond the pool. I lay on one of the loungers for more than an hour, watching the sky as it lightened, listening to the stirring sounds of the waking world: the mournful protests of pigeons, a donkey tittering, the whinny of a distant horse, all eager for the tropical sun to surge out of the ocean.

It stormed the heavens just after 6.20 in a crimson blaze, four times its midday size as it breached the horizon, and was greeted with excitement by a jabbering gang of black-faced monkeys that scampered bickering across the tin roof. In the dawn I glimpsed the silhouette of a distant island looming on the eastern horizon. Two fragile dragonflies were chasing each other, darting to and fro

11

above the swimming pool, pursued by a third like an angry husband. There was no sign of any house nearby so I plunged naked into the pool and swam a few lazy lengths before breakfast, watched intently by a pair of solemn kingbirds perched on the corner posts of the wall around the pool deck. Commuters back in London would already have struggled to work through the cold, grey morning streets, strap-hanging in crowded, sweaty carriages on the Underground, pressed up indecently against strangers and trying to pretend that they didn't exist. 'You lucky bastard!' Milligan had said. 'How come you always get sent on the jammy jobs?'

'Charisma,' I said.

Hare had sent me to Innocent to track down and investigate several suspected British multi-millionaire tax dodgers who were avoiding paying tax in the UK by claiming to be living in Innocent. OK, I know that everyone hates tax inspectors, and it's not much fun nailing little people whose only crime is to fiddle a few hundred quid here and there, and some of my colleagues are indeed absolute bastards. But we're not all like that, and most of us are good men trying to do our public duty to the best of our ability, and most of the time we're not after the small fry but the mega-millionaires who've avoided paying hundreds of thousands of pounds of tax every year for years, sometimes for decades. Somebody has to make them pay up: if we didn't the burden of tax on all of us would be much heavier, and if we don't pay our taxes who's going to finance the army, navy, air force, police and firemen who protect us, the doctors, nurses and ambulance men who heal and care for us, the roads we all use, the schools, the universities, the libraries? Yes, my job can be underhand at times, and sometimes I'm ashamed of myself because snooping and spying can be a grubby business, but I promise you I'm not a shit and I have plenty of friends who would tell you so. It's estimated that British tax-dodgers cost you and me several billion pounds a year in unpaid taxes, and that's just unacceptable. The problem is worst in a couple of handful of tax havens around the world like Andorra, the Bahamas, Belize, Bermuda, the Cook Islands, Kuwait, Monaco, even the American state of Delaware. And many of the havens are in the Caribbean: Anguilla, Antigua, the British Virgin Islands, the Cayman Islands, Innocent, St Kitts and Nevis, the Turks and Caicos. So to try to reduce the problem Hare had sent seven of us out to the seven Caribbean islands to sniff around and gauge whether it might be worthwhile building a permanent team of travelling inspectors to hunt down the wealthy British expats who are cheating us all, and he'd chosen me to go to Innocent.

There'd been a hell of a row at HMRC in London over the cost of sending us out on what a lot of the Big Cheeses reckoned was a complete waste of time and money and little more than a glorified jolly. Increasingly angry memos flew to and fro, voices were raised, meetings became acrimonious, and loud arguments rumbled along the corridors at Northumberland Avenue, but in the end Hare won the argument by persuading the Big Cheeses that it was well worth gambling a few thousand quid on each of us if we returned with only the scalp of just one dodger whom the Revenue could squeeze for hundreds of thousands of quid. He even persuaded HMRC to do us proud by renting expensive villas for each of us for a couple of months so that the expats we were going to investigate would think we were rich holidaymakers rather than shabby taxmen. Hummingbird House was elegant and expensive but still much cheaper than one of the island's overpriced tourist hotels. One night in a single room at the Sunshine Hotels resort cost £750, and to make it even worse you had to put up with hordes of loud Americans. Hummingbird House, by contrast, was a joy.

I showered and breakfasted on orange juice, grapefruit and poached eggs on toast on the verandah overlooking the pretty little garden with its palm trees, multi-coloured Match-Me-If-You-Can, and feathery flamboyants – the Flame of the Forest – ablaze with orange flowers. Cinnamon and saffron butterflies danced in the sunlight and a couple of feet away an iridescent green and purple hummingbird hovered with a blur of wings beside an hibiscus bush and sipped at one of its dewy red flowers. Two fat, lime-green lizards were flirting upside down on the roof of the verandah, gazing at each other for long motionless moments, then darting suddenly towards each other, the male boasting by inflating his throat like a giant balloon. A big black spider swung like a spindly Tarzan on a strand of its web, and a chunky caterpillar with vivid yellow stripes and a scarlet head trudged across the stone floor. The sweet scent of crimson, pink and orange frangipani drifted across the verandah, and the dry, rattling seed pods of a Shack-Shack tree – 'Woman's Tongue' – nagged away at the end of the garden.

I made a cup of coffee, watching a long queue of tiny ants commuting up the kitchen wall, turning around when they reached the roof and tramping back again. I returned to the verandah to enjoy the coffee and an aged gardener turned up on foot at seven o'clock wearing a battered old Paddington Bear hat, a threadbare tee-shirt that proclaimed I ♥ NEW YORK, and baggy trousers held up by a grubby pink-and-cucumber Garrick Club tie. When he saw me on the verandah he cried '*inside!*' and shuffled towards me. '*Inside!*' he cried again.

When he reached the verandah he swept his hat off and gave me a courtly bow. 'Good morrow, gentle sir,' he said. 'Greetings. Verily thou art thrice welcome by we beauteous isle.'

'Good morning,' I said. 'Thank you.'

'I's thy gardener. I's yclept Grandad.'

*Yclept*? Dear god, he was speaking some sort of Shakespearean English, the language brought to Innocent by the first English settlers in the early 1600s. I was talking to the 17th Century.

I stepped off the verandah and shook his horny hand. He seemed embarrassed by the handshake, as if instinctively his genes recalled the pain of some enslaved old ancestor who had once been whipped for daring to touch a white man at a time when no black man would ever dare to enter a white man's house.

'I'm David Barron,' I said.

He bowed again. 'Well met, Master Barron. 'Tis verily an honour to bid you welcome.'

'You keep this garden beautifully. It's lovely.'

His watery old eyes gleamed. 'I give you hearty thanks, kind sir, for I have toiled on these lands for nigh on thirty summers.'

'You've done a great job.'

'Thou art most bounteous in thy gracious praise,' he said.

'Tell me, Grandad. What's your real name?'

'Laoughlin Livingstone.' he said, as if clearing his throat of phlegm. 'I come of Irish stock.'

I laughed. 'I think I'll call you Grandad,' I said.

'Why, truly, sir, 'tis the common custom of the isle,' he said. 'When I were brought forth fresh from my dam's belly my sire vouchsafed that I resembled one of his ancient forebears, so henceforth I was know as Grandad far and wide.'

'And do you have grandchildren yourself?'

He straightened with pride. 'Forsooth, sir, verily. I have sired two score and five.'

Forty-five grandchildren! I must have looked startled.

'Indeed, sir, from six comely maids, two common strumpets, and thirteen childer.' He smiled. 'In my youth I were a fine, upstanding knave and swived many a fair maid. Methinks no wench was ever minded to say me nay.'

'I bet you were a terror.'

He smiled shyly. 'I was perchance somewhat of a rogue betimes, I do allow.'

'Tell me, Grandad. Your belt: it's very pretty. Where did you get it?'

He fingered the Garrick tie. ''Tis but a trifle,' he said. 'I purchased it these ten years gone for just one dollar in a sale of goods for charity by Jericho.'

'One US dollar?

'Barbados.'

About 35p. The Garrick Club would not be amused.

'And now it behooves me to commence my labours,' he said.

'Of course. It was good to talk to you, Grandad.'

'Indeed, sir, and thou also. Until we meet anon. And if ever thou needst to calm thy raging passions I nurture in a pasture beside my humble abode a handsome crop of finest hemp. Its fragrance is guaranteed to soothe the savage breast.'

He stood to attention, gave me a smart salute, and pottered away towards the little garden shed, where a few minutes later I heard a lawnmower cough and rattle into life. I gazed at him as he went, a living relic of the age of James I.

At 7.30 Miz Quaintance arrived on a wobbly little bicycle, looking awesome in her sturdy mountain climbing boots and vast, faded floral frock. How could I call her 'Gossamer'? Impossible. You might as well name an elephant Tinkerbell.

'Marnin', marnin',' she bellowed. 'You done sleep good, Lard David?'

What was the point of correcting her yet again? 'Very well, thank you,' I said.

'You not been chewed by de musk-eaters?'

'Sorry?'

'De musk-eaters, You Lardship. De insects what bite in de night.'

'Ah. Right. No, not at all. The mosquito net's fine.'

'OK. You have you breakfus'?'

'Thank you, yes: orange juice, grapefruit, poached eggs on toast, coffee.'

She nodded approvingly. 'Dat good. Mens mus' always keep up dey strengt' for de ladies. You got a lady, Lard David, back in Englan'?'

'Ah... no. Not at the moment.'

She looked worried. 'But dat a *terrible* waste, Lard David, fine man like You Lardship. We mus' find you nice lady quick quick.'

'That's very kind of you, Miz Quaintance, but...'

She raised a hand. 'No problem. I find you nice lady. You like big ladies wid big tops, big bottoms?'

'Really, I don't...'

'Me find you one wid big tops *an'* big bottoms. No problem. Den you got both.'

For one appalling moment I thought that she was about to offer herself. 'That's awfully good of you,' I said nervously, 'but there's really no need.'

She frowned. 'O' *course* dere's need. Proper mens *always* got a need for womans.' She looked suspicious. 'You not one o' dem anti-mans, is you, Me Lard? You not one o' dem homely sensuals?'

'Good god, no! I've been married. I have children. But I'm divorced.'

She looked relieved. 'T'ank de Lard,' she said. 'Anti-mans is a bonimation in de eyes of de Lard.'

I changed the subject hurriedly. 'By the way,' I said, 'there's an army of ants tramping up the kitchen wall.'

She shrugged. 'Don' worry 'bout dem, You Lardship. Ants 'as got clean feets. Not like flies: flies got dirty feets.'

She propped her bicycle up against the verandah railing, waddled inside, began to make housekeeping noises, and launched into a garbled verson of 'Rock of Ages' in a sweet, clear, girlish voice:

*Wreck of angels, left for me,*
*Let's invite myself to tea.*
*Lay de waiter, Andy Budd,*
*From my womb inside it flowed.*
*Be off, Cindy! Devil's Whore!*
*Stay from courtin', make me yours.*

After the third mangled verse she emerged onto the verandah with a basket of dirty laundry, waddled down to the end of the garden, and disappeared into a small wooden hut in the shade of a beautiful Travellers' Tree with huge feathery palm fronds fanned out like a peacock's tail. A raucous clanking and throbbing exploded from the hut as an old washing machine roared into action and the building itself began to shudder. Miz Quaintance's deep baritone voice echoed across the garden. 'Swine machine!' she bellowed. 'Chile of de Devil!' She kicked the machine twice with her hefty climbing boots. It whimpered, moaned and sobbed gently. She emerged from the hut wiping her hands on her dress so vigorously that she might have frightened even Mike Tyson.

'Is it usually that noisy?' I said.

'Alway',' she said grimly, 'bud I don't abide no nonsense from it, no sir. I got de measure of it, oh yes.'

I telephoned Snowflake to drive me into town. The banging and clanking from the hut became louder and an ancient, rusty washing machine lurched out of the door and advanced, trembling, across the grass towards me.

'Miz Quaintance!' I yelled. 'The washing machine's escaped!'

She emerged from the house at a steady trot, lumbering across the lawn towards the hut with the grim determination of a Churchill tank.

'Swine machine!' she grunted. 'Back! Back in you arse!'

She bent at the waist to block its advance and they met head-on with a sickening crunch, Miz Quaintance like a mighty rugby forward diving into the scrum, the machine howling at the impact and belching a cloud of soapy foam. For a few seconds the combatants were evenly matched, Miz Quaintance clutching the machine in a fearsome embrace, grunting, straining and bracing her gigantic chintzy buttocks. I gazed at her, mesmerised. I should have run to help her but I was paralyzed by the vision of her gargantuan rear. Grandad appeared in the corner of my eye, took one look at the scene and ducked back out of sight again

'Swine washer!' she bellowed. 'Chile of de Devil!' The machine began to wheeze and slowly she pushed it back into the hut, where I could hear her kicking it unmercifully with her hobnailed boots. 'Dat teach you, swine instrument!' she grunted, breathing heavily. '*Bad* boy. *Very* bad boy.'

The machine howled, whimpered, fell silent at last, and Miz Quaintance emerged from the hut, breathing heavily and hitching her knickers up with her elbows.

'You really should ask the landlord to buy you a new one,' I said.

'No way!' she growled. 'Dat machine ain' gonna get de best of me, no sir, no way. Dat 'ooligan appliance gotta learn 'oo am de boss.'

She stamped back into the house and Snowflake's battered yellow minibus arrived a few minutes later, a one-man global-warming disaster propelled by a foul cloud of exhaust. He crouched over the steering wheel, eyeing the house nervously.

'Marnin', marnin',' he said.

'Good morning,' I said. 'It's OK, Snowflake. She's inside.'

'Praise de Lord.'

I climbed into the taxi and as we drove away I tried to imagine what sort of giant superhero could possibly be Gossamer Quaintance's lover. The thought of her in the throes of uncontrollable passion was too frightening to contemplate.

'Snowflake,' I said. 'What kind of a fellow is Miz Quaintance's sweetman?'

'Belly-up Rubinson.'

'That's his name?'

'Dat he street name.'

'Why Belly-up?'

He sniggered. 'Dey say dat's de way she like it best!'

'And his real name?'

'Cedric Robinson.'

'*Cedric*? That must be a very unusual name in the Caribbean.'

'Nut at all. We gotta lot o' Cedrics, Cecils an' Cuthberts; from de ol' sugar days when de English plantation owners call de slaves like demselfs.'

'So what's Belly-up like?'

'Well, 'e'm a redskin.'

'A Red Indian?' Sioux? Apache? Cherokee? In Innocent?

'Nah. De redskins am black fellers wid bery light skin. We callin' dem redskins 'cos dey ain't bery black.'

'Ah.'

''e runnin' Miz Quaintance rum shop in Chicken Bone village.'

'She owns a bar?'

He nodded. 'An' a gamblin' den also. Lots o' fellows like gamblin' wid dominoes.' He sniggered. ''e be a bery small feller, ol' Belly-Up. Dey say 'e be so bery small 'cos her sittin' on 'im all de time!'


Snowflake dropped me off in town at the Thrifty car hire office by the harbour, where a little inter-island ferry was puttering away from the jetty. A dozen sailing boats rode languidly at anchor in the glittering bay and a woman in a fast-food stall, a converted van, was selling saltfish and ackee, goat water, breadfruit, roti, coconuts, soursop juice and sweet fizzy drinks called Ting and Caribe. The pretty little waterfront was lined with charming old 'skirt-and-blouse' buildings with ground floors of solid stone and sunny wooden balconies painted in pale pastel colours of greens, blues and pink.

I rented a small Japanese jeep with air conditioning and wandered off to explore the town. It wasn't really a town at all, just a small, higgledy-piggledy jumble of narrow streets, meandering alleyways, low ramshackle old wooden buildings and fragile corrugated iron huts, except for three or four modern two-storey banks and a couple of smart computer stores. Columbus may have been named after an Italian explorer but every corner was haunted by memories of the British Empire. There was just one main street (imaginatively called Main Street) and several little lanes led down to the sea: Spanish Alley, Pirates Lane, Cut-throat Corner, Gospel Road. Two streets, Prince Charles Drive and Prince William Lane, had been named not after our 21$^{st}$ Century Princes Charles and William but after the young men who went on to become King Charles I and King William IV.

The streets buzzed with cheerful pedestrians who shrieked with laughter, the men greeting each other slapping palms and bumping fists, some of the women with their hair in brightly coloured plastic curlers. I saw no beggars nor anyone in rags, but a demented middle-aged man lay on the pavement outside the Consolidated Bank of Innocent yelling obscenities at passers-by. Music boomed out of every doorway and vehicle, even those that were parked and empty. In the central square mobs of passengers jostled each other to board minibuses with names like ISLAND EXPRESS, **TRAMPOLINE GIRL**, STRESS ME, LORD. Cars and jeeps stopped suddenly without warning in the middle of the street so that their drivers could gossip with friends on the pavement.

I wandered down towards the sea, to Sailors' Pier and Hangman's Cove, where a dozen seventeenth-century pirates had stepped gingerly onto the gallows to gaze with final regret across the pretty little bay. Just off Prince William Lane was a busy little covered market – in Market Street, of course – where a score of women stall-holders were selling bananas, paw-paw, yams, breadfruit, mangoes, soursop and broccoli. I wandered on through the town past the solid, elegant old police station, where I bought a three-month driving licence from a stern young policewoman who refused to smile. Fixed to the wall beside her was a blackboard listing recent road deaths and traffic offences. DRIVE WITH CARE, LIFE HAS NO SPARE, it said; UNDERTAKERS LOVE OVERTAKERS; and IF U DRINK AND DRIVE, U SPILL DE DRINK. On another wall a large poster showed a worried girl with the caption I WAS ALWAYS AFRAID OF GETTING PREGNANT BUT I NEVER EXPECTED AIDS. A third poster urged pregnant girls who had been abandoned by their lovers to report them to the social security department.

Outside again, I walked on, past a shabby little fire station with one small, aged fire engine, and through a ruined old cemetery with weather-beaten, barely legible headstones commemorating lives that had ended as long ago as 1623: English colonists, Scottish soldiers, Welsh preachers, Irish labourers, indentured workers from the Orkneys and the Isle of Man, most of them not yet forty, a couple just infants, all felled by fierce tropical heat, disease, exhaustion and medical ignorance.

Beyond the cemetery a rowdy cricket match was underway and the sound of the chattering crowd and a lively steel pan band drew me onto the dusty little field to watch for a while. The entrance was manned only by a rickety little plastic table, a roll of pink cloakroom receipts, and a hand-written sign saying TICKIT'S. On the nearest boundary the blue, gold and green palm-tree flag of Innocent fluttered proudly from a flagpole above a small wooden pavilion. In front of the pavilion the metal numbers of a simple, hand-operated scoreboard clanked gently in the breeze: 112 for 3, batsman number one 58 not out, batsman number five 9 not out. A mangy goat was fielding at deep square leg, lazily cropping the grass, and a skeletal dog was emptying its bowels copiously at long-on. The two umpires wore grubby white coats and linen hats but only two of the players were in long trousers and only four in proper cricket whites: the others were all dressed in shorts, tee-shirts, caps, sunglasses and trainers of various colours and cleanliness. On the right-hand boundary a ramshackle wooden grandstand sheltered about a hundred noisy spectators, women and children as well as men, so that it was obvious that cricket was still as popular as ever in the West Indies. How strange it was that generations of black people in the Caribbean have inherited from England a deep love of cricket yet white Americans and Canadians of British descent have not and are often baffled by the game. On the third side of the playing field the four musicians in the steel pan band assaulted their assorted instruments with relish, and on the furthest boundary half a dozen men in striped pyjamas – five blacks and one white – were slashing unenthusiastically with scythes and machetes at a waist-high jungle of grass and weeds, watching the cricket and shepherded by a man wearing a khaki uniform, a black peaked cap, and carrying a thick stick.

I joined the crowd in the grandstand, climbed up to the top tier, and sat on a bare green plank a few feet away from a Rasta with dreadlocks, a chunky wooden necklace, and on his head a multi-coloured tea cosy. 'Good morning,' I said.

'Marnin', marnin'.'

'Who's playing?'

'Dis Columbus vee Jericho. Dey vyin' for de island championship.'

'And who's batting?'

'Dis Columbus, maan. De first innin's.'

I was surprised. 'They play two innings each?'

He looked at me as if I were an idiot. 'Of course, maan. Dis not some uncivilized 20-20 rubbish, dis proper t'ree-day cricket, for de island championship.'

'And who's the chap who's made 58?'

'Dat Shefton Martin, de best batsman on de island. Dey say he soon be pick for de Win'ward Islands.'

'He must be very good.'

'Sure t'ing, maan. He de best, an' he only eighteen. One day he play for de West Indies, dat for sure.'

'And the men over there in pyjamas, cutting grass?'

'Dey jailbirds, maan, from de prison farm, an' de feller wid de stick am dey prison guard.'

'He's a brave guy to let them loose with scythes and machetes when he's got only a stick. They might attack him.'

The Rasta gave a booming laugh. 'No way, maan. Dey not *violent* men: dey just maybe done kill dey woman for messin' wid udder men, or maybe dey been havin' a bit o' naughty wid very young girls, dat sort o' t'ing. Dey not real *criminals*. Dey not *harm* no one.'

'Ah. Right.'

'An' anudder t'ing, maan: if dey attack de guard an' interrupt de cricket de crowd gonna get real vex wid dem an' give dem all a good beatin'.'

Shefton Martin hit a four and the crowd erupted with glee. He then hit a six and another four and the crowd went wild.

'You show dem, Shefton!'

'You de best, Shefton!'

'You ma main man!'

A tall, skinny young fellow in the second row yelled 'you fuckin' magic, Shefton!' and a fat woman in front of him, clutching a long umbrella and wearing a straw hat liberally decorated with plastic fruit, turned and glared at him. 'You wash out you mouth!' she said.

''e fuckin' brilliant!' said the young man.

'You not speakin' like dat!' she snapped. 'You not sayin' dirty words like dat.'

'What dorty words?'

'You know good.'

'No. What dorty words?'

'De… f word.'

'OK, OK, OK.'

During the next ten minutes Shefton Martin hit two more fours but the other batsman did nothing but prod, block, nudge, nurdle and miss the ball all together. As the minutes dragged by and the goat proceeded to munch its way from deep square leg to deep mid-wicket, the crowd became restless and the tall, skinny young man increasingly impatient. When the number five batsman played and missed yet again he couldn't contain himself.

'Hit de fuckin' ball, maan!' he yelled. 'What you t'ink you playin', fuckin' ping-pong?'

The fat woman in front of him turned and glared. 'I not tellin' you again,' she said. 'Dat word vex me plenty.'

'He jus' fuckin' useless!'

'Right, dat's it!' she said, rising from her seat. 'Me fetch de police.'

'Fuck de fuckin' police!' he said.

She headed importantly towards the pavilion, swinging her umbrella purposefully like a walking stick, and approached a smart, pretty young policewoman who was standing beside the scoreboard, giggling and flirting with one of the batting team. The two women spoke for a minute, returned to the grandstand together, and the fat one pointed at the tall young man. 'Dat 'im,' she said. ''e'm a disgrace.'

The policewoman – trim in a smart navy blue cap, crisp white shirt, pressed navy skirt, white socks and highly polished black lace-up shoes, and equipped with a truncheon, handcuffs, a whistle and a silver badge that read PC27 – approached the young man, produced a notebook, and fixed him with a stern frown.

'Name?' she said.

'What?'

'You name?'

The young man looked incredulous. 'You *know* me name,' he said.

'I axin' you formally.'

'For why?'

'For me official report.'

'Dis stupid.'

'You gotta tell me you name. You don' tell me you name, you be arrest.'

The young man was indignant. '*What*? *Me*? *Arrest*? For not tellin' you me *name*? You *know* me name, Kimanda. You know me name for more dan twenty years.'

'Dat not de point,' said PC27. 'I gotta 'ave you name official. I gotta ax you name an' you gotta tell me.'

'Dat a waste of time.'

'Dat de law. Dat de rules.'

'So why you want ax me name?'

'Because you usin' darty words contrary to de law.'

'What dorty words?'

'De f word.'

'I don' know no f word.'

'You know de f word only too good.'

'What f word? Field? Finger? Fast bowler?'

'Now you vexin' me.'

'I dunno no bad f word.'

'You lie, Robelto Perkins.'

'Dere! You said it! You know me name already!'

'Dat not signify. You mus' tell me you name because you use de f word an' you break de law an' you offend dis lady. She done made a formal complaint.'

He laughed raucously. 'Dis *lady*? She not a lady. She me *mother*!'

'I know dat. Dat not signify nuttin'. She done make a complaint, sayin' you usin' de f word.'

'Me? De f word? Never!'

'It agains' de law to be swearin' in public,' said PC27.

'Dis nut public. Dis private cricket match.'

'Dis a public place. You give me you name or you be arrest.'

'By *you*, Kimanda?'

'Dat is so.'

'An' who else? You blow you whistle? You call de cops?'

'I *is* de cops, an' I done de judo.'

Robelto Perkins considered the alternatives. He shrugged. 'OK, OK,' he said. 'Me name Robelto Perkins.'

'Address?'

'Fuckin' 'ell, Kimanda! You *knows* me address! Dis ridiculous!'

'Dere! You done said it again. De f word. I gutta arrest you. De f word is agains' de law.'

'OK, OK,' he said. 'I sorry. OK?'

'No, it not OK. You done vex all dese people 'ere. Dey not wunt hear you usin' de f word all de time. Dey all disgust wid you.'

He turned towards the grandstand, spread his arms, and appealed to us all. 'Has me done vex you?' he said.

'No!' said most of the crowd.

'Yes!' said three or four.

'Has me done disgust you?'

'Yes!' said three or four.

'No!' said most of the crowd.

He faced PC27 again. 'See?' he said. 'I not vex nobody.'

'De law is de law,' she said.

The fat woman in the fruity hat had become increasingly impatient. 'Oh, let de little bugger go, Kimanda,' she said. 'He not worth de trouble.'

'She say *bugger*!' said Robelto Perkins. 'You gotta arrest her also!'

'You own *mother*?' said PC27. 'You want me arrest you own *mother*?'

'Whyfore not? She want you arrest me.'

The fat woman reached back across the front row of spectators and struck him hard on the head with her umbrella.

'Ow!' he cried. 'She done assault me!'

PC27 giggled. 'Dat serve you right,' she said. 'She you mother, she allowed to chastise her chile.'

'She done commit assault! Battery! Griev-ious bodily 'arm! She done broke de law.'

'I break you *head* in a minute, Robelto,' said the fat woman grimly. 'Now shut up you face an' hold you row so as we can all watch de cricket like proper Christian parsons.'

PC27 shrugged, nodded and tucked her notebook and pencil back in her pocket.

A loud shout from the fielders resounded across the ground: '*HOWZAT?*'

'Not out,' said PC 27, sashaying back towards the pavilion.

'Fuckin' nice arse, dat Kimanda,' said Robelto Perkins.

I watched the match for another fifteen minutes until batsman number five was clean bowled for 12 and young Shefton Martin had reached his century, stabbing the air exultantly with his bat. I left the ground and turned back towards the waterfront, discovering on the way a shady square with a broken fountain in the shape of a pelican and along one side an old stone courthouse crowned by a squat little toytown clock tower with the hands frozen at twenty past three on some unknown day in some past, forgotten century. A trial was in progress and three upright policemen guarded the doors at the top of the courthouse steps, living ghosts of the British Empire, resplendent in white colonial helmets topped by sharp silver spikes, white jackets with ornate silver badges and buttons, white gloves, gleaming black belts and boots, and dark blue trousers with thick red stripes down each side. I climbed the steps and asked the nearest policeman if I could watch the trial.

'Certainly, sir,' he said, opening the door. 'We have a public gallery. In Innocent the law is not only done, it is seen to be done.'

Inside the building I was frisked by a security guard, who scanned me with a metal detector and pointed me silently towards the 'public gallery,' three rows of hard, wooden benches beside an air conditioning unit that clattered so noisily it was difficult to hear the lawyers' questions. At the front of the court, in a high-backed chair on a raised platform, a plump, elderly black judge sat stern and dignified in a short grey wig, black gown and high, stiff collar. On a lower level in front of him a begowned and bewigged clerk scratched frantically at a pad, and it could almost have been a scene from the High Court in London for the barristers, too, all islanders, wore wigs, suits, ties and gowns, remarked regularly 'may it please Your Honour' and 'if I may crave Your Lordship's indulgence', and they all bowed low in the judge's direction whenever he or they entered or left the court. The accused, a weaselly little man with a nervous expression, sat at a small desk inside a sort of wooden playpen in the well of the court, guarded by a policeman with a sergeant's three silver stripes on his arm and flanked by a jury of twelve well-dressed men and women sitting on two rows of hard wooden benches at the side of the court. As I sidled into my seat a young, supremely confident barrister was on his feet, wearing an MCC tie, speaking in an impossibly refined Oxford accent and gazing with condescending contempt at the accused as if he were a worm that had somehow slithered into court.

'This… *fellow*…, My Lord,' said the barrister, 'saw fit to break into and enter Mr Thompson's residence at night, effecting entry by means of a window, and subsequently to invade Mr Thompson's refrigerator, to avail himself of a bottle of Ting that he discovered therein, and thereafter to consume the beverage, after which he proceeded to misappropriate and consume a corpulent slice of Mrs Thompson's homemade lardy-cake.'

The judge look concerned. 'The defendant does strike one as somewhat undernourished, Mr Baggott,' he said. 'Could it be that he availed himself of the lardy-cake because he was in serious need of some sustenance?'

'Your Lordship's perspicacity is a lesson to us all,' said the barrister. 'That is indeed the accused's contention. He alleges that he had not eaten for more than forty-eight hours and was desperately in need of provender.'

'As indeed he is still,' said the judge genially. 'This is not a defendant who needs to go on a diet.'

There was laughter in court.

'Which cannot be said of all of us.'

More laughter in court.

'Including myself,' he said.

More laughter.

'Not to mention several counsel as well as some members of the jury.'

More laughter.

'May it please Your Honour,' said the barrister, 'I must crave the court's indulgence by pointing out that I have ascertained that the accused had in fact consumed a banana for his breakfast that very morning.'

'One whole banana, Mr Baggott?' enquired the judge.

'I believe that to be the case, My Lord.'

'An *entire* banana?'

'I believe so, My Lord.'

'But not the skin, I trust.'

More laughter in court.

'I regret, My Lord, that I have no information on that aspect of the accused's breakfast that day.'

The judge smiled indulgently. 'I was teasing you, Mr Baggot. It was merely a jest.'

'And a most successful and amusing jest, if I may express an opinion, My Lord.'

'You may indeed, Mr Baggot. You may indeed. And the defendant consumed nothing more than a single banana that morning, with or without its skin?'

'I understand that is so, Your Honour.'

'No wonder he looks as if he is about to expire.'

'Me rumblin' 'ungry all de time,' blurted the accused. 'Me nut got no job an' me nut got no money.'

'Silence!' bellowed the barrister. 'You will *not* address my Lord unless he has addressed you first.'

The defendant looked at him defiantly. 'You Lord be my Lord also,' he said. ''e nut be just You Lord.'

The judge grinned. '*Touché*, I think, Mr Baggott,' he said.

The barrister bowed stiffly. 'If Your Lordship pleases,' he said.

It was then that I noticed that despite his immaculate wig, pinstriped suit, shirt, MCC tie and gown, Baggot the barrister was barefoot. His shoes and socks stood neatly together beside his seat.

I leaned towards a man who was sitting on my right in the 'public gallery.'

'Excuse me,' I whispered. 'Can you tell me why the lawyer is not wearing any shoes?'

'He wagglin' he toes at de judge, dat why,' he whispered.

'Waggling his *toes*? What for?'

'To put de hex on de judge, to persuade him to send de defendant to prison.'

'By waggling his *toes*?'

'Sure t'ing. Naked toes be strong magic when dey wagglin'.'

'Silence in court!' hissed the policeman.

The naked toe ploy proved remarkably effective and the weaselly little man was sent to prison for four months' hard labour.

I sat through one other case, in which a poor, shabby, retarded man and his elderly mother were prosecuted for committing incest and fined $500 each: money that obviously they did not have. I asked my neighbour in a whisper what would happen if they failed to pay their fines. 'Dey gunna go to de calaboose for attempt of court,' he said. Innocent was not paradise for all its inhabitants.

I left the courthouse, headed back towards the harbour and the jeep, and dropped into the Cost-Me-Less Calypso Superette for some supplies that Miz Quaintance would probably not have thought of buying. It was February but a dusty Christmas tree, still forlornly decorated with baubles and tinsel, sulked in a corner near the front door, and grimy fake snow still lurked in the corners of several windows. A light-skinned little man, whom I took to be the owner, was holding a bottle of wine, looking bewildered, and being bullied by an overbearing white woman.

'It's corked, Elroy,' she said.

He nodded uncertainly. 'OK.'

'I mean, it's *corked.*'

He nodded again. 'OK.'

She raised her voice. '*Corked*, Elroy, so I want another bottle to replace it.'

He frowned. 'But they're *all* corked, Mrs Jamieson.'

'You haven't a clue what I mean, have you?' she snapped. 'It's CORKED. That doesn't mean it's got a cork in it. It's CORKED. The cork has reacted badly with the wine. The cork has spoiled the wine. The wine is disgusting. So I want a replacement.'

He looked dazed. 'You want a new cork?

'No, you dolt! I want a new bottle.'

'With wine in it?'

'Of course with wine in it,' she trumpeted. She strode across to the wine section and seized another bottle from the shelf. 'You can always return it to your supplier,' she said. 'They'll reimburse you. And another thing: you're always running out of the big one-and-a-half-litre bottles of Smirnoff. They seem to fly off the shelves. And you're always short of tonic water, too.'

'They are both far too popular,' he protested. 'People buy them too quickly. As soon as we restock the shelves they disappear.'

She looked at him with disbelief. 'So why not order more, you silly man? Double your order. You'd double your sales. You'd double your profit. Don't you want to sell more? *Triple* your order, Elroy, you gormless moron.'

He gazed at her in amazement. A light seemed to switch on behind his eyes. 'Good idea!' he said with wonder.

As she left the shop he was walking in a trance towards a pretty young cashier who was bagging some groceries for a customer.

'This wine is corked,' he said, nodding sagely. 'This wine is *corked.*'

I bought a packet of Special K; a tub of Marmite; a tin of sardines; some Chilean wine; one of the rare, collector's item king-size bottles of Smirnoff, which cost just £10; the latest edition of the weekly newspaper, *The Innocent Gazette*; and a fascinating guidebook, *Caribbean Companion* by Brian Dyde, from which I was eventually to learn a great deal about the island's flora, fauna and folklore. Without it I would never have been able to tell the difference between a Green-Throated Carib, a Pearly Eyed Thrasher and a Doctor Bird. I'd never even have *heard* of a Pearly Eyed Thrasher.

I spent that first morning exploring the rest of the island. I could have driven round it in an hour but I took my time and stopped whenever I felt like it. The white beaches on the gentle west coast were caressed by the tranquil, translucent, green Caribbean, warmed by a golden sun, patrolled by massive red crabs and predatory pelicans, fringed by friendly palms and sea-grape trees, and teased by fussy little gangs of tiny sandpipers that scuttled busily through the foam. By contrast the black volcanic beaches on the east coast were harsh and rocky but with a rugged beauty of their own, pounded as they were by exhilarating rollers surging in from thousands of miles of unfathomable Atlantic ocean. Inland the vegetation was surprisingly lush, drenched as it was every afternoon by a brief tropical deluge and then soothed and cosseted by the sun, and further up the mountain the thick, impenetrable rainforest guarded the secrets of the volcano. On each side of the main island road, everywhere, wild bougainvillea and hibiscus tumbled over bushes and branches, even in the wildest jungle, and rampant creepers and vines with pink flowers smothered the rusty hulks of abandoned cars and vans that their owners had dumped many months or years ago in the bush. Birds and butterflies swooped and fluttered in and out of the shade: Purple-Throated Caribs; bright verdant Streamer-tails with their long black feathers; little Honeycreeper Bananaquits with their white-striped eyes and yellow breasts and bottoms. Small white Cattle Egrets with yellow beaks and legs stalked the edges of ponds and marshes, and the high, wide skies were patrolled by murderous red hawks, kestrels and boobies looking for victims.

All over the island the branches of trees and bushes had been decorated with sinister crudity with empty cans, plastic bottles and bits of string and ribbon as if they were bizarre, pagan Christmas trees. Monkeys and mongooses scampered across the road: the monkeys black-faced, white-chested and with green-tinged stomachs; the mongooses still slaughtering the island's rats, just as their ancestors had done centuries ago when they had been shipped in as four-legged slaves to protect the sugar cane fields.

I passed through several hamlets where nervous, thin-faced village dogs with twitchy, pointy, fox-like ears barked hysterically as I drove by. Some of the settlements consisted of no more than four or five shacks but every one supported at least one church and the larger villages had three or four. I counted more than fifty, and this to serve a population of just nine thousand – not only Anglican, Roman Catholic and Methodist churches but Kingdom Halls for Jehovah's Witnesses, congregations of Baptists and Plymouth Brethren, and about a dozen unique little churches that probably exist nowhere else in the world: the Columbus Jump-Up Church, the Innocent Independent Church of God, the Bethlehem Word of the Lord Tabernacle, the New Testament Born Again Community, the Hopetown Hallelujah Church, the Lazarus Rise-Again Temple – *Miracles Performed Twice Daily* – the Cotton Beach Holiness Worship Hall, the Jesus Nazarene Saviour Temple, the Armageddon Praise De Lord, the Twenty-First Century Resurrection Church, and the Reformed Eight Commandments Church, which I discovered later had discarded two of the Ten Commandments because its founder, a fisherman from Mosquito Bay, had decided that neither adultery nor coveting thy neighbour's wife could possibly be a sin because he enjoyed them both so much. And all over the island radios boomed from houses and cars, chastising their listeners with the ranting, hectoring threats of hellfire from dozens of frenetic Christian fundamentalist preachers.

Every corner of the island displayed vivid contrasts between the old and the new. Ancient ramshackle hovels were slowly disintegrating beside smart new air-conditioned houses. Little horse-drawn carts blocked the progress of huge, brand new 4x4s. The only traffic roundabout on the island had been built on the road north out of Columbus, but Innocentian drivers were so baffled by it that I saw one drive the wrong way around it, terrifying a driver coming the other way, and another bewildered local drove straight over the middle of it, taking with him a wooden direction sign, a bollard and a flowerbed. Most of the locals wore cheap, simple clothes, but some seemed surprisingly rich: the women in fashionable outfits and bling jewellery; the men with expensive suits, ties, gold rings and designer watches. Out in the countryside the rusty roofs of tiny tin-shanty chattel houses were decorated with gleaming satellite TV dishes. Ferocious Rastas – swathed in dreadlocks, the odour of marijuana, and tea-cosy headgear in the Ethiopian colours of red, green, gold and black – trundled past on new JCB diggers (back-hoes) and giving genteel hand signals as prescribed in the Highway Code. On one remote stretch of road I overtook a barefoot old man riding a donkey laden with firewood and speaking animatedly on a mobile phone. Miles from anywhere, out in the bush, I would suddenly round a bend and discover a ruined old sugar mill or plantation house hidden among the trees or covered by creepers and the bright pink flowers of the Bee Vine that crawled over everything. The abandoned old buildings, silent relics of the great days of the British Empire, had about them a forlorn beauty that bore witness to the lost dreams of generations of dead Britons, some brutal, not all of them noble, but most of them courageous. Once those elegant old Great Houses had throbbed with vibrant family life and hope, alive with noise and laughter, dinners, balls, soirées; waltzes, quadrilles, Scottish reels and square dancing. Now they were still and silent, inhabited only by the memories of ghosts.

Back home at Hummingbird House, Miz Quaintance was about to leave for the day but she had prepared a cold lunch for me: ham, melon, bread and cheese, tomatoes, some fruit, a bottle of Red Stripe beer. 'An' when you done eatin' you go to you room!' she said firmly.

'Sorry?'

'For you siesta,' she insisted. 'De arternoon too hot for you white folks. You must do you siesta every arternoon. You must lie on you bed an' turn on de fan, yessah. You listen to ol' Miz Quaintance. Me knows.'

She did, too. When she had gone I drank another bottle of beer, suddenly felt exhausted, turned on the ceiling fan in my bedroom, collapsed onto the bed, and slept like a zombie for most of the afternoon. Afterwards I swam in the pool and emerged cool, refreshed and relaxed. I poured myself an icy vodka and tonic, watched the sun go down, and felt happier than I had for years. All the miseries of the past few months, the rows with Barbara, the heavy silences, the meetings with lawyers, the sullen children, the loneliness and tension of the divorce, seemed to evaporate in the stillness of the tropical evening. The sky turned a gentle pink, then crimson, the clouds ablaze, and I sat and watched it until long after dark when a million stars sprinkled the heavens. Soon after nightfall the lights in the house flickered to a feeble, dirty brown and then died all together, a power-cut that lasted until after I went to bed, but I didn't mind at all because at about nine o'clock a huge, terracotta full moon, the size of a giant planet, lifted out of the ocean like an ancient god come to cleanse the world. I sat on the pool deck and watched it in awe for half an hour as it slowly rose in the sky, turning like a chameleon from the colour of dried blood to a glistening gold, then silver, laying a gleaming path towards me across the sea, transmuting the clouds into moody black silhouettes. Columbus had been right: this magical place was surely close to Paradise. Perhaps it was time I began to believe in God again.

# CHAPTER 3

## SMARTLY AND SWEETMAN

Whenever I begin a tax investigation in a foreign country I start with the editor of the local newspaper and pretend to be a visiting travel writer looking for local colour. Journalists are always helpful to reporters from abroad and well informed about their area, and most of them are cheerful, sociable types who love to pass on gossip, which is invaluable for someone in my job.

The editor of the local weekly tabloid, the *Innocent Gazette*, was no exception: Smartly Warner-Perkins was a thin, gawky, toothy black guy in his late twenties with an eager expression, earnest spectacles, and buck teeth so prominent that he could have munched an apple through the strings of a tennis racket. I dropped into his office the next morning, a tiny windowless attic on the edge of town that he shared with his three staff. Above his desk hung a mildewed portrait of the Queen when she was about twenty-five: even though Innocent had been independent for more than forty years it was still a member of the British Commonwealth and Elizabeth II was still its Head of State.

'Good morning,' I said. 'My name's Barron: David Barron.'

'It's afternoon,' he said.

I looked at my watch: 12.06. 'Well, only just,' I said.

'In Innocent you should never say "good morning" when it's after twelve o'clock,' he said, standing up. 'It's very rude. It means you're saying "you're ugly".'

'Good god! Sorry. Why?'

'Don't ask me, Mr Barron. It's just a traditional local belief. But – hell! – I don't give a damn. You can tell me I'm ugly whenever you like.'

We shook hands and I told him that I was writing a long travel piece for the London *Sunday Times*, and after some preliminary chat about my job, Fleet Street and my journey I asked him his real name, assuming that 'Smartly' was his street name.

He grimaced. 'Not at all,' he said. 'It's my real name, my mother's little joke. Like many West Indian parents mine are not married – I'm an outside child – and when I was born my father went back to his wife and told my mother to name me smartly, meaning that she should give me an elegant, distinguished name. My mother was so annoyed that he was abandoning her and me that she decided to enrage him by taking him literally, so she called me Smartly.' He cackled. 'My father was furious!'

'I can't imagine why,' I said politely. 'It's very distinguished, like calling a girl Honesty or Chastity.'

He hooted. 'You won't find many girls in Innocent called Chastity,' he said. 'Her parents would be laughed out of town. There's probably not a single girl here over the age of twelve who's still a virgin. If she hasn't been screwed already by her brother or the boy next door she's probably been had by her uncle or grandfather. We have a saying here that '12 is lunchtime': when a girl reaches 12 she's on the menu.'

'That's shocking.'

He shrugged. 'Well, you're right, of course, and incest is illegal, and men are often sent to prison for it, especially if the girl's very young. But it's pretty common, and some people don't think it's all that sinful. I heard one local preacher argue once on the radio that incest must be OK and is sanctioned by the Bible because Cain or Abel must have slept with his mother or the human race would never have gone on, and if Noah and his children were the only human survivors after the Flood they must have committed incest too for the human race to go on. Some families of seven or eight here sleep naked in one or two small rooms, and it's very hot, and girls mature much quicker in the tropics than they do in Europe or the States.' He grinned. 'We all have boiling testicles, you see.'

'Do you know who your father is?'

He looked surprised. 'Yes, of course. Illegitimacy is always quite open. My dad's the Prime Minister, Eustace Ponsonby. He's also the Minister for Foreign Affairs, Finance, the Interior, Energy, Health, Education and Tourism.' He cackled again. 'And the father of two legitimate and five outside children.'

'And nobody minds? Not even the women?'

'Certainly not. Well, some of the women get angry and possessive, like my mother, but it's widely accepted that a married man will spend Friday nights with his mistress and Saturdays with his wife. In fact I guess my father's won three elections in a row because the voters admire his stamina and fertility. Once again, the Bible itself urges us all to go forth and multiply, and Innocent is such a deeply Christian island that we take that injunction very seriously. The voters are greatly impressed by my father's devout obedience to the word of God.' He chuckled cynically.

'So why's your surname Warner-Perkins and not Ponsonby?'

'My mother's name,' he said.

'And are you married?'

'Yes.'

'Any children?'

He grinned. 'Only one legitimate one, I'm afraid, and one outside child. I'm not as devoutly Christian as my father but I'm working on it. Do you have any kids, Mr Barron?'

'Two teenagers.'

'And you're married?'

'Divorced. Two months ago.'

'I'm sorry.'

'I'm not. She's a bitch.'

He sighed. 'Aren't they all? I think it was God's little joke that he made us need them so much.'

'So you're not a Christian yourself?'

'Good God, no! Christianity has caused more misery for the last two thousand years than any two other religions combined.'

He seemed quite happy to talk completely openly about intimate matters that most Englishmen would avoid, so I asked him more questions that most Englishmen would consider impertinent and inquisitive.

'Are you close to your father?'

He grunted. 'I hardly ever see him. He spends months every year jetting around the world with his latest young girlfriend and begging for handouts from rich countries like Dubai and Abu Dhabi. They give him a few million dollars now and then and in exchange Innocent votes the way they want at the United Nations. You flew in by air?'

'Yes.'

'So didn't you wonder how a poor little island like Innocent could possibly afford to build such a lavish airport?'

'It did seem rather swish.'

'You can say that again, and so are our state-of-the-art cargo harbour and our luxurious TV station. At the moment my old man's in Singapore trying to scrounge several million dollars to resurface all the main roads.'

'So who runs the island when he's away?'

Smartly grimaced. 'Windy Billington.'

'Windy?'

'Chezroy Billington, the Deputy Prime Minister. His street name is Windy because he's a champion farter. In Cabinet meetings the ministers fight each other to sit beside an open window. And he's utterly corrupt. He takes a percentage on everything here, from government contracts, business licences and planning permissions to passports and visas.'

'Why doesn't your father sack him?'

Smartly hesitated, glanced at his three colleagues, and lowered his voice. 'Off the record,' he said, 'I think he's got some rather fruity photos of my father relaxing on a couple of his overseas trips.' He looked at his watch. 'Are you free for lunch? What about joining me for a drink and a bite on the beach?'

'Great idea.'

'Excellent,' he said. 'We'll go to Sweetman's Bar on Pelican Beach. Have you discovered Sweetman's yet?'

'Not yet. I've only been here a couple of days.'

'You don't know Innocent until you've been to Sweetman's. He and his bar are international legends, famous all over the world, and he serves sensational lobster and mahi-mahi and a lethal rum punch with a secret ingredient.'

He stood, reached for a panama hat, and nodded at a buxom black girl sitting at a desk on the other side of the room. 'Hold the fort, will you, Gwendolyn,' he said. 'I won't be long.'

'That'll be the day,' she said.

Smartly looked at me with a woebegone expression. 'See what I have to put up with, day after day? Rudeness. Insolence. Lack of respect.'

'Balls!' said Gwendolyn. 'And don't come back pissed.'

We left his steamy little office and crossed the road towards the jeep. 'Do you have a street name too?' I asked.

'Stupid.'

'I beg your pardon?'

'Stupid. No, not *you*. That's my street name.'

'Stupid?'

'Smartly, you see.'

Of course.

'And your father's street name?'

He grinned. 'When he was at boarding school in England thirty years ago they used to call him Choc, but now they call him Donkey. I can't imagine why.'


Sweetman's Bar was a thatched, wooden log cabin, brightly painted in stripes of red, yellow and green, on the edge of a long, sandy beach furnished with a dozen small tables and wooden benches under pretty little thatched umbrellas. Strung across the ceiling in the bar hung the tattered flags of a score of other nations – the Union Jack, the Stars and Stripes, the French *tricoleur*, the Japanese rising sun – the legacies of dozens of boozy tourists. A cataract of Bob Marley songs tumbled out of the loudspeakers – *No Woman No Cry, Three Little Birds, Stir It Up* – and the walls were plastered with dozens of photographs of Sweetman himself posing with some of the famous customers he had served here over the years: Hollywood stars, American politicians, British pop singers, Caribbean cricketers. He was smoothly black, probably in his mid-forties, and Smartly told me that he had become incredibly rich and that although his real name was Beauregard Beaumont he had been known for years as 'Sweetman' because of his insatiable taste for white women: 'He doesn't care how old or ugly they are so long as they're white,' said Smartly. 'His success rate is incredible: he only has to smile at a white woman and she drops her knickers.'

I could see why: Sweetman was remarkably youthful for his age: slim, fit, lithe and charming, with a deep voice, wide smile, infectious chuckle, and a slow, loping, muscly walk that was full of promise. He was wearing a blue baseball cap, an expensive Caribbean shirt, well cut red shorts, Gucci loafers, two diamond earrings and a fat diamond ring on the middle finger of his left hand.

'Amazingly Sweetman has been happily married for longer than anyone I know, even though he's always screwing other women,' said Smartly. 'His wife's a big fat girl called Mutryce and she adores him, no matter what he gets up to. He's an excellent father, too, unlike so many West Indian men. He really cares about his kids. They have three: a son called Merlot and two daughters called Chablis and Chardonnay.'

'You're joking!'

Smartly chuckled. 'Absolutely not. He loves French wine, and he flies on his own to the South of France for three weeks every summer to stay at the Carlton in Cannes and to drink champagne and eat caviar and cut a swathe through the finest wines and prettiest hookers on the Côte d'Azur. Very sophisticated, our Sweetman. He took his last white mistress – the wife of an American tourist who made the mistake of bringing her here on holiday – to spend a week at the Hôtel de Paris in Monte Carlo and they gambled thousands in the casino every night.'

Sweetman ambled over to us and greeted Smartly warmly. They touched fists the Caribbean way. 'Stupid!' he said. 'Hey, maan, long time no see.'

'I've been very busy.'

Sweetman shook his head. 'All work and no play, maan: not a good idea. You only got one life.'

I was introduced and impressed by Sweetman's firm handshake and direct gaze. This was no descendant of a line of cowed slaves with an inferiority complex, this was a man who was strong, independent and self-assured. No wonder women fancied him.

He treated us to two of his famous rum punches. I sipped mine and it nearly removed the roof of my mouth. Within seconds my tongue and gums were numb. 'My god!' I gasped. 'What's in it?'

'Cleaning fluid, I expect,' said Smartly.

'You been to Innocent before?' said Sweetman.

'No. This is my first time.'

'You like it?'

'I love it. It's beautiful.'

He looked ridiculously pleased, as though I'd paid him a personal compliment. He patted me on the shoulder. 'That's great, maan, great. Thank you for loving my island. Hey, you guys gonna eat? It's the chef's day off but we've still got the cook.'

'What's the difference?' I said.

'The cook ain't got no white hat.'

I laughed.

'OK,' said Smartly. 'We'll take a chance. You got lobster?'

'Yeah.'

'And mahi-mahi?'

'Sure.'

'OK for you, David?'

'Fantastic,' I said.

'No problem,' said Sweetman. 'Comin' up. And take care, Mr Barron: Stupid here's a dangerous guy and he's not as stupid as he looks. See you around.'

He moved away towards the kitchen to shout instructions through the hatch.

'He's easily the most famous chap on the island,' said Smartly, 'including my father. This place of his has been photographed and mentioned in newspapers and magazines all over the world, and more celebrities' buttocks have perched on these benches than any other restaurant in the world.'

'How's he done it?'

'Charm, hard work and bullshit. And excellent food.'

It was, too. An elderly waiter called Fauntleroy served us with two huge platters of lobster cooked in beer, grilled mahi-mahi, prawns in garlic butter, and a delicious island salad with a piquant coconut dressing, and we drank a surprisingly good bottle of Chilean white wine. 'He keeps the Californian muck for the Yanks,' said Smartly, 'and charges them twice as much. Hey, Faunty: tell Mr Barron why you're called Fauntleroy when your real name's Ishmael.'

'Well, sah,' said the waiter, 'when me chillen was small dey done said dey cain't pernounce Ishmael proper, so dey call me Fauntleroy.'

'Is that easier to say?' I said.

'No, sah, but dey say dey remember it better.'

'Innocentian logic,' said Smartly.

Four young white women came into the bar, one of them with a vivid purple birthmark across half of her forehead. Sweetman sat them down at a table and said gently to the disfigured girl: 'You been burned in a fire, young lady?'

She looked uncomfortable. 'No. I was born like this.'

'In that case,' he said softly, 'I'll never notice it again,' and he bent over her and lightly kissed her discoloured forehead. 'You have beautiful eyes,' he said.

I looked at Smartly. He nodded. 'I see what you mean,' I said.

We talked for more than an hour as the tables around us filled up with lazy laughter and people of all ages and colours, many of them American, Canadian and British tourists from the big Sunshine Resort a hundred yards further along the beach: people on holiday, relaxed and happy, the men in baggy swimming trunks and swigging beer from the bottle, the girls in bikinis, tiny shorts or bright sarongs and sipping garishly coloured drinks from frosty glasses. It had become a stunningly hot afternoon, the pale blue sky soft with small, fluffy white clouds, and sweat was surfing down my back. Five or six people were swimming in the sea and small yachts rode the gentle, glittering swell, their flags and sails fluttering in the breeze. In the distance a squat little ferry struggled bravely against the current towards some distant island. A giant white cruise ship lay paralyzed on the horizon as if stunned by the heat. Two of Sweetman's young waiters danced barefoot across the burning sand, balancing laden trays, as the sun reached its zenith and started to hang-glide towards the western horizon. Bob Marley and the Wailers gave way to UB40 – *Kingston Town, The Way You*

*Do The Things You Do, Higher Ground* – and then Bankie Banx, 'the Caribbean Bob Dylan': *The Gypsy Rides, Takin' Over, Busted in Barbados.*

We enjoyed a gloriously fresh fruit salad with chunks of pineapple, paw-paw, mango and banana, we ordered a reckless second bottle of wine, and Smartly gave me a list of people who might be worth talking to: a couple of local politicians; the British vice-consul; an elderly white English couple who'd been living in Innocent for forty years; a boozy Australian woman who ran a beach bar on the north of the island and was apparently having an affair with the Catholic priest. I steered the conversation around to the British expats whom HMRC suspected of tax dodging: Donald Rogers, allegedly a drug smuggler from Essex, and his wife, Tracey; Rupert Williams, an ex-public school conman from Surrey who had founded his own religion to worship Judas Iscariot; and Angela Fellowes, a mysteriously rich divorcée who was running several offshore investment scams thanks to Innocent's lax financial regulations. The French *fisc* had also asked me to sniff around a couple of dubious Frogs who had bought properties here: Michel Lecroix, a gay Provençal painter whom Paris suspected of laundering Mafia money; and Genevieve Savroche, an ex-prostitute from Marseilles who couldn't possibly have accumulated her huge wealth just by lying on her back for ten years in assorted hotel rooms.

'There are stacks of dodgy financial activities here,' said Smartly. 'Shell companies, offshore trusts, Ponzi schemes, Liberian registrations, anonymous bank accounts, money laundering, fictitious invoices, embezzlement, pyramid selling, all sorts of scams. And you'd better speak to Windy Billington, as well.'

'The deputy P. M.'

'Right. He's sleazy and corrupt and he drinks too much brandy, but he's also in charge of several government departments –

planning, fisheries, highways, youth, garbage, recycling – and he does run the island when my father's away. You'll need to slip him a friendly "present" first. A sweetener.'

'He's that obvious?'

'Blatant.'

'So how much?'

He thought. 'Five hundred US should be enough. For starters.'

Five hundred! More than three hundred quid, just for starters! Charlie Wilson in accounts would go into orbit when he saw £300 on my expenses claim 'to bribing Deputy Prime Minister.'

'Is there any chance of talking to your father too?'

He looked doubtful. 'Well, he's due back from Singapore on Wednesday week, but he's always changing his schedule at the last minute and sometimes he disappears for months at a time. You'd better go and see his secretary, Alopecia Martin, and ask her to let you know as soon as he returns.'

'*Alopecia*?'

'Sad, eh? Poor girl. Her parents just liked the sound of the word. They had no idea what it means. And when you talk to her, mention my name. I think she's got a soft spot for me.'

'And the British vice-consul?'

'Bernard Garwen. A mystery, decidedly unsavoury: barely able to speak English, and when he does he sounds like some refugee from Outer Mongolia. I doubt that he's even British. The local Brits loathe him and they're convinced he's involved in something decidedly unpleasant: drugs, maybe, or prostitution, the white slave trade, paedophilia, who knows? He gives me the creeps.'

'How on earth did he become the British vice-consul?'

'Nobody else wanted the job. It's hardly taxing but the local expats are an idle bunch and not one of them could be bothered.'

'Do Innocentians hate the British?'

He looked astonished. 'Certainly not. Why do you say that?'

'Well, our ancestors were slave owners, and some of them were brutally cruel. They kidnapped your ancestors, dragged them out of Africa in chains, shipped them over here, killed hundreds or even thousands of them, and worked them unmercifully until they dropped.'

Smartly nodded. 'OK, I agree it wasn't much fun for the earliest slaves when they came here, but today most of us are grateful to the British. They gave us British law, language, education, infrastructure, standards of honesty and behaviour. And cricket: what would we have done without cricket? And many of us are very grateful indeed that our ancestors were taken from Africa and brought to the Caribbean, because if that hadn't happened we'd all be living in Africa today and perhaps being beaten, tortured, starved and murdered by some monster like Mugabe or Al-Bashir or Obiang.'

'You're very tolerant and magnanimous,' I said.

'Not at all, just logical. It stands to reason: wouldn't anyone rather be here in our little paradise today than in Somalia, the Sudan or Zimbabwe?'

'Politically correct liberals in Britain and the States would go berserk if you told them that you were actually grateful for the slave trade.'

'The bleeding-heart PC brigade don't live in the real world,' he said. 'They live in some rose-coloured fantasy land.' He looked at his watch. 'Bloody hell! It's nearly four. I must get back. We go to press tomorrow and I've still got no front-page splash. Nothing much has happened this week. Hey, I know: I'll report your arrival with a headline saying FAMOUS ENGLISH WRITER PRAISES INNOCENT.'

'I'm not a famous writer,' I said.

'You will be as soon as I say you are.'

'I'd really rather you didn't.'

He sighed. 'Oh, OK, but you've no idea how tricky it is to fill a twenty-four page tabloid every week on an island where nothing ever happens. I'll have to make something up: MAN BITES MONKEY, maybe, or BUMPER TOURIST SEASON EXPECTED. Nobody'll know it's not true. But I'm not letting you off: you'll have to promise that before you leave the island you'll write a full-page article about it for me.'

'You're on,' I said, relieved, 'and lunch is on me.'

'That's very generous. Thank you.'

I called for the bill, and Sweetman brought it himself. 'Island prices, I hope,' said Smartly sternly. 'None of your fancy inflated tourist rates.'

'Of course not,' said Sweetman. 'What you take me for?'

'A rogue and a crook,' said Smartly, 'that's what.'

I paid the bill, left a decent tip and drove Smartly back to his office. 'Thanks for an excellent lunch,' he said, 'and it's been very good to meet you. We must do it again, and please call me if there's anything I can do to help with your research.'

It was well over ninety degrees when I got back to Hummingbird House and so humid that my shirt was plastered firmly to my back even though the jeep's air conditioning was drumming away as frantically as Ringo Starr. Flushed with rum, wine and too much food, hazy, weary and dazzled by reflections of the sun, I collapsed on the bed and slept for two wonderfully self-indulgent hours. In England I would have been ashamed of myself to sleep for so long in the afternoon, but here in Innocent the rules were completely different, all the rules: a long siesta was not shameful, racism just wasn't racism, adultery wasn't really a sin, incest and murder not really serious crimes, and Innocent wasn't innocent. Here anything might happen.

That night at about 8.30 the cable TV service died, and soon after ten o'clock the house was plunged into darkness. Another power cut. I sat on the pool deck again, gazing at thousands of glittering stars, spotting the occasional awesome meteorite streaking across the sky, marvelling at the cacophony of insects, but after an hour or so it was obvious that the lights were not going to come on again soon and I decided to go to bed. As I was cleaning my teeth in the dark the telephone rang suddenly, a shrill cry that made me jump. My heart was beating fast. I went into the bedroom and lifted the receiver on the bedside table.

'Hello?'

There was silence.

'Hello?' I said again.

Complete silence.

'Hello? David Barron here. Who is it?'

The line seemed to be alive, almost to breathe, but soundlessly. Some atavistic instinct told me that there was someone at the other end. And then there was a soft click, and the purring of the dialling tone.

So that was how it started.

# CHAPTER 4

## BOOZY SUZY AND DELCETA QUAINTANCE

I spent my first week in Innocent making contact with some of the people Smartly had suggested, but first I took the island's three main bank managers to lunch at the most expensive restaurants on the island: two charming old seventeenth-century stone plantation inns up in the hills and a modern, vulgar American monstrosity on the beach, the luxurious Sunshine Resort, where glutinous muzak oozed from the loudspeakers and the waitresses wore grass skirts that might just have been acceptable in Hawaii but looked ridiculous in the Caribbean. I told the bankers that I had a couple of million dollars to invest and was not too choosy about where to put it so long as it earned me some seriously high and possibly illegal returns, for which I would happily pay them a large commission. The eldest banker – a huge, pompous Bajan called Mr Small – was obviously keen not to jeopardise his pension, claimed stiffly that Innocent was no longer the haunt of financial pirates, that it had signed the international Mutual Legal Assistance Treaty to combat money laundering and had now been removed from the global offshore blacklist of rogue tax havens. He made it plain that he did not deal with nefarious investments nor with dodgy people like me. The other two bankers had no such scruples. The manager of the Consolidated Bank of Innocent, a shifty young 'redskin' the colour of milky coffee, looked over his shoulder before muttering that he could introduce me (for a fee) to Donald Rogers, the Essex shyster who was already on my hit list. The other manager, a Guyanese Indian who ran the Windward Co-operative Bank, giggled nervously and said that he could recommend me (for a fee) to one of my other targets, Angela Fellowes, whose skill at running several investment scams was apparently legendary.

I asked them to set up these meetings and drove over to Mosquito Beach to introduce myself to the Australian woman who owned the Tamarind Bar, Susan Macdonald. A red jeep with blackened windows followed me out of town and all the way along the coast road. I noticed it only because most Innocentian drivers have an irresistible compulsion to overtake everyone in front of them, even on a bend or in the face of oncoming traffic hurtling towards them, but this guy slowed down whenever I did and picked up speed again at the same time. I parked my jeep in the shade of a palm tree beside the bar and the red jeep pulled up and parked at the side of the road about fifty yards away. I was apprehensive. Who would phone me just before midnight and then say nothing? Who would want to follow me? Or could they simply be coincidence?

The Australian woman told me that everyone called her Boozy Suzy 'because I drink like a metho from Nuggetty Gully.'

'Where's that?' I said.

'Victoria. Outback. Beyond the black stump. Near Talbot. One-whore town – and she was a seriously ugly abo and all.'

She was probably in her late thirties but still attractive in an obvious way. She had cool, aggressive blue eyes, a neat figure, long brown legs, and was wearing very brief khaki shorts and a red tee-shirt over perky nipples and a white slogan that said SO WHAT THE FUCK DO YOU THINK YOU'RE STARING AT? She had bare, sandy feet and was perched on a bar stool under a palm tree, swigging a cold Carib beer straight from the weeping bottle, leafing through the *Innocent Gazette* and smoking a chain of untipped cigarettes. Her voice was as abrasive as sandpaper. A young black barman lurked behind the counter, pretending to polish glasses and trying not to look at her breasts.

'I'm David Barron,' I said.

'Well, don't blame me, mite,' she said. 'Jeez, another fucking Pom! You baastards get everywhere.'

'That's how we conquered half the world, including Australia.'

She put up her hands in surrender. 'Fair go, mite,' she said. 'OK. So what can I do you for? Beer? Rum? Vodka?'

'It's a bit too early for me.'

'*Early*?' She consulted her watch, a chunky job with a big square face. 'Come off it, sport. It's 10.30 already, almost time to move on to the haard stuff.'

'I never drink until twelve at the earliest.'

'Oh, la-di-da! Not just a Pom but a tight-aarsed, teetotal Pom as well.' She shrugged. 'OK, sport, so what're you here for if you don't wanna drink?'

'I need some advice.'

She laughed. 'From *me*? Fuck me, mite, you *must* be in trouble. I don't even ask *myself* for advice.'

'Well, I just need some background info about the island, the people here, and so on. I'm writing a travel article for the *Sunday Times* in London.'

'Bully for you. Sounds better than working. London, eh? I landed up there for a coupla years, way back, when I was nineteen, twenny. Lousy little apaartment in Earl's Court, five of us, all sheilas, coupla lesboes, coupla nymphos, and me. Earl's Court was all Aussies in those days. Great paarties, went on all night: hash, coke, shagging, the works. Outta my skull every weekend. Bonzer!'

She crossed her legs, treating me to a glimpse of soft brown upper thigh. The barman's eyes were like liquorice lollipops. I guess that as soon as he met her the poor old Irish priest had never had a chance. With a shape like hers he and his celibacy were goners right from the start: poor old bugger; goodbye, Paradise; hello, Beelzebub.

'OK, mite,' she said. 'Buy me a beer and I'll dish whatever dirt you need.'

It seemed po-faced not to join her so I bought two sweaty Caribs, sat on another bar stool, and raised my glass in her direction. 'Good luck,' I said.

'Up yer nose.'

She settled back and lit another cigarette.

I pulled a notebook and biro out of my pocket to make myself look like a reporter. 'Any celebrities live here?' I asked. 'The British are obsessed with so-called celebrities: pop singers, film stars, TV presenters, soccer players, preferably all shagging each other like ferrets.'

'Dunking the biscuit, eh? Spearing the bearded clam. Well, there's nothing much wrong with that.'

Such stylish slang, the Aussies. It's a different language.

'Celebs,' I said.

'Well, there's a fat old French poof from Martinique lives over at Jericho. They say he's huge in the aart world. He's huge everywhere else, too, with a mega beer belly: it's a massive verandah over the toyshop, and on the beach he wears obscene little budgie-smugglers.'

'You can't say *poof* any more.'

'You can here,' she said. 'They hate shirt-lifters in the Caribbean. That's one of the reasons I left Sydney: the place's crawling with the baastards: queers, fairies, turd-denters and aarsehole-bandits on every corner.'

I winced. I'm not all that politically correct myself but 'turd-denters' seemed to be pushing it a bit.

'So there's this gay Frenchman,' I said.

'Yeah. He's a so-called aartist, Michel Lecroix, sells his paintings for a million dollars a time. A million *US*! They say he's famous but I'd never heard of him till he came here. His paintings are crap, all complete bollocks, but he's stinking rich and has a stonking great place haalfway up the mountain where he spends most of his time buggering his little black bum boy.'

'So who buys Lecroix's paintings if they're so bad?'

'They say he sells them to the New York Mafia for a million each, pays haalf the money back into a Mafia account in the Caymans, and – bingo! – he's made himself five hundred grand and neatly laundered another five hundred grand for the Mob.'

'Clever. Is he on the island now?'

'I guess so. I saw his faggotty boyfriend cruising in Columbus one night laast week in tight little pink shorts and waggling his aarse. Jeez!'

I scribbled a couple of notes. She lit another cigarette. 'Any actors here?' I said. 'Film stars?'

'We get a few in the winter – Madonna, the Douglases, the Brangelinas – and two or three sail across from Barbados now and then for a day or two, but there's none living here. There's a Scottish guitarist who's got a big estate up at Westfield Ghaut, Rod...'

'... Stewart?'

'... Mackenzie. Roddy Mackenzie. But I'd never heard of him, either, before he came here.'

'Nor me.'

'It's bizaare how many drongoes you've never heard of seem to be so-called staars these days. All those skinny models with no tits and gormless reality TV aarseholes.'

'The celebrity culture,' I said. 'But give them another year or two and nobody will ever hear of them again. What about multi-millionaires? The British love reading about rich people they can hate.'

'We've got plenty of those, mostly Yanks and Canucks. A few Brits too, but not household names.'

'Who?'

'Couple of boring money men: Roger Conroy, Bill Martin, Gerry Molloy. God, I hate financiers and bankers: you can actually smell the greed; like rotten eggs. I guess *bankers* is just cockney rhyming slang. There's one, though, who's fun: a funky young Brit chick called Angie Fellowes. She runs some sort of shady financial shenanigans but she's up for anything. I've sunk a few jars with her, I can tell you.'

'Angie...?'

'Fellowes. Mind you, she's a tad too keen on the local young Rastas. I'm not talking about colour: I *like* black guys. But if you shag one of these young blokes they think you're trash and treat you like shit aafterwards. Mind you, Angie's a match for them. When she first arrived here she walked past three young guys who were lyming in town...'

'Lyming?'

'Hanging out. She walked past them and heard one say to the others: "yo, maan, new white pussy in town." She stopped, turned, smiled, and said: "*Old* white pussy, thank you *very* much".'

I laughed.

'I've got plenty of time for Angie,' she said. 'She's a cool sheila.'

'Any obvious crooks?'

'Only the police. The lawyers. And the politicians.'

'What about eccentrics?' I said. 'Any weirdos?'

'Fuck me, mite! You gotta be jokin'. Any weirdos? In Innocent? Is the Pope a Nazi? There's more weirdos here than fleas on a dingo's dick.'

'Like?'

'Well, let's see. There's the Featherstonehaughs, for a staart.' She pronounced it Feather-stone-haws. 'Coupla snooty old Brits, been here centuries.'

'They probably pronounce their name *Fanshaw*,' I said.

'What?'

'Fanshaw.'

'The Feather-stone-haws?'

'Yes: I reckon they call themselves the Fanshaws.'

'You're joking.'

'It's one of those quaint old English things, like Cholmondely's pronounced *Chumley* and Mainwaring's *Mannering*.'

'Quaint be buggered. It's just bloody stupid: typical Pom bollocks. Anyway, I don't give a tinker's toss what they call themselves. Their first names are poncy enough as it is: Peregrine and Venetia, would you believe, both with plums in their mouths and carrots up their aarses. He's an arrogant old baastard and she's as bonkers as a duck-billed platypus. They've been here for centuries and own haalf the island, bought it years ago when you could pick up ten slaves and a hundred acres for sixpence.'

'You don't like them much.'

'Well done, detective! They should make you chief of police. Jeez, I hate pretentiousness and snobbery. I drove into the Sunshine Resort the other day and I was stopped at the gate by a pompous security guard who knows me very well but said stiffly: "And what is your porpoise here today, madam?" What is your *porpoise*? "I'm here for a piss and the *New York Times*," I said.'

I laughed. 'Any others?'

'There's a Norwegian woman who runs bollock-naked through Columbus whenever there's a full moon, and there's a sinister bloke who's just been appointed the Brit vice-consul even though he can haardly speak English: Bernard Gaarwen, looks like a sheep-shagger. There's a German guy whose wife disappeared recently and everyone's convinced he's murdered her but no one can prove it. Then there's Sandy McDowall: he's a hypochondriac Scottish quack who keeps telling you about all his physical ailments and asking your medical advice. And there's my current squeeze, Brendan Mulchrone, an Irish priest who doesn't believe in God. "How can you carry on as a priest, then?" I said. "Isn't God going to get seriously pissed off with you?" *"Not if he doesn't exist,"* he said. "You deserve to be defrocked," I said. *"Me and half the rest of the clergy too,"* he said. But at least he's human and not a bloody paedophile like a lot of those left-footer God-botherers.'

'I suppose most of the expats here are British, Yanks or Canadians?'

'Pretty much, though a couple of Russkies turned up a few weeks back, Nikita and Anna, and they seem to be planning to stay. Moscow mafia, I reckon. They've got pots of money and already they've paid fifty thousand U.S. each to buy Innocentian citizenship.'

'You can do that? Just a few weeks after you arrive?'

'Sure. You don't even need to come here. Anyone can buy citizenship here so long as you buy property worth a million US or more. They've bought a bloody great mansion up the top of Goatshit Hill.'

'That's never its real name!'

'Why not? Goats have been crapping up there ever since Columbus sailed by and his entire crew was suddenly pole-axed by a severe bout of Barbados Belly and had to run for the handrail and dangle their aarses over the side for the rest of the day. It's on the other side of the island. Ever since then it's been called Shitten Bay.'

I laughed. 'So what about the Russians?'

She shrugged 'Who knows? They seem polite enough. Some people think they're KGB.'

'That doesn't exist any more.'

'Well, whatever it's called now: Putin's Polizei; Vlad's Impalers; whatever. They've got some huge aerials and satellite dishes on their roof, but what the fuck would the KGB want with a tiny speck of rock in the Caribbean like this one? Maybe they're just tax dodgers, like everyone else.'

'And the vodka's incredibly cheap.'

'So's the scotch,' she said, 'so you can buy me a laarge Famous Grouse. All this gossip is seriously thirsty work.'

I bought her a whisky and she told me some more wacky stories about the island, one of them about a bored old Canadian expat who kept trying to commit suicide but never got it right: even when he tried to hang himself the rope broke. About a crafty Danish woman who put a stop to her daughter's affair with a young black guy by seducing him herself and telling her daughter.

'There's an old French hooker called Genevieve Savroche over at Williams Ghaut who's completely bonkers, maybe because she's bonked all her brains out,' said Suzy. 'She said to me once: "Suzette, my 'usband 'e is vairy ignorant. 'e tells me all ze time 'you are a stupid count' an' he knows vairy well zat I am a countess'." White women go mad on this island if they stay too long. You can see them all over the place with their glassy eyes and fixed grins. Too much heat, booze and boredom.'

'You too?'

She chuckled. 'Not yet, but it caan't be long.'

'So how long have you been here?'

'Ten years now, and I wouldn't live anywhere else, but you do need a sense of humour. The locals would drive you mad if you took them seriously. They're always late for everything – there's something here called Innocent Time, which is two or three hours later than real time – and they don't turn up for appointments and they're unbelievably inefficient. The shops are always short of food, the internet keeps breaking down, the telephone system goes dead, and last night Cable TV suddenly went off the air because the company hadn't paid its electricity bill and the electricity company simply cut them off without any warning, even though the electricity and TV companies are both owned by the government.'

'That's mad.'

'You said it.'

'So why do you like living here so much?'

She lit another cigarette, inhaled deeply, and thought about it. 'There's an irresistible charm that I've never found anywhere else,' she said. 'Last year a couple of young burglars broke into one of my friends' houses and demanded money. He said he didn't have any in the house. They threatened to beat him up if he didn't fork out, so he said he could let them have a cheque, they said that would do, and the police were waiting at the bank the next morning when they turned up to cash it.'

I laughed.

'Another friend of mine had her handbag stolen one night with all her credit cards, driving licence, passport, etc, but the burglar returned the next night to return everything except the money. He left a note saying "sorry to rob you, lady. I need the money but you need these".' She chuckled. 'That's Innocent. There's a pace of life here, a gentleness and tolerance, that I've never found anywhere else. They know that there's much more to life than slogging your guts out so that you can earn more and spend more. You can take your time here. You can waste it. Life shouldn't be just about money. It's to be enjoyed and savoured. You ought to have time to gaze at the horizon.'

I took a chance. 'So if you're so happy why do you drink so much?'

She stared at me. 'You're a cheeky baastard, aaren't you?' Then she laughed. 'Good question,' she said. 'The answer is that I like the taste of booze and I like having a small buzz on all day – not to be pissed, just to take the edge off reality. Like the Rastas smoking ganja. It makes life a little lighter, a little more fun. Too much reality can be a killer.'

'So can booze. And cigarettes.'

'Well, you've got to die of something. I can never understand this modern obsession with health, jogging, exercise, all that crap.

People seem to think that they can eventually die in perfect health. No, they caan't: they're going to end up seriously sick, whatever they do. It's pathetic to be so hypochondriac and narcissistic.'

I wondered what had brought her here, what had brought all the expats here. 'So do all these expats have something in common?' I said. 'Something similar that drove them all to come and live on a tiny island?'

She thought about it, 'I guess maybe we're all fugitives. We're all hiding from something, running away from something: the taxman, wives, husbands, duty, security, responsibility, real life, maybe ourselves.'

'And have you succeeded?'

'Nah. The trouble is that wherever you run you have to take yourself along as well.'

I closed the notebook and put it away. 'Well, I'd better be off,' I said. 'I mustn't take up your whole morning.'

'I'm not going anywhere,' she said.

'You've been very kind. Thanks.'

'You're welcome,' she said. 'Any time. There's plenty more where that came from. You here long?'

'A month, maybe two. However long it takes.'

'Everything here takes three times as long as you expect. It's the island philosophy: *No problem, maan. Don' worry. Be happy.* Well, you know where to find me. If you want me.'

I realised suddenly how vulnerable she was, how lonely, perhaps, under all that raw Down Under brashness. I surprised both of us by stepping forward and kissing her on the cheek. 'Thanks,' I said.

She touched her cheek and smiled. 'I'm having a Valentine's Day paarty here on Wednesday night,' she said. 'Come along, meet some people. From 5.30 until.'

'Until what?'

'Until it ends. Whenever. You married?'

'Divorced.'

'Good. There'll be lots of girls.'

'It was only two months ago.'

'That's plenty of time to get over it. Time to get up and live again.'

'Well, I'd love to come, anyway. Thanks.'

'Great. See you then.'

She smiled again. She really was very attractive.

'*Ciao*,' she said.

No one in England has said *ciao* for twenty years. Unless they're Italian, of course.

As I headed back into town the red jeep with the blackened windows pulled out from the verge behind me and followed me all the way. On the outskirts of Columbus, bolder now that I was surrounded by witnesses, I braked suddenly and jumped out to see who my stalker was and to ask him what the hell he was doing, but the red jeep's windows were so dark that I could see nothing inside. It swerved, overtook me, and sped into town. I followed as fast as I could but found myself stuck behind a truck and a huge cement mixer in the middle of town and by the time we moved on I'd lost the red jeep somewhere in the maze of little alleyways running down towards the harbour.

I returned to Hummingbird House to cool off in the pool, nervous now. Why would anyone phone me and follow me? The sun was high, the day sweltering even though the clouds were fat and low. The two randy dragonflies were flirting just above the surface of the water and darted off to dance together across the wooden deck. A couple of huge terracotta butterflies fluttered beside a bougainvillea bush.

Miz Quaintance emerged from the house with a buxom black girl of seventeen or eighteen.

'Hello, Miz Quaintance,' I said. 'How's life?'

She frowned ferociously. 'Ah's *terrible*, Lard David,' she said. 'Me sure is vex. Me head bang bad an' me bottom belly walk.'

No, I didn't ask about her bottom belly: I didn't think I'd like to know the answer.

She pushed the girl towards me. 'Dis me neice, Delceta Quaintance, You Lardship. Go on, girl: say hello to 'is Lardship.'

The girl looked sullen and hung her head.

'Say hello,' growled Miz Quaintance, prodding her.

''ello,' mumbled the girl.

'Her am very pretty, no, You Lardship?'

'Yes, very,' I lied.

'She got nice big tops.'

I suddenly realised what was going on. Dear God, Miz Quaintance was pimping for me.

'Yes.'

'Also nice big bottom.'

'Yes. Very.'

She cackled. 'Big bottoms be good: more cushion for de pushin'!'

She cackled again. 'You like her, You Lardship?'

'Er… yes… um… well…'

Miz Quaintance winked horribly. She was shameless. 'You want her stay wid you a liddle after I gone?'

'Well, in fact I…'

'No problem. Her like you also, me can tell. Dat not so, Delceta? You tell 'is Lardship you likin' him lots, you want stay wid him a liddle.'

The girl looked at me with distaste.

'That's very kind of her,' I said quickly, 'but I'm very tired, Miz Quaintance. It's the heat, I think. I need a siesta.'

'Delceta like de siesta also. Dat not so, Delceta? You like sleepin' in de day.'

The girl shook her head morosely.

A brief shower of rain wafted across the garden, sprinkling us even though the sun was shining brightly, giving me a chance to change the subject hastily. 'When it rains but the sun's still shining it's known in parts of Africa as a Monkey's Wedding,' I said.

'Why dat?'

'I've no idea.'

'Dat blasphemious. Weddin's is for de Good Lard, not for de animals. Shame on dem Africans.'

The rain stopped as suddenly as it had started and Miz Quaintance and Delceta pedalled off on two wobbly little bikes into the steaming haze, Miz Quaintance looking peeved, Delceta relieved. Perhaps Miz Quaintance ran a brothel as well as a rum shop and gambling den.

I plunged into the pool, watched solemnly by my two tame kingbirds, and swam twenty deliciously cool lengths. It would doubtless be raining in London: not a sudden, exciting tropical downpour or the gentle sprinkle of a Monkey's Wedding but the whingeing, wheedling, insistent, bone-chilling wetness of grey English winter rain. It struck me then that a Monkey's Wedding was precisely what life was like in Innocent: one moment it felt like paradise but the next you were sorely vex or apprehensive. One moment you were extremely happy, the next your bottom belly walk or you realised that someone was following you. There's an old Arab proverb that seemed particularly appropriate now in Innocent: 'Life is like a banana: one moment it's in your hand and the next it's up your arse.'

The phone rang again that night, just before midnight, and again there was nobody there. The line seemed to whisper but without any sound. I double-locked all the doors and windows before I went to bed.

# CHAPTER 5

## SHADOWS OF THE BRITISH EMPIRE

It took me ten minutes on the telephone to persuade Peregrine Featherstonehaugh to meet me.

'I cannot see any possible value in such an encounter,' he said in a thin, querulous voice.

'I'd much appreciate it,' I said.

'No doubt you would, Barron,' he quavered peevishly, 'but I should not.'

He didn't have a title or even an OBE but he was the sort of snobbish Englishman who thinks he should have been knighted years ago.

'I'm told that you know more about Innocent than anyone alive, Sir Peregrine,' I said craftily.

'Or dead,' he said. 'Your information is correct.'

There was a hum on the line like an irritated mosquito. 'You say you are writing an article? For the *Sunday Times*?'

'Yes, Sir Peregrine.'

'I despise journalists.'

'Me too,' I said. 'I'm writing this piece only as a favour to an old friend. I'm really a novelist.'

'A *novelist*?' he said. 'I thought only women write novels, and moronic women, at that. So you intend to concoct a farrago of lies about us?'

'Certainly not, Sir Peregrine,' I said. 'I'd be quite happy to let you read and approve the article before it's published.'

'Hmm.'

The mosquito hummed and began to whistle.

'You *are* English?'

'On both sides, for generations.'

'How old?'

Rude old bugger. 'Forty-six,' I said.

'Hmm.' He thought. 'Decent school?'

Bloody cheek. And they say that an English gentleman is never rude unintentionally. He'd been to Eton, of course, and looked down on every other school.

'Harrow,' I said off the top of my head. I'd never been to Harrow nor any other English public school, but Harrow sounded respectable enough. Winston Churchill had been to Harrow.

'*Harrow*?' said Featherstonehaugh. 'Good God, Barron, I hope you're not one of those four-letter Harrow bounders who wear brown suede shoes. Even in *Town*.'

'Absolutely not, Sir Peregrine. Polished black Lobbs for me, always.'

'Hmm. University?'

'Cambridge,' I lied. 'Magdalene.'

'*Magdalene*? Good Lord! Fourth-rate college for drunken yobs, named after a Hebrew prostitute with grubby feet.'

There was silence for several seconds. The line crackled. The mosquito whined.

'Nevertheless I'm a Cambridge man myself,' he said in his shrill little voice, 'so I shall give you twenty minutes, tomorrow at 1630 hours. Here. Sugarmill Estate, just off the main road near Parrot Ghaut. Come straight up to the hice. And I cannot abide unpunctuality.'

'That's very good of you, Sir Peregrine,' I smarmed.

'Yes, it is' he said. '*Noblesse oblige*.'

I arrived ten minutes early just to be on the safe side. The old plantation house was hidden beyond tall, wrought-iron gates adorned with a pompous family crest and a Latin motto. I stepped out of the jeep to open the gates and glanced at the crest, which featured a dragon, a gryphon, a ship, an open book, and the motto *Noli Me Tangere* – 'Don't Touch Me'. The long gravel driveway was losing its battle with weeds and was lined on each side with the ruins of several small, abandoned stone buildings and two ancient, rusting copper sugarcane boilers. The house itself, a large stone mansion, lurked behind a thick riot of frangipani, poinsettia and Match-Me-If-You-Can.

I parked the jeep beside a pink oleander bush, climbed the wide, shallow front steps towards a tall mahogany door that was guarded by two hefty stone lions, and pulled at the heavy iron doorbell. There was a distant jangle of bells like the chimes of Big Ben. After twenty seconds or so the door was opened by a tiny, skeletal white woman, probably in her late seventies, with a blaze of frosty hair, pale blue translucent eyes, ochre skin, and surprisingly big bare feet with long, jagged toenails. She was wearing a pearl necklace, pink frilly blouse, faded blue shorts and a distant, vacant smile. 'Hello hello hello!' she trilled in a cracked falsetto voice. 'Welcome welcome! *Lovely*! *Su*per! Come in come in come in!'

'Good afternoon, Mrs Fanshaw,' I said, extending my hand. 'Barron?'

She glared at me. 'Certainly *not*!' she said indignantly. 'I have had *three* children!'

'I'm sorry,' I said. 'You misunderstand me. *I'm* Barron.'

She adopted a sudden, distraught expression. 'Oh, my *dear*!' she said, patting my arm consolingly. 'How *frightful* for you! I am *so* sorry! Children and grandchildren are *such* a comfort in old age. But the doctors can do wonderful things these days to improve your sperm count.'

'No, you misunderstand me. My *name* is Barron. David Barron.'

She looked bewildered for a moment and then gave a manic cackle. She grasped my hand in two skinny claws. 'How *silly* of me! Of *course* you are! Peregrine *is* expecting you. *Do* follow me.'

She skipped ahead like a child, humming loudly but tunelessly, and led me through several large, airy rooms where huge fans caressed the heat with little effect, and out onto a broad verandah with simple bamboo furniture and a stunning view high across the sea towards the distant hazy silhouette of a nearby island. I followed her down another cascade of generous stone steps, these guarded by fat stone dragons, and onto a grassy lawn surrounded by a blaze of red hibiscus, white bougainvillea, yellow, pink and crimson frangipani, red and orange Flame of the Forest. We crossed the lawn towards a small green pergola beside a wide swimming pool where a tiny, hairless old white man with huge ears was sitting at a wooden table and hunched over a laptop computer. He was wearing rimless glasses, a garish Caribbean shirt, khaki shorts, short white socks and sandals, and beige teeth. No English gentleman has ever worn socks and sandals. So much for Featherstonehaugh's snobbish pretentions. His wife skipped towards him trilling gaily 'la-la-*la*-la-la-la-la!' to the tune of *Lillibullero*, 'la-la-*la*-la-laaa-la!'

'For God's sake, Venetia!' he said peevishly. He looked up with dark, suspicious little eyes that were set too close together. 'What *is* it, woman?' he snapped in his piping voice.

'Mr *Barton*, darling! *You* know! Don't be *horrid*!'

'Barron,' I said.

'The man from *Anglesey*, Peregrine,' she said.

'England,' I said.

'Mr Baring.'

'Barron. David Barron. The *Sunday Times*,' I said. I offered him my hand. 'Sir Peregrine,' I said. 'How do you do?'

He looked at my hand with distaste and did not take it. He glanced at his watch. 'You're early,' he quavered irritably.

'Five minutes,' I said. 'I always think it's better to be slightly early rather than late.'

He sniffed. 'One should neither be early nor late. Both are impolite. I detest unpunctuality and impoliteness.'

I resisted the temptation to pick him up by his enormous ears and toss him into his swimming pool. 'I do apologise, Sir Peregrine,' I said.

He sighed. 'Very well,' he said. 'I suppose you had better be seated.' He waved me towards a lumpy, chintzy old sofa with its back to the sea. I sat and retrieved my notebook, resuming my pose as a journalist.

'Would you care for a *lovely* glass of champagne, Mr Beaton?' trilled Mrs Featherstonehaugh.

'Barron,' I said.

'Don't be ridiculous, Venetia!' he barked. 'It is still the middle of the afternoon. We are not *all* alcoholics.'

'Temper, temper!' she said. She pouted grotesquely, shuffling her false teeth.

'Go away, woman,' he said, flapping his hand at her. 'Go on, back into the hice. Go on.'

'Now you're being *horrid* again, so I'm going to go and get myself a *teensy-weensy* little brandy!'

He sighed. 'Dear God,' he said.

She skipped back into the house singing 'la-la-*la*-la-la-la-la! La-la-*la*-la-laaa-la!'

He closed his laptop, pushed it away and sighed heavily. 'So what do you want to know?' he said. 'I can spare you no more than fifteen minutes. I am extremely busy.'

'Of course, Sir Peregrine,' I said. 'I believe you first came here from Britain more than forty years ago?'

'That is correct.'

'Why?'

He glared. 'Don't be impertinent,' he squeaked. 'That is none of your business.'

It wouldn't have been to escape tax, not that long ago, when Innocent was still a British colony and residents paid British taxes. Perhaps he had been a son of one of those English families that used to despatch their embarrassing relatives to the colonies to get them out of the way.

'I'm sorry,' I said. 'I'm just interested in what made the island so attractive even then.'

He sat back in his chair and folded his prissy little hands across his lap. His beady little eyes pierced mine. From inside the house came the shrill warbling of Venetia Featherstonehaugh attempting to sing *Baa Baa Black Sheep*.

'It was a haven of sanity and decent, old-fashioned values in a world that was fast going to perdition,' he said. 'Innocent was indeed innocent then. It was utterly primitive when we first came here in 1965, when my wife and I decided to leave an England that was no longer the country that once we had loved. By then it was already in decay and infected with atheism, promiscuity, drug-taking, greed, crass television programmes, yobbishness, selfishness and self-indulgence. Ill-bred northern working class yobs were making millions by strumming guitars and shrieking, and men whose fathers had saved the world from Hitler were mincing about with flowers in their hair. England no longer seemed to have any moral standards or to believe in the old English virtues of decency, fair play, politeness, thrift and self-restraint. By contrast Innocent had no crime at all, and nobody locked their hizes even when they went out. There were only twenty-five Europeans here when we came, mostly English, and just seven motors. We had no television, telephones, electricity, running water or sewage system. We lit candles and gas or kerosene lamps, and collected rainwater in cisterns under the hice, and relieved ourselves in long-drop pit lavatories outside the hice. If we chose to invite people to dinner we would leave a verbal message for them with two old black women who used to spend all day sitting on the steps of the old court-hice in Columbus and they would pass on the invitation the next time your invitees passed by. Land was unbelievably cheap, wages extremely low, unemployment high because the sugar industry was already dying, and even a man who was comparatively poor in England could afford to buy a hundred acres here, build a big hice, and employ a dozen servants. Agriculture was difficult because the monkeys ate most of the crops. They still do, which is why you won't find many crops grown here – just a few paw-paws, mangoes, bananas and broccoli – but at first we farmed cattle and sheep and exported the meat to the neighbouring islands. There was only one hotel, the Nelson, which was built in Columbus in the eighteenth century for the shiploads of English gentry who sailed across the Atlantic to bathe here in the warm volcanic mineral water at Hot Springs. Innocent was still uncorrupted by the modern world. It was old-fashioned, law-abiding, decent, disciplined, polite and well-mannered. It reminded us of how England must have been in the Twenties and Thirties.'

'And it's still like that?'

'It has changed, of course. It was an English colony then and now it's an independent black state with a vote at the United Nations.'

'What, with a population of just ten thousand people?'

'Certainly. Why ever not?'

'Well, there are villages in England with bigger populations.'

'That's as may be, but the Innocentians are fully entitled to complete representation in the councils of the world, and they bring to those councils a wisdom, character and morality that is tragically lacking in the big western nations. They're very conservative and well aware of the cultural dangers that have begun to threaten the island: television, violence, drugs, materialism, and creeping Americanisation. Drug runners are increasingly using the islands of the Caribbean to smuggle cocaine from South America to the USA, with the inevitable result that crime and violence are increasing. Many of the young, who used to love cricket, are now playing baseball, netball, and carrying knives, and nowadays they insist on observing horrible, spurious American occasions such as Hallowe'en and Grandmother's Day. So vulgar. And the young now are less gentle and tolerant than their parents and grandparents. But despite all that, Innocent is still an oasis of quiet, old-fashioned courtesy and civilization in a world that is careering out of control towards the slime. Not only are they the nicest people in the world, they also still revere the old English values and traditions like morris dancing on St George's Day. They still celebrate the Queen's birthday each year with a garden party at Government House, and they still have a parliamentary system that is so democratic that just a handful of votes in just one of the six small constituencies can overthrow the government, and when the government is overthrown it goes, unlike those in so many other allegedly democratic Third World countries.'

'And is your wife as fond of Innocent as you are?'

He looked startled, as though he had never even considered asking her opinion. 'Of course,' he said. 'What an extraordinary question.'

I doubted whether Venetia Featherstonehaugh knew or cared where she lived or what the time of day might be, but she seemed happy enough in her childlike world. Looking up at the house from the pergola I could see her skipping about on the verandah and attempting without success to sing *The Lord of the Dance* in tune.

'What about racism?' I said.

'Very rare. You could not live here if you disliked black people, though I do remember that when one elderly Englishwoman first arrived a few years ago she enquired in bewilderment "what on earth are all these coloured people doing here?"'

He gave a shrill little laugh, the first hint that he might have something like a sense of humour.

'I meant the locals,' I said, 'anti-*white* racism.'

He looked bewildered. 'How do you mean?'

'I mean do the locals resent, dislike or hate white people?'

'Good Lord, no. There's never been anything like that here.'

'Why not? White people here are much richer than most of the blacks. Don't they resent you coming here and buying up all their land and living so much better than they do?'

'Certainly not. Some of us have been here longer than they have, and we've always treated them well. During the days of the Empire we always used to give our servants our cast-off clothes and shoes to wear, and we paid for their children to go to school, and we gave them all bonuses at Christmas, and for years I paid pensions voluntarily to a couple of our old retainers. Even in the eighteenth century the plantation owners gave their slaves their own plots of land and time to work on them to feed their families, and even nowadays a squatter can move onto a plot of empty land and if no one else has laid legal claim to it after twelve years that plot becomes the squatter's. Throughout the late nineteenth and early twentieth centuries the returns from growing sugar dwindled to such an extent that many of the plantation owners simply abandoned their hizes and estates to go to America, or back to England, and the locals moved onto the land, squatted, and eventually look legal possession of it. And during the wars of the eighteenth century, when the Caribbean bristled with warships and the English and French fought each other for possession of every island, the plantation owners here took the huge risk of arming their slaves with pistols and muskets so that they could help to defend the island against invasion. They trusted them with their lives, and the islanders have never forgotten or betrayed that trust.'

'Remarkable.'

'Many of them own their own homes and they appreciate white tourists and expatriates coming here and spending money to bolster the local economy. In fact the island's prosperity would collapse if there were no tourism or immigration, so they know that they need the whites. Tourism is the mainstay of the economy. You have only to look at the Sunshine Resort, which employs nearly forty per cent of the population, to realise that Innocent would be bankrupted if they ever pulled out. Until they built the resort the unemployment rate was seventy per cent but now it's negligible, and there's no real poverty here at all. You'll never see a beggar or someone in rags. The only racial tension here is between the Innocentians and the Indian immigrants from Guyana, and that is not so much racial as economic – because the Guyanese work harder, are more reliable, and are resented for stealing the locals' jobs. And the locals are deeply Christian, whereas the Guyanese tend to be Hindu.'

'Are there any Muslims here?'

'A couple of the Guyanese, I believe, but it's not a problem, thank the Lord. We're not likely to have any suicide bombers here. But I'll tell you what they do have here: an extraordinary level of class discrimination. The Innocentians are hugely snobbish. You'll never see a civil servant marrying anyone other than another civil servant or a teacher, doctor or nurse, someone professional.'

He looked at his watch. 'Gracious!' he squeaked. 'This is quite intolerable. You have detained me for far too long. You really must go now. My time is extremely valuable. I have a great deal to do.'

He flapped his hand at me, waving me away, and opened his laptop again.

'You've been very kind,' I said. 'Thank you. But there's just one more question I'd like to ask.'

'Really!' he said irritably. 'This is too much.'

'Tax dodging,' I said.

'I *beg* your pardon?'

'Innocent used to be notorious as an offshore haven for tax

dodgers, fraudsters and money launderers and all sorts of financial misbehaviour.'

'No longer,' he said, a little too quickly, and I knew he was lying. After years of conducting tax investigations I had learned to spot instinctively those who were not telling the truth. 'That used to be the case,' he said, 'but in recent years the Innocentian government has signed all the international treaties, and now it observes all the necessary regulations so that Innocent is no longer on the blacklist of rogue régimes.'

I didn't believe a word of it.

'You've been very helpful, Sir Peregrine,' I said.

'You will let me see anything you write before it is published?'

'Absolutely. You have my word, as a Cambridge man.'

He grunted and turned away.

'Don't bother to see me out,' I said, knowing very well that he had no intention of doing so.

I offered my hand. He ignored it.

'I trust we'll meet again before too long,' I said.

'I very much hope not,' he said. 'We do not mingle.' He might just as well have added 'with people like you.'

As I crossed the verandah Mrs Featherstonehaugh greeted me like an old lover, wrapping her scrawny little arms around me and kissing me wetly on the cheek. 'Goodbye goodbye goodbye!' she trilled, and as I descended the stone steps at the front of the house, past the giant lions and out to the jeep, I heard her singing tunelessly again in the depths of her old colonial mansion:

> *Goodbye-eee! Goodbye-eee!*
> *Wipe the tear, baby dear, from your eye-eee.*
> *Though it's hard to part, I know,*
> *I'll be tickled to death to go,*
> *So don't cry-eee, don't sigh-eee,*
> *Bonsoir, old thing! Cheerio! Chin-chin!*
> *Nah-poo! Toodle-ooo! Goodbye-eee.*

Madness obviously has its carefree compensations.

When I got back to Hummingbird House as the shadows lengthened I found that one of the two locks on the front door was smashed. Someone had tried to break in but had been foiled by the sturdy deadlock. I checked the back door and discovered that was damaged too. This was no longer funny. Maybe I should go to the police, but Smartly had said that they were useless and many of them related to many of the villains, so what was the point? I barricaded the doors, pushing heavy furniture up against them, and propped ornaments, crockery and glassware on all the window ledges so that if someone forced a window I'd hear them. When I went to bed I took a big kitchen knife with me and locked the internal door, but I slept badly, twitching and turning, and at 2.15 I heard three loud gunshots close to the house. Someone was trying to frighten me and they were making a damned good job of it.

# CHAPTER 6

## ALOPECIA AND WINDY BILLINGTON

I phoned Smartly in the morning to ask his advice. He sounded seriously concerned.

'Is it worth going to the police?' I said.

'Waste of time. They're hopeless.'

'Should I buy a gun?'

'It's illegal unless you have a licence, and the police are so slow you might have to wait two or three months.'

'So what the hell do I do?'

He thought about it. 'You'd be better off with a long machete. There's no law against having a machete: everyone has one. Or you could hire a security guard to patrol your grounds all night, but they're just as bad as the cops. In fact most of them *are* retired cops. And they're notoriously unreliable and tend to fall asleep on the job. Your best bet would be to move into a hotel.'

I didn't fancy that: too many tourists, too many loud Americans. I'd become very fond of Hummingbird House already. I'd rather improve the locks, have a few solid bolts fitted.

'So who could be behind this?'

Maybe one of the expats I'd come to investigate? Maybe s/he knew who I was and was trying to frighten me away? Maybe some corrupt taxman back in England had warned one of my targets that he was in the frame. It's happened before. We're not all angels, and taxmen are disgracefully badly paid.

'God knows,' I said.

'Well, take care,' said Smartly. He grinned. 'And don't take sweets from any strange men.'

Miz Quaintance was horrified when I told her what had happened. 'Dat *te'bble!*' she cried. 'Who be done dis?'

'I don't know,' I said.

'OK,' she said, 'I come sleep wid you ebery night.'

I swallowed nervously.

'Nobuddy mess wid me!'

'That's awfully kind of you,' I stammered, 'but it's really not necessary.'

'I sleep un de sofa, no problem, an' I bring me snickersnee. Somebuddy break in de 'ouse an' 'e get more dan 'e bargain for, yes sir!'

I managed to talk her out of it and persuaded her instead to call a locksmith and have the doors fitted with a second deadlock each and each window with a couple of bolts. Then I drove into town to make an appointment to see the Prime Minister. His office was in a smart new government building on the edge of town with gleaming white walls, green hurricane shutters and a bright green roof. It was surrounded by lush gardens sculpted around a pelican-shaped fountain that gushed into the middle of a fishpond with red, white and yellow water lilies. I drove up the short cobbled drive and parked in a space marked VIPS ONLY. Why not? People take you at your own estimation. An old friend of mine used to pretend that he'd achieved a Double First at Oxford and no one ever questioned it. As I stepped from the jeep a monkey strolled across the lawn, sneered at me and gave me the finger.

The front door was solid mahogany with a large, polished brass doorknob in the middle. Fixed to the wall was an elegant dark green plaque with gold lettering that read:

OFFICE OF THE PRIME MINISTER

THE HONORABLE EUSTACE Q. PONSONBY

MP, CBE, GPI, MA

*OFFICIUM ET DIGNITAS*

The Latin was a nice touch and I enjoyed especially the CBE, which meant that the Queen had made Ponsonby a Commander of the Order of the British Empire – a pleasant irony considering that he was descended from ancestors who had been enslaved by the same British Empire of which he was now a Commander even though it no longer exists. But the American spelling of *Honourable* annoyed me: unreasonably, I know; American spellings like *center*, *draft* and *thru* are much more logical than their British equivalents.

I pressed the bell and the door was opened by a young policeman wearing a white cap with a shiny peak, a spotless white jacket with insignia on the collars and gold buttons up to the neck, sharp blue trousers with a white stripe down each leg, and a highly polished black belt and boots. On his left breast was pinned a silver badge that identified him as PC 382. I entered the lobby and basked in the gentle coolth of air conditioning. Two well-dressed young women, both speaking on telephones, sat behind a broad reception desk: one very fat and jolly, one thin and serious. Innocentians seem to be descended from two quite different African tribes: one massively obese and fleshy, the other slim, tall and dignified, like the Masai of Kenya or the peoples of Ethiopia and Somalia. On the wall behind them hung the handsome portrait of the Prime Minister that I'd seen at the airport, the one with the naughty smile, and beside it the Innocentian coat of arms: the green volcano and palm tree bordered by gold for the beaches, blue for the sea, and the motto *Innocentia et Libertas*. Above the receptionists a glittery red-and-gold tinsel banner wished me a MERRY CHRISTMAS, even though we were well into February, and in the corner was a beaming, lifesize, blow-up model of Santa

Claus lounging against a large poster that exhorted the Prime Minister's visitors to JOIN THE CRUSADE AND VANQUISH AIDS – USE A CONDOM. Judging by what Smartly had told me about his father it sounded like extremely wise advice.

'Good morning, sir,' said the policeman. 'May I enquire as to your business here?'

'I'd like to make an appointment to see the Prime Minister,' I said.

He looked apologetic. 'I regret to inform you, sir, that the Prime Minister is abroad at present.'

'I know, but I'm hoping to make an appointment to see him as soon as he returns.'

He nodded. 'Very good, sir,' he said. 'Your name, please?'

'David Barron.'

'Your address?'

'I'm renting Hummingbird House. At Nelson's Rest.'

'I know it well. A delightful residence.' He indicated the girls at the desk. 'Please be so good as to sign the visitors' register,' he said, 'and then if you take the corridor over there on the right and follow it until you reach the third door on the left, you will find the Prime Minister's personal private secretary, Ms Alopecia Martin, who will undoubtedly be able to assist you.'

'Thank you.'

'Not at all, sir. It's a pleasure. Have a good day.'

I waited at the desk until the fat girl had finished her telephone conversation, giggling helplessly, her jowls, upper arms and massive breasts wobbling all the while, and I signed the book: name, age, nationality, passport number, permanent address, temporary address, telephone number, cellphone number, purpose of visit (Pleasure). I followed the right-hand corridor, which was lined with framed photographs of local worthies: a couple of Governor-Generals appointed by the Queen after Innocent had been given its independence; three Prime Ministers; prominent

Cabinet Ministers and MPs; High Court judges, magistrates and police chiefs; all the pomp and panoply of the modern sovereign State, even on a tiny Caribbean island. The third door on the left bore a plaque that read

MS ALOPECIA MARTIN

PRINCIPLE PERSONAL PRIVATE SECETRY

TO THE PRIME MINISTER.

I knocked and entered. She looked up suspiciously. She was probably in her late twenties, very black, short, scrawny, flat-chested and hyperactive, with a sharp, narrow nose that kept twitching. She wore two silver rings in one nostril, a silver stud pierced her lower lip, and when she spoke I saw two more puncturing her tongue. Should Smartly ever succeed in his baffling ambition to have his wicked way with her he would probably encounter a hidden assortment of safety pins, nails, ball bearings, nuts, bolts and tin tacks attached to various parts of her body, and as they screwed (joke) they would clank and clatter like a serious accident in the pots and pans department of an ironmonger's shop. Her frizzy hair was tied with red ribbons and piled high in two huge bunches, one on each side of the front of her head, so that she looked like Minnie Mouse. She was wearing a purple shirt, khaki dungarees, a fierce expression, and was sitting behind an empty desk, a silent telephone, and a hibernating computer. On the wall behind her hung the usual portrait of Eustace Ponsonby.

She glowered at me. 'Yeah?' she snapped. 'Wotcher want?'

She said *want* without pronouncing the *t*, in an unmistakably glottal London accent.

'Good morning,' I said. 'Ms Martin?'

'Carncher read?' she yapped. 'What's it say on the dowah?'

'Well, it says Ms Alopecia Martin.'

'That's me, then, cock, innit? Obvious. So wotcher wan'?'

*OK, OK, Alopecia,* I wanted to say, *keep your hair on,* but I didn't dare.

'I'd like to make an appointment to see the Prime Minister.'

''e ain' 'ere.'

'Yes, I know, but…'

''e's in Sig-na-po-ah.'

'Yes, but I understand that he might be back some time next week?'

She shrugged. 'Maybe 'e will an' maybe 'e won',' she said. ''E's unpredictaboo.'

'Your friend Smartly Warner-Perkins told me that he's sure you'd be kind enough to let me know as soon as Mr Ponsonby returns.'

She grimaced horribly. '*Perkins*? Me *friend*? That wanker? 'e finks I fancy 'im, the goofy littoo four-eyed prat. No way!'

Tough luck, Smartly: no naughties for you with this one.

'Well, I'd be very grateful if you would let me know when Mr Ponsonby gets back,' I said oleaginously. 'I'm writing an article about Innocent for the *Sunday Times* that should encourage more tourists to come here.'

'Gor blimey!' she said. 'We got too many of them buggers comin' 'ere awready, cloggin' up the streets, jostlin' you off the pavements, an' stinkin' the beaches aht wiv their bottoos of Amber Solitaire.'

'Well, I understand that the Prime Minister's very keen to encourage more tourists. May I leave my name and phone number with you?'

She shrugged. 'Suit yerself,' she said.

I wrote down my name and the Hummingbird House number. 'And you'll call me when he's due to return?' I said.

'If I 'member.'

'Thanks.'

'Zat it?'

'I'm just wondering,' I said, 'what a nice cockney girl like you is doing in a place like this.'

'Fuck knows,' she said. 'Me folks took me to England when I were free year old, an' when I left school lars year I fought I'd come back to find me roots 'ere. Jesus! Roots? 'ere? It's a shit-hole, innit? I were bored ahtta me skull wiv-in a week. There's sod-all to do excep' watch the telly, get pissed an' shag. I wish I never come but I carn' afford to go back till I got some dosh.'

'It's a very pretty island.'

'So's the Isle o' Wight, but you wooden wanna live there. Not unless you was 'alf dead.'

'The weather's great here.'

'Too bloody 'ot. I'm bored of sweatin'.'

'Well, the people are really nice and friendly.'

She looked at me as if I were a moron. 'You gotta be jokin'! Nice and friendly? Give over. They may be OK with you honkies but they treat you like shit if you're a local returnee. They fink we're all rich if we lived in England and some of them are real jealous bastards. I was broke into an' robbed me first week 'ere.'

I was running out of ideas. 'Well, at least this job of yours must be very interesting, being the Prime Minister's secretary,' I said.

'*In'erestin'*? Fuck me! It's *borin'*. There's nuffink to do. Prime Minister? Pull the other one. 'E's jus' a tinpot littoo parish councillor wiv a fancy name. I carn' wait to get back 'ome.' She shrugged. 'That's fuckin' life, innit?'

On my way out I stopped at the reception desk to make an appointment to see the Deputy Prime Minister, Chezroy Billington, some time. PC382 was still standing just inside the door, swaying gently back and forth on his heels, and the fat girl was still giggling into her telephone, wobbling her cheeks and chins. After a couple of minutes she stopped pretending that she hadn't seen me standing in front of her, muttered into her telephone – 'hold you'self, Janesha, I got some honky feller here' – and said to me belligerently: 'Yus?'

'I'm sorry to disturb you,' I said, 'but would it be possible to make an appointment to see Mr Billington? If it's not *too* much trouble.'

She glowered at me. 'Woffor?'

'I'm writing an article about Innocent.'

She sighed, murmured into her phone 'dis feller wantin' somet'in'. I call you back,' and replaced the receiver.

'What you wanna ax 'im about?' she said.

'I need to ask Mr Billington for some official information and I'd also like to discuss government policy with him.'

She sighed again. 'You name?' she said.

'Barron. David Barron.'

'Correct!' she said, as though I'd just answered an impossibly difficult question on *Who Wants to Be a Millionaire?* She pushed the visitors' book towards me. 'You fill in de register an' sign you signature,' she said.

'I've done that already,' I said. 'Just now.'

'You mus' do it again.'

'That's ridiculous.'

She glared at me. 'You callin' me ridiculous?'

'No, of course not.'

'I not here to be insulted.'

'Not *you*. I didn't say *you're* ridiculous. I said it's ridiculous to have to write down all my details again on the very next line after my previous entry.'

She tapped the page firmly. 'Dat am de rules. You wanna see de Deputy Prime Mister, you mus' sign again. No sign, no see.'

I considered filling the next line with a string of ditto marks but I guessed that if I did she'd refuse to deal with me at all, so I went through the whole rigmarole again: name, age, nationality, passport number, permanent address, temporary address, telephone number, cellphone number, purpose of visit (Pleasure).

I signed the book and pushed it back towards her. She turned it upside down and studied it suspiciously. Eventually she lifted her receiver and dialled an internal number. It rang for at least a minute before a gruff male voice barked: 'What?'

'We 'as a honky man axin' to see you, sir,' she said.

The voice rumbled indistinctly.

'He Doris Byron.'

'David *Barron*,' I said.

The male voice grunted.

'He from de *Sunday Time* newspaper in London. He say he writin' a travel article about de islan' an' he wanna ax you about de police.'

'About *policy*,' I said, 'not police. Government *policy*!'

The male voice growled.

'Yessah,' she said. She replaced her receiver and waved me dismissively towards the chairs beyond the reception desk. 'You wait.'

'I didn't mean I need to see him *today*.'

'You sit!' she said, pointing imperiously at the chairs.

I caught the policeman's eye. It twinkled. He winked. I sat and waited, and waited, and waited. In the end I waited for more than an hour, nodding at officials and visitors passing in and out, leafing through magazines, glancing at brochures about the island, WELCOME TO PARADISE!, gazing out of the window, contemplating the ceiling, listening for small variations in the humming of the air conditioning, watching the TV screen flickering silently and pictureless above the waiting area and the policeman shifting his weight from one foot to the other, creaking his gleaming boots, and the fat girl giggling into her telephone, and the thin girl working on and on: 'Good day. Innocent island government administration centre. Thank you for calling. Ivorcia speaking. How may I help you? Hold on, please. Trying to connect you with your party. Have a nice day.'

I began to worry about when exactly I should offer Billington the $500. How blatant could I be? Perhaps it would be best to pretend that it was a charity donation, 'a small gift for the poor children of Innocent'

Eventually the fat receptionist answered another telephone, snapped her fingers at me, and pointed brusquely towards the corridor on the left. ''E ready,' she said. 'You go. Now! Go! Go!'

I followed the corridor to the end and knocked at a door with a plaque that read:

THE HONORABLE CHEZROY BILLINGTON

MP, COI

DEPUTY PRIME MINISTER

He grunted.

I entered.

He was a huge man, at least twenty stone, with a vast belly, lounging back in a soft white leather chair and sweating heavily despite the air conditioning. His brow was low and deeply corrugated, his face fleshy, his eyeballs yellow, and he wore the angry, suspicious, bewildered expression of a Spanish bull that was about to be put to the sword. A bottle of five-star brandy sat on his desk and the room smelled of alcohol.

I approached him. 'Mr Billington,' I said. 'Good morning, sir. It's very good of you to see me at such short notice.'

He grunted.

I offered my hand.

He shook it reluctantly, wiped his hand on his shirt, and waved me towards a small, saggy sofa beside his desk.

'I'm David Barron,' I said. 'From England.'

He grunted again.

'I'm writing a travel article about Innocent for the *Sunday Times* in London, which I hope may help to bring hundreds more tourists to your beautiful island.'

He farted loudly.

'Windy' Billington! Smartly was right. A thin miasma wafted low across the room.

'I'd like to talk to you about your tourist trade and the government's tourism policy,' I wheezed.

He farted again, and I could have sworn that he did it deliberately. He sighed contentedly. 'Bake beans,' he said. 'I eat a lutta beans.' His voice was like gravel in a cement mixer.

He leaned back in his chair, patted his stomach, and belched. Five hundred dollars? No way was I going to give this oaf five hundred dollars. I pulled two hundred from my back pocket and held them up like carrots in front of a donkey.

'As a token of our appreciation the *Sunday Times* would like to make a donation to one of your island charities,' I said. 'For widows and orphans, perhaps?'

He looked at the money, cleared his throat, and projected a gobbet of phlegm into his wastepaper bin.

'On second thoughts,' I said, 'perhaps three hundred would be more appropriate.'

I produced another banknote and waved it at him.

He considered it with disdain. 'We gotta lot o' widows,' he growled, 'an' orphans. A lot.'

'In that case…'

I produced another note.

He stuck his little finger into his ear, swivelled it around, withdrew it, and studied its golden harvest with interest. Smartly had been right again: five hundred was obviously Windy Billington's basic call-out fee. I fished in my pocket for the fifth hundred. The accounts department in London would go berserk.

He smiled like a crocodile, nodded, took the money in a huge fist adorned with a chunky gold ring, and tucked it into the inside pocket of his jacket. I didn't dare ask for a receipt, even though it would help in trying to mollify the accounts department.

'Kudos to you, maan,' he growled. 'Respect. An' un behalf of

the widows an' orphans of Innocent I t'ank you for you gift.' He
fixed me with a penetrating stare. 'Now, you say you writin' an
article?'

'Yes.'

'The *Sunday Times*?'

'Yes.'

'In London?'

'Yes.'

'England?'

'Yes.'

'A travel article?'

'Yes.'

'About Innocent?'

Suddenly I felt nervous. I didn't like his light, almost teasing
tone of voice. I'd prepared a list of questions to ask him about the
tourist industry and the damage it was suffering because of the
worldwide recession. Tourist numbers were drastically down on
previous years and scores of hotel and restaurant workers had been
laid off. How were they coping? What was the outlook for the
future? Was it true that the government was thinking of licensing a
casino to boost the island's income? And wasn't there a risk that a
casino would encourage crime, drugs, and attract the wrong sort of
downmarket trippers and gamblers?

'Of course,' I said. 'About Innocent.'

He gazed at me with a mixture of amusement and contempt. His
eyes were dangerous.

'You t'ink I'm an idiot,' he growled.

'I'm sorry?'

'You t'ink I'm a fool.'

'Excuse me?'

'You lyin'. You not from the *Sunday Times*. I just called the
*Sunday Times* in London. They never heard of you.'

I blenched. I never thought that anyone would check up on my

89

story. 'There must be some mistake,' I stammered.

He nodded. 'Yes, *you* mistake,' he said. 'You liar.'

I thought with commendable speed. 'No, no, I assure you. I'm a freelance writer. I'm not on the paper's full-time staff, so my name wouldn't be on their staff list. I write for them only occasionally. And maybe you spoke to the wrong department. I write only for the travel section. The other departments wouldn't know anything about me.'

He jabbed his pen towards me. His eyes were like daggers.

'You liar again,' he said. 'I called the travel section. I gave you name: David Barron. I axed them if you writin' an article about Innocent. They never even *heard* of Innocent, an' they never heard of you. So what you up to, eh? All you chickens comin' home to roast, Mr Barron.'

I struggled to escape his interrogation. 'Perhaps you spoke to some temporary secretary,' I said in desperation, 'someone who doesn't really know what's going on.'

'I spoke to the travel editor.'

'Perhaps he was only…'

He smacked his fist on the desk. 'Enough!' he said. 'I want to know who you are, why you here, otherways you be deported on the forst plane to Barbados. Today! Right now!'

I had a moment of inspiration. I couldn't tell him the real reason that I was in Innocent. He would probably have me deported anyway if he knew that I was snooping around the island and its tax dodgers and investigating its flaky tax regulations without official permission. But I could admit to being an idiot. That would probably satisfy his need for an apology and to humiliate me.

I opened my hands in a gesture of submission. 'I'm so sorry, sir,' I crawled. 'I've been very stupid. I realise that now.'

He gazed at me with bottomless eyes.

'When I said I was writing a travel article for the *Sunday Times* I must have given you the false impression that they have *commissioned* me to write it for them. In fact I'm writing it on spec, on the off-chance, in the hope that when I've finished it they'll want to publish it.'

Did he believe me? How could I tell? His face was expressionless.

I grovelled. 'I've been a fool,' I said. 'I see that now, sir. I'm so sorry. I apologise. I should have been more precise. That was wrong of me. But I *am* writing an article about Innocent, and I *am* hoping that the *Sunday Times* will publish it eventually, and I *do* hope that it will help to encourage more tourists to come to your lovely island.'

He gazed at me. There was no way of knowing what he was thinking. I've always been quite a good liar: you have to be in this business because you find yourself constantly up against people who've been lying all their lives. But was this particular lie quite good enough? I tried what I hoped would be the clincher. 'And if for some reason the *Sunday Times* doesn't want the article,' I said, 'there are plenty of other British newspapers that might well take it, all of them selling hundreds of thousands of copies every week. And they all have fat travel sections every week, so I'm sure I'll be able to publish the piece somewhere eventually.'

He stared in silence at me for at least a minute, brooding, menacing, his brow creased, his eyes glowering and hooded. The air conditioning was humming gently but I found myself sweating even more than he was.

Eventually he leaned back in his chair and wagged his forefinger at me.

'You better beware, *Mister* Barron,' he said. 'You better take care of you'self. I watchin' you now. If bush comes to shrub, you make one more mistake an' you on the first plane out. You unnerstan'?'

I nodded. 'Of course,' I said. 'Perfectly. Thank you, sir. And I apologise again.'

He nodded curtly and waved me away towards the door, dismissively.

'Goodbye,' I said. 'Thank you.'

He grunted.

It was not until I was outside his office that I realised that he had answered none of my questions and that for five hundred dollars I'd learned nothing at all except that he was much sharper than he looked and that the Honourable Eustace Ponsonby, with the Honourable Chezroy Billington breathing down his neck, had better watch his back very carefully indeed. For Ponsonby to leave the island for weeks at a time did not seem like a very good idea.

Back in the lobby I nodded at the two receptionists. The fat one sniffed and glared. PC382 opened the front door to let me out. He grinned and nodded surreptitiously towards her.

'Women!' muttered PC382.

'They rule the world these days,' I mumbled.

'That is too true. I intend to ax God to send me back as a woman next time, for sure.'

'Good idea,' I said. 'Do you know, they say that women have *ten times* more fun in bed than men do.'

He flicked a glance at the reception desk and lowered his voice. 'And have you heard the *noise* they make?' he said.

As I drove back to Hummingbird House I realised that the red jeep with the darkened windows was following me again, and when I got home I found the body of a dead monkey had been crucified against the front door.

# CHAPTER 7

# ST VALENTINE'S DAY

I asked Grandad to bury the monkey at the end of the garden before Miz Quaintance arrived the next morning, but for several days and nights I was haunted by the grimace of agony on its horribly human face and its scrawny, furry, bloody little body nailed by its hands and feet to the front door in a grotesque parody of Christ's suffering at Golgotha.

Grandad shook his head. 'Verily, master,' he said, 'this truly be a foul misdeed and an evil omen.'

'Obeah,' said Smartly. 'Black magic. We still have witches and wizards in these islands.'

'Like voodoo?'

'Different.'

'So someone's put a curse on me?'

'Maybe.'

'So what's likely to happen?' I asked, trying to hide my alarm.

'Nothing,' he said, 'unless you're gullible enough to believe in it.'

Yet strangely I was plagued by no more sinister mysteries for several days after that. I was no longer followed by the red jeep, nor were there any more silent phone calls or attempts to break in. It was almost as if the monkey's death had been a necessary sacrifice to absorb and cleanse my fear. It was a couple of weeks before I felt threatened again, and during those weeks I began to discover some of the joys of living in paradise. But that was only a lull before the tempest, the still, calm eye of a hurricane.

On the morning of 14 February Miz Quaintance turned up early for work with a big, cuddly, golden teddy bear wearing a heart-shaped hat and a T-shirt that said HI, BIG BOY, BE MY VALENTINE, and she brought with her a big, cuddly girl wearing very little. The girl can't have been more than sixteen and she was not pretty.

'Happy Valentine's Day, Lard David!' cried Miz Quaintance, planting a big kiss on my cheek and handing me the bear. She pushed the girl towards me. 'Dis me udder neice, Sonita. Go on, girl: gib Lard David a nice big juicy Valentine's kiss.'

Udder was right: the girl pressed them both enthusiastically against me as she seized my arms and nuzzled my cheek.

'Her lovely, no?' said Miz Quaintance.

'Ah… well…,' I said.

'Nice tops an' also nice bottoms.'

'Er…'

'Her you Valentine's Day gift, Lard David. She wanna be you lovin' Valentine. She gonna love you lots.'

'That's very kind, but…'

Miz Quaintance looked at me with sympathetic affection. 'Don' you be *shy*, Lard David. You English mans always so *slow* an' so *polite*.'

'Well…'

'Sonita like a lot o' sex, oh yes. Not so, Sonita?'

'Dat true,' said the girl, licking her fat lips. 'Me love de big stick.'

'That's very kind, but…'

'Go on, Sonita. Give him a feel.'

I managed to extricate myself without being too rude and scuttled off into town as quickly as I could, nervous that one of these days Miz Quaintance would tire of pimping for me and would instead offer herself for my pleasure. If ever she gripped me seriously in a firm embrace I'd be a goner.

They go very big on St Valentine's Day in Innocent. They go very big on any day that gives them an excuse to stop work and have a holiday: Burns Day, Commonwealth Day, St Patrick's Day, St George's Day, the Queen's birthday, the storming of the Bastille, American independence, Hallowe'en, Guy Fawkes, Thanksgiving, and in September they take a whole week off to celebrate their annual Caribbean Culture Festival. But Valentine's Day is the biggest of them all. From the first of February even the chemists boost their sales of condoms and Viagra by stocking up on romantic cards decorated with plush satin hearts, doves, and simpering Cupids with golden bows and arrows. One supermarket had a vivid red poster by the check-out tills that said DON'T GET AIDS AS A VALENTINE'S GIFT: USE A CONDOM. The shops are piled high with boxes of chocolates, ribbonned bouquets, and cutesy little teddy bears in T-shirts with slogans like I LOVE YOU and GIRL OF MY DREAMS. Stores are festooned with crimson heart-shaped balloons and smoochy pink St Valentine's Day banners, and shop assistants wear badges proclaiming KISS ME QUICK, HELLO BIG BOY and ALL U NEED IS LOVE. When I drove past the cemetery on my way into town I passed a cheery sign, attached with balloons and coloured streamers to the railings around one of the graves, wishing the inhabitants of the graveyard a HAPPY VALENTINE'S DAY. I suppose that in a society where promiscuity is rampant it needs to be softened by an exaggerated camouflage of romantic love.

Boozy Suzy's Valentine's Day beach party at sunset on the Wednesday evening throbbed with sexual tension. The bar was packed with predatory men and obvious girls in all shades from pink to chocolate, some of them strikingly pretty, and Suzy herself looked delicious in a lacy, low-cut top and short skirt that made her smooth brown legs seem longer than ever. When I arrived soon after 5.30 she was telling a dubious joke to four adoring men and an ugly but mischievous-looking white woman of about forty. 'So there's this dog lying on the ground licking its balls,' said Suzy, 'and its owner says to his mite, "Jeez, mite, I wish *I* could do that," and his mite says "well, why don't you? It's your dog".'

We all laughed louder than it deserved.

'Did you hear about the little boy walking along the road?' she said. 'A priest stops his car and says: "Hello, little boy. If I give you a lolly will you come in my car?" The kid looks him up and down. "If you give me the whole bag, mister," he says, "I'll come in your mouth".'

She saw me and kissed me on both cheeks. 'G'day, Dave,' she said. 'Grab yourself a glaass of grog and I'll introduce you to some of these reprobates.'

I fought my way to the bar, claimed a vodka and tonic, struggled back, and she presented me to the mischievous-looking woman, who turned out to be Angela Fellowes, the feisty Englishwoman who had joked about her old white pussy, the first of the tax dodgers I was after. She was little more than five feet tall, with a face like a monkey, a little-girl voice, and a disconcertingly flirty manner.

'Welcome to Innocent,' she said, touching my arm, 'though you won't find much innocence here. Suzy's told me all about you.'

'I doubt it,' I said. 'She knows nothing about me.'

She winked. 'That's what *you* think.'

I disliked her on sight. She was too familiar and too pleased with herself. It's always helpful for a taxman to dislike his quarry: it gives you an added incentive to nail the bastard.

Next up was the Catholic priest, Father Brendan Mulchrone, allegedly Suzy's lover, who wore a gold cross on a chain around his neck but otherwise bore no resemblance whatever to any man of God I've ever met. He was well oiled already and looked more like a seedy layabout from one of the less salubrious English inner cities than one of the Pope's God-botherers. His expression as he leered at Suzy was blatantly profane. He was big, square, red-faced, unshaven, probably in his early fifties, with grey, curly hair, a broad forehead, a determined jaw, and a huge fleshy nose, which some women have told me is a promising sign, along with big feet. Maybe that explained his attraction for Suzy. He said 'fock!' and 'fockin' 'ell!' and 'fock me!' a lot, but then she was pretty handy with four-letter words herself, and what's to stop a priest effing and blinding if he doesn't believe in God?

'Great to meet yer, for sure,' he said, crushing my knuckles in an agonising handshake. 'Call me Brendan. So you're from de city of Satan?'

'London.'

'Dat's de one: de Great Wen, de Devil's own Babel, t'robbin' wit' sin, evil and vice.'

'Well, I wouldn't quite put it like that.'

'Lov'ly,' he said with a grin. 'Me favourite town, so it is. Oi lov' it, an' fock the begrudgers!'

'Tell me, Father…'

'Ach, fer Chroist's sake,' he said. ''Tis Brendan, not Father. Ye're not a Cat'olic, are yer?'

'No.'

'In dat case ye've no need to call me Father. Brendan I am to all me friends.'

'Right,' I said. 'Well, Brendan, you're just the man to tell me: why do we celebrate St Valentine? Who was he?'

He waved a hand. 'Take yer pick. Which one would yer loike? Dere's at least eleven of dem in de Cat'olic canon.'

'Well, who was the one who gave today his name?'

He shrugged. 'No one knows for sure, but it moight have been St Valentine of Rome, whose relics are in the Carmelite Chorch in Doblin, God rest his bones, or it moight just have been St Valentine of Terni.'

'So which was the romantic one?' said Suzy. 'The one who

inspired all these heaarts and flowers and cupids? I thought the saints were forbidden to have girlfriends.'

'Ach, sure they were, me darlin', but some had dozens, and even de perfect St Augustine loiked to dabble in a bit o' naughty from toime to toime. "Take dis cup of sin away from me, O Lord," he asked the Lord, "but not yet, O Lord, not yet".'

He laughed lewdly.

'So which St Valentine was the randy one?' I said 'Rome or Terni?'

He grinned. 'Oi rather think dey were both ravin' poofs, if the truth be told.'

'Wasn't one of them tied to a tree and shot with arrows?' said Suzy.

'Ach, never. That was all just sentimental bollocks. The saint was probably crucifoied or burnt aloive loike most of them early Christian martyrs. Fock the lot o' them!'

He'd obviously drunk very much more than I'd suspected at first. Even a priest who doesn't believe in God would surely not curse quite so publicly the sacred idols of his religion unless he were seriously pissed. 'But at least he's not a bloody paedophile,' she'd said, which was something. If your friendly neighbourhood sky pilot has to have a weakness then it's undoubtedly preferable for him to have a taste for the bottle rather than boys' bottoms.

'Brendan,' she said, 'you're becoming a bore. Bugger off and talk to someone else.'

'Sorry, Suze,' he said contritely, but he stayed where he was and gazed at her with adoration. He no longer worshipped his saints but you could see that he worshipped her.

She introduced me next to a nervous, worried-looking little Scottish doctor, Alex McDowall.

'How do you do?' I said.

'Och, *terrible*,' he said. 'I have this shooting pain in my right knee. Like a hot spike through the kneecap. Torture.'

'Cartilage,' I said.

'D'ye think so?' he said eagerly. 'D'ye think I should have an operation?'

'For God's sake, Sandy,' said Suzy. 'How the hell would Dave know? He's not a surgeon. Anyway, I thought that doctors hate talking about medical symptoms at parties.'

'Not their own,' he said, 'and this one's agony.'

'Ach, yer fockin' Presbyterian gobshite!' said Father Brendan. He belched. 'Try spendin' yer whole loife on yer knees in front of an altar: pray pray pray pray pray. Jaysus, dere's no end to it. Fockin' excruciatin', dat is, I can tell yer. Dere's not a priest in de whole chorch who's not crippled by de gallopin' arthritis. Did ya not see the Holy Father on de telly de other noight? Could hardly walk, de poor old bogger. Shufflin' up de aisle at St Peter's, he was, loike de fockin' hunchback of Notre Dame.'

I was introduced finally to an American couple, he a balding, fifty-something multi-millionaire from Baltimore, Washington Dempster, who had a ridiculous ponytail, a growly voice and a bottle-blonde wife called Baby with enormous buttocks, a couple of unfortunate facelifts, vast low-slung breasts, and one of those quacking voices that so many American women have.

'David Barron,' I said, shaking hands.

'Quack quack,' she said. 'Quack.'

He was one of those Americans who nod all the time. He nodded. 'You're a limey person from London, England, Yurp?' rumbled Dempster. 'Right, Dave?'

I hate people calling me Dave as soon as we meet. I don't mind it, of course, from an attractive woman like Suzy, but I do mind when it comes from a balding, middle-aged, American prat with a ponytail.

'Well, yes,' I said.

'Way da go!' he said. He smiled smugly, nodding, nod-nod-nod. 'I deduced such information at this moment in time as soon as we established visual contact and subsequently by a close analytical study and dissection of your distinctive speech pattern. I achieved such an insight, Dave, by paying especial attention to your verbalization of the words *quite, question, today, romantic* and *cartilage*. Right? You were abnormally precise, positively *anal*, in your pro-noun-ci-a-tion of every consonant in such words, especially the letter *t*. From long experience and careful application over many years, Dave, and given a level playing field, I have deduced that this anal over-pro-noun-ci-a-tion of the letter *t* is a widespread affectation of a certain genre of Brit, so that your pathological consonantization of such verbal communicants alerted me immediately to the powerful likelihood that you are almost certainly of a Brit persuasion. Right?'

I hate people calling the English 'Brits,' as well. We're Britons or British, not Brits. 'Brits' was first used as a contemptuous abbreviation by the IRA to sneer at the innocent people they were murdering. Nowadays you're no longer allowed to call people Japs, Chinks, Pakis or Eye-ties but everyone freely insults the British by calling us Brits.

'Isn't Washington *brilliant*?' quacked Baby, her eyes aglow. 'He's so *clever*. He does voices, too, you know: Obama, Jimmy Carter, Arnie Schwartzenegger, your English Sir Connery, Sir Jagger, Dame Mirren. He does 'em all. Show him, honey. Do your Jimmy Cagney.'

He adopted a menacing look. 'You dirdy rat!' he growled. In fact Cagney never said 'you dirdy rat!' but Dempster grinned and nodded, nod-nod-nod, the ponytail bobbing up and down. 'I have an undoubted talent for mimicry,' he said. 'Right? You only get out of life what you put into it.'

'Isn't Washington *fantastic*?' quacked Baby.

I couldn't do with much more of this. It was time to start taking the piss. I find most Americans pretty hard to take at the best of times, and these two Yanks were classic arseholes. 'You're right,'

I said. 'It's a beautiful city.'

'I meant *him*!' she quacked, jabbing a finger towards her husband.

'Ah, yes, of course. I'd forgotten. Tell me, Mrs Dempster, why was your husband named after a town?'

'He wasn't named after a *town*,' she quacked. 'He was named after a great American *President*.'

'President Dempster?' I said. 'Was he the one who quaked in his boots for three years before he could summon up the courage for the States to join the First World War? Or was he the one who quaked in his boots for two years before you had the balls to join the Second World War, and then had the cheek to charge Britain billions plus interest for saving the world from Hitler in 1940? Britain was repaying that loan for sixty years, until 2005. Or maybe your President Dempster was the guy who invented your Dempster garbage bin?'

'That's not a *Dempster*,' she quacked. 'It's a *dumpster*. Washington was named after *President* Washington, *George* Washington! Jeez, you Brits don't know nuthin'. No wonder you lost your empire.'

'We didn't lose it,' I said. 'We gave it away. Deliberately. You think George III was unhappy to lose the American colonies? Far from it, sweetheart. He'd been trying to dump them for years. "Bloody Yanks," he said, "always wanting more, always sponging, whining and complaining, even about a tiny tax on tea." He danced a jig as soon as he'd got rid of you, and he and Pitt the Elder got as pissed as parrots and caroused the night away at Windsor Castle.'

She looked at her husband uncertainly. 'Washington?' she quacked.

'And now I suppose you're going to ask me why William the Conqueror was stupid enough to build Windsor Castle right under the flight path from Heathrow.'

'Washington?' she quacked nervously.

'And then,' I said, 'we got rid of the rest of the Empire as soon as possible: India, Canada, Australia, New Zealand, Africa, Burma, the lot. The best thing we ever did, dumping the Empire. Whinge, whinge, whinge, the lot of you, ungrateful bastards, and after all we'd done to civilise you.'

She was frightened now. 'Washington?' she quacked.

Sad, really. No sense of humour. No concept of irony or sarcasm. How did they ever become the most powerful nation in the world? Do you remember George 'Dubya' Bush's remark about the French? 'The trouble with *lay Français*,' he said, 'is they don't got no word for *enter-pre-newer*.' Classic.

Suzy glanced at me, grinned, and turned away to talk to other guests, and I realised that Angela Fellowes, Father Mulchrone and Sandy McDowall had all melted away as well and that I was alone and completely at the mercy of the Great Bore of Baltimore.

I saw with relief that Smartly had just arrived and was fighting his way towards the bar. I didn't even make an excuse. 'Goodbye,' I said, and dived into the crowd to make my escape.

'Well!' quacked Baby. 'So *rude!*'

'Typical Brit arrogance,' said Dempster. 'They've always been arrogant, right back to the days of Julius Caesar, when the Brits daubed themselves with blue paint and ate toads and were conquered by the Romans but still believed they were superior. Right?'

'But was he right about all that history stuff?' she quacked.

He patted her cheek. 'Don't worry about it, honey. It was all a long time ago.'

I caught up with Smartly at the bar and called for another drink. 'Am I pleased to see you,' I said. 'I've been cornered for the last five minutes by the biggest bore in the western hemisphere.'

Smartly grinned, all tooth and gum, his spindly spectacles glinting in the setting sun. 'Washington Dempster,' he said.

'Got it in one.'

'They arrived on-island a couple of weeks ago and already strong men run for cover when they see him coming. Whenever I bump into him he gives me a long lecture about how to improve the paper. Right?'

'Right! So what are you doing here? Friend of Suzy's?'

'Not really. I write a gossip column in the paper, so the expats invite me to all their parties. They pretend to value their privacy but really they love to see their names in print.'

'A *real* gossip column? Who's sleeping with who? Divorces? Scandals?'

Smartly looked shocked. 'Certainly not,' he said. 'The *Innocent Gazette* is a quality newspaper for ladies and gentlemen of taste and discretion. My column is a genteel social diary. It's called *A Beachcomber's Jottings*.'

'A pity. I bet there's loads of juicy scandal you could write about. There always is when you get a crowd of bored expats together.'

He sniffed. 'I prefer not to contemplate such matters,' he said.

I decided to tease him. 'I met Alopecia the other day,' I said.

'Isn't she gorgeous?' he said eagerly.

'Fabulous.'

Should I tell him that he didn't stand a chance with her? That would be too cruel.

'Well, the best of British luck,' I said, 'but be careful not to impale yourself on one of her nails or needles. They could do you a serious mischief.'

Smartly introduced me to a couple of genial Innocentian businessmen, one of them the vague, absent-minded owner of the Cost-Me-Less Calypso Superette, Elroy 'Machete' Williams, who wore a dreamy smile and had had such difficulty in understanding the concept of corked wine.

'Why's he called Machete?' I asked.

Smartly chuckled. 'Because he's not very sharp.'

I met several more expats that evening, including the bizarre British vice-consul, Bernard Garwen, a wizened little man with a pinched, ratty face, shifty eyes, a ginger beard and a hunted expression, who spoke a strangulated version of English as though he came from Outer Mongolia. 'Eez pliz ah mit you,' he said, giving me a grisly smile and a damp, limp handshake. I'd have to ask Percy Holden in the Foreign Office to find out just how a man who could not speak English had been appointed a British consul.

Equally sinister were the two Russians, Anna Litvinova and Nikita Malenkov, even though they were frighteningly friendly. He was burly and gave me a suffocating bear-hug and a huge guffaw, but his eyes were as cold as a snake's. I could easily imagine him in the KGB, in the cellars of the Lubianka, pulling fingernails out with pliers. She too was on the hefty side, like one of those twenty-stone Soviet women Olympic shot-putters who speak with gruff voices and shave twice a week. She looked like Boris Yeltsin but was not as pretty. She kissed me hard on the mouth and kept stroking my arm.

'I jost *lurve* your *skeen*,' she said. 'Is so *soft*, so *smoove*. How you keep eet so *silk*?'

I thought of Hannibal Lecter and shuddered. She sounded as if she wanted to wear me. 'We most 'ave you for dinner,' she said, which frightened me even more.

The sun slipped into the ocean and the last few pelicans skimmed the surface of the sea, shopping for a fish supper, soaring high, plunging into the water like arrows, surfacing with a wag of the tail and a toss of the head. Strings of coloured fairy lights began to twinkle above the bar and in nearby trees and bushes. It was a gloriously clear evening, without a breath of breeze to disturb the palms or a cloud to smudge the horizon, and Suzy suddenly appeared at my side and insisted that we should scan the horizon together to try to spot the legendary Green Flash as the sun went down.

'You've never seen it before?' she said. 'Really? OK, then: *concentrate*. You don't want to blind yourself, so don't look straight into the sun too soon, but at the very laast minute you have to stare right into the middle of the tiny rim of the sun as it sinks into the sea, and then you'll see it: a brief, brilliant dot of bright green light.'

I stood beside her, expecting nothing, silenced by the beauty of the tropical twilight as the sky faded into gold and pink and crimson and the sun dropped suddenly out of the sky like a fat red boulder, surprisingly fast, and I gazed unblinking as its final scarlet sliver slipped beyond the horizon.

She grabbed my hand and squeezed it. 'There!' she whooped. 'Fantastic! Did yer see it? Jeez, that's beautiful. Did yer see it?'

I shook my head.

'You *didn't*?'

'No. Sorry.'

'I caan't *believe* it! You caan't be *serious*! It was bright green!'

'Sorry. Not a thing.'

'You caan't have been *concentrating*.'

As the evening darkened the barmen lit flaming braziers along the beach and the stars began to glitter in the deep black sky, just Venus at first, the evening star, then a dozen, then fifty, then hundreds. A thin new hammock moon rose low and silver across the bay, lying flat on its back, quite unlike the parenthesis moon that we see in the far northern hemisphere. The shadows deepened beyond the palm and sea-grape trees and a dozen fireflies cruised through the darkness, their lights flickering bright in the night like tiny aircraft. On the foaming shore the surf gleamed gentle with phosphorescence, and a couple of couples slipped away from the party and wandered hand-in-hand along the beach in search of each other and magic.

'It's time you met some nice girls,' said Suzy.

'I don't think so,' I said.

'Of course you must.'

'I'm not really…'

'Get a grip, Dave. It's *Valentine's* Day.'

'But I don't…'

She grabbed my hand and pulled me towards the bar. 'Jeez, mite, stop being such a fucking wowser and do as you're told. This is meant to be a *paarty*, for Chrissake.'

She led me towards a barefoot young woman who had just turned away from talking to a group of men. 'Hi, Shermelle,' said Suzy. 'I'd like you to meet Dave Barron. He's just arrived from England. Dave, this is Shermelle Donaldson.'

She was stunningly pretty: mid-twenties, toffee-coloured but with deep green eyes and long black hair; slim, elegant, gloriously feminine, wearing something bright and flimsy that I barely noticed because when she smiled at me I forgot everything else. Her eyes and teeth sparkled. She was the sort of girl who inspired middle-aged men like me to make fools of themselves.

'We've met already,' she said in an immaculate Oxford accent. She gave me her hand. 'Hi.' She smelled of oranges.

Of course. The customs officer at the airport when I arrived.

'Hello,' I said. My voice was croaky. I cleared my throat. 'Of course,' I said. 'The airport. You're Eve, but with clothes.'

She laughed deliciously.

'That sounds *very* interesting,' said Suzy. 'Have fun, you two.'

She winked and moved away.

'Shermelle,' I said. 'Pretty name.'

'Thanks.'

'Unusual.'

She shrugged. 'Typically Innocentian,' she said. 'Parents here like to name their children by joining their own names together. I suppose in a way it's a sort of substitute for actually getting married. My mother's name is Cherie, my father's is Melvin. Join the two and you get Shermelle.'

'Or Melcher,' I said, 'which wouldn't sound nearly as nice.'

She chuckled. 'Or Chevin, which would be even worse. Or Rievin. God!'

'Close shave,' I said.

We laughed. It was lovely to hear her laugh.

'It's good to meet you again,' I said.

'You too.'

'I didn't recognise you out of your uniform.'

She looked mischievous. 'You like girls in uniforms?'

'Only customs officers,' I said.

She grinned. 'Flatterer! So what do you think of our little island?'

Her lips were perfect as they shaped the words, her dimples enchanting. I felt acutely vulnerable. *Don't be ridiculous*, I thought. *She's half your age, young enough to be your daughter.*

'It's lovely,' I said, 'and the people are wonderfully friendly.'

'Have you seen much of it yet?'

'Not nearly enough. I've driven right round the island once but that's only enough for a superficial impression.'

'I'll show you around, if you like,' she said. 'Give you the guided tour.'

*If you like? Do birds sing?*

'I wouldn't want to impose on your time,' I said stupidly.

'It's not an imposition at all,' she said. 'I'd enjoy it. Really. We're all proud of our little island and we want to share it and make everyone else love it too. What are you doing on Sunday?'

If I'd had an appointment with the Queen I'd have cancelled it.

'Nothing,' I said. 'Nothing at all.'

'Great. Where are you staying?'

'I'm renting Hummingbird House. At Nelson's Rest.'

'I know it. Pretty old wooden place, yellow and white. Lovely garden.'

'That's it.'

'Lucky you. I'll pick you up there at nine on Sunday, OK? And we'll spend the day looking around, have a picnic somewhere nice.'

'That sounds wonderful,' I said. 'Are you sure?'

She smiled again. It weakened me.

'Of course I'm sure,' she said.

'Well, that'll be great,' I said. 'Thank you. And I'll bring the food and drink.' Her glass was empty. 'Do you fancy another?'

She hesitated and looked at her watch. 'No, thanks,' she said. 'I'd better go. I'm on duty early tomorrow and I need my sleep.'

I imagined her in bed with her hair fanned out across the pillow. Breathing gently. The moonlight soft across her lovely face. Naked.

'Sunday, then,' I said, a trifle hoarsely.

'You getting a cold?'

I coughed. 'I don't think so. Just a frog in the throat.'

'Sunday, then. Nine o'clock, and bring your swimming gear. I know a perfect, secret little beach.'

'Fantastic.'

She flashed me a final glorious smile, wide, deep and generous, and disappeared around the edge of the crowd towards the car park. Even her back looked irresistible as she walked away, her feet sandy, her bottom trembling in the moonlight, her long hair drifting on the breeze.

And then I remembered something that she'd said at the airport. 'There's nothing poisonous here,' she'd said, 'except my mother-in-law.' Oh, shit! So she had a mother-in-law, so she had to be married.

*So what?* I thought. *Stop mooning about like a pimply adolescent. Of course she's married. Why wouldn't she be married? She's gorgeous.*

But then why would she offer to spend all Sunday with me? What could she possibly see in an old fart like me? Suspicion tickled the edge of my desire. Could she be a honeytrap? Could someone be using her to blackmail me? Windy Billington, perhaps, who knew only too well that I wasn't a journalist? Or one of the rich tax dodgers I was after? Could someone have tipped them off that I was here and an HMRC investigator? Lovely girls in their early twenties just don't come on to middle-aged old goats as soon as they meet them. *Beware: this girl is dangerous, the sort of girl who inspires sad, middle-aged men to delude themselves into thinking that they're young and attractive again.*

I'd probably had too much vodka, and the lazy hammock moon, and the whispering surf, and too many lonely nights mourning Barbara and the death of our marriage. Time to go. I went over to thank Suzy for the party. She was telling a group of admirers another Australian joke:

'So this guy takes his pet crocodile into this baar miles away in the outback, way out beyond the black stump. "Give us a nice cold tinny, mite," he says to the baarman, "and an abo for the croc." The baarman hands him a beer and tosses an aborigine to the crocodile. Aafter a while the customer orders another round: "a beer for me and an abo for the croc." This goes on for five or six rounds, "same again, mite" every time, "a tinny for me an' an abo for the crock," but eventually the baarman says: "I'm sorry, mite, but we're clean out of abos. Would the croc fancy something else? A coupla dwarfs, maybe?"

'"Jeez, no!" says the customer. "For Chrissake! There's no holding him once he gets onto the shorts".'

Father Mulchrone laughed so much that I thought he was about to have a seizure. The guy standing next to him banged him several times on his back until he'd calmed down.

'Fockin' erseholes,' said the man of God. 'Jaysus, Mary an' Joseph, dat's a good won.'

I touched Suzy's shoulder. 'I've got to be off,' I said. 'Thanks for the party. It's been great fun.'

'I'm glad you could come,' she said. She kissed me on both cheeks. 'How'd you get on with Shermelle? She's lovely, isn't she?'

'Very pretty,' I said nonchalantly, 'but I didn't get to meet her husband. Was he here?'

'They're divorced,' she said.

I could hear my heart beat.

'Didn't she tell you?'

'Uh… no.'

She gave me a cheeky grin. 'She hasn't even got a boyfriend. Would you believe it? A lovely girl like that?' She laid a hand on my arm. 'I'm sorry about dumping you with Washington Dempster like that. They only arrived on-island a couple of weeks ago and they don't know anyone, so I thought it'd be kind to invite them. Never again!'

'I don't blame you,' I said. 'He bores for Baltimore. And a *pony*tail! At *his* age.'

She grinned. 'Well, you know what you'll always find under a ponytail.'

'What's that?'

'An aarsehole.'

I laughed.

'See you around,' she said.

On my way towards the car park I felt a hand on my elbow: Angela Fellowes, her little black eyes glinting in her little monkey face.

'You leaving so soon?' she said.

'Yes. I have to work.'

'And what work's that?'

'Collating my notes for this article I'm writing.'

She looked at me as though she didn't believe a word I said. 'Ah, yes,' she said dismissively. 'Suzy told me you said you're a journalist.'

'It's better than working,' I said.

She smiled with her mouth. 'We never had a chance to talk.'

'Yes, I'm sorry. Everyone was so friendly that I didn't meet half the people I'd like to have done.'

'Let's make up for that,' she said. 'What are you doing on Saturday night? I'm having a little dinner party. Will you come?'

I wanted to say no. I didn't like her, I didn't trust her, I guessed that she didn't trust me either, and I was pretty sure that most of her friends would be decidedly flaky. But she was one of my targets and it would be a way of getting to know her.

'That's very kind of you,' I said.

'Not at all. It's a treat to meet someone new and nice.'

I stared at her. Her eyes were like stones in the dark. I couldn't decipher whether she was challenging me, threatening, or taking the piss.

'Well, thanks,' I said.

'Great. Seven o'clock. Very informal. The Old Manor. It's the first big stone plantation house on the left as you drive out of Hopetown towards Cotton Beach. You can't miss it. There's a big sign right on the main road, two wrought-iron gates, and a security guard.'

'I look forward to it,' I said.

She stood on tiptoe and kissed me on the cheek. This sudden outbreak of necking with strangers was becoming an epidemic.

'It'll be great to get to know you,' she said.

I should have refused that invitation, too. I know that now. There were a lot of things I should have done and a lot more that I shouldn't.

That night I dreamed of Shermelle. We were together in the Garden of Eden, both naked, and she was smiling and eating an apple, her lips lingering lasciviously on the skin, juice dripping down her chin, and I knew, as somehow you do in dreams, that slithering silently somewhere unseen was a snake in the grass.

# CHAPTER 8

# MOTHER TERESA AND THE HAUNTED MANOR

Angela Fellowes's secluded old manor house just outside Hopetown was protected by a long, high stone wall topped with shards of broken glass and wrought-iron gates crowned with vicious spikes. Just inside the gates a humourless security guard emerged from his hutch, demanded my name, checked it against a list, shone a flashlight into my eyes, grunted and reluctantly opened the gates. The gravel drive to the house was at least half a mile long and lined on both sides by rows of elegant Royal Palms and dignified Victorian street lamps lit now by electricity rather than gas. Immaculate lawns, flowerbeds and rockeries stretched away into the darkness, and a small lake shimmered in the moonlight. The house itself was a solid, three-storey stone mansion, probably eighteenth-century, with a colonnaded porch and a broad terrace punctuated by big stone jars and *jardinières* tumbling with colourful flowers. Along the entire length of the terrace large iron braziers blazed with orange flames, and towering open doorways spilled light across the garden from every room. Whatever Angela Fellowes' investment scams might be they were obviously damned successful.

I was greeted at the massive mahogany front door by a suave, bald little butler whose ebony skin gleamed as if it had been polished again and again. He was wearing a dinner suit, black tie and white gloves, so that I felt seriously underdressed in my slacks, short-sleeve shirt and brothel-creepers. To the right of the door, on a tall pedestal, stood a large silver birdcage that contained a brilliantly red, blue and green parrot with a savage black beak. It glared at me.

'Fuck off!' it said.

'Good evening, sir,' said the butler, bowing slightly. 'I must apologise for the creature. Its louche interjections amuse Mistress Fellowes. My name is Gascoigne.'

'Arsehole!' said the parrot.

'Hello,' I said. 'I'm David Barron.'

The parrot cocked its head and looked at me sideways, as if it were listening intently. It watched me with one cold, beady eye.

'Indeed, sir,' said Gascoigne. 'I have already been well apprised by Mistress Fellowes as to your expected arrival and I am honoured to welcome you most humbly and heartily to our illustrious establishment.'

'Bollocks!' said the parrot. It cocked its head again, listening, twitching its head from side to side, glaring at the butler, then at me, then at the butler again, as if it were watching a Wimbledon singles final.

The butler was assiduous. 'May I be so bold, sir, as to enquire whether, prior to enjoying an aperitif, you might require to avail yourself of our domestic facilities?'

'I'm sorry?'

'Would you care to visit the comfort station, sir?'

'Ah. No, thank you.'

The parrot gave a loud wolf whistle. It stared at me coldly, its eyes like little black stones, and shifted on its perch. It scratched its ear with a horny claw. 'Hello,' it said. 'My name's David Barron.'

'What an extraordinary bird,' I said.

'It is in fact an infernal nuisance,' said Gascoigne. 'Were I allowed to have my way I would wring its neck. Unfortunately Mistress Fellowes appears to be inordinately fond of the creature.'

113

He smiled sweetly. 'May I prove to be of any further service in any regard before we proceed unto the drawing room to encounter your hostess and fellow guests?'

'I don't think so, Mr Gascoigne. Thank you.'

He looked affronted. 'Not *Mister* Gascoigne, sir, *please*. Just Gascoigne. I abhor over-familiarity between master and servant. It leads to anarchy.'

'Wanker!' said the parrot. It made a loud clicking noise, ruffled its feathers and yawned.

'In that event please be so good as to follow me, sir.'

'Hello, I'm David Barron,' squawked the parrot. 'Thank you. That's very kind of you. I'm sorry? Bollocks!'

'Does the parrot have a name?' I asked.

Gascoigne grimaced. 'Mistress Fellowes calls it Mother Teresa.'

I laughed. 'It's female?'

He shrugged. 'Who knows, sir? It would require a decidedly intrepid investigator to attempt to decipher its nether regions.'

He ushered me across a wide hall that was furnished with exquisite mats, ugly antiques and garish tropical ornaments. 'My name's David Barron,' croaked the parrot. 'That's very kind of you. I'm sorry?' From the drawing room drifted the sounds of clinking glasses and a dozen competing voices. The room was vast, with high ceilings and sparkling chandeliers, but I was relieved to see that the women were all wearing trousers or simple cocktail dresses and none of the men had a jacket or tie. They were drinking champagne.

The butler cleared his throat loudly. 'Ladies and gentlemen,' he announced. 'I have the honour to present Mr David Barron, Esquire.'

Angela Fellowes wafted towards me, wearing a bright green and yellow kaftan. 'Dave!' she said with exaggerated enthusiasm, advancing on me with lips pouting and arms flung wide. I grabbed her hand and shook it.

'Hello, Angela,' I said. 'What a wonderful house.'

She flashed me a glance of irritation, her little monkey face twisted in a grimace, her little simian eyes glittering with annoyance, and then she gave a bark of a laugh, stood on tiptoe and pecked me on the cheek. She was obviously not used to anyone denying her anything.

She clapped her hands and raised her voice. 'Listen up, people,' she said. 'I want you all to meet Dave Barron, who's just arrived from England. He's Suzy's latest conquest.'

A couple of women giggled and a man sniggered. So Boozy Suzy had a reputation, did she? She emerged from the pack and came over to kiss me on the cheek. 'Grite to see yer, mite,' she said.

Father Mulchrone was there too and nodded genially, the Russian gave me a bear-hug, his frightening woman kissed me wetly on the lips, and Angela introduced me to her six other guests: a smooth black property developer and his beautiful Guyanese wife, an elderly retired Canadian couple and – *bingo!* – another of my tax investigation targets: Donald Rogers, a stocky, heavily-built, forty-something businessman from Essex with a close-shaven, five-o'clock-shadowed head and a skinny redhead trophy wife, Tracy, who was probably half his age and looked monumentally bored.

'So what's your racket, then, Dive?' said Rogers, facing me full-on and planting his feet firmly apart, like Henry VIII, while Gascoigne presented me with a glass of champagne.

'I'm a travel writer,' I said.

He looked at me aggressively. 'Yeah? That a full-time job?'

'Well, sometimes.'

'D'ya make much wonga in that racket, then?'

'Not a lot.'

'So why d'ya do it?'

'I enjoy it. I like travelling and I like writing.'

'*Writin'*?' he said. 'Never 'ad much time for that meself. Nor readin', neiver. Poncy waste o' time, if yer ask me. So 'ow much d'ya make in a year, then?'

'Come off it, Don,' said Angela. 'Stop being so bloody nosy. You can't expect him to tell you that.'

'Why not?' he said belligerently. 'You got issues about moolah? I don't mind tellin' anyone what I made last year: free mill, it were, give or take a few fousand, an' four mill the year before.'

'I bet you didn't tell the taxman that,' said Angela mischievously.

'No need, darlin',' he said jovially. 'I'm kosher non-resident, that's why. All above board, an' stamped wiv the Inland Revenue seal of approval.'

'So how many days did you spend in the UK last year, then, Don?' she said playfully.

'Sod off, Ange,' he said.

'More than the ninety days you're allowed, I'll bet.'

'Do me a favour, darlin',' he said. 'Shtum. Walls 'ave ears.'

'Come on, Don,' she said. 'We're all friends here.'

He looked directly at me. 'Let's chynge the subject,' he said.

'Fock me!' said Father Mulchrone lugubriously. 'Four million quid! In jost one year! Jaysus! Oi'm locky if oi clear four t'ousand, so Oi am.'

'That's very impressive, Mr Rogers,' I said.

'Don,' he said.

'Don.' I smiled encouragingly. 'I'm sorry to say that writers don't make anything like that sort of money, not unless you're Jeffrey Archer or Jilly Cooper.'

'Can't see why ya do it, then, meself,' said Rogers. 'Not if there's no spondulicks in it. What's the point if there's no spondulicks? Waste o' time.'

'Money isn't everything,' suggested the Canadian woman timidly.

He glanced at her with contempt. 'What is, then?'

She looked nervous. 'Well, love and kindness…'

He laughed cynically. '*Love*? Stone me! Do us a favour, lady. We're talkin' about real life 'ere, not *Peter Pan and Wendy*. Give us a break!'

'And there's generosity,' she said defiantly. 'And charity. Helping others. Self-satisfaction.'

He jabbed a forefinger at her. 'I'll tell ya somefing for nuffink, missus,' he said. 'I get plentya satisfaction makin' loadsa wonga, that's for sure. My glass is always 'alf full, not 'alf empty. Four mill a year comes wiv a whole loada satisfaction, let me tell ya. Me an' Trice don't go short on no satisfaction nor nuffink else, neiver, do we, Trice?''

'Nah,' said Tracy. 'Nuffink.'

'Meself an' her got loadsa satisfaction, fanks very much. Isn't vat right, Trice?'

'Yer,' she said. 'Right on. Yer not wrong there, Don.'

'We got big 'ouses in Billericay an' Torremolinos an' Cape Town an' 'ere, and an apartment in Noo York, an' we got skivvies in all of 'em, an' a Roller an' a Lamborghini an' a Porche for 'er, an' I got free kids at posh boardin' schools in the UK, an' meself an' Trice we 'ave two long luxury cruises every year, lars year in the Souf Pacific an' the Artic Circoo, isn't vat right, Trice?'

'You're not wrong, Don,' she said.

'Well, that's *wonderful*,' I said. 'You've obviously done fantastically well for yourself.'

He looked defiant. 'Yeah, well,' he said. 'Stands to reason, dunnit? I 'aven't wasted me time wiv readin' and' writin' an' all that poncy crap. I bin aht there in the university o' life, livin' 'igh an' makin' lotsa wonga.'

'Four million quid!' said Father Mulchrone, shaking his head.

117

'Jaysus, Mary an' Joseph!'

'And what exactly *is* your line of business?' I said.

'I'm a director, inn'I?'

'Films?'

'Nah nah. Comp'nies. I'm on lotsa boards.'

'Companies that do what?'

He looked wary. 'This an' that.'

I raised an eyebrow.

'Import, export, that sorta fing.'

'Importing and exporting what?'

'Well, this an' that.' He tapped the side of his nose. 'Confidential, see.'

'He's a crook,' said Angela Fellowes cheerfully in a tone that suggested she wasn't joking. 'You only have to look at Don to know that he's as bent as a lavatory pipe.'

''ere, Ange!' he protested. 'Oi'll 'ave ya fer libel!'

'No chance,' she said. 'Libel has to be written down. And now for God's sake stop talking about money. It's so vulgar. Didn't you ever learn that in your University of Life? Now, how are your drinks? Gascoigne! More bubbles!'

We drank and made small talk for nearly an hour as Gascoigne liberated bottle after bottle of champagne and two young Innocentian girls, both wearing neat red uniforms embroidered in gold with our hostess's intertwined initials, offered us tray after tray of *hors d'oeuvres*: delicate pieces of smoked salmon and *foie gras* on tiny pieces of toast, quails' eggs with celery salt, impossibly thin slices of miniature salami, chunks of strong cheese and pineapple on sticks, exquisite little cocktail sausages with three different mustard sauces, all served with elegant little Irish lawn napkins also embroidered *AF* in gold. The snacks alone could have qualified as an entire meal.

To escape Don and Tracy Rogers and the Russians I homed in on the local property developer and his beautiful wife, Winston and Samira Williams. Why is it that so many West Indian men, yet so few Englishmen, have been named after Winston Churchill, the greatest British hero of the twentieth century? I know of only two Englishmen who have: John Winston Lennon, the Beatle, and the politician Denis Winston Healey, the one-time British Chancellor of the Exchequer. You'd think that hundreds of British boys would have been called Winston during and after the Second World War, but they weren't. Could it be that West Indians were more patriotic and British than the British themselves? Perhaps Peregrine Featherstonehaugh was right: that Innocent is still more British than Britain.

This Innocentian Winston told me that a couple of years ago he had barely been able to build enough new houses to meet the demand from rich American, Canadian and British expats looking for holiday homes in the sun, but that demand had now evaporated almost completely during the recession. 'I have had to lay off a couple of dozen of my workers,' he said sadly, 'hard-working men with wives and families, and that is heart-breaking. Skilled men are trying to find work as labourers, women are feeding their families with catfish, offal and pig's snout, just like the old slave days, and children are going to school hungry. It's a tragedy, and all because of a few hundred greedy international bankers and financiers who brought the world to its knees.'

'Winston gets so upset,' said his wife softly in a sweet little sing-song voice. 'He lies awake at night worrying.'

'It can't last forever,' I said, unconvinced.

Later I joined the Canadians, a pleasant but dull couple from Toronto who flew south to the Caribbean every winter to escape the ferocious northern winter.

'We're snowbirds,' she chirped happily. 'Six months in T'ron'o and six months here.'

'Sounds wonderful,' I said.

She beamed. 'It's perfect. Henry was in plastics until he took early retirement.'

'Ah.'

'Mouldings,' said Henry, nodding sagely.

'Fascinating,' I said.

'Four years ago,' he said.

'Don't you ever get bored here? I mean, I don't suppose there's much to do.'

He smiled contentedly. 'That's the joy if it,' he said. 'There's nothing to do *at all*.'

'The rat race,' she said. 'Henry couldn't wait to get out of it.'

Why are nice people so often so boring? It was a relief to be summoned eventually to dinner by Gascoigne, who stood in the elegant archway between the drawing and dining rooms and struck a small copper gong three times. 'Ladies and gentlemen,' he announced importantly, 'dinner is served.'

The dining room was smaller than the drawing room but still generously proportioned, with lofty ceilings and stylish chandeliers. Engraved silver cutlery, monogrammed crockery and delicate crystal glasses glittered on a long, beautifully polished antique mahogany table. I was disappointed to see that Suzy had been placed at the far end of the table while I was near the head, on Angela Fellowes' right, with Anna Litvinova on my right and the appalling Don Rogers opposite, picking his nose and examining the result. Beside him the timid Canadian woman watched him, appalled and mesmerised. It looked like being a long evening and I had to remind myself that I was not here in Innocent on holiday: Fellowes and Rogers were both on my hit list, and this was my chance to learn more about them.

The two young maids served a first course of delicious prawns with a piquant garlic sauce, crisp lettuce, chopped celery, cherry tomatoes and thin slices of homemade brown bread, while Gascoigne poured slim, chilled glasses of a silky Pinot Grigio and chunky tumblers of fizzy San Pellegrino water. I noticed with surprise that both the Russians declined the wine. Odd. I thought Russians were notorious alcoholics. Maybe these two were on the wagon. Then she lit a cigarette.

Rogers glared at her and waved a hand theatrically in front of his face. 'Do us a favour, missus,' he said. 'Smokin' durin' a meal: vat's out of order.' She looked bewildered.

'It's disgustin',' said Rogers. 'Smokin' at the table.'

'Eet eez my greatest pleasure,' she said.

'Madam,' said Rogers, 'my greatest pleasure is *fuckin'* but I don't do it at the table between courses.'

Litvinova glared at him, took a deep lungful of smoke, and stubbed her cigarette out in the remains of her prawns, lettuce and garlic sauce.

'It's a wonderful house,' I said hurriedly to Angela Fellowes.

'Not bad, is it?' she said. 'Built in 1718 by an English plantation owner called Mullins. Apparently twenty-eight slaves died while they were building it. Three floors, eight big bedrooms with dressing rooms ensuite, four reception, a library, study, billiard room, huge kitchen, pantries, wine cellar, laundry, servants' quarters. I'll show you around after dinner, if you like, give you the guided tour. There's even a windowless dungeon where Mullins punished his slaves by locking them up and having them flogged, and there's another dark underground room which still has wrist and ankle shackles bolted into the walls where they say his young female slaves were chained so that they could be raped again and again by the lustiest male slaves to provide Mullins with his next generation of workers.'

'What a bastard,' I said.

Anna Litvinova gave a grunt like a wounded animal. I glanced at her. Her eyes gleamed. She licked her lips. 'Fas-kin-a-tink,' she said.

'The basement is said to be haunted by the ghost of one of the girls,' said Angela. 'They say she runs screaming silently from the shackle room at three in the morning on several nights of the year.'

Rogers snorted. 'Loada bollocks!' he said. 'She were black, eh? This slave? So 'ow couldja see a black ghost, then, eh? You'd never see it in the dark, wouldja? Not in the middoo of the night, bein' black an' that.'

'Maybe ghosts are colourless,' said Angela.

'Nah,' said Rogers. 'It's all bollocks. Stan's to reason, dunnit? Yer'd never see nuffink, not wiv 'er bein' black an' all. You ever see 'er yerself?'

'No, but it's mentioned in three old diaries that I found in the attic,' she said with irritation, 'and there's an icy chill in the basement even on the hottest days. Two of my maids have left over the past three years because they were frightened by something in the cellars, and I don't like going down there myself even in daylight.'

'Sounds creepy,' I said. 'When did you buy the house?'

'Sixteen years ago. It stayed in the Mullins family for two hundred and fifty years, until the mid-1960s, but the family fortune was devastated by UK death duties and they had to sell almost everything to pay the taxman. Then their business went bust and they sold the house to a South American drugs baron who kept it for eight years until the Americans kidnapped him and sent him to prison for life in Florida. Then it was bought by a Portuguese pimp who opened it up as a brothel until he was stabbed to death one night by an angry customer.'

Anna Litvinova grunted again with pleasure.

'Murdered?' I said. 'Here? In the house?'

Angela nodded. 'In the drawing room, where the girls paraded every night for the punters. He was stabbed in front of a dozen witnesses and the killer was hanged in Columbus six months later.'

'*Fas*-kin-a-tink!' said Anna Litvinova, breathing heavily, her eyes alight. 'Zey still 'ave 'angink 'ere today?'

'Oh, yes. A couple of months ago they topped one guy who'd

cut his woman's throat because he thought she was having an affair. Amnesty International and all the bleeding-heart liberals kicked up a hell of a stink about it, but West Indians are great believers in capital punishment because they reckon that criminals should pay for their crimes and victims should be revenged. After all, they revere the Bible here and the Old Testament tells them to demand an eye for an eye.'

'An' a toof for a toof,' said Rogers. 'Bloody right, too: 'ang the bastards, I say! An' I'd chop their goolies off first, an' all.'

'Are zere many killinks here?' said Litvinova eagerly.

'Three or four a year. Usually young gangsters shooting or stabbing rivals. It's usually over drugs, sometimes girls.'

'Scum,' said Roberts. 'Vermin. Let 'em cut each uvver's froats, that's what I say. No loss.'

'But at least no whites have been killed here for more than ten years,' said Angela. 'The last was a gay English bloke who tried to pick up the wrong guy late one night. West Indians don't have much time for homos: they call them anti-men.'

The maids served us with wonderfully rare, tender roast beef, gravy, horseradish sauce, perfect little Yorkshire puddings, fresh peas, carrots and broccoli, and Gascoigne poured fat goblets of a smooth French Brouilly. I noticed that Don and Tracy Rogers were both swigging the wine like water. 'Great mouf-wash, this Broo-illee, Ange,' said Rogers, smacking his lips. His face was red and he was sweating freely.

I lifted my knife and fork to enjoy the feast when the lights suddenly flickered and died. In the darkness a bare foot caressed my left ankle and urgent fingers caressed my right thigh. I flinched: two brazen women simultaneously, one on my left and one on my right, and both repulsively ugly! I twitched my legs away, and in the bowels of the house a distant generator rumbled into life and the lights came on again.

Anna Litvinova gave me a lascivious grin and Angela Fellowes looked more than ever like a po-faced chimpanzee. 'Happens all the time,' she said, 'the power cuts. We get one or two a week, sometimes more. Usually at night, always at the most inconvenient moment.' She chuckled. 'A couple of years ago an American tourist at the Sunshine Resort switched his electric razor on to shave before dinner and the whole place was plunged into darkness. He nearly had a seizure because he thought his razor had fused the entire island. Sometimes several villages are cut off for hours at a time, but we've got our own generator that kicks in automatically whenever it happens.'

'Why does it happen so often?' I said.

'The locals forget to top the generators up and they can't be bothered to service or repair them. They buy new equipment, run it until it breaks down, dump it in the bush to rust, and wait for someone else to replace it. The British government has given the island several powerful generators over the years but they've simply been run into the ground.'

'Morons,' said Rogers with contempt. ''alf of 'em 'ave only just come down outta the trees.'

'I wouldn't say that too loudly, Don, if I were you,' she said. '*Pas devant* Gascoigne.'

'Pa what?'

'They'll chuck you off the island.'

'Fuck' em,' he said. 'I'm spendin' a lotta spondoolicks on this island an' if they don't like to 'ear the troof I'll just go an' spend 'em somewhere else. There's lotsa plices would love to 'ave me an' Trice spendin' our wonga.'

'You are not being a cistern, then?' said Litvinova.

'Come again?'

'You haf not become an Innocent cistern?'

Rogers looked baffled.

'I think she means *citizen*,' I said.

She glared at me. 'Me an' Nikita ve are both Innocent cisterns.

Fifty thousand US dollar each. Now ve haf ze yellow Innocent passport, yes.'

'Bloody 'ell!' said Rogers. 'Fifty grand for a poncy littoo coon passport? You won't get *me* payin' fifty grand for vat, I can tell ya. Nor Trice, neiver. I'm a Brit, an' prahd of it.'

You can't win: now even some of the British were calling themselves Brits.

The food was a great deal better than the conversation. The beef was delicious, the Yorkshire pudding soft and fluffy, the vegetables succulent, the wine nectar. This woman certainly knew how to live well. But how did she do it?

'So what happened after the Portuguese pimp was killed?' I said.

'The hookers were all sold off to some brothel in Venezuela...'

'*Sold?*'

She smiled condescendingly and patted my hand. 'You dear, sweet, naïve man. Slavery still exists, you know, but nowadays not all slaves are kept in chains. Then a Canadian zillionaire bought the house, moved in with his wife and six kids in the '80s, and set about transforming it. He modernised the whole building – air conditioning, bathrooms, kitchen, redecoration – and he completely replanted the garden and built ponds, fountains, a gazebo, and a huge swimming pool. But eventually he got bored and ran off with a pretty little local girl from Jericho. The wife shacked up with a Rasta from Dominica who beat her up regularly, stole all her money, and then dumped her for a ditsy young English heiress he met on the beach.'

'Gawd knows what these stoopid white slappers see in these black buggers,' said Rogers.

Angela lowered her voice. 'Shut up, Don,' she murmured. '*Pas devant les domestiques.*'

'What?'

She nodded towards Gascoigne, who was standing to attention

at the far end of the room.

''*im*?' sneered Rogers. 'Vat littoo black runt? I don't give a tinker's fart what '*e* finks.'

'Per'aps zese black boggers 'af certain... ah... *special* qvalities,' said Anna Litvinova with a leer.

'That's all bollocks!' said Rogers. 'About 'em 'avin' bigger cocks van what we do. I bet my cock's just as big as any coon's. Bigger.'

'Yer not wrong, Don,' said Tracy. She hiccuped. She turned towards Angela. ''e's not wrong, Ange. Honest. Don's todger is '*uge*.'

'I think that's more information than we need,' said Angela.

An uneasy silence hung over the table. Somebody had to break it.

'So what happened after the Canadians split up?' I said.

'He divorced her for adultery, which was bloody cheeky, considering what he'd been up to himself,' said Angela. 'Then he chucked her and the kids out, and sold the house to me in '94.' She laughed callously. 'Ruthless bastard, he was. Almost as much of a shit as my own ex.'

'You are dee-forced?' asked Litvinova.

'Yeah.'

'Zis I did not know.'

'Seventeen years ago, just before I moved here. Lazy little Italian bastard. Christ knows why I ever married him. Never did a day's work in all the eight years we were together, just sponged off me. When we got divorced he even claimed maintenance and the bloody judge agreed. I'm still paying the little shit alimony.'

I enjoyed a guilty frisson of pleasure to learn that in at least one English divorce case a man had managed to take a woman to the cleaners for a change.

'Balls!' squawked the parrot in the hallway.

I laughed. I couldn't help it.

'You vere alvays rich?' said Litvinova.

'Well, not right at the start,' said Angela, 'but I got lucky soon after I set up my first business.'

'What was that?' I said, a little too quickly.

She looked at me with amusement. In that moment I had an inkling that perhaps she knew more about me than I realised.

'I started in the rag trade,' she said, 'in the '80s. Cheap clothes made in the Far East, piled high, sold at bargain prices. They went a bomb.'

'So that's bought all this?' I said. 'I'm impressed.'

She smiled sardonically, and again I felt that she knew something about me. 'No,' she said, 'but I started investing the rag trade profits, playing the markets, cautiously at first, then more adventurously. I seemed to have the knack of buying and selling almost always at just the right time. So I started making serious money, expanded into financial services, hired a couple of dozen good people, fancy offices in the West End, took on rich clients, and began to do very nicely, but I was paying so much tax in England that it made sense to move to a tax haven and I've been here ever since.' She stared at me. 'All perfectly legal,' she said. 'I've got nothing to hide.'

'Well, of course not,' I said uncomfortably.

She patted my hand. 'Now, that's quite enough about me. What about you? Are you *really* a writer?'

I felt decidedly uncomfortable now. 'Yes, of course,' I said.

She gazed at me. Mockingly? Why didn't she believe me. What did she know?

I needed to divert attention. I turned to the Russian woman. 'And what brought *you* here, Anna?' I said.

'Anchela invite us for dinner.'

'No, I meant what brought you here to Innocent?'

'Ah, vell, ve vas fed up of ze vezzer in Moscow in ze vinter, zo now ve is 'ere November/May.'

'You and your husband are retired?'

'Nikita? Eez not my 'usband. Eez only my lover.'

'Ah.'

'Eez ver' good lover.'

'Excellent,' I said.

'Eez ver' imaginate. Inventeef.'

'Ah. Fine,' I said. 'Jolly good. Well done.'

'My real 'usband, Anatoli, 'e eez in Vladivostok fockink bloddy Chinky vooman viz no tits.'

Rogers leaned forward eagerly. His face was red. 'Is it true that Chink birds' wotsits go sideways instead of up an' down?'

'Well, *really*!' said the Canadian woman.

Litvinova looked at Angela. 'Vat is votsits?'

'Don't bother,' said Angela. 'He's talking rubbish as usual. Don't be such a gormless prat, Don. You can't really believe that old crap.'

'Never 'ad a Chink bird,' said Rogers morosely. 'Nor a black, neiver, come to that. Never fancied black birds: fat lips, flat noses, an' pubes on their 'eads, Gawd 'elp us! Mind you, I 'ad a Malay bird once, in Koala Lumpy. Nice bit o' brown. Cracker, she were. Firteen year old and cost fuck-all. A few dollars for an 'ole night, an' all night she were like "Come on, mister, do it again," so after the fird time I go "bloody 'ell, girl, I'm knackered," an' she goes "come on, big boy, gimme some more," an' I went "shit, girl, you'll kill me," but we did an' she was like "see?" an' we did it again in the mornin'. Best bonk I ever 'ad. Ever been ter Koala Lumpy?'

We shook our heads, stunned by this tasteless revelation. Tracy looked thoroughly pissed off. She also looked thoroughly pissed. Wisps of hair straggled across her forehead and her eyes had that wild, glazed look of a woman who has had several glasses too many and is not quite sure where she is.

'Yer wanna go ter Koala Lumpy airport,' said Rogers. 'Best

curry in the world at Koala Lumpy airport.'

'You've travelled a lot, then,' I said to Rogers.

'Me? Everywhere, mate. Me an' Trice, we been all over. Globetrotters, that's us. Jetsetters. We been everywhere. We enjoy life. We make the most of it. Me glass is never 'alf empty, it's always 'alf full.'

The pudding was a perfect *crème brulée* with tiny wild raspberries and glasses of Beaumes de Venise that were finally to do for Tracy.

'I 'ear you've bought a small pline,' said Rogers to Anna Litvinova.

'Pline?'

'Aircraft.'

'Pliz?'

'An aeroplane,' said Angela. 'Jesus, Don, isn't it time you had some elocution lessons?'

'What?'

'Learn to speak properly.'

He bristled. 'Yer got issues wiv the way I talk? Yer want me to talk all 'oity-toity? Like Prince Charles an' all them snobs?'

'No, Don, just learn to speak your own language well enough for people to understand what the hell you're saying.'

He bridled. 'Yer fink I should talk all toffee-nosed, yer mean, all lah-di-dah, like I got me balls in a vice. Let me tell yer, darlin', there ain't not nuffink wrong wiv the way I speak. It's down to earf, traditionoo London talk what ordinry peopoo speak.'

'You're not wrong, Don,' said Tracy with difficulty. 'You tell 'er, shnooty ol' cow.'

'Did I hear you call me an old cow?' snapped Angela.

'Yeah,' said Tracy. 'An' an old bitch an' all.'

The entire table fell silent.

'You've just bought an aeroplane?' I said to Anna Litvinova, but it was no good. Tracy Rogers was in a tailspin and going into a serious nosedive.

'Fuckin' old cow,' she slurred. The wheels had finally come off.

'Take her home,' said Angela to Rogers. 'She's as drunk as a skunk.'

'Nah, she's fine.'

'I said "take her home, Don." She's as pissed as a newt. Completely bladdered. She's also fucking rude.'

'Nah, not my Trice. Give over, Ange. I 'aven't 'ad me dinner yet, an' anyway, me good lady wife's never rude.'

'She is tonight. Look at her: she's paralytic. Take her home and put the stupid little tart to bed.'

Rogers dropped his knife and fork. He looked about to explode. 'You *what*?' he said. 'Stupid little *tart*? You talkin' 'bout me missus?'

'Just take her home, Don.'

Rogers was belligerent. His big red face glistened. 'You got some sorta issue wiv us, eh, Ange? You frowin' us out? You showin' us the red card, yeah?'

'Yes.'

'Well, fuck you, lady.' He pushed his chair back and stood up, only just keeping his balance. He tottered along the table and put his hands on his wife's shoulders. 'Come on, then, Trice, love. Time to go. The ugly old bag's chuckin' us out.'

'That's it,' said Angela. 'Out!'

'Come on, Trice. Ups-a-daisy, gel. Time for beddie-byes.' He tried to lift her out of her chair but failed and staggered back. In an instant Gascoigne was at his side and had hoisted Tracy onto her feet.

'Take yer dirty black 'ands off 'er, ya fuckin' baboon,' said Rogers.

'Out!' said Angela. 'Nobody speaks to my staff like that! Get out!'

The Rogerses staggered together towards the front door. 'Fuck the lotta ya,' he said.

'Good evening,' said Mother Teresa as they crossed the hall. 'How very nice to meet you. Do come again. Cocksucker!'

As the front door crashed shut conversation started up slowly again around the table.

'Yobs.'

'Bloody rude.'

'*Nouveaus* from Essex. No manners.'

'Well, what do you expect? No class.'

'More money than sense.'

'A pair of flamin' Pom drongoes.'

The maids served us with glowing bowls of peaches, plums, nectarines, apples, grapes, walnuts, and a sumptuous cheeseboard laden with a gooey Brie, a spongy Camembert, a gloriously mature Roquefort that smelt like a rugby players' changing room, a rich, sloppy Saint-Félicien, and some powerful, hard, black-skinned cheese from the Pyrenees that I'd never tasted before; and all accompanied by salty biscuits, small homemade rolls and glasses of red, fourteen percent Rioja.

Afterwards there was Jamaican Blue Mountain coffee or herbal tea, Belgian chocolates, Bendicks bittermints, cigars, cigarettes, a choice of port, brandy, malt whisky, Provençal *marc*, calvados and grappa.

'What a fantastic banquet,' I said to our hostess. 'Can you buy all this stuff on the island?'

She snorted. 'Good God, no. I fly it all in from Martinique, which is heavily subsidised by France. The Frogs like to pretend that a handful of Caribbean islands four thousand miles away are still a part of mainland France. Isn't that typically French and utterly illogical? The Frogs like to pretend that they invented logic but in fact they're completely irrational.' She chuckled. 'I'll tell you how illogical they are: they call a penis *une verge* (which is feminine) and a fanny *un vagin* (which is masculine). Ridiculous, eh? I asked a Frenchman once how a penis could possibly be feminine and a vagina masculine. "Eez *très facile*," he said. "Ze penis is ze property of ze vooman an' ze vagina belong to zee man".'

The Rusian woman gave a filthy laugh. '*Da!*' she said. 'Zis I like!' and she squeezed my thigh so hard that I yelped.

'Dave?' said Angela. 'You OK?'

'Yes, fine,' I said, rubbing my thigh. 'Just a touch of cramp. I get it quite a bit.'

'You need to eat more salt,' said Angela, 'and calcium.'

'Magnesium,' said the Canadian woman.

'Quinine,' said Litvinova.

When we left the table to return to the drawing room Suzy was telling her end of the table another of her dreadful jokes.

'She says to the doctor, "I'm having terrible trouble with me aviaries, doctor."

'"You mean your *ovaries*," he says.

'"No, no," she says, "I'm sure it's me *aviaries*."

'So he lies her down on the couch, tells her to open her legs wide, and has a good look up her fanny. "Bloody hell!" he says. "You're absolutely right. You've sure had a cockatoo up there".'

They howled with laughter. How did she get away with it? No matter how outrageous she was, people forgave her. Because she was a woman? Because she was good looking? Because she was an Aussie and utterly unpretentious?

A local string band called the Sandpipers was waiting for us in the drawing room: a young man playing a shrill little silver fife homemade out of a piece of pipe; another strumming a guitar; an old guy plonking away at a banjo; another blowing into a long tube, a sort of didgeridoo, that made a deep, farting noise; a young boy with a couple of drums and another with a triangle and castanets made out of the dried seed pods of a shack-shack tree. The simple music that they made with these unsophisticated instruments was hauntingly primitive – light, catchy and cheerful, with a whiff of Africa – as they stood in a circle at the far end of the drawing room, facing shyly inwards towards each other and pretending that they had no audience. They played for twenty minutes or so and when they finished we all stood up and applauded but they didn't acknowledge or look at us at all and filed silently out of the room without even a glance in our direction. I imagined their eighteenth-century ancestors playing perhaps the very same instruments in this very room to the brutal Mullins and his guests.

'That was delightful,' I said to Angela. 'Absolutely magical.'

We were standing slightly away from the rest of her guests. She leaned towards me. 'Now, let me give you the guided tour of the house,' she murmured. 'Just the two of us.'

I knew what would happen if I let her lead me away from the others. She would back me into a dark corner and it would end in embarrassment.

'That'd be great,' I said, 'but some other time. I'm very tired. It's been a long day.'

'Why not stay the night?' she muttered. 'Save yourself the drive home.'

'That's sweet of you,' I said, 'but I'm really knackered and I need to be up early tomorrow morning.'

She gave me what she obviously thought was an irresistibly coquettish smile. 'You sure?'

'Absolutely.'

She played with her hair. 'Quite certain?'

'I'm shagged out.'

Not the best choice of verb in the circumstances, but there you are.

'Very well,' she said brusquely. 'Some other time, then.'

I said goodnight to everyone, Suzy blew me a kiss, Anna Litvinova tried to stick her tongue in my mouth, and Angela waved

Gascoigne away and saw me herself across the hall and to the front door.

'Wanker!' said Mother Teresa.

'I can't imagine where that bird learned such dreadful language,' said Angela archly. She kissed me on both cheeks. 'We must do this again, Dave,' she said. 'Just the two of us.' She gave me a penetrating look. 'I could tell you a great deal about Don Rogers.'

I tried to be nonchalant. 'Really? Would that be particularly interesting?'

'Very.'

Did she knew about me? I was sure that she knew or at least suspected something. Could I bring myself to sleep with her just to nail Don Rogers? No way. No chance. Never.

'You surprise me,' I said. 'I assumed that Rogers is just a vulgar slob with a tacky wife.'

'Oh, there's much more to him than that,' she said. '*Much* more.' She hesitated. 'You *sure* you want to go?'

'I must.'

She shrugged and opened the front door.

'I understand you've met Chezroy Billington,' she said.

The deputy Prime Minister, who knew very well that I wasn't a journalist.

'Yes.'

'Interesting, isn't he? And he's very interested in you. He told me a lot about you.'

'Really?'

'Yes. He's a very good friend of mine.'

We looked at each other for a long moment.

'Be careful, Dave' she said, and closed the door behind me.

'Arsehole!' squawked Mother Teresa, and I had a horrible feeling that the bird was right.

# CHAPTER 9

## THE BLACK CHRIST AND A SECRET BEACH

Shermelle picked me up at Hummingbird House at nine o'clock the next morning, the Sunday. She was driving a natty little pink Japanese jeep and wearing a pretty blue blouse, very short khaki shorts, red trainers, dark glasses with red frames, and her long, dark hair was tied with a red ribbon into a ponytail that made her look even younger than I remembered. She looked gorgeous with her lovely face, green eyes, wide smile and flawless brown skin. But could I trust her? Quite frankly I didn't care. That's what a girl like that can do to you.

I kissed her on the cheek. She smelled of peaches.

'You look great,' I said.

She had lovely dimples. 'Thank you, kind sir,' she said. 'You don't look so bad yourself.'

I dumped my beach things and a couple of small deck chairs that I'd found in the garage on the back seat and into the boot a Koolie bag packed with cold beers, white wine, ham, cheese, fresh bread, ice cream, a pineapple and bananas. I slipped into the front passenger seat. She was playing a lyrical CD by Ben's Brother. It was one of those gloriously warm, clear Caribbean mornings when fluffy little cottonwool clouds dance across a pale blue sky, the sea is a shimmering turquoise, and palm trees tremble in the breeze. Somewhere beyond the main island road a bird was warbling and a coven of cicadas was gossiping in the bush. Out on the ocean a dozen tiny sails – white, yellow, red – flirted like butterflies with the horizon. In England, according to the online weather report that morning, it was a typically grim Sunday afternoon in February: low grey cloud, a nagging drizzle, dark already at two o'clock, achingly cold. In London the pubs would be packed with raucous boozers pretending to be having fun and drinking too much so that they could sleep the rest of the dismal day away.

She drove well, shimmying around the potholes and dodging the sheep and goats that wandered gormlessly along the middle of the road. Her fingers were long, slim and efficient on the wheel, her nails unvarnished, just one simple ring on the fourth finger of her right hand. I was absurdly pleased to see that she was wearing neither a wedding nor an engagement ring. Why should it matter? But it did. I very much wanted her not to be married. I glanced at her face now and then as she drove. She was perfect: her eyes sparkling, her pretty little nose adorable, her lips irresistibly soft. I imagined what my children would say if they knew how I felt: 'Ah, *gross*, Dad! She could be your *granddaughter*. You turning into some sort of old *perv*?' And I didn't give a damn what they thought. Her voice caressed my soul and the sound of her laughter was pure joy. She was simply delicious, and my heart sang.

After a mile or so we turned off the main road onto a rough track and stopped at an old, abandoned sugar mill at Wilson's Ghaut, where moss and ivy fingered the fat, conical stone tower and long weeds guarded a graveyard of ancient, rusting plantation machinery: coppers, pumps, tanks, giant wheels, cogs, levers, pistons. We climbed out of the jeep. On the left of the tower the surface of a small, circular, stone reservoir glinted in the early sunlight; on the right a tiny, rotting, wooden chattel house with a broken roof slumped to one side, exhausted, surrounded by acres of sullen, overgrown cane fields. A heavy silence hung over the place, as though it was weighed down by the unbearable memories of forgotten generations. Some small creature scurried through the undergrowth: a lizard, perhaps, a mouse or a mongoose. A huge bumblebee lumbered by, humming to itself, so big that it seemed aerodynamically impossible. A breeze shuffled the tall grass, a loose shutter clattered in the chattel house, a mournful pigeon lamented the passing of time.

'Sad,' I said.

She was standing beside me, so tantalisingly close that the hairs on my arm stood up. Something passed between us like an electric shock.

'I think it's beautiful,' she said softly.

For several minutes we basked in the silent, haunted melancholy of the place until eventually, wordlessly, we both turned and climbed into the jeep. She drove back onto the main road and for another mile or so we said nothing, hypnotised by the timeless atmosphere of Wilson's Ghaut, until she stopped at the Heritage Village, where the island's Historical Preservation Society had reconstructed the various types of dwelling that had been built on Innocent over the centuries, from the brutal hovels of the earliest cannibals to the small round huts of the peaceful Arawak Indians, the flimsy shelters of the ferocious Caribs, the pitiful little pens of the West African slaves, the wooden chattel houses of the first freed men, the simple two-room brick shelters of the early twentieth century. Each dwelling was furnished appropriately for its times: flint and stone implements for the cannibals, with a few disturbingly real bones and skulls scattered about; primitive pottery, baskets, gourds, shell necklaces and hammocks for the Arawaks; clubs, bows and arrows for the Caribs; the slaves' mats, crude West African masks and pathetically precious little trinkets; the first rough chairs, tables and beds.

'My grandfather lived in a shack like that,' she said. 'He had to walk four miles each way to work every day.'

'Is he still alive?'

'Yes. Not that he knows it.'

'Alzheimer's?'

'Whatever: senile dementia, madness, disappointment, a lifetime of backbreaking labour, who knows?'

'That's very sad. And your grandmother?'

'She died last year.'

'I'm sorry.'

'No need to be.' She smiled gently. 'She was ready to go, very happy. She believed in God, you see.'

'And you?'

'Not any more.'

Another mile or so around the island we came to a huge, modern, blue building standing high, remote and lonely beside the main road, overlooking the sea. It looked like a multi-screen cinema but a large sign announced that it was in fact the Bethlehem Word of the Lord Tabernacle. A Sunday morning service was underway and we could hear a hymn, beautifully sung, wafting across the scrub towards us.

'Let's go in,' she said, 'just for a while. I don't believe in God but I do believe in theatre. They baptise their children in the ocean. It's a great ceremony.'

We slipped into the church through a side door and found seats at the back. There must have been more than three hundred people in the congregation, the men and boys wearing suits and ties, most of the girls in white frilly dresses and with ribbons in their hair, the women resplendent in their Sunday best, many of them wearing long white gloves and fancy hats. Some wouldn't have been out of place at a Buckingham Palace garden party. In fact one little old lady, who was wearing on her head what appeared to be a purple upturned chamber pot, strongly resembled the late Queen Mother, right down to the cunning expression and crooked brown teeth.

Inside the building it was even more like a luxury cinema. The floor was covered by thick, green, wall-to-wall fitted carpet, the seats were wide, plush and comfortable. Above the altar, where the raised platform boasted a flashing neon crucifix, the words of the hymn were projected onto a huge white screen and singled out by a lively little ball that bounced along above each word as if this were a karaoke party. The singing was lusty and magnificent, led by a white-robed choir and accompanied by a feisty synthesiser, guitar, flute, drums, cymbals, and rhythmic clapping from the congregation. In front of the choir four black women – one mountainous, one chunky, one tiny, one tall and slim – sang in glorious harmony, swaying rhythmically from side to side. Each of them sang one verse as a solo in voices so pure that they sounded astonishingly like Aretha Franklin, Ella Fitzgerald, Tina Turner and Whitney Houston. When all four sang together the marriage of their voices was so sublime that my spine tingled and I felt a deep sense of regret that I had lost my faith so many years ago. The stirring beauty of the singing took me by the throat and humbled my atheism with the simplicity of these faithful worshippers, who loved their god without a flicker of doubt and believed profoundly that they would live on after death with him in heaven.

When the hymn came to an end the congregation sat and a small, bald, middle-aged black man in a smart grey suit with collar and tie strode across the stage to the lectern.

'The Reverend Henry Stapleton,' Shermelle whispered. 'During the week he runs a bakery in town.'

He stared straight at me with piercing eyes and raised his voice. 'Welcome, brother, to our sacred tabernacle,' he said in a deep, booming voice enlarged by a microphone and loudspeakers that echoed around the church. 'We thank and bless thee for honouring us by sharing our worship on this holy day.'

The entire congregation swivelled in their seats to look at me. I nodded nervously, embarrassed.

'Tell us, friend,' boomed the reverend gent, 'whence do you hail?'

Shermelle nudged me. 'You'd better stand up,' she whispered.

I stood, the cynosure of more than six hundred eyes. 'From London,' I said.

'A fine city,' he said in his resounding voice. 'The capital of the greatest umpire the world has ever known.' He raised his hands. 'Sisters and brothers!' he cried. 'Let us show our appreciation for this worthy descendant of the great British Umpire that protected and nurtured this our beloved island, who has graced us with his presence by sharing our worship on this holy day.'

'Ay-men!' cried one of the congregation.

'Ay-men!'

'Ay-men!'

The applause was deafening.

'Kindly vouchsafe for us a few facts about yourself, sir,' said the Rev. Stapleton, 'so that we may truly welcome you as a brother in Christ.'

I told them my name.

'No need to be shy, here, brother,' he boomed. 'Here we are all brothers and sisters in the Lord, all friends you have yet to meet. Speak, brother!'

So I lied about my job, confessed that I was divorced, mentioned the children, said how much I was enjoying Innocent, and they listened in absolute silence. When I had finished another torrent of applause cascaded around the room.

'Ay-men!'

'Hallelujah!'

'Yea, Lord!'

'Thank you, brother,' boomed the Rev Stapleton, raising his voice and addressing the ceiling. 'O Lord, we give humble thanks to Thee for bringing to us across the wide oceans this our brother in Christ, Brother Byron from London, England, and this our fallen, sinful, wicked sister, Shermelle Donaldson, who hath strayed from Thy path of light and righteousness and into the darkness of the valley of sin.'

'Ay-men!' cried the congregation.

'Hallelujah!'

'Yes, Lord!'

'Bloody cheek!' muttered Shermelle. 'Sinful sister? God, he's a hypocrite! He's slept with half the women in this congregation!'

The preacher launched into a loud, long sermon of fire and brimstone, lapsing into the local pronunciation, haranguing, cajoling, bullying, denouncing, bellowing at his audience, threatening them with Hell and eternal torment and damnation. His theme was the need for us all to keep our promises and to 'back up de chat'.

'You ull gutta back up de chat in you lifes,' he bellowed. 'Like Jesus.'

'Hallelujah!' cried one of the congregation.

'Jesus…'

'Yea, Lord!'

'Praise Him!'

'Tell it! Tell it!'

'JESUS, HE BACK UP DE CHAT ALL HE LIFE!' bellowed the Rev. Stapleton. 'When He gone to de Temple to punish de evildoers an' de money lenders an' de adulteraters he done jus' dat: He punish dem hard; He back up He chat. When He promise to feed de five t'ousan' wid jus' t'ree loafs an' five fishes, He done jus' dat: He back up de chat. When He promise He disciples He gonna save dem, He done jus' dat: he back up de chat. When He tell de t'ief on de cross nex' to He dat dey will be togedder dat day in paradise, He done jus' dat: He back up de chat.'

'Yes!'

'True!'

'Hallelujah!'

'Praise Him, Lord!'

'Like dat Winstun Charchill when he say to dat bad man Hitler, "you a bad man, mister, an' I gonna kill you," he back up de chat.

He done kill him good in de bunker in Berlin.'

'Tell it!'

'Like dat Margaret T'atcher, de Ironing Lady, when she done seen de Argy-bargies is invadin' de Folklan' Islan's, she is telling dem "dose islan's is mine, you evil Argie-bargie sonofabitches. You attack dem an' I gonna kill you all," an' she done jus' dat. She done come an' kill dem all. She back up de chat.'

'Bear witness, O my soul!'

'Praise de Lord!'

'Like de great West Indies cricket captain, Chris Gayle, when de Englan' team come by we de las' time. He am tellin' de Englan' captain, dat Andrew Straws, "you come by de Wes' Indies, we whippin' you bad, boy," an' so it is. We done beat dem 1-0. Big Papa an' de crew, dey bangin' dem hard! Dey back up de chat.'

'True!'

'Yea, Jesus!'

'Pity us, Lord!'

'An' dat is what we must all do all we lifes: we must back up de chat. When we makes a promise we must back up de chat. When we does marry a good parson and does vow to love an' honour until death does us part, we must back up de chat.'

When eventually the tirade ended after at least half an hour, the choir began to sing another beautiful happy-clappy hymn, and we slipped out through the back door and made our escape.

Shermelle was furious. '*Sinful sister*? Cheeky little sod! He's been trying for years to get me to sleep with him, ever since I was thirteen. Dirty old goat!'

We climbed into the jeep and drove on, turning off the main road again a mile or so later, bumping up the mountain along another track through thick jungle and driving into a big butterfly sanctuary. As soon as we left the jeep we were surrounded by scores of fluttering wings of all sizes and iridescent colours: blues, reds, terracottas, yellows, greens, white. Their carefree beauty, the joy with which they flirted in the sunshine, lightened the heart. Is it true that a butterfly lives for no more than a few days? If so these had chosen the perfect place to be born and die. Where else but in Innocent would they ever have been so happy?

'Aren't they gorgeous?' she said. 'Do you know what the lady caterpillar said to the gentleman caterpillar as they sat on a twig and watched a butterfly flutter by?'

'No. What?'

'"You'd never get me up in one of those things!"'

We wandered through the butterfly sanctuary and into a small orchid farm where hundreds of brilliantly coloured, delicate blooms – pink, red, yellow, mauve, blue, white – dangled from nets with their roots drifting free in the open air.

'How do they survive without any soil?' I said.

'They suck nourishment and moisture from the air.'

'Just out of the air? That's amazing.'

For twenty minutes we relished their beauty and inhaled their sweet fragrances, some streaked with several different colours, some light, some dark, and when we could take no more perfection we clambered back into the jeep and drove on down another rough track until we reached the ruins of a small stone fort that sat on a cliff top with a fine view across the sea.

'The French built it after they captured the island from the British in the 1780s,' she said. 'They were here for several years but eventually the British plantation owners drove them out with the help of their slaves. That's why there are still a few places on the island with names like Grasse, Orleans and Auribeau.'

We sat for a while on a broken stone wall and gazed out beyond the palms towards a tiny deserted island a few hundred yards out to sea. Boobies wheeled above our heads, crying piteously. Pelicans cruised the distant shore, ungainly yet gliding effortlessly on the thermals without moving a wing. Frigate birds patrolled the sea, as silent, black and sinister as Stealth bombers. A donkey brayed in the distance. The sun was hot now on our skin and the breeze ruffled her hair and caressed her blouse and breasts. She looked magnificent. She had closed her eyes and was savouring the ozone so that I was able to gaze at her for a minute or more. God, she was lovely.

She opened her eyes, saw me looking at her, and smiled.

'What's the island called?' I said, embarrassed.

'That's Jumby Island.'

'Does anyone live there?'

'It was a nest of pirates in the seventeenth century, but there's no one there now. They say it's haunted.'

'Really? By ghosts?'

'By jumbies. Evil spirits. And duppies.'

'Duppies?'

'The malignant ghosts of evil babies. They can curse you with bad luck, sickness and death.'

'How can babies be evil?'

'Perhaps if they're evil people reincarnated?'

'You don't believe in reincarnation!' I said.

'*There are more things in heaven and earth, Horatio, than are dreamt of in your philosophy,*' she said. She grinned.

'Bloody hell!' I said. 'You've read Shakespeare?'

'At school. Of course we did, and we did the plays. I was Lady Macbeth. We're not savages, you know, David.'

I loved the way she said 'David.' It had never sounded so intimate or musical: *David*, like a saxophone whispering.

'We're quite well educated here, you know,' she said. 'I passed four A-levels.'

'Good grief! I got only three.'

She shrugged. 'Well, it's no big deal. A-levels were much more difficult when you took them twenty or more years ago. Anyone can pass them nowadays. I've seen some of the papers from your days: I wouldn't have passed any of them.'

How many young women would be that honest and generous?

'You're being modest,' I said.

'Not at all. It's true. Everything's easier now, except life.' She sounded sad, almost resigned.

'So tell me about jumbies, then,' I said, to lighten the mood.

She settled herself more comfortably on the wall. 'They say they're the spirits of our ancestors and they can influence your life and predict the future. Sometimes they're vicious, sometimes just mischievous, playing tricks on you, but a lot of the old people say that they're always hoping to jump into your mouth and control you.'

'Spooky.'

'They say that if you mistreat or ignore a jumby it can turn nasty and steal babies. Have you noticed how many doorways here are painted blue?'

'No.'

'Well, they are, and that's to keep the jumbies out. They're meant to be frightened of blue, like vampires are afraid of garlic, and parents tell their children always to go into the house backwards so that a jumby can't sneak in behind them. You know how so many kids wear their caps back to front?'

'Yes. It's ridiculous.'

'Not if you believe in jumbies. If you wear your cap back to front they think you can see behind you or that you're walking backwards, so they don't try to slip past you. And then there are funeral processions, where the jumbies jostle around the coffin trying to molest the corpse. When a funeral passes by people lock all their doors and windows to keep the jumbies out.'

'What do they look like? Frightening? Ghosts?'

'They say there's one really powerful jumby called a *soucouyant* which looks like a wrinkled old crone during the day but at night sheds all of its floppy old skin, like a snake, hides the skin in a secret place, and turns into a gorgeous young woman, always beautifully dressed in a gown with long sleeves and gloves, before going out to entice and seduce men, drink their blood, and leave them dead. They say that the only way to defeat a *soucouyant* is to find her skin and pour salt all over the inside, so that when she returns just before dawn to put her skin on again the salt stings her raw flesh so agonizingly that she can't bear to wear the skin, and if she's skinless when the sun comes up, she dies.'

'Maybe you're a *soucouyant* yourself,' I said.

She chuckled. 'Not pretty enough.'

'False modesty again. So Innocentians are obviously very superstitious.'

'Incredibly. They're also terrified of something called the Jack o'Lantern, which they say has fiery, burning hair and such an avid taste for human flesh that a lot of the older people lock their doors at twilight and refuse to walk out alone at night. Some swear that they've seen strange lights flickering on the beach at night and they say it's the Jack o' Lantern looking for victims.'

'You can't believe any of this rubbish,' I said.

'Not much of it, no, of course not. Those lights on the beach at night are probably just young guys giving themselves some light to catch crabs, which they do by filling a bottle with kerosene, stuffing a bit of cloth into the neck, and lighting it. But most Innocentians are also terrified of *crapauds*, the huge, brown, horny toads that we have here and can grow a foot long. There's also a frog called a Mountain Chicken, which is what its long, powerful hind legs taste like. It can jump a couple of metres and they say it likes to leap onto your face, clamp itself across your eyes, nose and mouth, and cling on so strongly that the only way you can remove it before it suffocates you is to burn it off. When I was a kid I once saw our gardener chasing a Mountain Chicken across the grass, trying to drench it with diesel and set it alight.'

'Yuk.'

'And some of the older people believe in a mischievous spider,

Anansi, that can turn itself into other creatures, including a man with a squeaky lisp. Most of those superstitions are obviously rubbish, but I'm not so sure about some of the legends.'

'Like what?'

I loved to hear her voice. I didn't take in half of what she was saying, I just wanted to keep her talking so that I could watch the shapes of her lips.

'Well,' she said, 'legend has it that twelve sailors were slaughtered here in the seventeenth century by Henry Morgan, Blackbeard the pirate, and they say that he stuffed their bodies, along with all the fabulous treasures he'd collected, into two sugar coppers...'

'Coppers?'

'Big copper bowls for boiling sugar cane. He put the sailors into the coppers, bolted them together, buried them halfway up the side of the volcano, and forced the dead men's souls to guard the treasure until he could return to claim it. He never did return and nobody knows where the treasure is buried, but the legend says that once every century the lost souls of the twelve desperate sailors break out and try to set themselves free by slaughtering twelve living men to replace them.'

'You can't *believe* all this rubbish.'

'I don't know.'

'Come off it, Shermelle. It's superstitious balls.'

She nodded. 'You're probably right, but here's a strange thing. One of my school friends lived high up the mountain and roughly in the area where the treasure and the dead men are said to be buried. Late one night she woke to hear her father screaming in terror, and when she burst into his bedroom she swears that he was levitating six feet above the floor and howling for mercy. When she ran into the room, she said, he crashed to the ground, breaking an arm and shattering his coccyx, and his body was covered with a hundred and twenty deep, inexplicable wounds that were oozing blood and black pus. He told her, the doctors, police and the papers that he had heard the twelve dead men calling his name and howling for him to come and replace them, and he swore that he had felt their hundred-and-twenty long, filthy, four-hundred-year-old fingernails digging into his flesh, lacerating it, as they tried to drag him to their copper tomb.'

'He was drunk.'

'He was teetotal.'

'OK: hallucinating.'

'What about the hundred and twenty wounds?'

'Your friend was exaggerating, then. Pulling your leg.'

'No. She was never a liar and she swore she'd seen him hovering six feet in the air when she ran into his room.'

'Then *she* was hallucinating. Or having a nightmare. She'd only just woken from a deep sleep. She was probably still groggy.'

Shermelle shook her head. 'No, David, she was absolutely terrified, and her father died of shock a few days later. I only hope his soul escaped before the dead sailors could take it prisoner.'

'I thought you didn't believe in souls. I thought you were an atheist.'

She grinned. 'An agnostic, but *there are more things in heaven and earth, Horatio…*'

'Get away,' I said.

As we rounded the northern shore of the island we dropped into another church in the little hamlet of Gethsemane to see its unique, roughly carved crucifix, which depicted nailed to the cross a coal-black Christ with exaggeratedly woolly hair, flattened nose and thick lips. Heavy chains hung from the wrists and ankles, the chest was scarred with whiplash wounds, blood dripped from the nose, mouth and side, and nailed above the top of the cross was a crude sign that read INRS: IESUS.NAZARENUS.REX.SERVIUM. *Servium*? It was a long time since I'd done O-level Latin.

'*Servium*?' I said.

'It's from *servus*, a slave,' she said.

'You did *Latin* at school?'

'Of course. It's the genitive plural: JESUS OF NAZARETH, KING OF THE SLAVES.'

I was stunned. *Latin*? I think it was then that I fell in love with her. Until then I'd fancied her rotten but this was something else. This was a very special girl indeed.

'It's at least three hundred years old,' she said, 'and no one knows who carved it.'

'It's awesome,' I said, 'unbelievably moving.'

She squeezed my hand. 'I'm so glad you think so,' she said softly.

We stood together and contemplated the crucifix for a minute or more. Some desperate, tormented, mutilated eighteenth-century slave, whose wife and daughters had perhaps been tortured, raped or murdered, had determined to bear witness to the horrors of his age for the enlightenment of later generations. *This is who we were*, it seemed to say. *Remember us.*

We returned to the jeep in a melancholy mood through an untidy churchyard where the ancient, crooked gravestones were all so weather-beaten that they were illegible except for two that faintly recorded the death of Matilda Abbot in 1614 and Lazarus Morton in 1618. Poor old Lazarus: still unresurrected after nearly four hundred years.

We drove for another ten minutes and turned off the main road into a heavily wooded area and along a small, barely visible, track where the trees and bushes scraped against the jeep on each side and swallowed us up as soon as we passed. It was a track where the sun never penetrated and so muddy that the jeep became bogged down a couple of times, but she used her four-wheel drive to power us out of the mud and onward.

'You can see why no one drives down here,' she said.

'Unless she's mad.'

'But that's why the beach is secret. No one ever comes here. No one knows about it. I discovered it by sheer chance when I was a little girl.'

For several minutes the little pink jeep struggled through the bush, snarling at the undergrowth and growling at the mud, until suddenly the trees released us and we found ourselves in a small clearing on the edge of the most perfect little beach I'd ever seen. It curved in a gentle, white crescent in its own private bay, completely hedged in from east to west by thick green bush so that the track we had used was the only way out. The sand was pristine, untouched by any footprint. The aquamarine sea was protected from the open ocean by a line of coral reef so that its lazy waves merely tickled the soft white sand. A dozen palm trees rimmed the beach, offering shade from the midday sun. Half a dozen pelicans perched superciliously on the reef, pink crabs scuttled towards their holes, and a nervous tribe of sandpipers skittered along the edge of the surf.

'Oh, wow!' I said. 'Fantastic.'

'You can be my Man Sunday,' she said.

She killed the engine and we were enveloped by a silence so complete that even the waves made no sound. We might have been alone in the universe.

'A drink first or a swim?' I said.

'I'd love a beer.'

'Me too.'

I opened a couple of ice-cold bottles of Carib and set up the beach chairs on the sand in the shade of one of the palms. I pretended not to watch Shermelle as she slipped out of her blouse and shorts to expose a very brief red bikini, an astonishingly small waist, and very long legs. She untied the ribbon in her dark, glossy hair, which cascaded down to her waist, flopped into a chair, and drank straight from the bottle.

She closed her eyes. 'Heaven,' she said.

'The Garden of Eden.'

She smiled lazily, her eyes shut. 'You Adam, me Eve.'

'Not quite. You've still got clothes on.'

She chuckled. 'Not for much longer,' she said, and my heart skipped.

I looked at her perfect profile, her small but immaculate breasts, her neat little mound of Venus, her long brown legs, and I thought I would burst. I wanted her very much indeed.

She opened her eyes, saw me watching her, laughed, swigged the last of her beer, slipped her bikini off, and ran naked into the sea, hair flying, diving into the water and swimming out towards the reef. She was a strong swimmer, leaving barely a splash behind her. I shed my swimming trunks, followed her into the sea, floated on my back, realised that I had an erection as perky as a submarine's periscope, and rolled onto my front to swim for a moment underwater, relishing the water rippling cool through my hair. I'm going to make love with this beautiful girl, I thought. Today. I know it. Nothing can stop me now. The deep blue sky was streaked with thin white cloud and a small aircraft puttered above the bay, the purr of its engine accentuating the peace. The Russians, perhaps, off on some nefarious KGB mission or maybe just spying on us.

Shermelle swam up silently beside me, her breasts gold under the shimmering water. 'Lazy sod!' she said, poking me in the chest. 'That's not proper swimming.' Her eyes were dancing and her hair was wet and wild.

'It's too hot for anything energetic,' I said.

'Don't be so feeble. I'll race you to the shore.'

She won, of course, and she was back in her bikini before I reached the beach. I put my trunks on again, feeling strangely shy and vulnerable because she was watching me, and we walked along the shore to dry off in the sun, frightening the sandpipers, annoying a big crab that glared at us and waved a red claw, picking up the prettiest, daintiest pastel coloured shells, a handful of sand dollars that she said she would make into a necklace, and one magnificently spiky conch shell that was splashed inside with pale pink and deep crimson. At the far end of the bay we found five big red starfish basking in a row in the shallows.

I sighed. 'This really is paradise,' I said.

'I told you when you arrived. At the airport. Come on, I'm starving.'

I opened the Koolie bag and a frosty bottle of Santa Rita Chilean chardonnay and she set out the bread, ham, cheese and fruit on paper plates on a small paper tablecloth printed with dancing palm trees. I ate greedily, my appetite excited by the fresh air, the ozone, the sunshine, the beauty all around us, and by her. After the ice-cream we spread our towels on the sand in the shade of a palm tree and lay beside each other, close but not touching. My balls flooded with warmth. I was ridiculously nervous. It was years since I'd last propositioned a woman. I'd always been faithful to Barbara, god knows why: she'd given me plenty of reasons not to be. I wanted to touch Shermelle, take her hand, feel the cool delicacy of her long, slim fingers on my skin, but it was too soon. Shyness, even at my age? Difficult to believe, maybe, but also the feeling that a grown man shouldn't rush it. I wasn't a boy any more. What was it that Shirley Bassey had sung? '*An Englishman needs time.*' Yes.

'Tell me about yourself,' I said. 'Your parents, your family, your home.'

She rolled over onto her side, tucked her arm under her head, and gazed at me. In the sunlight and the salt of the sea her green eyes had faded to a pale emerald.

'Why?' she said.

'I don't know anything about you.'

'Why would you want to?'

Because I'm going to fuck you.

152

'I just do.'

'OK.'

She told me about her parents, both mixed-race teachers, and their simple, comfortable three-bedroom house on a hillside above Jericho, and her two older brothers and younger sister, and how she'd been to the grammar school in Columbus and then to the University of the West Indies in Antigua to read for a degree in travel and tourism before returning to Innocent to gain some experience at the sharp end of the tourism industry, first as a trainee in one of the plantation hotels and now as a customs officer.

'You're wasted in that job,' I said. 'You deserve something much more exciting and challenging.'

She nodded. 'I know. I'm hoping to get a job soon in the Ministry of Tourism in Columbus.'

'You deserve much better than that, too. Why are you still here at all? Why aren't you beginning some high-powered career in London or New York?'

She thought about it and smiled. 'I love it here, you see,' she said. 'I love my island and my people and I want to do what I can to help them. Tourism is vital for Innocent. It's the bedrock of our economy. Without it we'd have huge unemployment, hunger, despair and people would turn to drink, drugs, crime and violence. You've only to look at some of the other Caribbean islands to see what can happen. If I can do something with my life to help to protect Innocent from all that I'll feel that I've lived it well.'

'What about marriage, and children?'

She told me that she'd married a childhood boyfriend when she was far too young, only eighteen, because she was pregnant, and how he'd treated her badly right from the start, staying out every night, sleeping with other women, drinking too much, coming home late and hitting her.

'He must have been mad,' I said.

She shrugged. 'It's a male West Indian thing,' she said. 'It's not personal.'

One night he had punched her so hard in the stomach that she had lost the baby, and her parents had insisted that she return to live with them. When her husband had come after her, threatening to kill her, brandishing a knife, her brothers had beaten him up so savagely that he had barely survived, and they had been sentenced to serve five years each in Columbus prison. She had divorced her husband but her brothers were still inside.

'So where's your ex-husband now?' I said.

'I don't know and I don't care. He went off to Trinidad and hasn't been seen since. Good riddance. I hope he rots.'

'Why did you marry him in the first place? Nobody else here seems to bother to get married even if they're pregnant.'

She sighed. 'I did it for my parents, I suppose. They're very religious and old-fashioned. I couldn't upset them by having an illegitimate baby. My father's just about unique here: he's never cheated on my mother, I'm sure about that. They believe firmly in duty, discipline and responsibility, and they're convinced that many of the island's problems are caused because men are selfish and feckless and don't stay with the mothers of their children. So the children grow up without rules, discipline or a male role model. The family used to be an important central focus of life here, but not any more. Fathers are absent, mothers have to go out to work, and their children are left without security or guidance. It's a huge problem that's growing all the time.'

'So who's the man in your life now?'

She gazed at me. 'No one.'

'I can't believe that.'

'Why?'

'You're lovely.'

'Looks aren't everything.'

'You're lovely inside, too.'

'How do you know?'

'I just know. I can tell. Don't the young men come after you all the time?'

'Yes.'

'So?'

She shrugged. 'They're too young for me. Too gauche. Too cocky. Too West Indian. They think they're God's gift to women. They never leave you alone. They pester you day and night. It drives you mad.'

'So you're going to do without a man for the rest of your life?'

She looked at me sharply. 'If necessary, but I hope I'll find the right one eventually.'

'How?'

'He'll come along.'

'And what'll he be like.'

She looked straight at me. 'He'll be older than I, and he won't be West Indian.'

*Older than I.* Such perfect grammar: 'older than I *am*', not 'older than me,' as an English girl of her age would say.

'And what about you?' she said.

I told her again the lie about being a journalist, and hated myself for doing it, but everything else I said was true: my dull, lower-middle-class childhood in a dreary English suburb; my miserable marriage to Barbara; my vain efforts to save it; the cruel lies she had told during the divorce; the unbridgeable gap between me and my children, who chose to believe her.

She squeezed my hand. Her fingers were gentle. 'That's sad,' she said. 'I'm so sorry. But you'll find someone else.'

'I doubt it.'

'You will. You're a really nice man.'

'Nice means boring.'

'It doesn't mean that at all,' she said. 'It means kind, considerate, tolerant and understanding. It's what we should all try to be. And now I'm going to have a little nap. Beer in the afternoon always makes me sleepy.'

She fell quickly into a doze. I gazed at her for ten minutes or more, mesmerised, enchanted. Her salty, dishevelled hair cascaded down across her shoulder. There was sand on her cheek. A thin line of sweat dampened the tiny hairs above her upper lip. Her lips were slightly parted and her teeth glistened. It was all I could do not to lean across and kiss her mouth. Her soft brown breasts rose and fell gently with her breathing and I watched them without any sense of shame. Why should I feel ashamed? They were beautiful, their magic enhanced by the shadow that lurked between them. It was all I could do not to reach across and touch them. Instead I touched her sandy fingers again, and in her sleep she smiled.

I fell asleep myself after a while, lulled by the afternoon heat and alcohol, and woke perhaps an hour later with a small headache and a large erection. I glanced towards her quickly in case she had noticed it but she was no longer lying beside me. I propped myself up on my elbows and could see her swimming out almost as far as the reef. The afternoon was slowly dying, the sun already sinking beyond the western headland, the western sky light with a touch of pale yellow, shadows creeping across the sand. A pigeon was moaning in a sea-grape tree, a lovesick cicada chirping plaintively in the bush, and a pelican drifted low along the shore as dark, sinister and ungainly as a Nazi Junkers heavy bomber. I followed her into the sea, refreshed by the coolth of the water, and swam slowly out towards her, nothing flashy, no showing off, just a gentle breaststroke. As I neared the reef I could hear that she was singing some gentle lullaby.

'Hi.'

'Hi.'

'Nice song. Nice voice.'

'Thank you. I'm happy.'

'Me too. Very. Did you sleep?'

'Like a baby.'

'I never know why people say that. Both my kids seemed to howl all night when they were babies.'

We swam for a while, relishing the cool caress of the water, the peace of the bay, the fading light, the solitude. Just us, just the two of us. It was perfect.

'We ought to go,' she said eventually. 'Mosquitoes soon.'

'I suppose so.'

'I'll drive you home.'

We packed up the ruins of the picnic and she tunnelled the jeep through the bush and undergrowth back onto the main road, and drove back to Hummingbird House. It was almost dark when we got there. I didn't want to let her go. I didn't want the day to end.

'Come in for a drink,' I said.

She hesitated. 'I'd love one,' she said, 'and then you can fuck me if you like.'

*If you like?* Dear god.

And then, suddenly, inexplicably, it came to me. The crucifix of the black Christ in the little church at Gethsemane. IESUS.NAZARENUS.REX.SERVIUM. What early 18th Century African slave would have understood Latin, let alone been able to write it? The crucifix can't have been carved by a slave. It had to be a fraud. It must be a forgery.

'Don't you want to fuck me?' she said. 'You've been dying to do it all day.'

# CHAPTER 10

# JOY, MISERY AND JUDAS ISCARIOT

Shermelle was a magical lover: passionate, tender, generous. She came to Hummingbird House every night, even after working a late shift at the airport, and stayed until dawn. Every night I buried my face in the sweet scent of her long, dark hair and I lost myself in her, revelling in the softness of her firm young body, her warmth, her touch, the taste of her tongue, the fine invisible hairs on her upper lip, the delicious little corners of her mouth, the flavour of her tiny toes, her glorious smell. Her skin was as smooth and brown as toffee, the tender inside of her thighs pale caramel, her ears like little shells under my tongue, her navel an intricate marvel, and I feasted on her lovely little breasts and tight, eager little nipples, the musky flavour of her armpits, the naughty, damp cleft at the top of her buttocks, and I drank with wonder from the sweetness of her secret garden and shamelessly plundered its depths two or three times a night. She would tease me unmercifully with the tip of her tongue and take me far into her mouth, bringing me time and again to the brink, tracing wicked pathways of glorious pleasure in places that no other woman had ever mapped. Sometimes she swallowed my fountain with relish, as if her thirst would never be quenched, and sometimes she licked me where I'd never been licked before, and sometimes she rode me, rearing high above me, throwing her head back, gripping my sides with her knees, whimpering, shuddering, spilling her hot juice over my groin. She liked me to take her from behind, her face pressed deep into the pillow while she gasped and groaned, her perfect golden buttocks gleaming under my fingers in the moonlight. She came easily and every time, more than any woman I'd ever known, with a moan or a shout, and she would reach down and squeeze my balls when she knew I was about to come, making them explode, making me feel as if I were made of iron and twenty-five again and inexhaustible. In her arms I felt as if I'd become an immortal young god. 'With my body I thee worship,' they say during the marriage ceremony, and I worshipped Shermelle and her body with mine. I felt invincible. She became my own private religion, my personal route to salvation, with no need for priests or ceremony or superstitious mumbo-jumbo. In her I found my own true paradise.

Afterwards her eyes were always a deep green, and sometimes she wept.

'Why are you crying?' I said.

'Because it's so good. Because I'm so happy.'

No one had ever told me before that I was a good lover, or had wanted me as much as she did, or had relished my body the way that she did, or had given me so much abandoned joy. She liked to wake drowsily from a deep sleep in the middle of the night to find me inside her again and moving yet again, relentlessly. She liked to pretend to be still asleep but when I groaned and filled her she would tighten herself around me several times, squeezing me dry, smiling and licking her lips. Afterwards, when she slept again, I would lie on my side in the darkness listening to her gentle breathing, gazing at her silhouette, relishing the acrid perfume of our lovemaking and mourning all those lost years, all those wasted days and nights of my loveless marriage. Where had she been all my life? Why had I had to wait for her until now?

'Why me?' I said on the second night.

She poked me in the chest. 'West Indian girls love sex,' she said mischievously. 'That's why. Any man will do.'

'No, seriously: why me?'

'Why not?'

'Because I'm twice your age and hardly irresistible.'

'Who cares about your age? Young guys think they know it all but most of them know diddly-shit. Most of them are boring, vain and arrogant, and the better looking they are the more boring they are, always strutting around and smirking at themselves in the mirror. You're much more interesting: you know so much and you've been around, and you're not obsessed about yourself. And you're lovely, and kind, and funny, and a wonderful lover. My god, you're not old in bed, that's for sure.'

I woke each morning charged with energy and enthusiasm. We would always make love yet again when we woke, just after dawn, languidly, taking our time, but she always left before Miz Quaintance arrived, more for my sake than hers, she said. I don't suppose Miz Quaintance would have minded at all, considering her own rackety love life, but Shermelle said that Innocentian women are incredibly jealous and critical of other people's behaviour. 'They love to gossip and bitch and run people down,' she said. 'It's one of our less attractive characteristics.'

'Talking of running other people down,' I said, 'I reckon that the guy who carved that crucifix you showed me is a fraud.'

'Really?'

'It's a fake. I don't believe it was carved by a seventeenth century slave. I think it was done much more recently.'

'Why?'

'The Latin at the top of the cross. No seventeenth century African slave would ever have known Latin.'

She hesitated. 'I never thought of that.'

'Sherlock Barron,' I said.

She thought about it. 'Well, maybe some educated white man told him what to write.'

'A slave wouldn't have known how to write at all, let alone in

Latin.'

'Maybe the white man wrote it for him. Maybe one of the Irish indentured labourers.'

'They wouldn't have known any Latin, either.'

'Yes, they would: they would have been Roman Catholics; they would have been spouting Latin every time they went to church.'

'I suppose that's possible, but there's still something… spurious about it. It's just too politically correct for the seventeenth or eighteen centuries.'

'You're a cynic.'

'Yes.'

'You don't take anything at face value.'

'No.'

You can't if you're a tax inspector.

'I like that,' she said.

Knowing that I would see her again each night, I went to work every day with a new determination. I spent half-an-hour with Don Rogers over coffee at the Galleon Café on Prince William Street, pretending that I had a couple of million to invest in one of his dodgy schemes, hoping to find out just how crooked he was, but he was suspicious.

'You said you was skint,' he said aggressively. 'You said what all writers is skint, so 'ow come nah yer gotta coupla mill to spare, eh, cock? Lotta spondoolicks, a coupla mill, for a guy what got nuffink.'

'My father left me a bit.'

'Oh yeah? An' *my* farver knew Lloyd George, an' all, an' Lloyd George knew me farver.'

So now Rogers *and* Angela Fellowes mistrusted and suspected me. Not a good start. She kept telephoning Hummingbird House and although I left the answerphone on so that I could hear who was calling, she started leaving messages for me with Miz Quaintance as well. 'Dat Mistress Fellowes,' said Miz Quaintance slyly. 'She am dat English woman what got de big 'ouse up by Hopetown?'

'Yes.'

'Dat nice. I t'ink she am very, very rich, Lard David.'

'Yes, I believe you're right.'

'So you am she sweet man, You' Lardship?'

'Certainly not,' I said.

'She am callin' you all de time.'

'Well...'

'She am callin' you every day.'

'On business.'

Miz Quaintance hooted with laughter – 'oo-oo-oo!' – her whole vast body wobbling like jelly. 'On *business*!' she cackled. 'Yessir! So you is doin' de business wid her! OK! Dat am just what me t'inked! So now you not needin' no more for me to find you nice girl wid big tops an' big bottoms. Dat good. Me beginnin' to t'ink dat you's impertinent an' cannot raise de big stick no more.'

She started changing the sheets every other day, whenever she came to clean the house, making suggestive remarks about the state of my bedclothes.

'All mens must 'ave sweet womans,' she said, 'oh yes, an' is best if white mens be goin' wid white womans an' not wid some o' dese bad black girls, no sir. Some o' dese bad girls not all clean, dat for sure.'

And this was the woman who'd kept trying to pimp black girls for me. Gee, thanks.

She wagged her finger. 'Some wicked girls got lots o' germ, dat for sure. Some o' dem dey got de hiv an' de gone o' rear. You don' want nuttin' to do wid dem dirty girls, no sir. You want to keep puttin' it in dat nice clean Mistress Fellowes, dat am de fact. She not got de gone o' rear, dat for certain.'

'Miz Quaintance,' I said emphatically, 'I am *not* having an affair with Ms Fellowes. Is that clear?'

She sniggered. 'If you sayin' so, You' Lardship.' She winked. 'But dese sheet am always very dirty every marnin'.'

I dropped in on Alopecia Martin to see if there was any news yet that the Prime Minister might be returning soon, but he was still away on his travels, holding out his begging bowl as usual in Libya or Qatar or somewhere. She seemed even more metallic than when I'd met her: a large nut and bolt were screwed together into her previously uninhabited left nostril and a safety pin pierced her left earlobe. Her mood was hard and metallic, too. She was wearing a T-shirt that snarled WHAT YOU STARING AT, ASSHOLE? She glared at me. 'I *towdja*,' she barked. 'I *towdja* I'll letcha know when 'e's back.'

'Yes, I just thought...'

''e's still away.'

'Right. Do you know when he might be back?'

'No effin' idea, squire.'

'A week? Two weeks?'

'I ain't got the foggiest.'

'A month, then?'

'Look 'ere, sunshine,' she said with menace. 'You fink I'm a fortune teller or somefink? 'e don't tike me inna 'is confidence, does 'e? I ain't 'is confidentioo seckertry. All I know is 'e's in Swisserlan' or Monica or somefink.'

'Monica?'

'Inna Souf o' France,' she said with contempt. 'You never 'eard a Monica? Cor, you ain't 'alf hignorant.'

'Ah: Monaco.'

'Yeah, Monica. So nah you can naff off, then, OK?'

In the corridor outside her office I bumped into Chezroy Billington, who was emerging from his own office and smelling strongly of brandy. He stared at me with yellow eyes.

'Good morning, sir,' I said oleaginously.

He grunted.

163

'Do you happen to know, sir, by any chance, when the Prime Minister might be back from his travels?'

He frowned. His brow was as low as the floor of a chattel house and as thickly corrugated as its tin roof. 'Why you wantin' 'im?' he growled.

'Well, this article I'm writing…'

He snorted and waved me away as if I were an irritating insect. ''e'm on big guv'ment business, maan,' he rumbled. ''e'm too busy for wastin' 'e time wit' jornalists,' and he stamped ahead of me down the corridor, farting as he went.

As I left the building the fat receptionist remembered me and glowered.

'Nice to see you again, sweetheart,' I said.

I called in at the *Innocent Gazette* to see if Smartly Warner-Perkins knew where I might find Rupert Williams, the English conman who had founded his own religion to worship Judas Iscariot.

Smartly looked at his watch. Just after midday. 'Time for a tincture?'

'A bit early, isn't it?'

'Nonsense. This is the Caribbean: it's never too early or late. Let's repair to Sweetman's again.' He glanced at his assistant. 'Hold the fort, will you, Gwendolyn. I won't be long.'

She cackled. 'That'll be the day.'

Sweetman's beach bar was as busy as ever, packed with tourists. He welcomed me with a powerful hug. I winced. 'Where you been, maan?' he said. 'I ain't seen you a long time.'

'It's only been a couple of days.'

'Too long, all de same.' He touched fists with Smartly. 'Yo, Brains,' he said.

'How's Mutryce?' said Smartly.

Sweetman adopted a pained expression. 'She drivin' me mad, maan,' he said. 'She gone by Barbados to spend me money. Spend

spend spend, that's Mutryce.'

'That's all of them,' said Smartly. 'That's women. Anyway, you mean old bastard, I don't know why you're complaining. You're as rich as Croesus.'

'Creases?'

'An old Turkish king. Sixth century B.C.'

'What he got to do wid me?'

'He was a rich, tight-fisted old bastard too, just like you. And how are the kids?'

'They wid that Mutryce and they all also spendin' me money, god-dammit! They all just like her. They all chips off the old black,' and he roared with laughter.

We claimed the last small table under one of the thatched umbrellas. 'You wantin' a Scarlet Scorpion?' said Sweetman.

'No thanks,' I said hastily. 'My mouth is still recovering from the first one you gave me.'

He chuckled. 'That the whole point of it, maan. OK, you want somethin' for the brain?'

'The brain?'

Smartly sighed. 'Ganja. Cocaine. Crack. E. Special K. Crank. GHB. You name it, he sells it.'

Sweetman spread his hands. 'You gotta make a livin'.'

'You're quite rich enough already, you old rogue,' said Smartly. 'You ought to be in prison.'

We ordered a couple of Caribs and watched the boats bobbing out at their moorings. The temperature was well into the eighties, there was barely a breeze, and the sun's reflection off the sea was dazzling. A few youngsters were careering on jet-skis across the bay, buzzing like hornets, trailing foam. Burned sunbathers lay on the beach, painfully crimson and sweating profusely. 'I'm constantly baffled that so many white people want so desperately to be brown and so many brown and black people want to be white,' said Smartly.

'Do they?'

'Absolutely. Innocentians spend a fortune on skin-lightening creams and hair-straighteners. I blame Michael Jackson. Did you hear what Jay Leno said on TV when Jackson was acquitted of being a paedophile? He said: "Of course he was acquitted. What jury in California would convict a white man?"'

I laughed. 'That's sad. I thought that black is meant to be beautiful.'

'Not for everyone. Do you know why Ray Charles was always laughing?' Smartly grinned. 'He didn't realise he was black.'

'That's really tasteless.'

'It's a niggers' joke. Black humour.'

The beers arrived and he told me what he knew about Rupert Williams. 'He's got a large property that he calls the Independent Republic of Judasia up in the hills at Misery,' said Smartly.

'Odd name, Misery.'

'That's what the slaves called it in the old days, when a brutal old slave master lived up there in the 1700s. Williams decided it was just the place to build a little chapel dedicated to the memory of Judas Iscariot.'

'How's he got away with doing that? Most Innocentians seem to be fervent Christians. I'd have thought they'd have burned the place to the ground and lynched him for blasphemy.'

Smartly shrugged. 'We're pretty tolerant here, especially towards outsiders. We're used to eccentric honkies: the Caribbean has always been full of them. We're only vicious towards each other, our own. And we're lazy: Misery is way up in the hills, so nobody can be bothered, and Williams doesn't actually hold religious services or have any congregation. The chapel is really just his office and he calls it a chapel only so that he can claim that he's running a religious charity. It's just a place where he keeps his records and sends out books and parcels of magazines and pamphlets about Judas, and sells his Republic of Judasia documents: things like spurious citizenship certificates, passports, ID cards, bogus driving licences, credit cards and insurance policies.'

I was puzzled. 'Why would anyone buy them? I don't suppose they're actually recognised anywhere in the world.'

'Some countries do: the usual suspects; Iran, North Korea, Sudan, Somalia, Congo, Zimbabwe. They'll recognise anything that irritates the West, and there are plenty of officials, police and government ministers in Africa and the small island nations in the Pacific and Indian Oceans who are quite happy to accept anything so long as you bribe them.'

'I'm surprised the government here lets him claim that his property is an independent state.'

Smartly shrugged again. 'Who cares? Nobody takes any notice. He's not hurting anyone or causing any trouble, and he pays his property and business taxes. He employs a couple of local girls to print and post his books and documents, and he pays their social security charges, and he spends a fortune on postage. He's generous towards several local charities, and always buys a fistful of tickets for the Carnival and the police ball, and I'll bet he bribes Windy Billington with at least thirty pieces of silver several times a year.'

'How old is he?'

'Williams? Late thirties, I guess.'

'English public school?'

'Harrow.'

'I should have guessed. Dodgy chaps, Old Harrovians. Four-letter men, Peregrine Fanshaw told me: an entire school of uneducated, semi-literate bounders, cads and rotters. Apparently they wear brown suede shoes! Even in Town! Even on weekdays! Married?'

'No: divorced and living with a young girl from Jericho, Tonicia, almost a child, can't be more than sixteen or seventeen, but they say he's still screwing his ex-wife, Polly, even though she's now married to a Canadian called Holloway.'

'He sounds like a major shit.'

Smartly smiled. 'Not at all: in fact he's utterly charming. You'll like him. Everyone does.'

I drove up the mountain towards Misery after lunch to investigate the Independent Republic of Judasia for myself. The road was a rugged dirt track and the jeep's tyres were threatened constantly by sharp stones, the suspension by fat boulders and deep ruts. No wonder the locals couldn't be bothered to trek all the way up here. After a couple of miles I came to a small hut with a neatly printed notice saying PASSPORT CONTROL and across the track a red-and-white striped barrier with a large, embossed, oval consular coat of arms in the middle that depicted a monkey and a pelican on each side and a corpse hanging from a tree with purple flowers. In an arc across the top of the barrier were the words INDEPENDENT PEOPLE'S REPUBLIC OF JUDASIA and across the bottom the Latin motto IUDAM VENERANDUM VENERARI. *Iudam*? The Latin accusative of Judas, maybe. *Venerandum*? *Venerari*? My thirty-year-old Latin was so rusty that I could hear my brain creaking as it searched the empty, cobwebbed files of my adolescent memory. Venerated? Venerable? Shermelle would know, damn it.

There was no security guard in the hut nor any intercom so I raised the barrier and drove on up the track through thick jungle and unruly undergrowth. At the top, after a few hundred yards, I reached a clearing and then a lush garden that surrounded a large house with a small, purple chapel to one side. On the roof of the chapel, where a Christian church would display a cross, there was a miniature tree with a rope dangling from one of its branches.

I tooted the horn, climbed out of the jeep, and a tall, slim young white man emerged from the house. He was blond, suntanned, and wearing shorts, a garish Caribbean shirt, and that privileged, self-confident, self-satisfied look of the well-bred, well-fed, upper-class

Englishman.

'Dr Livingstone, I presume,' I said facetiously.

He laughed. 'Mr Henry Morton Stanley, of course,' he said, 'or should I say *Sir* Henry?' He seemed surprisingly well-informed for an Old Harrovian: Stanley had indeed been knighted but how many people know that?

We shook hands. His were small and soft, unaccustomed to physical work.

'David Barron,' I said.

'Rupert Williams.'

'I thought you must be.'

'Yes?' He raised an elegant eyebrow.

'I've heard quite a bit about your church and your republic.'

'From whom?'

'The editor of the *Innocent Gazette*.'

'Ah: Smartly.'

'Yes.'

'Good man, Smartly. Excellent fellow. Heart in the right place. Chap with bottom.'

'He speaks well of you, too.'

'Glad to hear it. So what can I do for you?'

I braced myself to trot out the feeble old cover story, a lie that was becoming less convincing every time I told it. 'I'm writing a travel article about the island for the *Sunday Times* in London,' I said, 'and I'm fascinated by the story of your church and independent state. So I'd very much like to talk to you about them. Not now, necessarily, of course. Only when it's convenient.'

'Now would be fine,' he said. 'Not much on. Slow down after tiffin. Too hot. Come in.'

'That's very kind of you,' I said.

It's extraordinary how many people, even intelligent, sohisticated people, will agree to talk to you, even tell you the most intimate things, if you say you're a journalist, and especially if you don't take any notes while they're talking. They assume you won't quote them if you're not taking notes. How naïve can you be? Even the most unscrupulous gossip columnist would never dream of alerting his victim by digging out a notebook in front of him. As a big sign used to exhort reporters in the newsroom of one of the old Fleet Street tabloids, MAKE IT EARLY, MAKE IT SHORT, MAKE IT UP.

I followed Williams into the house and through several rooms, all blissfully cool with air conditioning and huge, idle, overhead fans. The furniture was simple Caribbean: bamboo chairs and sofas upholstered in light, airy materials decorated with red-and-blue parrots, yellow monkeys and green palm trees. Primitive local carvings stood on every bamboo table: charming little donkeys, parrots, mischievous monkeys, frogs, turtles, crabs, fish. Slatted wooden blinds protected each window from the ferocious afternoon sunshine and the walls were bright with paintings of colourful Caribbean scenes by Jill Walker, Kate Spencer, Rosey Cameron, Eva Wilkin, Howard Pain, Juliet Lewis: portraits of shady old plantation inns, workers in cane fields, fragile chattel houses, rowdy bars, busy street scenes in Barbados and Antigua, tiny fishing boats that looked too frail to sail, beaches, flaming sunsets, solemn old people with sad eyes full of memories, children laughing. Rush mats were scattered across the pale tiled floors, intricately carved oriental camphor-wood chests guarded several corners, the glum, amputated head of a monkey stared down from a wooden shield high up on one of the walls, and in the corner of one room a bubbling aquarium glittered with garish, darting, tropical fish.

We reached a large, light, airy, enclosed verandah, where at one end birds twittered and fluttered around a spacious aviary. Williams gestured towards two comfortable armchairs. I sat. 'Cooler inside,' he said. 'Gargle? Beer? Wine? Scotch?'

At four in the afternoon? 'I'd love a cup of tea,' I said.

'Good God! A *journalist*! *Tea?*'

'We're not all alcoholics.'

He laughed. ''Course not. Partial to a cup meself. Earl Grey?'

'I'd rather have Indian, please, if you have it.'

''Course. Foul stuff. Never drink it meself. Coolie juice. But everything here. Liberty Hall. Caribbean Fortnum's.' He raised his voice. 'Tonicia!'

A huge, very young, very black girl emerged from a nearby room, one of the monstrously fat tribe of Innocent. She could have given even Miz Quaintance a run for her money in the obesity stakes, even though she was still a teenager. Her breasts were as massive as giant watermelons, her waist the size and shape of a barrel, her vast buttocks as mobile as a fistful of balloons, but she had a sweet face and a gentle smile.

'Tonicia, dear heart,' he said, 'this is Mr Barron. Journalist. English. From London.' He gestured towards her. 'Tonicia. My other half.'

Other *half?* Good grief! Other four fifths, I'd have said, but how can you blame her for being fat? Like so many poor West Indians she'd probably been raised in a hard-up family on a diet of starch and sweet fizzy drinks.

I stood up to shake her hand. Her palm was rough. 'How d'you do,' I said.

Like so many Innocentians, she wouldn't look me in the eye. Many of them look shyly down or away when you speak to them, a reticence that maybe stems from the olden days when slaves were perhaps forbidden to look directly at their white masters. 'I'm good, sir,' she said in a tiny little-girl voice with a strong West Indian accent. 'T'ank you, sir.'

'Please call me David,' I said.

She giggled nervously, hiding her mouth behind her hand.

'Tonicia, old thing,' said Williams. 'Two teas: one Earl Grey, one Indian muck. Would you? There's a dear.'

'No prublem.'

'Milk, David?

'Please.'

'Sugar?'

'No, thanks.'

'I does it,' she said, and waddled out of the room.

He watched her go, her buttocks wobbling like a family of ferrets in a sack. 'Big girl, eh?' he said. He chuckled. 'Love big girls. Always have. Bigger the better. You?'

'Well…'

'Recommend 'em. Juicy. Lots of meat. Bloody great handfuls. Sensational arses. And black, really black. Love that. You?'

'I've never…'

'Don't know what you've missed. Delicious. Skin like midnight and huge purple nipples.'

'Yes?'

He nodded. 'Monumental. Couple of inches across, easy. Get your money's worth. Really get your teeth into 'em.'

Now I was embarrassed.

'Still,' he said. 'Not here to discuss Tonicia's humungous bristols, are we?'

'Talking of purple,' I said hurriedly, to change the subject, 'I noticed on the way up here that the coat of arms on your barrier at the entrance depicts a tree with purple flowers. And your chapel is painted purple, too.'

'Judas-tree. *Cercis siliquastrum. Caesalpinia* family. Small pink or purple flowers. Also known as redbud. Judas hanged himself on one, poor bugger.'

'And the motto?'

'*Iudam venerandum venerari.* To Worship Holy Judas.'

'You believe he was *holy*?'

'Undoubtedly.'

'But his betrayal of Christ, the kiss in the garden, the thirty pieces of silver.'

'All balls.'

'Really?'

'Completely.'

'How come?'

He looked intently at me. 'Interested?' he said. 'Really?'

'Absolutely.'

He considered me for a moment, then nodded. 'Very well. Legend of Judas's treachery quite untrue. Not even mentioned in the earliest books of the New Testament. He died in about AD30, yet St Paul had never even heard of him. Paul would surely have heard of him if he really was a traitor.'

'I didn't know that.'

'Not many people do. About thirty years ago an old Gnostic document, *The Gospel According to Judas*, turned up in Egypt. Second century, maybe. Reported that Judas was doing just what Jesus wanted. Jesus *told* him to betray him, *begged* him to betray him. Judas refused at first, argued, wept, but Jesus told him it was his destiny. He was *obeying*, not betraying him. He identified him to the High Priest's soldiers because Jesus *wanted* to be crucified, killed, his spirit freed from his body and the ancient prophecies fulfilled. Most loyal apostle of all, Judas. Truly believed Jesus to be the long awaited Messiah. Some Muslims even say he *defended* Christ in the garden and was crucified in his place, so that Jesus escaped and lived into old age.'

'And eloped with Mary Magdalene to the South of France, I suppose,' I said flippantly, 'and raised a family.'

'*The Da Vinci Code*? That's rubbish, of course,' said Williams. 'Jesus was undoubtedly crucified, and died, and Judas was so distraught that he hanged himself afterwards in grief, not because of guilt. Broken heart. Loved him, you see, and by hanging himself he hoped to be reunited with Jesus. And Jesus told him he would be the greatest disciple of them all.'

'That seems unlikely.'

'Why?'

'Didn't he tell St Peter the same thing? "You are the rock on which I will build my church"?'

'Quite possibly, but the rock was simply the firm foundation. Judas was destined to be placed on the highest pinnacle. Judas was destined to become the spire. Which is why his enemies have been traducing his name for centuries. Jealousy. Spite. Envy. They said he was a traitor. Said he was homo. Said he fancied Jesus. Said he embezzled apostles' money. All lies. Said he was called Iscariot from *sicarius*, Latin for murderer. Another lie. He was called Iscariot because he belonged to a patriotic group of fervent Jewish nationalists, the Sicarii, who swore to drive the Romans out of Palestine. And he came from a town in Judaea called Kerioth, and in Hebrew *Ish Kerioth* – Iscariot – means "the man from Kerioth".'

I was disconcerted by this cascade of unusual but maybe utterly spurious erudition. Was it really possible that for two millennia the entire western world could have got Judas so wrong? Could he in fact have been not the lowest of the low, the scum of the Christian world, but the greatest martyr of them all? Or was this just another religious fairytale to excite the gullible? I had to demonstrate some scepticism. 'So what about the thirty pieces of silver?' I said.

Williams laughed. 'Only thirty? *Peanuts*. Worth about five US dollars in modern money. The price of the cheapest foreign slave in ancient Rome. Blood money then was a damn sight more than thirty pieces of silver.'

'But he took the money.'

'And threw it back at the High Priest afterwards.'

'He still took it.'

'Only as camouflage, to fool them into thinking that he really was betraying Jesus.'

It was time to lighten the atmosphere. I grinned. 'You're very persuasive,' I said. 'Perhaps I ought to join your church!'

'Any time,' he said. 'Would you like an application form? The subscription is only fifty dollars a year.'

'And what would I get for that?'

He grinned. 'You'd save your soul,' he said.

Tonicia came wobbling in with a tray and two pots of tea, two elegant china cups on dainty saucers, a matching jug of milk, and a plate of biscuits: wholemeal digestives, chocolate fingers, ginger nuts, big round Maries for dunking, custard creams. We could have been in Wimbledon or Weybridge.

'Thank you, my precious,' said Williams, patting a massive buttock.

She smiled shyly, dimpled her dimples, fluttered her eyelids, and wobbled out of the room. He watched her go with fascination. 'Just look at that arse,' he said. 'Magic.'

He reached for the first teapot. 'Shall I be Mother?'

I glanced up quickly, suspecting that he was pulling my leg, but he looked completely serious. 'Please,' I said, and he poured the tea.

'So how many members do you have in your church?' I said.

'Here? None at all. Well, except for me and two girls I employ. Honorary members. Bad form otherwise. Even Tonicia refuses to leave her church to join mine. She's in the Born Again Church of Galilee. Fair enough. But around the world? About ten thousand.'

Ten thousand members at fifty dollars each a year: that's half a million a year just in membership subscriptions, never mind the books, magazines, pamphlets, and all the dodgy documents he sold.

'Impressive,' I said, impressed. 'And you're still a British citizen?'

'Oh yes.'

'But you're resident here?'

'Yes. Have been for years.'

'The usual ninety days a year rule?'

175

'Absolutely.'

'Do you go back to the UK much?'

He chuckled. 'You sound like a tax inspector.'

I held his gaze.

'I obey the law,' he said, 'as much as possible.'

'Sounds like a great life.'

'Oh, it is. Perfect. Paradise, just as the posters say. Now, tell me about yourself.'


I left an hour later, none the wiser but a little better informed. He had indeed been married and divorced, and he was still very friendly with his ex-wife, Polly, who still lived on the island, and mentioned her fondly. 'Led astray by the old willy once too often,' he explained ruefully. 'Never could keep me trousers on. Still can't. Weakness of mine. Old girl couldn't take any more. Caught me in bed one day with some big black totty. Bad luck. Careless. Didn't mind too much if they were white or brown but drew the line at black. Bad show.'

Tonicia?

'Good shag. Jolly keen on it. Willing. Girls here love a good shafting, specially the big ones. No sense of shame, you see, not even in the Born Again Church of Galilee. No guilt. But obviously not serious. Couldn't be. Not much brain. Fun for a few months, maybe, but then time for something different. Maybe Guyanese. Some of the Guyanese girls here are very pretty. A bit small and thin but nice tight fannies. Get bored easily, though, you see. Need to move on. Variety. Spice of life.'

His ex-wife had married again. 'Canadian wanker called Holloway. Works for some do-gooder charity. Big, red-faced prat with curly ginger hair. God knows what she sees in him: big tool, I suppose.'

Sometimes he still missed England: country pubs, rugby,

autumn afternoons, the Savile Club – and he returned a couple of times a year to spend a few weeks fertilising his roots. 'But never for more than ninety days a year,' he said. 'Even though I've been resident here for several years those Inland Revenue shits never let go. Suspicious bastards.'

'It's not called the Inland Revenue any more,' I said, and immediately regretted it.

He gazed at me. 'Really?'

'Well, so I believe,' I said, a fraction too hastily. 'I understand it's now called HMRC.'

'Her Majesty's Robbers and Crooks, I suppose.'

'Her Majesty's Revenue and Customs.'

He gazed at me a little more. 'How quaint,' he said. 'You're very well informed.'

After that, I left as soon as I could.

'You must send me a copy of your article when it appears,' he said with a hint of what I thought might be sarcasm.

'Of course,' I said.

Bugger! Now all three of my main targets suspected that I was a British taxman and looking for quite a bit more than thirty pieces of silver.

# CHAPTER 11

## ASCOT RACES

Shermelle had a day off the following Sunday, so we didn't get out of bed until after ten, incredibly late for the tropics. *Please let this last for ever*, I prayed. *I need this woman for the rest of my life.* I'd never been so happy and I'll never forget exactly what happened every minute of that wonderful, terrible day.

She lay on her side and brushed my lips with hers. 'Bacon and eggs?' she said.

'Fantastic.'

'Coming up, but let's have a swim first.'

She leaned over me, tickling my chest with her breasts, kissed me on both eyelids, swung out of bed, and wandered away naked towards the bathroom. I watched her go: so young, delicious and carefree, and my heart turned over.

We swam naked in the pool, revelling in the caress of cool water, watched as usual by my two faithful, solemn kingbirds, which had taken to fluttering onto the fence around the pool deck as soon as I appeared every morning to say hello. Afterwards she cooked fried eggs and bacon with sausages, mushrooms, tomatoes, baked beans and toast and marmalade – the sort of huge, glorious, disgraceful breakfast that I hadn't had in years. We drank chilled orange juice and ate on the verandah overlooking the pretty little garden with its red and orange Flame of the Forest, the crimson and pink frangipani, the rattling of the Shack-Shack trees, the

178

blurred wings and iridescent flash of a hummingbird hovering beside an hibiscus. We listened to the pigeons calling mournfully in the tamarind tree and the green tree frogs whistling and beeping from beyond the mangos. I don't think breakfast had ever tasted so good. I was always starving after a night of making love, and that meal was like a Sunday sacrament, a jubilant affirmation of life and hope, the last for many months. We drank deep mugs of rich Jamaican coffee and the smell of it lay across the Sunday morning like a promise.

'Let's go to the races this afternoon,' she said.

'What races?'

'Horses, of course. What do you think? Donkeys?'

'There's a racetrack? Here?'

'Don't sound so surprised. It's called Ascot.'

'You're joking.'

'Not at all. It's down on the coast, near Goatshit Hill.'

'Seriously?'

'Don't be so snooty. We're not savages, you know. And we're still sort of British.'

'So they have proper meetings?

'Of course. Six a year and six races at each. Just like England.'

'What time's the first?'

'1.30.'

I looked at my watch. It was 12.30 already. 'We'd better get going then,' I said.

She laughed. 'There's no hurry. They never start on time. Nothing *ever* starts on time in Innocent. Quite often it's nearly four o'clock before the off, and sometimes the last race has to be run in the dark.'

We lounged under fat, white umbrellas by the pool for a couple of hours, me reading a book, she flipping through some magazines, and at 2.30 we shared a lunch of beer, bread, cheese and fruit before setting off in her little pink jeep. She drove north along the coast road until we reached a derelict petrol station surrounded by the corpses of wrecked cars and rusting trucks, and then turned off towards the sea, bumping, jolting and juddering down yet another track garnished with potholes, rocks, ruts and ridges. Before and behind us stretched a long line of noisy cars, jeeps, vans and painted buses, one called AH'M COMIN LORD, another DANCE LAK A BUTTERFLY, another FEELIN LUCKY, PUNK? They beeped and tooted at the crowds of pedestrians who ambled down the middle of the road, some carrying blaring radios, some shouting at each other, waving, singing, shrieking with laughter, banging their fists and hands on the roofs and bonnets of passing vehicles as the drivers picked their way slowly through the throng to a chorus of jeers and catcalls.

'Where you goin' so fast, darlin'?'

'Why you in a hurry, girl? De first race not started yet.'

'Dis ain't no race for vee-*hickles*, lady. Dis a race for *horses*.'

Eventually we reached the racecourse, a small, hot, dusty field with a ramshackle little wooden 'grandstand' right beside the glittering ocean. Seabirds wheeled and shrieked above the track and the thunder of waves pounding on the rocks below drifted across the course along with a pungent stench of horseshit from a small group of tin-roofed stables. The few shady parking spots under the palm trees had all been taken and Shermelle had to park the jeep in the pitiless sunshine. The field was unfenced and spectators wandered in and out of the grounds without any checks or controls, but I thought I ought to do the decent thing and bought two entrance tickets from a wrinkled, toothless old woman who was sitting at a rickety table between two sagging gateposts.

'Hi, Eunice,' said Shermelle.

''ello, darlin',' croaked the old woman, her face crumpling into an ancient smile. 'Dis you new man?'

'Yes. Isn't he lovely?'

She giggled. 'He sure have nice big feets.'

Between the gateposts hung a rotting gate with a lopsided, hand-painted sign that said ASCOT RACECOURSE: SILVER RING. Shermelle squeezed my arm. 'You bought a *ticket*,' she said fondly.

'Of course. Two.'

'Two? Nobody *ever* buys a ticket. That's sweet, so English, so *honest*! That's really nice.' Beyond the palms, a mile or more out to sea, in the direction of Barbados, a small, deserted lump of rock punctuated the ocean.

'What's that called?' I said.

'That's Cocobé Island.'

'Cocobé?'

'It must be French. It means leprosy. For a couple of hundred years lepers were banished there.'

'To die?'

'Probably, but they had a boat to go fishing, and now and then their friends and relatives would row over and leave food for them on the shore.'

We walked across a dry, stony 'paddock' that was filling up with crowds of people and bordered by stalls selling fast food: greasy hamburgers dripping with slices of slimy, plastic packaged cheese, hot dogs, breadfruit, salt fish and ackee, goat water, rice an' peas an' t'ings, mammees, ugli fruit, soursop ice-cream. Smoke and the smell of cooking meat and barbecue fluid wafted from a dozen stalls and the paddock was strewn with rubbish: cans, bottles, cartons, plastic bags, sweet wrappers, newspapers, cigarette packets. We headed towards the grandstand, a small, rickety wooden structure with a tin roof and six horizontal rows of planks staggered one above another to provide perhaps fifty spectators with an elevated view of the track. At the top several small, open cubicles were marked PRESS, OFFICIALS, VIPS, JOCKEY CLUB and PRIVATE BOXS. On the ground floor at the back of the stand a small, grubby, area was marked CHAMPAGNE BAR, a rough counter was marked BETTING, two lavatories were designated for STALLIONS and FILLIES, and a little staircase was labelled STRICLY RESTRICTED ENTRY: OFFICIALS AND PRIVATE BOXS ONLY. TRESPASSERS WILL BE PERSECUTED. In front of the grandstand a small area surrounded by a flimsy wooden fence boasted a tipsy sign that read ROYAL ENCLOSURE: BADGES MUST BE WORN.

I laughed.

'What?'

'Nothing.'

'You're laughing at us.'

'Never. It's just so… perfect.'

'Quaint, you mean.'

'Yes. Like a drink?'

'Mmm. Please. A Coke would be great.'

'Not a glass of champagne?'

She looked at me as if I were mad. '*Champagne*? Where on earth are you going to get champagne?'

'From the champagne bar. Where else?'

She giggled. 'They don't sell champagne!'

'It's called the Champagne Bar.'

'You dear, sweet, naïve man! This is *Innocent*. The gents' lav is called STALLIONS but you don't have to have four legs to use it.' She giggled. 'Or a two-foot-long willy.'

I struggled towards the bar and spotted Boozy Suzy, Father Brendan, Angela Fellowes and Alex McDowall wedged together in a corner, clutching glasses. The priest was wearing a garish Caribbean shirt and was obviously drunk already, on his Sunday communion wine, I suppose. Suzy kissed me on the cheek. 'So how's it going with Shermelle?' she said.

I frowned. 'What?'

'You and Shermelle.'

'What do you mean?'

'Jeez, Dave, come off it. Everyone knows you're shagging the

182

aarse off her. The whole bloody island knows.'

'I...'

'You caan't keep anything secret here. Scratch your balls and the whole island will know by nightfall.'

'Bastard!' said Angela Fellowes 'So *that's* why you've been ignoring my messages.'

'I'm sorry,' I said. 'I've been very busy.'

'Sure,' said Suzy, 'shagging the aarse off the prettiest girl on the island. Well, fair do's, mite. Good on yer. Aaren't you glad I introduced you? I knew from the staart you two'd get it on like a coupla koalas in a coolibah tree. I knew you had it in you.'

The priest guffawed. 'We knew you had it in *her*, too!' he chortled.

'Brendan,' she said.

'Yes, me oul' darlin'?'

'Shut it.'

'Roighty-ho.'

'Whatever you're doing,' she said to me, 'you're doing it right. I've never seen her looking so good.'

So everyone knew about Shermelle and me, did they? And I didn't care. I was proud of it.

'Catch up with you later,' I said.

'Bastard!' said Angela Fellowes.

I elbowed my way to the bar, eventually managed to buy a Coke and a Carib, and struggled back to join Shermelle. I spotted Smartly up in the Press box and waved. He glanced at Shermelle and gave me a thumbs-up and a lascivious wink. So everyone *did* know about us.

Most of the spectators were black but I recognised some expats in the throng – the Dempsters, the Rogerses – and a few tourists had turned up as well. The Russians approached and the woman looked Shermelle up and down with disdain. 'An' 'oo eez zeez black vooman?' she said. 'Eez prostitute?'

'I *beg* your pardon?' I said.

'Zeez black woman 'ere. Eez prostitute? You pay 'er for fockin'?'

'Certainly not!' I said angrily. 'This is Mrs Shermelle Donaldson. She's a respectable senior officer of the Royal Innocentian Customs and Excise Department, and you'll apologise to her right now.'

Litvinova looked her up and down again, slowly.

'Apologise!' I said.

'She look like prostitute,' she said, turning on her heel and walking away. Malenkov shrugged and followed her.

Shermelle was almost speechless. 'How dare she? How *dare* she?'

'She's Russian. They're not renowned for their manners.'

'I don't give a damn who she is, *no* one talks about me like that.'

'She's jealous of you: your youth, your beauty.'

'I don't give a toss what she is. What's the bitch's name?'

'Anna Litvinova.'

'I'll have her guts for garters.'

I'd never seen her angry. She looked even more beautiful.

I had a sudden inspiration. 'You could have their plane impounded.'

'Their plane?'

'Yes. They've bought a small plane. As a customs officer you could have it impounded for non-payment of import tax or something, or for contravening some flying regulation. Or maybe they haven't got the right licences or permissions.'

'That's a brilliant idea,' she said. 'What's *his* name? The husband?'

'They're not married. It's Malenkov: Nikita Malenkov.'

'I thought I recognised him. Yes. He brought the plane in a few weeks ago.' She kissed me. 'I'll get the bitch, I swear it. How *dare* she?'

The loudspeakers crackled into life. 'Testing testing testing,' said a male voice. 'One two three four five. Alpha beta gamma delta.'

The loudspeakers boomed, whined, developed a high-pitched hum, and settled for a hollow echo.

'Ladies and gentlemen,' they announced. 'The first race, the 1.30 Sunshine Resort Stakes, will begin in ten minutes.' I looked at my watch: 3.45. Not too bad: just two and a half hours late. 'So place your bets, ladies and gentlemen, and runners and riders are requested to make their way to the starting line.'

'Who's the announcer?' I said.

'Zekey Ponsonby. He's a disc jockey with Radio Innocent.'

'Ponsonby? Related to the Prime Minister?'

'Maybe. Who knows? Almost everyone here is related to everyone else.' She poked me in the ribs. 'That's why I like going to bed with you: at least I know I'm not screwing my uncle!'

'Charming,' I said. 'Now, where can I buy a programme? If we're going to bet we should look at the list of runners.'

'A *programme*? Don't be silly. This is *Innocent*. They just chalk the names of the horses up on a blackboard. Come.'

We battled over to the betting counter, where the names of three horses were chalked on a blackboard under the scrawled heading 1.30 SUNSHINE RESORT STAKES: 1 Bananaquit, 2 Carnival Queen, 3 Manchineel.

'Just three runners?' I said.

'Sometimes there are only two.'

'What about the odds?'

'Oh, you don't get odds. It's a tote. If your horse wins you share the pot with anyone else who's bet on it too, depending on how much each of you have bet.'

'OK,' I said, 'then let's go and have a look at the horses, see which one we fancy.'

We circled the grandstand and headed towards the starting line, where a tall, glum jockey was sitting astride an emaciated little horse with his legs almost touching the ground. He was wearing a multi-coloured Rasta tea cosy, a stained grey tee-shirt with the slogan WORLD CHAMPION, dirty jeans, and a grubby pair of trainers.

'Hi, Latto,' said Shermelle. 'How's things?'

'Not too bad, t'anks, Sherm.'

'Great. And Uniqueko?'

'She also fine.'

'And Cleffroy? And Latrine?'

'Dey good too.'

'Excellent. So what's your horse called?'

'She Carnival Queen.'

'Any good?'

'Te'bble. Like a nelephant wid de hemroids.'

'So which one d'you think'll win?'

'Number t'ree: Manchineel.'

'Unlucky name.'

'Mayhap, but she easy de best.'

'Thanks, Latto. Are you riding in any more races?'

'All o' dem.'

'All six?'

'Yeah.'

'Well, good luck.'

'T'anks, Sherm. I sure gonna need it. Dey all *te'bble*.'

We returned to the betting counter.

'*Latrine*?' I said.

She laughed. 'His daughter. She's two.'

'But *Latrine*?'

'I know. But *his* name's Latimer and his girlfriend's called Katrine, so…'

'Poor kid.'

She shrugged. 'There've been worse names. I know one kid

whose parents are Arlette and Solomon.'

I thought about it. I worked it out. 'No! Not...'

'Yes.'

'Arsol?'

'Yes.'

I laughed. 'That's *dreadful*.'

'Yes.'

'That's *terrible*.'

'Yes.'

'Don't the other kids take the mickey out of the poor little blighter?'

'No. He calls himself Aerosol.'

'Clever.' I laughed again. 'And why did you say that Manchineel's an unlucky name for a horse?'

'The manchineel's a very poisonous tree. Its fruit looks just like a small, green apple, but it burns you if you touch it, and it makes you very sick if you take even one bite out of it. If you chop it down it gives off poisonous fumes, and if you burn it the smoke damages your lungs. Even if you shelter under it when it's raining, the drops of water dripping off its leaves can burn your skin.'

'Nasty. Still, he did say it's the best horse.'

'I don't care. I'm not backing a horse called Manchineel.'

Absent-mindedly I held out towards her a $20 note.

She frowned. 'What's that for?'

'Your bets.'

She looked at me. 'I don't need your money, David. That's not what this is about.'

'I'm sorry. I thought...'

'I'm not your *wife*.'

Ouch. 'I just thought...'

'Well, don't. I can pay my own way. I'm not your kept woman.'

'Of course not. I'm sorry. I didn't mean to...'

She kissed the back of my hand. 'But thank you. It was really generous of you to think of it.'

She bet two of her own dollars on Bananaquit – 'maybe it'll fly,' she said – I put five on Manchineel, and we returned to the track to watch the race. Bananaquit, a pretty little filly with a tiny jockey wearing proper racing colours, had joined Carnival Queen at the starting line, but there was still no sign of Manchineel. The announcer broadcast an appeal for the jockey to bring his mount onto the track. After ten more minutes and two more increasingly desperate announcements the horse pranced alarmingly out of the stables, eyes rolling, and danced towards the start as its jockey cursed and struggled to control it.

'Ah, Manchineel, at last!' boomed the announcer jovially. The loudspeakers emitted a piercing whine that so startled the horse that it took off along the course like a bullet galloping towards the sea with its jockey clinging on precariously and eventually falling off on the far side of the track. The horse thundered riderless around the course three times, rolling its eyes and neighing at the grandstand, until eventually it slowed to a stop and ambled back towards its stable, where a couple of young lads approached it warily, grabbed the reins and led it out of sight.

'Ladies and gentlemen,' boomed the announcer, 'we can but apologise for this unfortunate development, but we hope to run the race in a few minutes with the two remaining runners, Bananaquit and Carnival Queen.'

It was 4.20 before the 1.30 race began at last, and Shermelle was right: by comparison with Carnival Queen, which appeared to have heavy weights on its hooves, Bananaquit flew like a bird and won by several lengths.

'Well done, darling,' I said. 'Let's go and collect your winnings.'

A crowd was jostling at the tote counter, surging forward, waving betting slips and shouting. It seemed that almost every punter had taken one look at poor old Carnival Queen and had bet instead on Bananaquit, so that almost everyone had won. Eventually, after a lot of pushing and shoving, we reached the counter and a harassed tote official took Shermelle's $2 betting slip, tapped some numbers into a calculator, and gave her $1.25 back as her winnings.

'One-twenty-five?' I said indignantly. 'That's even less than she bet.'

'Tax,' said the bookie, 'an' the tote percentage. Next!'

'That's outrageous!' I said. 'And I want my stake back, please. Here's the slip. I bet $5 on Manchineel and the horse didn't even run.'

'Dat you bad luck,' he said. 'No refun's. Next!'

'What d'you mean, no refunds?'

'Racecourse pulicy. No refun's.'

'But the horse didn't even start!'

'Dat you problem, maan. Act of God. No refun's.'

'Come on,' said Shermelle.

'This is daylight robbery!'

'No, this is Innocent. We do things differently here, so stop grumbling.'

We watched all six races and I lost another $20 backing Green Monkey, Beachcomber, Jahweh's Prophet and Full Moon. Well, racing isn't much fun unless you've got money on one of the horses. Quite frankly, they all look the same to me. I'd probably have lost another $5 had there been more than one runner in the fourth race, Sweet Papaya, which had a walkover. The fifth race actually managed to attract five runners, apparently a record for Ascot, but by then it was 6.45 and so dark that the horses were invisible in the distance as they galloped towards the sea and the far side of the track. By then the course had become incredibly noisy. Half a dozen unbelievably loud radios were tuned to different local stations, on one of which a furious preacher was threatening his listeners with Hell and damnation. Rap and reggae music pounded at full blast from a dozen boom boxes, a live steel pan band had started playing raucously near the entrance, and people were laughing uproariously and shouting so as to be heard above the din. More stoves and bonfires had been lit, clouds of smoke and smells drifted across the field, and the air was thick with a powerful whiff of marijuana and horseshit.

'Come on,' I said to Shermelle. 'Let's go.'

'OK,' she said, 'but first I need to go to the loo.'

'OK. Me too. I'll see you by the gate.'

I joined the STALLIONS queue and then went to wait for Shermelle by the gate. After a minute or so I spotted her near the bar talking heatedly to a tall, thin young black man as if they were having a row. I started towards them but he saw me coming, said something to her, turned and walked away.

She looked extremely angry.

'Who's that?' I said.

'No one.'

'Come on, darling. Who is he?'

'It doesn't matter.'

'But he's upset you.'

'He's nothing,' she snapped.

The ex-husband, maybe? No, he was in Trinidad. A previous boyfriend? A brother? No, they were both in prison.

I took her arm. 'OK,' I said. 'Let's go.'

She hesitated. 'I've been thinking. Let's stay on for a couple of hours. The fun's just starting.'

I battled with my better nature. It lost. 'To tell the truth, darling, I'm knackered. I don't think I'd be up to another couple of hours.'

'But it'll be fun. There's music, and food, and dancing. It'll be great fun.'

No it won't, I thought: it'll be horribly noisy, smelly, and everyone will get drunk or high on drugs, probably both. What I wanted was to go home, have a swim, a shower, a long, cold drink, and watch an old movie on cable TV. But I didn't say so: I didn't want to remind her that I was a tired, dreary old fart twenty years older than her.

'So you'd like to stay on?' I said reluctantly.

'Well, yes, if you don't mind.'

'Of course I don't mind,' I lied, 'but I need a swim and a shower, so I'll go home and see you later.'

She seemed relieved. 'OK. You take the jeep. I'll get a lift home later, and I'll call you tomorrow.'

I was disconcerted. 'Tomorrow? You won't come back tonight?'

Did she look a bit shifty? She did. 'No, David, I'll see you tomorrow. I could be late, and I have an early start in the morning.'

I was suddenly overwhelmed by a surge of suspicion and jealousy. Why did she want to stay? Five minutes ago she'd been quite happy to leave, so why had she changed her mind? Was she going to meet someone else? The young black man she'd been arguing with? Some other boyfriend? Jealousy is a terrible curse: it can kill a love affair as quickly as infidelity.

On the far side of the crowd I spotted Suzy and Brendan Mulchrone heading towards her jeep. 'I know,' I said to Shermelle. 'You keep the jeep. Suzy and His Holiness are just leaving: I'll get a lift with then.'

'You sure?' she said. 'OK.'

Once again I thought she seemed relieved. She wanted to get rid of me. I was sure of it.

I kissed her on the cheek, burning with unhappiness. 'See you,' I said.

'See you.'

I hated to leave her there alone. She looked so small, so vulnerable.

'I love you,' I said.

'I know,' she said, but she said it sadly.

I caught up with Suzy and the priest and cadged a lift back to Hummingbird House. Mulchrone stank of whisky, staggered when we reached the jeep, and tumbled into the back seat. 'Where's that sexy little darkie of yours?' he slurred. 'Fockin' noice tits. Noice erse. Lov'ly.'

By the time Suzy dropped me off at Hummingbird House he was slumped in the back seat and snoring. I asked her in for a drink. 'Better not,' she said. 'I should get the old bugger home.'

'Why do you put up with him?'

She shrugged. 'Christ knows.'

'I doubt whether Christ and he are acquainted.'

'Well, he needs me, and who else would have me?'

'Lots of men.'

She smiled wearily. 'You're sweet,' she said, 'and a fucking bad liar.'

I shut the door of the jeep.

'So long,' she said.

'Tell me something,' I said. 'That guy Shermelle was talking to by the bar. D'you know who he is?'

'Which guy?'

'Tall black guy. Young. They were having an argument.'

'Never saw him. Why?'

'I just wondered. She wouldn't tell me who he is, and now she's decided to stay on at the racecourse.'

She looked at me in silence for a moment. 'Don't lose her,' she said gently, 'not now that you've found her. Don't ask too many questions. Don't drive her away.' She put the jeep into gear. 'G'night, mite,' she said, and drove away.

I watched her tail lights flicker and disappear as she drove through the gates and into the blackness beyond. There was no moon that night, and nothing is darker than a moonless night in the tropics. You can almost taste the darkness. The house was blind behind me. I turned, stumbled onto the verandah, fumbled with the key, struggled to find the lock, opened the door, swore to oil the squeaking hinges, and reached for the light switch. The house was silent, yet something audible seemed to lie within the silence. A faint smell of cigarette smoke lingered on the air, and I knew immediately that someone had been in here while we'd been out, that someone might still be here. I grabbed a big umbrella from the stand beside the front door. It was furnished with a strong, sharp tip: not as good as a club or walking stick, maybe, but better than nothing.

'Hello?' I said. 'Hello? Who is it? Who's here?'

My ears were alert for the slightest sound. The lightbulb fizzed quietly above my head. The fridge hummed in the kitchen. A fly buzzed repeatedly against a window pane. A mosquito whined past my ear.

'Anyone here?' I said, gripping the umbrella.

Sweat was pouring off me, my face was awash with it, a river dribbling down my spine, my shirt stuck to my back. A floorboard creaked in the bedroom. The tin roof gave a sudden crack, as loud as a gunshot, making me jump, as it cooled after the heat of the day. And then the telephone rang, shrilly, slicing through the silence. I jumped again. I let it ring four times before lifting it.

'Hello?' I said.

I could hear someone breathing, then a click, then the dialling tone.

'Hello?' I said, but there was nobody there.

# CHAPTER 12

## SERGEANT POMEROY AND THE MISSING LAPTOP

I locked and bolted the front door, dumped the umbrella back in its stand, armed myself with a kitchen knife and a hammer that I found on a shelf in the utility room, and moved warily through the house as if I were a burglar myself, checking each room, opening cupboards, peering behind furniture and under beds, locking each door and window behind me as I went. There was no obvious sign of any intruder yet something alien seemed to hang in the air, some odourless smell, some silent sound, some absent presence that had not been there before. In my bedroom I checked the bedside table: a pair of Shermelle's silver earrings lay on it and my gold cufflinks were still in the top drawer, so the intruder was obviously not just a simple thief. I lifted the earrings, held them in my palm, and felt a pang of loneliness. Silly: she'd only be gone one night; tomorrow she'd be back.

I'd been using one of the spare bedrooms as an office and I opened all the drawers to check if anything was missing. My wallet still in the top drawer with a wad of pound notes as well as dollars, my credit cards and cheque book all intact. Yet for some reason I felt almost certain that something had been moved. Something wasn't quite right, something seemed to be out of place. The paper knife? The mug full of pens? The telephone? A branch tapped against the window. I jumped. My skin crawled. Was there somone out there in the night, looking in at me through the lighted window? I crossed to the window, bolted it, and stared out into the darkness. No one. Not a sign. But the night was as black as I'd ever known it, and even the stars had abandoned me, smothered by passing cloud.

*This is ridiculous*, I thought. *You're imagining things. There's no one here, and nothing missing.* And then it hit me: I realised that my laptop was no longer where I'd left it, beside the telephone.

Oh, *shit*! All my phone numbers gone, all my email addresses, future appointments, all the research I'd done and the notes I'd made about Rogers, Williams, Fellowes, and the others – all gone. Any one of them might have stolen it. Or perhaps Chezroy Billington. Who else? Whose suspicions had I aroused? Whom had I offended? There could be a dozen people, for all I knew.

I was still sweating profusely but I didn't fancy the idea of a swim in the dark, not now that I knew that someone had been in the house and might still be lurking outside, so I closed and bolted all the shutters, drew the curtains, switched on all the outside security lights, took a shower, and emerged invigorated. I sprayed my arms and legs with mosquito repellent, poured myself a stiff vodka and tonic with a slice of lemon and several hefty chunks of ice, and sat in the armchair in the living room trying to concentrate on the latest issue of the *Innocent Gazette*. A small fishing boat had been lost at sea. A man from Jericho had been charged with committing underage incest with all three of his teenage daughters. A youth from Columbus had been wounded in a knife fight with another boy, possibly over drugs. The Minister of Agriculture, Forests, Fishing and Crafts had claimed that the cotton crop would be the best for years. The Chief Medical Officer had reported an alarming increase in the number of AIDS cases. An unidentified light aircraft had been seen landing mysteriously a week ago on the Ascot racetrack in the middle of the night. Windy Billington had delivered a speech to the Hopetown Women's Institute on the subject of morality and honesty. That would have been interesting, I thought cynically: Billington on morality. But I couldn't concentrate. Who could the intruder have been? Why would a burglar leave the money, credit cards, earrings and cufflinks?

I poured a second large vodka and decided to call the police. If I waited until the morning to report the theft the trail might well have gone cold. Perhaps there were footprints around the house that might be washed away overnight. Perhaps there were fingerprints, DNA, other clues. The police would surely know all the local villains and which of them was most likely to commit this sort of crime.

I found the number for the central police station in Columbus. The telephone rang ten or twelve times before a bored male voice said: 'Yo.'

'Police?'

'Right.'

'Good evening.'

'Good night.'

I never got used to them saying 'good night' instead of 'good evening.'

'I need to report a break-in.'

'You been burglarized?'

'Yes.'

'You who?'

'My name's David Barron. You don't know me, but…'

'Sure: you de English guy what's boffin' Shermelle.'

Bloody hell! Did everyone here know *everything*?

'I don't know what you mean,' I burbled.

'You de guy stayin' up by Hummin'bard House?'

'Yes,'

'OK, you de one been boffin' Shermelle. You one lucky guy.'

'I've been burgled,' I said firmly.

'OK. Den you needs to call de Nelson's Rest precinct.'

'Right. Do you have their number, please?'

'Nah.'

'Where would I find it?'

'Try de phone book.'

His casual idleness annoyed me. He probably had the number pinned up above his phone but he couldn't be bothered to look at it. 'Oh, of *course*. *Silly* me! Will do. Good night.'

'Not good *night*: good*bye*. Good night is when we talkin' first. When we done talkin', dis is good*bye*.'

'Right.'

'OK, maan. An' *hey*! Good boffin', OK?'

It took me ages to find the number for the local cop-shop in the telephone directory. There was nothing under Police, Constabulary, Nelson's Rest, Law Enforcement, Justice, Ministry of Justice, Ministry of the Interior or Interior Ministry. After trawling through almost every page in the book I found it eventually under R: *Royal Innocent Police, N.R. Precinct.*

I dialled the number. This time it rang at least twenty times before a female voice said: 'Yus?'

'Nelson's Rest police?'

'We closed.'

'I beg your pardon?'

She yawned. 'We closed. 6pm to 8am.'

'But I've just been burgled.'

'You mus' call in de marnin'.'

'I'm sorry?'

'You mus' call in de marnin'. No one here. All de p'leece gone 'ome.'

'*You're* there.'

'I de cleanin' woman.'

'I don't believe it!'

'Is true. You mus' call de precinc' termorrer.'

'But I need someone to come and take a statement, check for

197

clues. There may be footprints, fingerprints.'

'Dey not do no fingerprint. Dey not got de 'quipment.'

'You're joking.'

'Not me, sir. You call de precinc' termorrer.' And she put the phone down.

I was angry. Suddenly the lazy, laidback, smiling charm of Innocent seemed decidedly less charming. How could a police station be closed all night? What if someone was murdered or raped?

And then the bloody lights went out. Another power cut. I felt my way into the kitchen, groped for the torch that I knew was on a shelf beside the cooker, found some candles and matches, and lit a couple of candles. As soon as I'd done so the lights came back on again.

Irritably I blew the candles out and called the Columbus police station again.

'Yo.'

'I'm sorry to bother you again,' I said in my best British self-effacing manner.

'You de guy wit' Shermelle, right?'

'Look here. I've told you…'

'OK. Sure.'

'Look, I'm calling you again because the Nelson's Rest precinct is closed.'

'Dat right. Frum 6pm to 8am.'

'So why did you tell me to call them.'

'Not tonight. In de marnin'.'

'But there may be footprints, fingerprints. They might get washed away by the rain.'

'It rainin' up by you?'

'Not at the moment, no, but…'

'Den we got no problem. You call de precinc' in de marnin'.'

'Look here, officer…'

'Sergeant.'

'Sergeant.'

'Sergeant Pumeroy.'

'OK. I don't want to make trouble, Sergeant Pomeroy, but I really do think an officer ought to come here tonight to examine the crime scene. I don't want to be difficult, but I'm sure the Prime Minister would not be pleased to know that one of his senior policemen...'

'I not senior. I just a sergeant.'

'... one of his policemen couldn't be bothered to visit a crime scene and take a statement from the victim.'

'You know de Prime Minister?'

'Yes,' I lied.

'You friends?'

'Very close.'

Sergeant Pomeroy gave a deep sigh. 'OK, maan,' he said. 'I comin' soon as pussible.'

'Thank you. I'll expect you. Good night.'

While I waited for him I assembled an easy, quick meal – sardines on toast with lemon juice and black pepper, a fruit salad of pawpaw, mango, banana and grapefruit, a glass of Chilean Merlot. As I ate it alone at the kitchen table I realised how much I was missing Shermelle. Just as the intruder's unseen presence had been almost palpable, so was her absence equally physical. There was an empty space where she had been, a vacuum that was sucking my new happiness and optimism into it. In just a few days she'd already become the centre of my life. Why had she been so keen to stay at the racetrack? Where was she now? Who was she with? What was she doing? I was tormented by suspicion. Who was the tall, young, black guy with whom she'd been arguing with such passion? Her ex-husband? An old lover? God help me, maybe even a *new* lover? I couldn't help it: another spasm of jealousy surged through me.

It was three hours before Sergeant Pomeroy arrived, by which time I had almost given up on him and was about to go to bed. He arrived in a small, battered old jeep and tooted the horn.

'Inside!' he called.

I peered at him through the shutters. He was a skinny little man, probably in his thirties, standing in a pool of light just beyond the verandah and wearing a red baseball cap turned back to front, a grubby string vest, torn blue jeans and dirty grey trainers.

'Inside!'

I opened the shutter cautiously. 'Yes?' I said. 'Who are you?'

'P'leece,' he said. 'Sergeant Pumeroy.'

I looked him up and down. 'You don't look like a policeman. Why aren't you wearing uniform?'

'I'se in plain clothes.'

'You could be a burglar.'

'Not me.'

'Let me see your police ID card, then.'

'I not got one.'

'So how can I be sure that you're a policeman? You look like a tramp. Or a burglar.'

He grinned broadly. 'T'ank you, sah. Dat's me ingenious disguise.'

'Why should I believe you?'

He shrugged. 'Everybody knows I'se de p'leece. Everybody on de island.'

'In that case,' I said with devastating logic, 'what's the point of wearing a disguise?'

'Eh?'

'If everyone knows you're a policeman, why bother to wear plain clothes?'

He looked blank. 'Ah never t'ought o' dat.'

I unlocked and unbolted the door. No burglar would have known that I was expecting a policeman this late at night, let alone that he would be Sergeant Pomeroy. 'OK,' I said. 'I'll have to take a chance. Come in.'

He did, wiping the soles of his trainers carefully on the mat by the front door. 'Nice place you got,' he said.

'I'm only renting it for a while.'

'Sure, I know dat. It belong to ol' Freedom Bunter, from Cotton Beach way. You on holiday?'

'No, I'm writing an article about the island.'

'Dat good. We need de publicity. You got a beer?'

'Yes.'

'I got a big t'irst.'

'I thought policemen don't drink on duty.'

He grinned. 'We does in Innocent.'

I fetched him a bottle of Carib from the fridge and poured myself another glass of red. He took a generous gulp and belched loudly. 'Dat de proper stuff,' he said. 'From Trinidad.'

'The crime scene,' I said.

'OK.'

I led him through to the spare bedroom and showed him where the laptop had been on the desk.

I showed him what the thief had left: the money, credit cards, cufflinks, Shermelle's earrings. He picked the earrings up.

'I don't think you ought to touch anything, should you?' I said. 'Not before your fingerprint guys get here and dust everything.'

'We don' do fingerprints. We not got de 'quipment.'

'DNA?'

'What dat?'

'Never mind.'

He stroked the earrings. 'Dese jus' like Shermelle's,' he said.

I said nothing.

'Dey be jus' like hers.'

Jealousy flared again: how the hell did he know what her earrings were like?

We took the torch and went out into the garden, which was brightly lit by the outside security lights. He looked around without enthusiasm, peering under window ledges, poking in flowerbeds, and generally pretending to search for clues. We found nothing and after about fifteen minutes he said that there was nothing he could do in the dark.

'Shouldn't I give you a statement?' I said.

'Not me,' he said. 'You go do dat at Nelson's Rest precinc' in de marnin'. It be dere jury's diction.'

'I see.'

'Dey will take all de details.'

'Do you think they'll know who did it?'

'Mayhap an' mayhap not.'

'But they must know all the regular criminals in the area.'

'Dat true, but dey don' catch many.'

'Why's that?'

'Dey jus' country boys, dese cops here. Dey not as smart as we proper cops in de big city, an' dey not as smart as de big city crooks.'

'Oh, that's great,' I said. 'So there's no point at all in my going to the local police station tomorrow.'

'You gotta do dat. It illegal not to report a burglarizing.'

'Well, thanks for coming out,' I said. 'Good night.'

He looked at his watch: just after midnight. 'Not so,' he said. 'It not good *night*: it be good *marnin'* now.'

And then the lights went out again.

'Fuck!' I said.

'Dat word against de law,' said Sergeant Pomeroy.

'Fuck the law!'

He shrugged 'OK,' he said.


I fell into a deep sleep and dreamed that Shermelle and Sergeant

Pomeroy were cavorting together across the huge, cold flagstones of a vast hall in an old Scottish castle where the walls consisted of hundreds of whirring tape recorders. They were dressed in frilly shirts, tartan kilts and ferociously dancing the Gay Gordons. He threw her into the air and tried to catch her as she fell, but she crashed to the ground.

I was jolted awake by the shrill screech of the telephone. Heart pounding, I glanced blearily at the green glow of the bedside clock: 3.07. Bloody hell, I thought, who phones at three in the morning? I lifted the receiver. 'Hello?' I croaked.

'You still in bed, you lazy bugger?' It was Milligan in London.

'Of course I'm still in bed!' I snarled. 'It's three in the morning.'

'Ah. Really? Yes. Well, sorry about that. I forgot the time difference.'

'How in the name of buggery can you forget the time difference? I'm nearly five thousand sodding miles away and you think it's the same time as London?'

'Sorry.'

'Jesus!'

'Sorry, David. Still, now that you're awake I might as well tell you what it's about.'

'I'm not awake, you bastard.'

'It's Hare. He wants to know how far you've got with the investigations and why you haven't reported back yet even though you've been away for two weeks.'

'I'll email him in the morning.'

'I'm afraid he wants an answer right away.'

'At three in the bloody morning?'

'Well, you know what he's like. He reckons you're loafing around all day lying on a beach drinking rum punches and knocking off some tasty black floozie all night.'

'Cunt!' I said.

'Precisely.'

'Ho bloody ho.'

'So what do I tell him?'

'Tell the fat bastard that I've established contact with all three of the main suspects and my enquiries are progressing.'

'Hmm. Not enough. I don't think that's going to keep him quiet.'

'Too bloody bad. Now I'm going back to sleep. Goodbye.'

'Well… OK. Good night.'

'No it's not,' I said grimly. 'It's good morning.'

I crashed the receiver back into its cradle.

After that I lay awake for most of the night, dozing fitfully, dreaming in spasms: Shermelle and Brendan Mulchrone running around the racetrack, both naked except that she was wearing Pomeroy's baseball cap; Anna Litvinova sticking her razor-sharp tongue down my throat so hard that it spurted blood; Pomeroy in a pink, frilly miniskirt and Shermelle's earrings; Angela Fellowes with Gascoigne perched on her shoulder like a parrot. When I wasn't dreaming I was worrying what the hell to tell Hare in the morning. The truth was that I'd made no real progress at all apart from merely meeting Rogers, Williams and Fellowes, all of whom claimed to be resident in Innocent and never to return to the UK for more than ninety days a year. If they were telling the truth then none of them had committed any offence, and Hare was right to think that I really should have discovered much more after two weeks. But how was I to prove that they were lying? That could be done only in England by running their names through the immigration computer records to see exactly when they had entered and left the country over the past year or two and totting up the totals. But I was hardly going to suggest that, not when I'd just discovered Shermelle, because Hare would have ordered me to return immediately to London and stop wasting any more of the taxpayers' money. Sod the taxpayers: I wanted to stay here for much longer. I'd have to invent a pile of excuses and a list of new suspects.

I rose as soon as the sun came up like a rocket at 6.15, as huge as a giant balloon and as red as a furnace, and I dived into the pool to swim twenty lengths and wash away my sleeplessness. The air was wonderfully clean and fresh, the water cool against my skin and scalp. How could I abandon this paradise to return to cold, grey, damp, wintry London? And how could I leave Shermelle? That would be impossible.

Miz Quaintance arrived as I was having breakfast on the verandah, wobbling massively top-heavy on her ramshackle little bicycle. She was wearing what appeared to be a large tent made out of red, blue and green curtain material, a straw hat decorated with long pink ribbons, and a pair of rugby boots.

'Inside!' she bellowed.

'Good morning,' I called.

'Marnin', marnin',' she roared, approaching the verandah. 'You good, Lard David? You sleep good?'

'Not really. We had a break-in last night. Well, yesterday afternoon when I was out at the races.'

She looked shocked. 'A robbery? Here?'

'I'm afraid so. There's no sign of a break-in but they took my laptop: you know, the little computer that I keep on the table in the spare bedroom.'

She was furious. 'De swine! I find it, You' Lardship, no problem. I get it back for you. I know all de bad boys on de islan'. I find it quick.'

'Well, that's very kind but I've already called the police.'

'De p'leece?' she said with contempt. 'Dey no damn good! Dey useless!'

'Sergeant Pomeroy came out here to investigate last night.'

She snorted. 'Pomeroy? 'e de most useless of all!'

'He told me I should go to the Nelson's Rest police station

today, put in a report, make a statement.'

'Don' waste you' time, milard. De p'leece round here is all relatives to all de thieves. Dey all be brudders an' sisters an' kissin' cousins. De juries, also: all relatives.'

'Oh, great.'

'I much better dan de p'leece. You give me de description of de computer an' me find it for you for sure.'

'Pomeroy said it's illegal not to report a crime.'

'Pooh! Pomeroy! 'e know *nuttin'*. You leave it to me, You Lardship. Ah fix 'em.'

After breakfast I retreated to the pool deck while she terrorised the furniture and assaulted the house with a malignant hoover, a feather duster, a sickening sweet spray that smelled like a Bulgarian whore's boudoir, and a powerful disinfectant that stank like a paint-stripper factory. I concocted an email for Hare in which I assured him that I'd made some serious progress in my investigations and had established beyond doubt that Rogers, Williams and Fellowes were all undoubtedly deeply involved in all manner of nefarious financial shenanigans but that my enquiries were taking much longer than expected because I was hampered constantly by thieves, the local police, mafia, security guards, tropical infections, ferocious thunderstorms, forty-eight-hour power cuts, heatstroke, a computer crash, and deliberate obstruction on all sides, not least from the decidedly sinister Deputy Prime Minister. Even so, I lied, I firmly expected to make two serious breakthroughs in the next few days, and I added: 'I was most amused by your suggestion that I have probably been lying on the beach all day and cavorting all night with the local beauties, every one of whom would make a fifty-ton hippopotamus look glamorous.'

Except Shermelle. I telephoned the airport, asked to speak to her, and was told that she was not working there that day. Strange: she'd said she would be. I called the harbour and was told she wasn't there, either. I called the ferry jetty with the same result. I was baffled. Why wasn't she at work? She'd told me quite specifically that she was working on the early shift. I tried her mobile phone. It was switched off. That really was odd: she never turned her mobile off. I left a message for her to call me back and started worrying. Had she overslept? Had an accident? Been rushed to hospital? I rang the hospital. No, she wasn't there. Well, that was a relief, anyway. And then suspicion slithered back like a worm into my mind. I pushed it away but it slithered back. I stamped on it but it grew a second head. I drowned it but it floated to the surface again. Perhaps she was with another man. *Don't go there. Don't even think about it. She wouldn't do that to me. Never. Not my Shermelle.*

I tried to think about anything else at all. She was probably on some special mission. That's it: perhaps she was in some government office where she had to turn her mobile off, making enquiries about the Russians' plane and going through their immigration, customs and air licence records. That's it. Of course she was. And I'd suggested it myself. She'd be back tonight. Of course she would.

I didn't bother to report the theft to the local police. What was the point if they were all related to the criminals? And Miz Quaintance was right: she probably did know all the local villains and was quite frightening enough to terrify the culprit into returning the laptop before the day was out. The best thing I could do was to get back to work and wait for Shermelle to call. She would eventually. Of course she would.

So: how to nail Rogers, Williams and Fellowes? Williams struck me as being pretty harmless: a conman, yes, and a religious nutter, but probably not a tax dodger unless we could prove that he did spend more than ninety days a year in Britain. Don Rogers was a different matter, a nasty piece of work who must surely have plenty of enemies. Maybe the best way to nail him would be to bribe someone close to him, someone who was privy to his financial and business operations. Her Majesty's Revenue and Customs would never admit to encouraging bribery, but in exceptional cases it has been known to look the other way so long as the bribe cost less than the tax recovered. But whom could I bribe? The shifty young 'redskin' manager of the Bank of Innocence, who had initially promised to introduce me to him, seemed a likely candidate. He'd struck me as being eminently corruptible and untrustworthy. Or what about Rogers's wife? On the face of it she had too much to lose: she probably owed him everything and depended on him completely; but if he were banged up in Wandsworth Prison for five or six years she'd have grounds for a very lucrative divorce. The English courts nowadays are as disgracefully biased towards divorcing wives as they are in California, even if the bloody woman has been married for no more than three or four years. Or might Tracey Rogers be vulnerable to blackmail herself? Her Majesty's Revenue and Customs does not normally encourage blackmail, either, but HMRC doesn't always ask inconvenient questions. So how could she best be blackmailed? Adultery? Whispers that she had a black lover or a taste for little boys?

As for Angela Fellowes, I was wary of her friendship with Windy Billington and the protection he could obviously give her, and in her case blackmail would be a waste of time because she was unmarried, childless, confident, unconventional, owed nothing to anyone, and didn't give a damn what people thought of her. I could threaten to expose her as a lesbian sado-masochist with a perverted affection for goats and she'd laugh in my face and tell me to get stuffed. The only way I could get at her files would be to sleep with her, which was too horrible to contemplate, or to bribe someone. Gascoigne, maybe, her butler? No, he seemed to be devoted to her. The security guard on the gate? Or one of the young maids who'd been serving at her dinner party? Perhaps she treated them badly. That was worth some more investigation.

I drove into town and began to make some discreet enquiries about them all: Rogers's wife, Gascoigne, the maids. Smartly told me that Angela Fellowes was notorious for arrogance, intolerance and bullying her staff. Gascoigne was commendably loyal to her but the maids hated her, and one of them was living with one of Smartly's friends' wives' brothers, and might be bribeable. He promised to find out more.

'May I ask why you want to know?' he said.

'No.'

'Fair enough.'

That's one of the many things that I liked about Smartly: for a journalist he was remarkably incurious.

I found Suzy as usual at her bar on Mosquito Beach. She was sitting alone and forlorn on one of the stools and there was no sign of the barman. She looked tired. I kissed her on the cheek.

'That was fun yesterday,' I said. 'The races.'

'Yeah, wasn't it?' she said without enthusiasm.

'You OK?'

'A bit crook.'

'Hangover?'

'Nah: personal stuff.'

'Can I help?'

She shook her head. 'But thanks for aasking. Fancy a beer?'

'Why not?'

Actually I could think of several reasons why not, including the fact that it was only 10.30am, but she seemed to be so low that saying 'yes' was a kindness. Perhaps she'd had a fight with Mulchrone. That wouldn't be difficult. Or perhaps she wanted company. Perhaps she needed to talk. Perhaps it was just the wrong time of the month. But whatever it was, she needed to be taken out of herself and to think of someone else's problems rather than her own. She opened a couple of beers and I asked her about

Don Rogers's wife.

'He's a baastard to her,' she said. 'Keeps her short of money, even though he's rolling in it, and treats her even in public like she's a moron. You saw him the other night, at Angela's dinner paarty. I know she *is* a moron, but that's not the point.'

'Any gossip about her? Has she got a secret boyfriend?'

'What's this all about, Dave?'

I hesitated for a few seconds and then told her everything. I don't know why, but I trusted her. There was something honest and dependable about her forthright Aussieness. I swore her to secrecy, and then told her who I really was and why I was in Innocent, and why I needed to nail Don Rogers. I didn't mention Angela Fellowes because Suzy and Angela were friends, but I did mention Rupert Williams and the French painter and hooker. I don't know why I told her. Well, yes, I do, actually: I was getting nowhere with my investigation and I needed to come up with some decent results pretty soon or Hare would call me back to London, and I wanted someone else to know what was going on, just in case anything happened to me. The burglary had shaken me more than I cared to admit because it was obvious that the intruder had not been an ordinary burglar. An ordinary burglar would at least have taken the money. Someone else was behind this, someone who was after my notes, records and contacts.

'Jeez, Dave,' she said. 'You craafty old baastard!'

'I thought you might have suspected.'

'Never. Why would I?'

'I don't think I'm the most convincing journalist, am I?'

'Actually you're perfect: a complete aarsehole.'

'Thanks.'

So I told her about the break-in and why I suspected that there was more to it than at first there'd seemed to be.

'So who do you suspect?' she said.

'Billington?'

She nodded. 'I wouldn't be at all surprised. He's a sinister old baastard. Never could understand why Angela gets on with him so well.'

I told her about Shermelle as well. Christ knows why I did. I wish now that I hadn't, but you know what it's like when you really love a woman but suddenly you suspect her of being unfaithful. Suddenly the ground no longer seems to be firm under your feet, and you need to tell *someone* about it, and the only someone here that I trusted, apart from Shermelle, was Suzy. Why wasn't Shermelle at work when she'd said she would be? Why had she turned her mobile off? Who was the young black guy she'd been fighting with at the races? God help me, I even resurrected my very first unworthy suspicion, when she suggested that we should spend that first Sunday together and I wondered why a pretty young girl like her would want to spend the day with an ugly old fart like me, and I wondered whether she had some ulterior motive. God help me, I couldn't stop wondering now whether she'd been playing a part all the time and had faked all those wonderful nights of passion, because why *should* she have been so excited by someone like me?

And then it hit me like a blow to the back of the head: maybe it was *she* who had taken my laptop, to pass on to somebody else, perhaps, maybe even before we'd left the house to go to the races. No wonder there was no sign of a break-in. Maybe a break-in hadn't been necessary. And I hated myself for even thinking these things.

'You've got to snap out of this, Dave,' said Suzy. 'She adores you. Truly. I promise. She's told me so more than once.'

'But why me? I'm twenty years older and I've never considered myself God's gift to women.'

'Maybe that's why. So many blokes think they're the dog's bollocks, which is always a huge turn-off. You don't.' She hesitated and looked down at the sand. 'You don't seem to realise how attractive you aare.'

She blushed. Bloody hell! Now there were *four* women here who fancied me. What was it about the women on this island? Before I knew it Miz Quaintance would be trampling naked all over me in her rugby boots.

'Shermelle's gorgeous,' said Suzy. 'She could have any man she wants but she's chosen you. Don't knock it, Dave. You ought to be bloody grateful. But don't crowd her. Don't harass her with questions. Don't get suspicious or you'll lose her. Whatever she's doing, she has her reasons and you'll just have to wait and let her explain. Jeez, this agony aunt stuff is bloody thirsty work. Let's have another drop of the amber liquid.'

# CHAPTER 13

## A DEMENTED CHICKEN AND ABERDEEN

I returned to Hummingbird House and waited all afternoon for Shermelle to call but the phone never rang. As the sun went down I sat on the verandah, pretending to read the paper but watching the gate, straining to hear her jeep in the distance, but the only sound was the chatter of gossiping insects. As darkness fell I called her mobile again but it was still turned off. She *never* turned it off. I rang the airport to see if she was working the evening shift but she wasn't there. Nor was she at the harbour, nor the jetty. I rang the hospital. I rang all four police stations on the island. I rang a couple of bars and a restaurant where we'd been together. Nothing. I swore at myself because I'd never asked her where she lived or whether she had a landline phone there. I'd never needed to know: she'd always come to me.

I poured myself a stiff drink and made myself some supper, but at nine o'clock there was another power cut and I couldn't bear the thought of sitting alone in the dark with a couple of candles. I jumped into the jeep, drove into town, and cruised slowly along every street in the hope of spotting her or someone who knew her. I poked my head into a couple of bars and the only nightclub in town, the Crimson Cockatoo, which was empty except for a couple of bored Spanish whores. I walked along the jetty, around the harbour, and glanced into the customs booths at both, but there was no sign of her. I drove out to the airport, spotted a customs officer in the deserted arrivals hall, and asked him if he'd seen her.

'She gun home,' he said.

'So she was working here today?'

'Sure.'

'Thanks.'

'No prublem.'

'Do you know where she lives?'

'I t'ink somewhere up by Aberdeen way.'

'Where's that?'

'By Inverness Rock.'

'Right. Thanks.'

'No prublem.'

So she'd been avoiding me deliberately, and she'd told her colleagues to lie if I called and asked for her. In God's name, why? On Saturday night we'd been as wonderful together as ever, we'd stayed in bed for most of Sunday morning, we'd had fun together all afternoon at the races, and I'd kissed her when I left. So what had changed? Why was she hiding from me? Why had she turned her mobile off all day? It had to have something to do with the row she'd had with the tall black guy at the races. It had to be that.

I took the car-hire map out of the glove compartment. Why's it called a *glove* compartment, anyway, for God's sake? Who wears gloves these days, let alone keeps them stuffed in a cubby hole in front of the passenger seat? I switched the interior light on and searched the map for Aberdeen and Inverness Rock but neither was marked anywhere: they were obviously tiny, insignificant settlements. I went back into the airport terminal to ask for directions but the customs officer had disappeared and a couple of cleaners were closing up and locking the building. The last flights had gone and no more were expected tonight. The flickering arrival and departure screens announced that the time was 0916 and the date was 1 January 1901.

I drove back to Hummingbird House in a fog of bewilderment.

Why was she avoiding me? If she'd had a row with her ex-husband or boyfriend, surely she'd want a sympathetic ear and a loving shoulder to lean on. But she'd told her colleagues to lie to me. I couldn't believe it. Why? What had I done wrong?

I poured myself another stiff drink and watched the 11 o'clock TV news on BBC World. It was 3am in London so the newsreader was a nervous, inexperienced young woman who looked as if she were on the verge of tears and kept fluffing her lines. Not that it mattered much: BBC World is the dreariest TV channel on the planet and its news bulletins are unrelentingly dull and gloomy: there's never anything cheerful or optimistic, let alone a smile or a joke. The 'BBC' in BBC World might just as well stand for Bloody Boring Crap. I zapped the TV off, switched the iPod on and played some random, shuffled songs: Elton John, Nina Simone, Rod Stewart, Emmylou Harris, Tracey Chapman, Dire Straits. The booze and the music dulled my bewilderment enough to make me angry. How dare she treat me like this? How dare she simply cut me off without any explanation? Who did she think she was?

Just before midnight I tried her mobile again but it was still switched off. This time I left a message. 'What's going on?' I said. 'Why are you avoiding me? Please call me. I miss you. I love you.'

And then we had another bloody power cut.

I fell asleep surprisingly quickly and dreamed that Shermelle, Barbara, Hare and Sergeant Pomeroy were playing a slow-motion game of tennis and I was the ball. At the end of the dream Shermelle smashed me through a big picture window and in the dream I screamed. I woke with alarm, startled by what I thought was someone screaming. I looked at the clock: just after 1am. As I came awake I realised that the noise I'd thought was screaming was in fact a chicken squawking outside. Bright moonlight was streaming silver through the bedroom window. I looked out into the garden but saw nothing. The sound of the demented chicken was coming from around the corner of the house, outside the window of the spare bedroom that I used as an office, and now I could hear the murmur of human voices as well. Dear God: what now? Burglars again? I crept naked into the spare bedroom, peered through the curtains, and saw under a tree a few yards away six people chanting in a circle around a small bonfire. In the centre was a huge black woman whose face was smeared with white paint and who was wearing a garish costume of tattered, bloody rags, a necklace of what looked like beaks, teeth and bones, and a gaudy headdress of red, green and blue parrots' feathers. She was brandishing a long knife and about to cut the throat of a black chicken. A skinny little man stood beside her, holding a huge toad and licking its skin as though in a trance. Another was carrying a small cage containing a massive, hairy spider, chanting in a lisping, high-pitched voice, and the tree above them was festooned with broken bottles that clanked in the breeze and a black flag with a big red X in the centre. A second woman was reverently sprinkling a bowl of soil into a hole in the ground, and another was breaking eggs and tossing the eggshells into the hole.

With a primitive cry of triumph that lanced up my spine and back again, the woman severed the chicken's head, tossed it to the ground, and squirted a fountain of blood from its body into the hole. Its head lay on the ground, its eyes startled, the beak still quivering, as though it couldn't believe its fate, like some of the headless but still living victims of the guillotine during the French Revolution as their severed heads bounced into the basket.

'*Obayifo oreko eee!*' bellowed the woman, or something that sounded something like that. '*Obayifo oreko eee! Na wonye obayifo ah, wuntwa wo annie!*'

Suddenly I realised who she was: Miz Quaintance! It had to be, with that massive bulk and booming voice. Miz Gossamer Quaintance with a white face, bloody rags, a feather headdress, and a sturdy pair of rugby boots.

'*Obayifo kumm wadi wamma mee!*' shrieked her companions, though I wouldn't swear to the exact words. '*Na onkum wamma mee na eswa!*'

The body of the headless chicken staggered away from the fire, hunching its bloody shoulders, unable to see, hopelessly intent on escape, before it collapsed in a heap a few feet away, twitched, and lay still. The second woman poured more of her carefully hoarded soil into a cloth bag, tied it tightly at the top, and suspended it on a branch above the fire.

Miz Quaintance bellowed again, a long incantation that is quite beyond me to reproduce, and her acolytes chanted and shrieked along with her and danced around the fire.

Obeah, I thought: witchcraft; ancient African sorcery. I was appalled yet riveted. This ceremony probably stretched back thousands of years and three thousand miles to the steamy jungles of West Africa when Christ had yet to be born. I watched through the chink in the curtains, mesmerised, loath to move or interrupt in case I let loose some primitive, supernatural force.

And then I wondered whether this ceremony really was truly pagan, because Miz Quaintance pulled what looked like a bible from under her rags and began to read what sounded like one of the Old Testament psalms: 'O Lard God to who vengeance belong, show youself. Lift up youself, you judge of de heart'. Rend a reward to de proud. Lard, 'ow long shall de wicked triump'? 'ow long shall dey utter an' speak hard t'ings? An' all de workers of inni-kitty boast demselfs...'

This went on for several minutes, punctuated by the crackling fire and cries of *yes Lord!* and *praise him!* and *hallelujah!* from her acolytes. So they'd grafted a sort of Christianity onto the ancient rituals of pagan Africa to create a bastard Caribbean religion that was both repulsive and compelling. I watched, appalled, right until the end, when eventually Miz Quaintance gave a bloodcurdling howl and fell to the ground, apparently in a coma. Should I try to help? Call for an ambulance? Better not, I thought. This was obviously not the first time that she had gone through this performance, and after a few moments she roused herself, shook her head groggily, and lurched to her feet while her acolytes stamped the fire out, filled in the hole with the eggshells in it, collected the bag of heated soil, the chicken's head and corpse, the broken bottles in the tree, the black flag with the red X, and made off muttering into the night.

After that I took ages to get back to sleep and I slept very badly, tormented by a dream in which Shermelle, Barbara, Hare and I were covered in feathers and dragged to the guillotine, where Miz Quaintance was sitting beside the basket of heads, knitting and grinning.

I woke exhausted and the rising sun was like a brutal searchlight in my eyes.

Miz Quaintance arrived right on time for work at nine o'clock, teetering dangerously as usual on her tiny bicycle and whistling *God Save the Queen*.

'Inside!' she bellowed.

I flinched. My head resembled an echo chamber.

'Marnin', marnin',' she rumbled cheerfully. She looked as if she had slept for eight or nine hours.

'Good morning.'

'Is a bootiful marnin'. You good, milard?'

'A little tired.'

'Why dat?'

'I didn't sleep too well.'

'Why dat?'

'The chicken at one o'clock in the morning,' I said.

She looked thoughtful. 'Ah. Yus. You done see dat?'

'I did.'

'We wakes you?'

'Yes.'

'I sorry, but is de powerful magic. Is de way to find de t'ief.'

'Come again?'

'De t'ief now gonna get sick, an' 'e know if 'e don't bring de computer back 'e gonna die soon, oh yus.'

'Really?'

'For sure. You see: de computer 'e come back quick-quick, all by 'eself. An' now me does de larndry.'

After breakfast I went to the desk in the spare room, closed the door to ensure that Miz Quaintance couldn't hear me, phoned Smartly, and told him what I'd seen.

'That's obeah, all right,' he said. 'It's quite common in some parts of the island, and a lot of older people still believe in it. Some of them are absolutely terrified of it, and they say that if someone really believes in it and learns that he's been cursed by an obayifo – an obeah man or woman – he'll just give up and die. It's sheer superstition and mumbo-jumbo, of course, but it's no more absurd than many Christian beliefs and ceremonies. I mean, think of it, really: the body and blood of Christ; the resurrection of the dead; angels and heaven; the right hand of God. All mumbo-jumbo, and obeah is no more ludicrous than Christianity.'

'One man last night was licking a huge toad,' I said. 'He looked completely spaced out.'

'He probably was. The toad's skin is apparently hallucinogenic and they say that licking it strengthens the obayifo's magic.'

'So Miz Quaintance is a witch?'

'Sounds like it. You say she was dressed in rags and feathers?'

'Yes.'

'That's typical of obeah.'

'There was also a guy last night with a big, hairy spider in a cage.'

'Anansi. Another West African legend. A lot of the old folk are seriously afraid of a spider they call Anansi.'

'I remember. Shermelle told me.'

'It's said to be frighteningly cunning and mischievous and to cause all sorts of mayhem. They say it can turn itself into anything it chooses, especially a man with a high-pitched lisp.'

'Yes! This guy last night had a very squeaky voice. And they dug a hole and sprinkled some soil into it.'

'Dirt from a grave, I expect. That's powerful magic.'

'Miz Quaintance told me that it would make the thief return my organiser.'

'Who knows? Maybe it'll work if the thief believes it will.'

There was still no word from Shermelle. I telephoned the airport again, and the harbour, and the jetty, and her mobile, without any luck. It was as if she'd disappeared completely. I asked Miz Quaintance how to get to Aberdeen and I set off in mid-morning, determined to find her. Maybe she'd been attacked, or had fallen ill and was lying helpless at home. Or maybe she'd been kidnapped, or called away suddenly: a sick relative, perhaps.

Aberdeen was a tiny hamlet at the end of a dirt track up in the hills at the northern end of the island, a settlement of no more than four or five little corrugated iron shacks amid a cluster of mango and banana trees, a small brick bungalow with a lovingly tended little garden, and a tiny Presbyterian chapel built perhaps three hundred years ago by some homesick Scottish exile. I couldn't imagine her living in one of the shacks so I knocked on the front door of the bungalow. There was no reply. A couple of small children emerged from one of the shacks and stood outside the gate, watching me solemnly. I peered in through every window but saw nothing that was obviously hers. 'Shermelle?' I called. 'Shermelle?' but nothing moved.

I walked to the nearest shack to see if anyone was in.

'Inside!' I called, and an old woman opened the door suspiciously.

'Good morning,' I said.

'Marnin', marnin',' she mumbled.

'I'm sorry to bother you but I'm looking for Miss Donaldson.'

'Ah, you wunt Shermelle,' she croaked. 'Me t'inks she workin' dis marnin' but mayhap she back tonight.' She grinned wickedly. 'Dat if she not wid her new sweetman all night!'

'Who's her new sweetman?'

She cackled. 'Some new honky feller over by Nelson Rest. She dere wid 'im every night, all night, dis week past.'

At least I hadn't been replaced, not yet.

'Thank you,' I said. 'So where does she live?'

She pointed at the brick bungalow.

'Thank you,' I said. 'That's very good of you. You've been very helpful.'

I fished an American $10 note out of the back pocket of my trousers and offered it to her. She looked at it as if my fingers were contaminated.

'What dat for?' she said.

'Well, to thank you for your help.'

The $10 note hung limp between us in my fingers. She looked at me with contempt. 'Me don' need you money for bein' polite.'

'Of c-course not,' I stammered. 'I'm sorry. I just thought…'

'You 'mericans t'ink you can buys anybodies wid you dirty dollars.'

'I'm not American,' I said, but she'd closed the door. I drove away feeling ashamed and strangely unclean.

'Honky!' yelled the children, running after me. 'Darty Yankee dullar honky!'


I returned to Aberdeen after dark in the hope of finding Shermelle at home. She was. Her pink jeep was parked outside and light splashed out of the little bungalow and across the garden. Through the open window I could hear a lazy, lilting guitar and James Blunt singing his sweet, gentle love song *Carry You Home*.

I parked the jeep, opened the little wooden gate, and walked up the path to her door. An army of insects squeaked in the balmy night and a dozen flickering fireflies flirted in the darkness. My heart thundered. I was nervous and breathless, even though it was barely twenty-four hours since I'd seen her. I was suddenly frightened of what she might say. Had she discovered that I'd lied to her: that I wasn't a journalist at all but a sort of spy? Had she decided after all that I really was too old for her? Had she just become tired of me? Had she found another lover? Please no: not that; I couldn't bear that.

I didn't shout 'inside!' You don't shout 'inside!' to someone you love. I knocked on the door. She opened it and looked stricken when she saw me. My heart missed a beat. I'd almost forgotten how beautiful she was. I couldn't let this woman go, no matter what she or I had done. This woman was mine, and always would be. I'd never let her go.

'Hello, stranger,' I said.

She stepped back. 'No, Dave.'

I'd almost forgotten already the lovely caress of her voice.

'What do you mean, *no*?'

'I mean you can't come in.'

'I'm in already,' I said, stepping over the threshold and closing the door behind me. She retreated as if I were contagious. I wanted to reach out for her, hold her, kiss her.

'Please go away,' she said.

'I can't.'

'Please leave me alone.'

'I can't. You know I can't.'

'You must.'

'Why?'

'Because.'

'Why?'

'It's over.'

'Over?'

'You and me.'

'That's not possible,' I said. 'I love you.'

'Please don't,' she said.

'I love you.'

'No you don't. Maybe you just think you do.'

'There's no maybe about it. I know. I love you.'

'Whatever that means.'

'You know what it means. It means how much we care for each other. It means what we've been doing together for more than a week.'

'Fucking.'

The word hit me like a bullet between the eyes.

'What?'

Her face was stiff. 'Just fucking, that's all. That's all we've been doing. Like enjoying a meal. Nice, but that's all.'

'I can't believe what you're saying.'

She shrugged. 'Did nobody ever tell you that West Indian girls love fucking? We *love* it. We'll do it with anyone. It doesn't matter who so long as it's good. But we don't fall in love with a guy just because we let him fuck us.'

I flinched. 'I wish you wouldn't keep using that word.'

'What word would you prefer, then? Screwing? Shagging? Balling? Bonking? Poking?'

Cold fingers touched my heart. She looked like a stranger, her face tight, her body tense, her eyes like icy emeralds, yet I knew every inch of her. 'What we've been doing is none of those things,' I said. 'We've been making love.'

'Come off it, Dave. *Love*! Don't make me laugh. Admit it: you just wanted to shag me.'

'No! We were making love. With passion and tenderness. Just

223

yesterday morning when we were in bed you…'

She put her hands over her ears and backed away. '*Don't!*'

'I adore you.'

'No.'

'You know I do. I love you so much it hurts.'

'Don't say these silly things!'

'They're true.'

'You're imagining it.'

'No I'm not, and you know it.'

'I don't know anything except that it's over.'

'You can't just say that without telling me why. At least you owe me an explanation.'

'I don't owe you anything. I don't have to explain anything. I'm a grown woman with a mind of my own. I can do what I like, and that includes telling you it's finished and choosing who to fuck and who not to fuck.'

'But *why*?'

She glared at me. '*Because I say so!*'

I was stunned. I stared at her. I was dumb. She really meant it. She'd had enough of me. Suddenly. In the space of just one day.

'There's another man,' I said.

'Don't be so childish.'

'There must be.'

'Why? Do you think I can't function without a man? Grow up, Dave. Get real. Now go. Please. I mean it, or I'll call the police.'

The *police*? I was paralysed with disbelief. How could she do this to me? How could she treat me as if I were a complete stranger, an intruder who had broken into her house and threatened her?

'You really mean it,' I said.

'Yes.'

'And you're not going to tell me why.'

'No.'

'Why not?'

'Why should I?'

'Because we had so much. We shared so much.'

'Our bodies,' she said brutally. 'Just our bodies. I lent you mine for a few nights, and it was quite fun, but that's it and now it's over. Now you can go and find yourself another easy black girl to fuck.'

I couldn't believe that she was capable of saying something as vicious as that. *Quite fun?* Had I really meant nothing to her at all? Had those magical nights really amounted to nothing more than two animals grunting in the dark? Had I really fooled myself so totally?

There was silence. James Blunt had stopped singing and so had my heart. A clock was ticking. A mosquito cruised by, humming to itself. I couldn't deal with this. I gazed at her with a bottomless sadness and shook my head. A hole had opened up inside me and misery had entered in.

She went into the kitchen and started clattering plates and cutlery. Just like that. No 'goodbye.' No 'thanks for everything.' No 'nice to have known you.' No 'see you around.' Just 'it's over, now sod off.'

I turned and left her little house without another word. As I walked back to the jeep I thought I could hear her weeping.


At 4am the telephone rang. Bloody London again. I lifted the receiver. 'Do you know what time it is here?' I said.

'I don't give a toss,' said Hare. 'I want you back here, Barron. Pronto. Your email yesterday was a disgrace. "Making progress"? Bollocks! It's quite obvious you've been doing sod-all ever since you've been faffing around the Caribbean. You've been away two weeks and you've come up with nothing.'

'That's not true.'

'Yes it is. I want you in my office first thing tomorrow morning.'

'I may not be able to get a flight in time.'

'Yes you will. You're booked on the BA flight from Barbados to Gatwick at 5.50 tonight. Be on it.'

He cut the connection.

Ah, *shit*!

I phoned the airport as soon as it opened at 6.30 and discovered that there was only one Carib Airlines flight to Barbados, at 8.30, that would connect with the BA flight to London that night. There was only one seat left on it. I booked it. There was no time for me to say goodbye to anyone. I had a quick final swim, packed my bag, and left a note and a handsome tip for Miz Quaintance and a message on Smartly's answerphone. I tried Shermelle's mobile again, hopelessly, God knows why, but it was still switched off. Perhaps she'd bought a new one so that I couldn't pester her. I dropped the jeep off outside the Thrifty office in Columbus, pushed a note through the letterbox, and took a taxi to the airport, saying a series of silent, sad farewells as we passed all the places I'd known along the way: Sweetman's bar, Hopetown, Cotton Beach, Suzy's place on Mosquito Bay, a passing bus called CHEEKY LADY. At the airport I poked my head into the customs hall, aching for a glimpse of her, just one last memory, just *something* to take with me, but she wasn't there.

A couple of passengers ahead of me were checking in for a flight to St Vincent and were being made to stand with their luggage on an ancient, clanking weighing machine.

'Why d'you have to do that?' I asked the man afterwards as they turned away from the desk.

'It's a very small aircraft to St Vincent, maan,' he said, 'just six seats, so they weigh us all to be sure we're not too heavy.'

'And what if you're very fat?'

He grinned. 'You pay for two seats or they kick you off the

flight.'

As I left the check-in desk myself the Russians emerged from the immigration hall. The woman spotted me and advanced with a leer.

'Zat prostitute,' she said, 'wiz you at ze 'orses race.'

'She's not a prostitute,' I said tightly.

She sniggered. 'Then vy did I seed her yesterday at 'ospital medicine lab-or-a-tory?'

'I've no idea.'

'Ha!' she said. 'She vas hafink ze test for Aids. Yes? For ze prostitute disease.'

The blood drained from my brain. Shermelle? Aids? Oh God, no. No. It wasn't possible.

'Is better you sleep wiz nice clean Rossiyan gorls,' she said.

'Fuck off!' I said.

*Ah, Jesus! Aids: not Shermelle; please; no; not her.*

As the incoming flight from Barbados landed there was a murmur of excitement and a surge of activity as some VIP disembarked from the plane and was surrounded by deferential officials who escorted him into the terminal.

'Who's that?' I asked a local passenger who was standing beside me in the departure lounge and watching the arrival through the big picture windows.

'You don' know, maan?'

I shook my head. 'Is he famous?'

'De most famous man in Innocent,' he said, 'de finest man in all de island. Dat de Hon'rable Eustace Ponsonby, de Prime Minister. He been away on a trip all around de world but now, praise de Lord, he back.'

The sun was blazing as we left the terminal building and crossed the runway to board the plane, but suddenly, out of a clear sky, we were sprinkled with a light shower of rain: a monkey's wedding, just like Innocent itself; sun and rain simultaneously, tears and laughter, joy and misery.

*Oh, Shermelle, Shermelle, Shermelle.*

As the aircraft took off and soared over the volcano, and the island slipped away so bright and green beneath us, I found it difficult to swallow. The lump in my throat was as solid as the pain in my heart.

*Goodbye, my love. Goodbye, my darling girl.*

# CHAPTER 14

## AN ENGLISH SUMMER

We landed at Gatwick just before 6am on a typically miserable February morning: sad, damp and gloomy with a nagging drizzle and a bone-achingly icy wind. It was bad enough having to fly in economy instead of in business class, as we used to do, cramped and uncomfortable thanks to the government's latest austerity cuts, but the nine-hour flight from Barbados was also an alarming roller-coaster ride as winter gales buffeted us time and again high above the Atlantic. I'd failed to sleep at all, as usual, and in the middle of the night, when the plane suddenly lurched, dropped a few hundred feet and staggered to right itself, some stupid woman behind me started sobbing and screaming *'we're going to crash! We're all going to die! Let me off! Let me off!'* At 38,000 feet! Children began to whimper and when we finally landed at Gatwick the cabin resounded to a burst of relieved applause.

The airport was deserted, its corridors echoing eerily, and only two irritable immigration officers were checking passports. The luggage took forty-five minutes to appear on the carousel and I had to stand for another fifteen on an open railway station platform in slanting rain and a cutting wind before I managed well after 7.30 to catch the Gatwick Express into Victoria. Through the blackened Sussex and Surrey countryside we clattered through Reigate, Croydon and Clapham Junction, the rows after rows of cramped little houses squatting beside the railway line all the way into town huddled together in the frozen dark like frightened rabbits. All those alien, unknown lives, all those hopeless hopes and doomed dreams. Why do we all still live in this dreadful climate on this tiny, crowded, tired old island that has long lost its pride and dignity? Why don't we fly south like birds to raise our faces to the sun and bask in the light and warmth of places alive with life, places like Innocent?

I took a cab to my small, rented, one-bedroom flat in a weary old converted Victorian house in the grottiest part of Battersea, where the pavements are piled with black bags full of rubbish, garbage rots in the gutters, rats scuttle between the back yards and hooded youths with shifty eyes slouch on street corners and finger their twelve-inch knives. Until a few months ago Barbara, the kids and I had shared an elegant four-bedroom house with a lovely garden in a pretty village in Surrey, but when we divorced she kept the house, the kids, and a large chunk of my salary as monthly maintenance. Take my advice: don't get divorced in Britain if you're a man; it's become as biased in favour of women as California. If you've got to get divorced then go somewhere civilized like Iran or Saudi Arabia, where you have only to tell your wife 'I divorce thee' thrice and the job's done. In Britain nowadays it's taken for granted that the man is to blame even before any evidence is given. The British courts are stuffed with women barristers and judges who believe that all men are selfish bastards, sexist monsters, wife-beaters, rapists and skinflints who deserve not only to be taken to the cleaners but to have their shirts ripped off their backs and their pockets turned inside out as well. Apart from the house I'd had to give Barbara eighty per cent of our meagre savings, half of my pension fund, and monthly maintenance amounting to forty per cent of my salary. And not just Barbara: her girlfriend had moved in with her and I seemed to be supporting her as well even though she had a well-paid job. A one-bedroom rented flat in the nastiest part of Battersea was the best that I could afford, and I was going to die a poor old man.

I bought some bread, butter, milk and eggs from the little Paki shop on the corner of the street – sorry, *Pakistani* shop, not Paki. You're not allowed to call a Paki a Paki any more, even though it's just an abbreviation: apparently it's racist. This country's gone mad with its whimpering political correctness. I let myself into the flat. The smell of damp, mould and sour drains hit me like a hammer. I switched on all the lights just to brighten the place but succeeded only in showing up dark stains on the faded old wallpaper and grubby cracks across the ceiling. I turned on the central heating and hot water and lit the gas fire. The water tank shuddered, the pipes groaned, the radiators creaked, and the fire hissed at me. A baby started howling in the flat below, on and on, as though it was being tortured. It probably was: torturing babies has become a major sport in England over the last few years. Molesting children sexually is increasingly popular too. Most English people have given up playing all other sports all together – not surprisingly when you consider how pathetic the national soccer and rugby teams are, let alone the tennis players. Thank goodness for the cricketers, who do manage occasionally to beat some of the weaker Test teams.

I cooked myself a couple of eggs for breakfast, and after half an hour took a feeble lukewarm shower. I needed to sleep but I knew that Hare would not tolerate any further delay, and even the office would be warmer and more welcoming than this dump.

I walked north through the dirty, windblown, depressing back streets, wearing a thick overcoat, gloves and a scarf, crunching across the frosty grass of Battersea Park beneath its naked winter trees and past the empty playground and silent bandstand, and across Chelsea Bridge towards the Embankment and Grosvenor Road. It was nearly 10.30am but so murky that it could have been dusk. It would probably be at least two more months before we had even a glimpse of the watery sun. The river was grey and sluggish, the ducks shivering on the surly mud banks. I caught a number 24 bus to Trafalgar Square that was packed with grey-faced people sniffing, sneezing, wheezing and coughing, and walked down Northumberland Avenue to the office, a stylish old Edwardian building that was far too smart for a few hundred tax officials. The public would have a fit if they knew what it cost to run the place.

I took the lift to the fourth floor and told Hare's secretary that I'd returned. She was one of those bossy middle-aged women with a fine moustache who once ran the British Empire and now thrive in the lower echelons of the civil service. She looked pointedly at her watch. 'He's been asking for you all morning,' she said.

'How sweet of him.'

'He's not happy.'

'He never is.'

I descended to my nasty little neon-lit rabbit hutch in the basement, which consisted of several dozen nasty little hutches separated from each other only by thin plasterboard partitions just five feet high so that heads kept popping up suddenly above them like nervous meerkats.

'Nice tan,' said Milligan, popping up from the hutch beside mine. 'Good trip?'

'Bloody awful.'

'Excellent. That makes me feel much better.'

'Jealous bastard.'

'I'd better warn you: Hare's hopping.'

'How very appropriate.'

There was a mountain of tiresome dreck piled on my desk: memos, scribbled notes, telephone messages, letters, forms, documents, magazines, leaflets, regulatory updates. I dumped the lot in my wastepaper basket without looking at any of them. If anything was really important someone would send it on to me again.

Hare summoned me ten minutes later. He was a small, bald man with tiny black eyes set far too close together and an unattractive sneer. 'Had a nice holiday?' he said sarcastically.

'If only.'

'Really? So what the fuck have you been doing, then, for the past two weeks?'

'Checking out the suspects that you sent me to investigate.'

'And?'

'Williams is just a religious nutter and maybe a bit of a conman, but Rogers and Fellowes are definitely bent.'

'I could have told you that ages ago. So?'

'They both claim to be residents of Innocent and to come to the UK for no more than ninety days a year, so I need to check if that's true.'

'How?'

'Immigration records.'

'Good God! That would take you weeks.'

'No. They're all computerized these days, both for people entering and leaving the country.'

'Only for the last year or two, since digital passports came in. For anything earlier than that you'd have to go through all the individual airlines' records. That could take months.'

'They've all been computerized for years.'

'But how many airlines do you check? Every one? And for how many years? And how long would it take to get court orders to force every airline to show us their records? You never heard of the Data Protection Act? And what if they flew in on a private jet, or some airline you've never heard of? Or what if they used pseudonyms or different nationalities? They've probably got Innocentian passports as well as British ones, maybe others from the US or some tin-pot Caribbean or South American republic. It could take years to check them all.'

He was right about the pseudonyms and passports. If they used those I'd never be able to track their movements.

'I'll start by just trying the last two years, then.'

Hare looked at me with open contempt. 'No you won't,' he said. 'You've wasted quite enough time on this enquiry already. I'll get someone reliable to do it.'

'I resent that.'

'Oh, do you? In that case you could always resign.'

At my age? When nobody hires anyone over forty any longer? In the middle of a recession?

'I wouldn't give you the pleasure,' I said.

At least he couldn't sack me. No one has ever been sacked from the British civil service: it's about the only organisation in the world where a job is still a job for life and still carries an inflation-proofed pension. But I went back to my hutch fuming. It was true that my enquiries in Innocent hadn't been hugely successful. I hadn't even begun to investigate Michel Lecroix or Genevieve Savroche but I was sure that I'd have found out much more about Rogers and Fellowes if I'd had another week or two. I hadn't yet had a chance to nobble Angela Fellowes's disgruntled maid or Don Rogers's wife, let alone to touch base with any of their dodgy business contacts.

Over the next few weeks Hare's bitch of a secretary took great pleasure in loading me with piles of desperately boring paperwork that he had allocated to me, and each time she approached my desk she did so with a smirk. For weeks I was trapped in the office and chained to the desk in my horrible little hutch, dealing with mundane problems, checking other people's work, and seething. You wonder why it takes so long to get a reply from any UK tax office? We're bored out of our skulls, that's why, and we resent our jobs, our bosses, our failure to find something more interesting to do, and we resent you.

Did I dare to resign? Of course not. I couldn't afford it. I had barely any savings, Barbara and the kids would continue to cost me a fortune for years to come, and I was still too young to take early retirement and my pension. Hare had me by the short and curlies.

That first evening back in London, immediately after work, I went nervously to a private clinic in Chelsea to have a blood test for Aids. How ironic it would be if I had picked up the dread disease from a girl I truly loved. Ah, Shermelle, my love. Not Aids. Not *us*.

'Do not be worrying if you are being tested positive,' said the grinning little Asian nurse as she slipped the needle into my vein. 'There is no major cause for alarm. HIV is not necessarily terminal these days, not always, by God no. Jolly good.'

Thanks a bunch.

'You are just having to give up having sex, that is all.'

Oh, great.

'Except of course with other peoples who are having HIV also, oh yes. That is jolly acceptable if you are both agreeing to exchange fluids in full knowledge that such fluids are contaminated.'

Can we get on with it, please?

'Jolly good,' she said. 'You are not fainting at all.'

'Should I be?'

'Well, it is always being the big men who are fainting when they are seeing the needle going into their arm and their own blood pumping and frothing into the syringe, believe me.'

I felt queasy and gripped the arm of the chair with my needle-less hand. I'd been fine until then.

I was shamefully nervous as I waited for the result but it turned out to be negative, thank God, and I prayed that Shermelle's test had been negative too. No matter what she'd done to me, no matter how hurt I was, she didn't deserve that. I wept suddenly, pathetically, as I thought of her, and felt ashamed of myself and my self-pity. Where was she now, today? What was she doing? Who was she with? And why had she dumped me so suddenly and brutally? The days stretched out long and empty in front of me, and especially the nights. What was I going to do without her? When would life begin to feel worth living again?

To compound my self-disgust I drank far too much in a pub near the office one boozy Friday night with Milligan and three or four other colleagues and found myself just after midnight in a shabby hotel off the Bayswater Road in bed with a prostitute who had picked me up in Hyde Park. She was young and almost pretty but that wasn't a good enough excuse. When finally I got back to the flat I stood in the shower for twenty minutes, until the water was cold, soaping and scrubbing over and over again and hating myself. I felt lonelier than I'd ever been even in the unhappiest days of the divorce.

Spring came and went, if you can call it spring, and what passes nowadays for an English summer – one cold, wet week in June – and I tried to banish the loneliness by having a brief affair with a sad, forty-year-old divorcée from the accounts department whose vagina was always mysteriously cold and who let her three cats sleep on her bed. Neither of us derived much pleasure from our dogged encounters, and I thought of Shermelle and was revolted with myself again, and the affair fizzled out as feebly as it had begun. For five months I toiled away at the dreariest tasks that Hare could devise for me, never leaving the building, and although I couldn't bring myself to see Barbara again I took the children out to restaurants for lunch on a couple of weekends and asked them about their lives and interests.

'How's school?'

A shrug.

'You still playing cricket?

'Nah.'

'Why not?'

'I got bored of it.'

'Bored *with* it.'

'Yeah.'

'That's a shame. You were pretty good.'

'I gived it up.'

'*Gave* it up.'

'Yeah, that's right.'

'No, I mean you should have said "I *gave* it up".'

'Whatever.'

'And you, Jenny? How's the painting coming on?'

'I don't do it no more.'

'*Any* more.'

'Yeah, sure.'

'And your friend Maureen?'

'Her an' me fell out.'

'*She* and *I*.'

She shrugged.

'That's a shame. You were such good friends. Why?'

'She's a fuckin' cow, that's why.'

'Jenny!'

'OK, then: she's a fuckin' bitch.'

What's the point? I gave up.

'And how's your Mum?'

'OK.'

'Is she happy?'

'Who knows?'

She might just as well have said 'who cares?' They were surly, almost hostile, and I tried to imagine what lies Barbara and her girlfriend had told them about me. How sad it is when love wilts and is replaced not by hatred but indifference. Where had those two beautiful, laughing, loving infants of ten years ago disappeared, and who were these two gawky, remote strangers who had stolen their identities?

By the beginning of August, which was wet and cold as usual, I was beginning to need a proper holiday badly. I was entitled to take three weeks off some time before the end of the year, but every week in August had already been booked by colleagues who had children who were on their school holidays and still talking to them. Most of September, though, was still available. But where should I go? Somewhere warm and sunny, of course, and it had to be reasonably cheap, but where? A Greek island? Menorca? Tunisia? And who with? A holiday alone is not to be borne: the loneliness would be intolerable. But who could I ask to go with me? Not the sad divorcée in the accounts department: that would be cruel and a terrible confession of failure. Nor any of the men in my department: most of them were married and the others desperately dull, and I wasn't up to facing all those crass jokes about being gay. I needed to find a woman to ask, and a woman would expect to be screwed, and I didn't fancy anyone at all.

And then, in the second week of August, I had an email out of the blue from Boozy Suzy. God knows where she'd found my email address: from the travel company that had booked my rental of Hermitage House, perhaps, or the Thrifty car rental office in Columbus.

'hi dave,' she wrote, 'long time no c how's trix good I hope but were missing u out here in paradise y not cum n stay u r welcum 2 doss down at my place any time n stay long as u like. Itd be great 2 c u.'

Suddenly I felt hot. My heart pounded and I found it difficult to breathe. Go back to Innocent for my holiday? Of course! Why hadn't I thought of it myself? It would be cheaper than anywhere else in the world if I flew economy and stayed with Suzy. I knew enough people there by now, so I wouldn't be on my own. And Shermelle: I'd bump into Shermelle; of course I would. How could we possibly not on such a small island? And I'd make her talk to me, and maybe after more than six months apart she might explain where we'd gone wrong. My heart lifted, and I marvelled suddenly at the glistening beauty of the coloured raindrops sliding down the window pane.

I asked Hare for my three weeks' holiday in the second, third and fourth weeks of September. He could hardly refuse: I was entitled to time off and the holiday roster for those three weeks was completely blank. He asked suspiciously where I was planning to go and I took great pleasure in not telling him. 'I haven't decided yet,' I said. 'I'll probably stay at home and redecorate my flat.' He looked indecently pleased that I would be having such a dreary holiday, happily agreed to let me go, and I booked a cheap, out-of-season economy flight to Barbados and emailed Suzy to tell her when I was coming. She replied with just one word: 'beaut'.

*Shermelle. Shermelle, my love. Again.*

# CHAPTER 15

# COMING HOME

The flight to Barbados was as smooth as my previous flight had been turbulent. We took off from Gatwick precisely at 11.15am and landed at Bridgetown at 2.50pm, bang on time. I had an aisle seat this time so that I could at least flex my right leg every now and then, and the guy on my left was small, thin, and kept his elbows to himself. In Barbados I had to wait little more than an hour at Grantley Adams airport before my connection to Innocent, which also took off exactly on time, at 4pm. The little nineteen-seat Carib Airlines Twin Otter was packed tight as usual with massive Innocentian passengers as it puttered into the rosy sunset. They all seemed to know each other and I was the only honky: mid-September is low season in these parts because it's so hot and wet that tourists tend to keep away until December. It was airless and like an oven inside the plane, and I was jammed up against the man on my right so firmly that neither of us could move, but the cabin resounded with such cheerful insults, ribald jokes, and high-pitched laughter that I felt light-hearted and happy, as if I was coming home. I felt as if I belonged here, among these smiling people with their simple joys and sunny enthusiasm for life. My heart lifted as we approached the island, the peak of the volcano wispy with cloud, the mountain slopes spreading lush and green towards the Caribbean lapping turquoise at the golden shore. I knew then that one day, some day, soon, I'd leave sad, dreary old

240

England for good and come and live here. What would I need? Just a shack on the beach and £100 a week.

When the ground staff opened the aircraft door a blast of hot air surged into the cabin like the belch of a dragon, and as we crossed the tarmac I started sweating even before we reached the terminal. Suddenly I felt clumsy and nervous. My heart started beating hard and fast. Would she be on duty in the customs hall? Why not? Would she be the one to check my suitcase? And what would I say? A pulse pounded at the base of my throat. *Is this really paradise?* I'd said. *Then you must be Eve.*

The immigration hall was blissfully cool with air conditioning. WELCOME TO THE HONOURABLE EUSTACE Q. PONSONBY INTERNATIONAL AIRPORT. I filled out the immigration form and joined the queue under the sign that said UNBELONGERS. One day, I promised myself, I'd be entitled to join the line for BELONGERS, not that it would make much difference because once again there was only one immigration officer on duty and the two queues merged into one. She was an ugly but jolly little woman whose hair was elaborately braided close to her head in small, tight black and brown plaits. She sat in her glass cubicle pouting like a goldfish. When I reached her she glanced at my passport and me and my passport again.

'I know,' I said. 'I'm not exactly pretty, am I?'

She gave me a huge white smile. 'Nor am I,' she said, 'but we beautiful inside,' and suddenly she wasn't ugly any more. 'Welcome to paradise, Mr Barron.'

'Thank you.'

'You un business or huliday?'

'Holiday.'

'How lung?'

'Three weeks.'

'You been here afore?'

'Yes. Seven months ago.'

She was surprised. 'You back so soon?'

'Yes. I love it here.'

She beamed. 'Thank you, sir, Mr Barron. Thank you kindly for loving my island. I will give you a one month visa in case you wunt to stay longer. After that you can always extend you stay at the police station in Columbus.'

'That's very kind of you.'

'Nut at all.' She stamped my passport with a flourish. 'Have a great stay,' she said, and gave me another huge smile.

'Thank you. I will.'

My heart was pumping hard again. *Shermelle*. The luggage emerged through the rubber curtain from the baggage bay and trundled out onto the carousel. My case was one of the first. I plucked it off the belt and wheeled it towards the customs hall. My heart was battering my ribs. My throat was dry, my legs weak.

I pushed through the swing doors towards the customs counter. pulling my case behind me. I peered ahead, half-blinded by the glare of the neon lights. Two customs officers were checking the cases: a man and a woman. I walked in a trance towards the woman. *Shermelle*? Just seven months ago. Was that all it was, just seven months? It felt like a century. *So you must be Eve*, I'd said.

*Eve?* she'd said. *Not me.* She'd winked. *I love clothes.* She'd loved taking them off, too.

She wasn't at the customs desk. Of course she wasn't. That would have been too much of a coincidence. This woman was older, with huge, aggressive breasts and a severe expression.

'Cheer up,' I said jovially to hide my disappointment. 'It might never happen.'

She frowned. 'You what? You cheekin' me, maan?'

'No, no. Just trying to be friendly.'

'I not here to be friendly.'

'No, of course not.'

'I here to catch smugglers.'

'Absolutely. Excellent.'

'It is an offence to attempt to be friendly with an officer of the Royal Innocent Customs and Excise Department, especially a female officer. It is an offence punishable by a fine of five hundred US dollars or a prison term of seven months with hard labour.'

Bloody hell, Shermelle: I never realised we were living so dangerously.

'I'll remember that,' I said.

'You better.' She pointed her breasts threateningly at me. Even her blue and gold epaulettes looked accusatory. 'You anything to declare?'

'No. Nothing.'

'No drugs? Marijuana? Cocaine?'

'Good grief, no!'

'Open you suitcase.'

'Sorry?'

'Open the suitcase.'

'Really?'

'You not hear me? I said OPEN THE SUITCASE.'

Not even *please*.

'Of course,' I said.

I opened the case. She went through everything, lifting my shirts and trousers out, shaking them, piling them on the counter, holding up my underpants, feeling inside my socks, squeezing some toothpaste out of the tube onto the back of her hand and inspecting it before wiping it off with a tissue. She unscrewed a bottle of Listerine mouthwash and sniffed it. She switched my electric razor on and off. She found a packet of contraceptives and held them up with distaste between thumb and forefinger.

'You hopin' to get lucky?'

'Always.'

She looked me up and down. 'In you dreams,' she said.

She broke the seal on a little tub of Provençal sea salt that I'd brought as a present for Suzy, opened it, and sniffed it. 'Cocaine?' she said.

'Certainly not.'

'Heroin?'

'Of course not. It's sea salt. From the Camargue.'

'Car mark?'

'It's in France. Southern France.'

'I do not approve of France. They are dirty an' immoral. What it for, this salt?'

'Putting on your food.'

She licked her finger, dipped it into the salt, and licked it again.

'It's salt,' I said.

She grunted with disappointment.

'Do I really look like a drug smuggler?'

She stared at me coldly. 'This it is my duty to discover. Why do you bring this so-called "sea salt" to Innocent? We have our own salt in our own sea. What is wrong with our sea salt?'

'There's nothing *wrong* with it. You just don't package it and sell it. The French do.'

She stared at me for several seconds, as if debating whether to clamp my wrists instantly in handcuffs. At the counter beyond, her smiling male colleague was happily waving all the other passengers through without checking any of their luggage, but this monstrous Gorgon was determined to nail me for some offence, even if it were only for smiling at an officer of the Royal Innocent Customs and Excise Department. She rummaged further in my case, coming up with a packet of loose Black Dragon Formosa Oolong tea that I'd bought at Whittard in Chelsea as another little treat for Suzy.

'And what is this?' she said silkily.

'Tea.'

'You admit it?'

'Of course.'

'Ganja?'

'Eh?'

'Ganja?'

I was pretty pissed off by now. I raised my voice. 'Of course it isn't! Come off it! It's tea!'

She fixed me with a cold expression. 'Do not become violent with me, mister.'

'I'm not becoming violent.'

'Violence or abusive behaviour towards an officer of the Royal Innocent Customs and Excise Department, especially a female officer, is punishable by a fine of five hundred US dollars or seven months imprisonment with hard labour.'

For a moment of madness I thought it would almost be worth seven months to smack her in the chops.

'Tea is a slang for ganja,' she said. 'It is also called marijuana, pot, hash and weed. You tea is called Black Dragon: this is also suspicious; "chasing the dragon" is a common drug smuggler word for consuming drugs.'

'I don't give a damn what it's called, lady,' I said.

'I am not a lady.' Her epaulettes bristled. 'I am an officer in the Royal Innocent Customs and Excise Department. It is an offence to call me a lady, punishable...'

'... by a fine of five hundred US dollars or seven months' imprisonment with hard labour.'

'You gettin' cheeky again.'

'Look, madam... officer: this is just ordinary tea. Tea leaves. From bushes. From Taiwan. For putting in boiling water. For drinking with lemon or milk and sometimes sugar. English people drink it all the time.'

She thought about it, tugging at her earlobe for concentration. There was not much earlobe to tug. I read somewhere that people with no earlobes are almost certainly psychopaths. I could well believe it.

She grunted. 'I let you off this time,' she said reluctantly.

'Let me off what, exactly?'

'You cheekin' me again. You cheek me again, mister, an' I sure be vex.'

I said nothing. In the circumstances silence seemed the wisest option.

'I am deciding not to arrest you.'

'That's extremely good of you,' I said sarcastically. 'Very generous.'

Sarcasm was wasted on her. 'That is so, but be aware, mister: I watchin' you. I keepin' my eye on you. You be best you keepin' you nose clean. You unnerstan'?'

I ground my teeth. 'Perfectly.'

'Now go,' she said, and waved me away contemptuously with a flick of her fingers.

I couldn't believe this unfriendly reception, so different from Shermelle's smiling welcome when I'd arrived seven months ago. *There's nothing poisonous here except my mother-in-law,* she'd joked. Oh yes, there is: there's this bolshie colleague of yours. I looked at the woman's name badge: 'Orecia Billington.' First thing tomorrow I'd report her to the heads of the customs department and tourism authority.

I collected my scattered clothes, repacked my suitcase, and headed for the exit. I was not a happy bunny. Apart from the Deputy Prime Minister, this woman was the first unpleasant Innocentian I'd ever encountered and it came as a shock to realise that they were not all smiley, laidback and friendly. Miz Orecia Billington could have come from a different planet.

Then it struck me: Billington; the same surname as Windy Billington. A relative? Maybe even his wife? Surely not. Would a deputy Prime Minister allow his wife to work as a lowly customs official? Well, here, in Innocent, yes, maybe. The rules were different here.

In the entrance hall I was welcomed by the huge photograph of the Honourable Eustace Q. Ponsonby, MP, CBE, GPI, MA, looking smug. I was determined to meet him this time, if only to find out what Smartly's father was like. The computer screen above my head announced that our flight from Barbados had been delayed and would now not arrive for several days. As I passed the check-in desk I bumped into Angela Fellowes as she was checking in to take the return flight to Barbados. Her butler, Gascoigne, was loading half a dozen suitcases onto the scales. She looked me up and down with her greedy little simian eyes. 'So you're back,' she said with distaste. 'Suzy told me you were coming. Well, rather you than me. You know there's a hurricane coming?'

'Of course,' I lied. A hurricane? Shit! But I wasn't going to give her the pleasure of admitting I'd had no idea.

She looked amused. 'And you still decided to come? How *brave* you are. I'm getting out before it hits, back to London tonight for a couple of weeks. I went through a hurricane once before and I don't recommend it.' She smiled unpleasantly. 'Don't worry: I won't exceed my ninety days a year.'

So she knew about me being a taxman, no doubt about it.

'You must be *awfully* keen to see Suzy again if you flew out straight into the teeth of a hurricane,' she said sarcastically. '*What* a lucky girl she is. Won't that little black trollop of yours be upset?'

I clenched my jaw. 'She's not a trollop.'

'Really? I heard she had Aids. What *dreadfully* bad luck for her. And for you, of course. But then there's a lot of it about in these parts. Most of the girls are riddled with it. They'll fuck anyone at all, you see. People really ought to be more careful when they fuck the locals.'

'You should know,' I said.

I didn't owe Hare any favours, but as soon as I got to Suzy's I would ring him in London, even though it was already 9.30pm there, and suggest that he sent Angela Fellowes's photograph to the immigration people at Gatwick to look out for her off the flight from Barbados in the morning and see what she was calling herself and what passport she was using. And while she was away in London I'd get into her house at Hopetown, go through her records, and see if I could find anything revealing.

Outside the sliding glass doors of the air conditioned airport the heat hit me like the blast from a furnace. I gasped. It had never been nearly this hot back in February. It must be nearly 100 degrees. I could hardly breathe. And this was at 5pm: God knows what it was like in the middle of a steamy afternoon. The only taxi waiting at the rank was a battered old yellow Mitsubishi minibus with GLADIATOR splashed in red across the front. The driver emerged as I approached and opened the boot for my suitcase. He was old and almost toothless.

'Goodnight, sah,' he said.

'Snowflake!'

He looked at me blankly.

'Yessah?'

'Don't you remember me? You drove me to Hummingbird House seven months ago. At Nelson's Rest? You introduced me to Miz Quaintance.'

He looked baffled.

'You told me about her sweetman: Belly-Up Robinson.'

'You know ol' Belly-Up?'

'No, but you told me all about him. The last time I was here. Seven months ago.'

He looked completely lost. He had no memory of me at all.

'Never mind,' I said. 'I remember you, Snowflake.'

'T'ank you, sah.'

I climbed into the taxi. 'Mosquito Beach, please. The Tamarind Bar.'

'Yessah.'

'And could we please have the air conditioning on?'

He looked mournful. 'De air-con he done died.'

I opened the window, hoping for a breeze, but the air was sluggish. The sun was settling towards the horizon as we jolted along the coast road at 20mph, trailing a noxious cloud of black smoke and dodging potholes, goats, donkeys, monkeys, and careering buses with names and slogans emblazoned in garish colours across the front: funky monkey, **I AM DE EGG MAN**, broken dreams. Pedestrians waved. Palm trees whispered. We trundled past lush, vivid hedges of bougainvillea, hibiscus, oleander and poinsettia, splashes of red, yellow, white and purple, the beach on the right turning as pink as a tourist's sunburn in the setting sun, the pelicans hovering high and motionless for a moment and then plunging straight down like rockets into the glittering sea. God, it was good to be back. Yes, it was incredibly hot, and I was dripping like a tap already, but it was great to be back. My anger began to fade. Even the monstrous Orecia Billington couldn't spoil the golden, laidback magic of this beautiful place.

'So what's new, Snowflake?' I said.

He turned and looked over his shoulder at as the traffic hurtled perilously towards us. 'New, sah?'

'Anything important happened here since I've been away? In the last seven months?'

He thought, sucking his four or five remaining teeth.

He thought some more.

'Nuttin',' he said eventually. 'Nuttin' at all.'

'Excellent,' I said, settling back in the seat. 'That's just how it should be.'

'Never-de-*less*,' he said with a touch of pride, 'dere been a murder in Jericho two month past.'

'A murder?'

Crime, even shoplifting and burglary, was almost unheard-of in Innocent, let alone murder.

'Yus. Two boy be fightin' over a girl. De one done stab de udder, done kill him.'

'That's terrible.'

'De fust morder in ten year,' he said with satisfaction.

'That's dreadful,' I said.

'Not at ull,' he said. 'De boy what got kill was a bad boy, a t'ief. He rubbish. An' de udder boy, he rubbish also, in one o' de gangs. 'e been smugglin' de drugs. Dey gonna hang him high in de prison soon soon, oh yus.'

After a few seconds Snowflake spoke again. 'An' de po-leece station in Columbus done burn down to de ground, two, free mumfs gone.'

'But how could that happen? It's right next to the fire brigade station.'

'Dat so, but de fire appliance been empty. No wutter. De firemens done forget to fill de fire engine wid wutter.' He tittered. 'Dey done use all de wutter de previous week for fillin' de po-leece chief swimmin' pool.'

After a long silence Snowflake offered another piece of news. 'An' you jus' in time for de carnival dis week.'

'Is that fun?'

''tis very fine fun. An' we also got a big 'urricane comin' dis week.'

'I heard.'

'Yessah. Dey am callin' it 'urricane Kylie. You jus' in time for dat also.'

'I thought you never get hurricanes this far south.'

'Dey is very unusual. Dey is more customary up nort'. Dis am de first one here since 1980. Before dat de last one was 1955.'

Oh, great. A hurricane every thirty years or so, and just as I arrive.

'De one in 1955, 'urricane Janet, done kill eighteen parsons.'

'Parsons?'

'Yussah.'

'Priests?'

'Nut priests: *parsons*.'

'Preachers?'

'*Peoples*.'

'Ah: persons.'

'You got it: parsons.'

'So when's this Hurricane Kylie due?'

'De TV say mayhap four, five day.'

'How long do they last?'

He shrugged. 'Two, free day.'

'That doesn't sound too good.'

'No problem, sah. Screw up you courage to de stockin' part. 'urricanes not always very bad. Sometime jus' a lot o' wind an' wutter.'

He dropped me off at Suzy's bar and the minibus belched away into the pale evening. There was not even the smallest breeze to ruffle the trees and the sea was so flat and still that there wasn't even a ripple where it kissed the shore. It glinted like a mirror. Sweat swamped my forehead, puddled under my armpits and trickled down my spine. After the long flight from London I stank like a tramp.

The young barman was polishing glasses and Suzy was sitting on a stool smoking a cigarette and drinking a beer. Her skin was tanned dark brown, her hair bleached by the sun, her eyes deep blue. She was barefoot and wearing extremely short yellow shorts, no bra, and a bright yellow tee-shirt with a green slogan that said YOU TALKIN' TO ME? I'd forgotten how good she could look. She gave me a dazzling smile. 'Hi, Dave!' she said in her husky voice. 'Welcome back.'

She slipped off the stool and gave me a kiss on the lips that took me by surprise. She'd never done that before. 'Grite to see yer, mite,' she said, 'but – Jeez – you're as piss-poor pale as a Caarmelite nun's tit. Don't you bloody Poms *ever* get *any* sun?'

'Not much.' I dumped my suitcase in a patch of shade beside the bar. 'It's been a bloody awful summer in England, as usual.'

'You poor baastards. Christ knows how you put up with that fucking awful climate of yours. Right: jew fancy a quick shaarpener first or jew wanna go up to the house, unpack and sluice yerself down?'

Even the beach was airless, the sun melting into the sea. 'A beer would be brilliant.' I said. 'Bloody hell, it's hot.'

'You can say that again.'

'Bloody hell, it's hot.'

'Christ, your sense of humour hasn't improved.'

'Sorry. Long journey.'

'Yeah. It's hot, all right. And caalm. There's a hurricane on the way: Hurricane Kylie, so called aafter our mighty musical midget from Melbourne. It's always like this a few days before a hurricane: stifling hot and dead caalm. But it's real bad luck for the organisers of the caarnival: that's due to staart tomorrow and it's meant to go on for a week, but they'll have to cut it short before the storm hits. A beer for the Pom, Tafaari.'

'Sure thing, Suze,' said the barman, digging into the fridge behind the bar, cracking open a wet bottle of Carib and handing it to me. It was wonderfully cold. I sank it in less than a minute.

'Give the poor baastard another,' she said.

He did.

'You been through a hurricane before?' I said.

'Yeah. Gordon in '94. Bahamas.'

'Was it rough?'

She shrugged. 'A bit blowy.'

'And this one?'

'Pretty strong, they say: category 3, maybe 4.'

'That's serious?'

She blew a perfect smoke ring that hovered in the still air. 'Winds about 130, 140. Lotta rain: it pisses down like a cow on a flat roof. Heavy sea surge, landslides. Roofs blown off, windows smashed. No worries. Could be worse. Could be category 5.'

Cool customers, these Aussie sheilas: tough old slappers; ballsy. In fact they've usually got more balls than their blokes. No wonder so many Aussie men are poofs and sheep-shaggers: anything to avoid their terrifying women.

'You should have warned me,' I said. 'I could have postponed my trip.'

She looked amused. 'Come off it, mite! You're not afraid of a bit of a breeze and a wet, aare you? Whatever happened to the famous Pom stiff upper lip?'

'It's just above this flabby, trembling lower one.'

'Old joke.'

'Well, I've only got three weeks here and it won't be much fun if we have to spend half of it huddled indoors for days on end.'

She chuckled. 'Oh, I dunno,' she said. 'I'm sure we'll find something to do,' and she winked.

*Bloody hell*, I thought. *She's flirting with me. Is that why she invited me to stay? To get me into bed?*

'How was the flight?' she said.

'Great, but when I got to customs here a bloody woman called Orecia Billington gave me some serious grief. She emptied everything out of my suitcase and accused me of being a drug smuggler.'

Suzy grimaced. 'That's typical. She's famous for it. Put her in uniform and she turns into Hitler.'

'She was bloody offensive. First thing tomorrow I'm going to make a formal complaint about her – unless she's the Deputy Prime Minister's wife. That could be tricky.'

'Windy Billington? No, no problem. The corrupt old baastard's dead.'

I was speechless for a moment. '*Dead*? Billington? But he can't be more than about forty-five.'

'Forty-four, but he staarted to feel crook soon aafter you left, took to his bed and just got weaker and weaker. The quacks couldn't work out what was wrong with him. The rumour was that some old obeah witch had put a curse on him. Billington was incredibly susperstitious – a lot of these guys are – and they say that if you believe in obeah and you think you've been cursed you're so terrified that you just accept that you're going to snuff it. They believe it's inevitable, they give up all hope and just curl up and die.'

Bloody hell! Miz Quaintance!

'The weird thing was that the same thing happened at the same time to his chauffeur. He just wasted away, too. The word is that they were probably both involved in some racket and the victim paid an *obayifo* to curse them.'

Miz Quaintance, white-faced and wearing bloody rags, bones and feathers, and the chicken squawking and bleeding in the moonlight, and the organiser stolen from my desk. *De t'ief now gun get sick*, she'd said, *an' 'e know if 'e don' bring de computer buck 'e gun die soon, oh yes.*'

No, that's not possible. This is the twenty-first century. We don't believe in witchcraft.

'They say that Billington and the chauffeur were so shit-scared they just went to bed, turned their faces to the wall, and wasted away, and bloody good riddance. The man was a monster and a major crook who didn't give a flying fuck about the island or the people. All he cared about was getting rich and he didn't care how he did it. They say he killed at least eight people who got in his way.'

Witchcraft? Surely not. That just wasn't possible.

'At Billington's funeral several people stoned the coffin, spat in the grave and jostled the mourners. They said he'd stolen their land titles and savings. They hated him. The police had to be called to keep order.'

I was seriously disconcerted by all this. I knew that Innocent was different, that its rules, beliefs and morality were not the same as anywhere else, that life and time danced to a different drumbeat here. But was it really possible that reason, logic, common sense and science could exist on an alien plane as well?

'You can't really believe all that stuff,' I said.

She shrugged. 'Who knows? They say Jesus raised the dead, so why shouldn't another wizard strike them down? Maybe Jesus was an *obayifo* too.'

Suddenly Orecia Billington didn't matter any more. As the sun went down on the beach a squadron of mosquitoes zeroed in on me like a flight of night fighters. 'I need some mozzie juice,' I said.

'Come on, then,' said Suzy. 'That's enough beer. We don't want you faarting all night. Let's get you up to the house. You look like you could do with a shit, shave, shower, shampoo and an early night. Hold the fort for me, will you, Tafaari. I'll be back later to lock up.'

'Sure thing, Suze,' said the barman. He winked at me. 'Good luck,' he murmured as I walked away. 'Give her one for me.'

Cheeky bugger.


She lived in a pretty little whitewashed two-bedroom bungalow half a mile up the mountain with a wide verandah, small swimming pool, colourful little garden, and a glorious view of the apricot sunset. After the long flight from London and the sweaty afternoon I couldn't resist the pool and I plunged in. Bliss. Then I showered, changed into shorts and a thin, short-sleeved cotton shirt, smothered my arms and legs with anti-mosquito spray, sank a large vodka and tonic, and she rustled up a couple of delicious herb omelettes with chunky brown bread, a luscious, homemade *crème caramel* and a bowl of fruit. She opened a bottle of Chilean Santa Alicia Cabernet Sauvignon and we enjoyed the meal out on the verandah with flickering candles and hundreds of insects nattering in the dark and the full moon splashing a silver path across the sea.

'This is heaven,' I said. 'Thanks for having me.'

'I haven't yet,' she said with a cheeky grin, 'but we've got three weeks.'

Bloody hell! She really was going to try to seduce me. And why not? She looked pretty good. Her eyes glistened in the candlelight, her tits were full of promise and her legs were endless. Why not? But I knew very well why not: Shermelle.

'So what've you been up to for the last few months?' she said.

I told her.

'Sod that! You ought to resign, tell 'em to stick the job up their aarses. You caan't work for people like that. Jeez, doesn't it drive you round the twist working in an office with wankers like that every day?'

So I told her too about Barbara and her lesbian girlfriend and the hefty maintenance payments and the grotty little flat in Battersea.

'Fuckin' 'ell!' she said. 'You've really been stitched up good and proper, you poor baastard. Why don't you just do a runner? Just dump all your problems and scaarper? Get the hell out?'

'If only I could.'

'Of course you could.'

'She'd come after me with a court order to pay the maintenance. She'd have me arrested for contempt of court.'

Suzy snorted. 'Let her try. Stay here. Live here. The courts here don't give a toss for any foreign court orders, and they get very bolshie if their old colonial masters try to tell them what to do now they're independent. You could live here for years before anyone could catch up with you. Or you could change your name, get an

Innocentian passport. It's a great life. And – hey, yes! – I could do with a manager. Really. Why didn't I think of that before? I'm serious, Dave. Really. I couldn't pay you much, but you could stay here until you found your feet and I'd feed you and pay you enough for pocket money and a gaargle or three.'

Suddenly it sounded a brilliant idea. Why not? The prospect of another winter in England didn't bear thinking about. But if I stayed here I'd have to sleep with her. Of course I would. And I couldn't do that. I couldn't: Shermelle.

'I don't think Brendan Mulchrone would like that much.'

She sighed. 'Poor old Brendan. He's not here any more. He left three months ago in disgrace. His aarchbishop heard about him and me, and his drinking, and he's been transferred to a teetotal parish in the Middle East, the poor baastard.'

'I'm sorry.'

'I'm not. It was time to end it. I don't know how I got into it in the first place, to tell you the truth. He made me laugh at first, with his Irish jokes and his Irish accent and his wonderful Celtic way with words. They're so much more inventive with the English language than the English aare themselves. And I suppose I felt sorry for him because he was lonely and – even worse – he'd lost his faith. He no longer believed in God, and that's a hell of a burden for a Catholic priest. He knew he was going to Hell. No wonder he drank so much. But then he become a major embarrassment and a pain in the aarse, and he was drinking far too much. Kept falling over and insulting people and falling asleep. So he's gone and I'm back on the maarket.' She looked at me boldly. 'You got a girl back in Pomland?'

'No.'

'You still carrying a torch for Shermelle?'

I nodded.

'Jeez, Dave.' She lit another cigarette. 'You've got to forget her. It's over.'

257

'Not for me. Not yet. Not until she tells me herself.' I hesitated. 'Is she OK?'

'Fine, so far as I know.'

'What about the Aids test?'

She looked surprised. 'You know about that?'

I nodded. 'The Russian bitch told me just as I was flying out in February. Anna Whatsername. She took great pleasure in it.'

'She would. Well, it's no problem. Shermelle's completely clear. No wucking furries, mite.'

'Thank God.'

She seemed to read my mind. She gazed at me and shook her head. 'She's not here, you know. She left soon after you did. Some people gave her such a haard time about the Aids test that she needed to get away. She said there were too many memories here.'

'So where is she?'

Suzy lit a cigarette. 'I've no idea.'

'Come off it, Suzy. Of course you know.'

'No. Honest. She wouldn't tell me where she was going. She said she'd keep in touch but she hasn't.'

'Barbados? Another island?'

She shrugged. 'Who knows? Could be anywhere: the States, the UK, anywhere. She had friends and relatives in both.'

'Someone must know.'

'Why? If she wouldn't tell me I doubt whether she's told anyone else. We were grite friends: she told me almost everything. She'd been through a hell of a lot, you know: you, and the Aids test, and the gossip and whispers and rumours. She wanted to disappear, to change her life completely.'

'She loved me.'

'Yes.'

'I know that.'

'Yes. She told me she did, more than once. She said the age difference didn't matter a damn. She wanted to live with you. She said she'd go anywhere with you.'

My heart began thumping again. 'So why did she dump me the way that she did? It was brutal. I was miserable. She wouldn't even tell me why.'

'She did it for you.'

'Come again?'

'She did it to protect you. You remember the guy at the races that day? The guy she was having a row with? The guy you aasked me about? That was her ex-husband, and he'd just told her that he'd got Aids and she ought to have the test. She was furious at first and accused him of catching it by going to the Spanish brothel in Conch Alley while they were still married, but afterwards she was afraid, and then she was terribly worried about you. She felt horribly guilty that she might have paassed it on to you. She said she didn't dare to sleep with you again in case she had it herself, so she told you it was all over. She pretended she didn't want you any more.'

'She was *cruel*. Unbelievably cruel.'

'Of course she was. She had to be ruthless, to drive you away. She tried to make you hate her. She *had* to make you hate her because otherwise she knew you'd never leave her alone, but it broke her heart.'

Oh, God. Shermelle!

'She had the test at the lab in Columbus the next day and when the result came through it was negative. She was so happy that day, but by then you'd gone. She tried to get in touch with you but all I could tell her was that you worked for some tax office somewhere in England. But there are dozens of them. She didn't know where to staart. She phoned and sent emails but nobody seemed to know who or where you were.'

Oh, God.

Suzy took a drag on her cigarette. 'So she gave up and left the island a couple of weeks later. She couldn't face all the people here who found out that she'd had an Aids test. The rumours and gossip were terrible, and it made it worse that people thought she'd picked it up from some honky tourist. She missed you so much. She cried a lot.'

'I'll find her.'

Suzy shrugged. 'You can try, but I don't know where you'd staart. She's even changed her e-mail address, and she's probably changed herself, aafter all she's been through. She probably wants to forget you because you remind her of too much.'

'Not if she loved me.'

Suzy hesitated, then: 'She may well have found another man, to wash you out of her hair.'

'No!' I couldn't bear the idea. 'She wouldn't do that. If she loved me seven months ago she loves me still.'

Suzy looked sad. 'I wouldn't bank on it, Dave. We're fickle creatures, women. We can change our minds like an old frock and our emotions like an old pair of shoes. Don't hang too much hope on Shermelle. You might be very hurt if you do. She may even have married again.'

'No!'

'She's moved on, and so should you.'

'No. I'll find her. I'll get her back. And if she's got another bloke I'll kill the bastard.'

She smiled affectionately. 'OK, Dave, whatever you say.' She stubbed her cigarette out. 'Well, good luck with the search, and you know I'd help if I could. But now I guess it's time you went to bed. You must be knackered.' She looked at her watch. 'Eleven o'clock. Jeez, that means that it's three or four in the morning for you. Get some kip. I'll go back to the baar and lock up, and tomorrow we'll staart taking some serious precautions against the hurricane. There's a lot to do.'

She stood up as I sat at the table and bent to kiss me, lightly on the forehead this time. 'Goodnight, Dave,' she said. Candlelight danced in her eyes and her teeth glistened and she smelt of something good. 'Sweet dreams,' she said. 'And it really is grite to see you again.'

When she was gone I quenched the candles and crawled into the bed in her second bedroom, under a big white mosquito net, and I fell immediately into a deep sleep, and just before dawn Shermelle came to me in a dream and she smiled at me, and I knew that I had to find her and that nothing else mattered.

# CHAPTER 16

## CARNIVAL, KYLIE AND THE MYSTERY OF MISSING MALENKOV

I drove into Columbus the next morning to make a formal complaint about Orecia Billington. There was something odd and unsettling about the road into town. At first I couldn't work out what it was until I realised that many of the palm trees beside the road were different from how they'd been in February: they looked diseased, with drooping fronds turning yellow and brown and bald, forlorn crowns that had lost all foliage.

I couldn't find anyone to complain to about Billington at the customs office, which was closed for the day like all the other offices and shops. It was stiflingly hot, the streets packed with Independence Day carnival revellers, and I had to park the jeep on the edge of town and walk in on foot. Music blared from every door, window and balcony, and a long, rowdy procession was winding its way slowly through the streets, led by the police brass band playing off-key as usual. They were followed by an exuberant parade of colourful floats and a dancing, singing mob wearing flowers, exotic headgear and garish costumes. Many were dancing along in couples, the men pressing close behind the women, rubbing, thrusting and grinding their groins lasciviously against the women's generous buttocks. Their blatant sexuality was startling, even indecent, but why? Innocentians, unlike the puritan, easily embarrassed English, accept and revel in the power of sex.

After the band, on the back of a lorry decorated with flowers, sitting on a purple velvet-covered throne and wearing a golden cardboard crown, came the Carnival Queen, a pretty chocolate-coloured girl in a sparkling ball gown with a gold and scarlet sash across her body that said MISS INNOCENT. She didn't look innocent at all. She was surrounded by six equally pretty girls who didn't look innocent either and were throwing pink and white petals onto the heads of the crowd. One of them caught my eye, winked at me and waggled her tongue salaciously. I waved, grinned, and waggled my tongue in reply. She pointed at me and dissolved into giggles. Why do pretty girls never waggle their tongues at me like that in England?

They were followed through the streets by groups from youth clubs, schools, sports teams, nurses, shops, banks, a crew from the ferry, jugglers, acrobats, men on stilts, a Punch and Judy show in the front bucket of a JCB backhoe, a gaggle of Morris Dancers prancing about with flowers in their straw boaters, bells tinkling on their knees, their hands fluttering with white handkerchiefs. Several raucous bands vied with each other: a ragged bunch of reggae singers; the Caribbean Rhythms rock group pounding guitars and drums; a jazz combo from Jericho; a calypso band from Coconut Bay; a church choir; a hairy old Rasta riding a milk float and playing an accordion; a young man blowing his trumpet as though it were the Day of Judgment; a Radio Innocent DJ broadcasting pop music; a cacophony of nursery-school children squealing, squeaking, banging drums, clanging triangles, waggling tambourines and shaking shack-shack pods; and finally the Purple Pelicans string band, led by none other than Hummingbird House's ancient gardener, Grandad, resplendent in his Paddington Bear hat and Garrick belt, beautifully playing an enchanting silver fife and dancing what appeared to be a medieval gavotte.

The fire engine had turned out, equipped with three firemen but probably no water, and an ambulance with its siren howling, and floats to represent whole villages and plantation inns, with Sweetman driving an open truck adorned with a harem of nubile girls in tiny bikinis. The procession took more than an hour to crawl through the town and assembled on the cricket field, where the grandstand filled up with spectators to watch the Romantic Amateur Dramatics Association (RADA) perform a melodramatic account of the history of Innocent in which Christopher Columbus was portrayed by a twenty-stone giant wearing a sombrero and singing *Viva España*, and Queen Elizabeth I was played by a very black dwarf in a pink tutu. Scattered around the edge of the ground were several stalls and sideshows, including a coconut shy, a lucky dip, and a rude blindfold contest that had the women shrieking with laughter: Pin De Dong On De Honky.

I forced my way back out of the melée and escaped to the peace and quiet of Suzy's house, where I dived into her swimming pool and washed away the sweat and dust of Columbus. 'And it usually goes on for four days,' she said, 'but this year they'll have to stop after one or two because of the hurricane.'

'I noticed that lots of the palm trees on the way into town are turning yellow,' I said.

'Yeah, it's really sad. They've been infected by something called Lethal Yellow Disease, which kills them in four or five months and leaves them with bare trunks.'

'That's dreadful. The coast is looking horribly bare. Can't they be treated?'

'Well, they say you can inject them with a vaccine called oxytetra-something but it's a long, expensive job.'

'They ought to do something about it. Parts of the beach look as if they've been devastated by a nuclear holocaust. Why doesn't the government do something? They could at least chop the dead trunks down: if they leave them like that the tourists'll never return.'

Suzy looked at me with a pitying expression. 'This is *Innocent*,

Dave. They caan't be bothered to do anything for themselves: they just wait for someone else to do it. In the end it'll be the conservation society and a bunch of expat volunteers who'll clear the mess away.'

The shops were open again the next day and when I went into town I was surprised to see how many people had mobile phones nowadays: almost everyone seemed to be talking into one. We spent most of the day preparing for the arrival of the hurricane, which we tracked on the weather channel as it approached the island slowly but relentlessly from the east. Already a wind was fretting the nervous palm trees and there was neither sight nor sound of a bird. A strong smell of rain leaked in from the sea and the ocean was restless, surly with whitecaps. There wasn't a boat or yacht to be seen: they'd all run south before the wind for the sheltered bays of Trinidad and South America. Unusually for the Caribbean there was not a cloud in the deep blue sky: they'd all retreated from the anger of the tempest, blown away to the west by the advancing gale.

We closed the beach bar, boarded it up, and turned Suzy's bungalow into a fortress, checking all the doors, windows and wooden shutters, tightening screws, securing loose objects that might be torn off by the wind, nailing roof tiles and gutters, dragging the furniture and plants off the verandah and pool deck into the house. We turned the fridge/freezer up to its highest setting, filled the bath and basins with water, checked that the radio, telephone, cell phone and generator were working, and I drove her jeep into Columbus to fill the tank with petrol and buy a couple of cans of diesel for the generator, a small paraffin stove, two powerful torches, a flashlight, batteries, candles, matches, a dozen rolls of lavatory paper, a hefty first-aid kit furnished with enough medical equipment to satisfy a brain surgeon, and enough bottles of water and tinned and frozen food to last us for a week. In some of the stores the shelves were almost bare but in the Cost-

Me-Less Calypso Superette a jolly Father Christmas still dangled from the ceiling and coloured lights still twinkled on a plastic Christmas tree in the grubby window of Véronique's Exclusive International Glamour Boutique ('All the Latest Modes, Styles and Fashions from London, Paris and New York').

I bought a copy of the *Innocent Gazette*. The front page lead reported the approach of the hurricane and speculated that it might mean the cancellation of a Caribbean Prime Ministers' conference that was due to meet in Columbus in a few days' time. On an inside page it ran a check list of all the vital items people needed to protect themselves. Another story reported that in Hopetown an elderly woman had been beaten up and raped. First a murder, now rape: what was happening to Innocent? Another reported that a teenager from Frenchman's Creek had been sentenced to twelve lashes of the cane and six months in prison for burglary. A seventy-four-year-old man from Pottery had been jailed for four years for committing incest with his thirteen-year-old great-granddaughter: he claimed that the child was a Jezebel who had tempted him beyond endurance. And a mysterious light aircraft had been seen again landing and taking off from the racecourse at night.

I dropped into Smartly's office on the way back to Suzy's house. 'David!' he cried. 'Hey, man, where've you been hibernating? One day you were here and the next you'd gone.'

'I was called back urgently to London.'

'You didn't even say goodbye.'

'No. I'm sorry. I had to leave in a hurry. But I did leave a message on your answerphone.'

'I never got it. Bloody Gwendolen! I've told her time and again not to delete messages until I've heard them. I reckoned that you and Shermelle had eloped.'

'No such luck,' I said. 'I don't even know where she is. She's disappeared. Do you have any idea?'

'Not a clue. Sorry.'

'Any idea who might know?'

He thought about it. 'You could try the chief customs officer, Cleon Melville: he might have a forwarding address. Or her neighbours up at Aberdeen. Are you with us for long?'

'Three weeks.'

'Excellent. We must have lunch again as soon as the hurricane has passed. Let's hope Sweetman's survives the storm. He's had quite enough trouble recently without having his bar damaged.'

'Why? What's happened?'

Smartly chuckled. 'He discovered a couple of months ago that his barman was stealing from the till, but the guy's got a wife and four kids, one of them handicapped, and Sweetman's a soft-hearted fellow, so instead of sacking him he hired a second barman to keep an eye on the first. But the second barman started robbing him, too, so he's had to sack them both, and now they're taking him to court for wrongful dismissal. Where are you staying?'

'With Suzy McDonald.'

He raised an eyebrow. '*Really*?'

'No, it's *not* like that,' I said, 'not at all.'

He grinned. 'Of *course* not.'

'And what about you? Any excitements since I've been away?'

He hesitated, glanced at me, made up his mind, and grinned again. 'D'you remember Alopecia Martin? My father's personal secretary?'

'The Cockney girl from London? How could I forget her? The one who's held together by nuts and bolts.'

'And screws,' he said. He sniggered. 'Now she's got personal with me, too, and she's... fantastic.'

So he'd done it, the randy young bugger. When they were in bed together they must sound like a steel pan band.

'Congratulations,' I said.

He looked modest.

'And what about your wife? How does she take to this new development?'

He waved a hand dismissively. 'Oh, like most Innocentian women she fully accepts that a man is entitled to have an outside interest.'

'How very civilized.'

'Oh yes, she is. Innocentian women don't get jealous or possessive. They know how to behave. They accept that fellows are born promiscuous.'

Fellows. Fellowes. Angela Fellowes.

'D'you remember,' I said, 'that before I left you offered to introduce me to one of Angela Fellowes's maids?'

'You wanted the key to her house.'

'Yes, I still do.'

'OK, I'll try her again. She'll probably want a tip.'

'Of course. Fifty dollars?'

'Plenty.'

'You're a star.'

He grinned. 'Twinkle, twinkle,' he said.


All afternoon and evening the winds increased their intensity, moaning in the eaves, whining under the doors, rattling the shutters, bullying the trees and nagging the surface of the swimming pool, which slapped the flap of the skimmer noisily to and fro, to and fro, dementedly. Despite the wind it was incredibly hot and after a simple lunch of bread, cheese and beer I tried to take a siesta but the racket of the approaching storm made it impossible to sleep. In the evening, after a couple of sundowners and a supper of prawns, angel-hair pasta and fresh fruit salad we tried to watch the BBC World news but the signal was broken up constantly by jagged lines, lost sound, error messages, and eventually it cut out all together. At about 9.30 the lights flickered, faded to a dim brown, and died.

'Shall I run the generator?' I said.

'Better not,' said Suzy. 'We ought to conserve the diesel until we really need it.'

She lit some candles and we sat for a while in the flickering gloom as the shutters banged and clattered unmercifully. She spoke fondly of Brendan Mulchrone and said how sorry she was that because of her he was convinced he would go to Hell.

'I thought he didn't believe in God.'

'He doesn't, but he believes in the Devil and Hell. At his worst moments he thinks that maybe the Devil *is* God.'

'That's terrible for a priest.'

'He calls it his Cross.'

'No wonder he drinks.'

'Poor baastard.'

'So what else is new?' I said. 'What's the gossip?'

She told me that Sweetman had a new white mistress, the young, very pretty wife of some unsuspecting off-shore financial adviser from Miami.

'How does he pull so much white totty?' I said.

'Big black cock, I expect.'

'Is that enough?'

'Sure. Why not? They say he's got WENDY tattooed along the length of his tool but when he gets a haard-on it reads WELCOME TO DE WEST INDIES. HAVE A NICE DAY.'

I laughed. 'You're dreadful!' I said.

She reported that she'd fallen out with Angela Fellowes and had heard a rumour that Don Rogers was being investigated by Interpol over one of his more outrageous financial scams; that Rupert Williams had started marketing a board game in which the players had to try to stop Judas Iscariot hanging himself; that Bernard Garwen had been sacked as the British honorary consul and been replaced by the hypochondriac Dr Alex McDowall, who had succumbed immediately to a genuine disease at last, shingles, but not before he'd had Venetia Featherstonehaugh sectioned and sent to a mental hospital in Barbados; that Michel Lecroix's black boyfriend had run off with a Tongan transvestite from Venezuela; and that the Russians had erected a high electrified fence all around their mansion and a sinister array of searchlights, alarms, aerials and satellite dishes on their roof.

I tried to talk about Shermelle, about where she might have gone, whether she had any friends or relatives who might know, why she hadn't tried harder to contact me, but Suzy kept changing the subject. She talked instead about the new Deputy Prime Minister who'd replaced Windy Billington: Shefton 'Old Money' Molloy, a smooth, clever young lawyer who was already lining his pockets with retainers from the Sunshine Resort, which was hoping to open a new casino on Casuarina Beach. Suzy shuddered, 'A casino!' she said. 'Can you imagine it? In Innocent? On the best beach? They're ruining the island already with their plans to build dozens more houses and condos, not to mention a vulgar new American-style shopping mall by the jetty, all tacky souvenir and jewellery shops. One of the joys of this place is that it's so quiet, slow, polite and old-fashioned, and the laast thing we need is some loud, chrome and neon palace attracting every crook and hooker from a thousand miles around. Molloy argues that the island desperately needs the extra money, taxes and employment that a new casino would bring, and he's right, but they'd also bring crime, violence and the Mafia. If that happens I'm off.'

'Where'd you go?'

She shrugged. 'Christ knows. There aaren't many quiet, unspoilt little islands left. Nevis, maybe? Anguilla? The Seychelles, or somewhere in the south Pacific.'

'Doesn't the Prime Minister realise the dangers of allowing a casino?'

'Ponsonby? The bugger's never here. Laast week he flew off

again on another jolly, this time to Tokyo to try to persuade the Japs to resurface the entire main island road.'

'You can't call them Japs any more.'

'I'll call them what I bloody well like. Then next week Ponsonby's off to Brussels to stick his begging bowl under the noses of the EU.'

At about 10.30 the power was still off, the candles were burning low, and we decided to go to bed. She gave me a brazen look and after a bottle of Chilean Merlot, in the flickering candlelight, with her hair tumbling across her shoulders and her long, bronzed legs stretched out along the sofa, it would have been easy to weaken, but she was one of Shermelle's closest friends and to sleep with Suzy would have been a shameful act of betrayal.

I yawned, sighed, stretched and stood up. 'I'm knackered,' I said. 'I must get some sleep. Goodnight, Suzy. And thank you for having me to stay. It's really kind of you. I do appreciate it.'

She smiled wanly. 'No worries, mite. It's grite to see you again,' and I bent and kissed her chastely on the forehead. 'Sweet dreams,' she said, 'but I reckon we won't get much kip with this gale howling around the house all night.'

It was a big, soft bed and I fell into it like a condemned man, but I tossed and turned all night even though I was still exhausted after the long flight. I dozed in brief snatches, dreaming of a beautiful woman whose face was in shadow but who I knew was Shermelle; of Brendan Mulchrone screaming silently, surrounded by flames; of Smartly wearing earrings made of razor blades. I kept waking with a start as the wind tested every nail and rafter, and the window frames clattered, and the roof groaned and sometimes gave a loud crack that sounded like a rifle shot. The shutters banged and rattled all night, on and on and on, bang, rattle, bang, rattle, bang. At about four in the morning the rain started, drumming on the tin roof, hammering a ceaseless tattoo against the shutters, pouring noisily into the cistern under the house and cascading like a waterfall off the gutters.

Dawn came late and grey and it was 7.30 before I could see much beyond the fence around Suzy's little garden. The rain was relentless now, a solid deluge, the wind pitiless, the mountain invisible in a thick murk. The swimming pool heaved and tossed as frantically as the Bay of Biscay, dancing with fallen leaves and brimming with overflow. Puddles flooded the verandah and every palm tree bent low before the wind in homage to the approaching storm. Smaller trees trembled and ferns and bushes shuddered at the fury of the wind. Just beyond the fence three sodden donkeys huddled together beneath a mango tree, staring miserably into the gloom.

Suzy emerged from her bedroom wearing just a tee-shirt and knickers, dishevelled hair, dark rings under her eyes, looking small and vulnerable. I wanted to give her a hug except that she was hardly dressed and the gesture might have been misinterpreted.

'Sleep OK?' I said.

'Sod all.'

'Nor me.'

'Those bloody shutters. I'm going to fix them good and tight when this is over.'

We tried to switch the TV on to check the weather channel but there was still no electricity.

'Shall I start the generator?' I said.

'Let's wait. We don't know how long we'll need it when we really need it.'

She switched her battery radio on but the only sounds that emerged were whines, whistles and shrieks, a battalion of banshees howling at the universe. In the kitchen I lit the little paraffin stove and brewed a couple of mugs of tea and some boiled eggs.

'D'you reckon this'll last much longer?'

She laughed wearily. 'This is just the overture. It hasn't even *staarted* yet.'

'You serious?'

'You'd better believe it. This is *nothing*, mite: peanuts. Wait till the *real* storm hits us in about three or four hours. That's going to be a humdinger.'

'It gets worse than this?'

'*Much* worse.'

The full force of the hurricane hit us soon after noon and I can barely describe the nightmare of the next three days and nights. The power of a tropical cyclone is truly terrifying. You cringe and cower beneath its awesome majesty, and even if you're an atheist you pray: not to God but to the hurricane itself, to Mother Nature, beseeching her to spare you. The noise alone is enough to make you whimper: an unending, deafening cacophony of splintering wood, clattering metal, smashing glass, screaming goats, howling dogs, stricken donkeys and moaning cattle, and a shrieking chorus of crashing palm trees. Add to that a wind powerful enough to rip your roof off and blow you off your feet, a ceaseless torrent of water, and a darkness blacker than anything you've ever known, and you understand at last how weak and defenceless we are and how close to cowardice. This is what it was like for Noah and his ark, for the citizens of Atlantis as their civilization sank beneath gigantic waves. We spent hours curled up in bed, living by torchlight, and every moment was frozen with fear as we waited for the roof to be torn off the rafters at any minute, the doors and windows to explode, the house itself to be wrenched from its foundations and carried away. It was barely possible to talk and at the height of the storm Suzy lay down beside me and begged me to hold her tight, and I did.

We decided to keep the water in the bath and basins for drinking and cooking, not washing, so we became dirtier and sweatier by the hour. Early on the first evening I struggled outside to try to start the generator in the garage and was immediately blown over and dragged by the wind for several yards across the ground. In seconds I was soaked and my hands, knees and elbows were bleeding. When eventually I reached the garage I found that the doors had been ripped off and carried away, and the generator was so wet that it was twenty minutes before I could get it to start. It did so with a feeble cough and a belch of foul black smoke, and for a moment the lights flashed on in the house, but then the engine spluttered and died and I never could get it going again. Four times in three days and nights I tried to start the damned thing, in vain. For three days and nights we had no electricity, no water pump, no running taps, no baths or showers, no flush in the lavatory. I remembered the instruction in the lavatory at Hummingbird House that had amused me on my first day in Innocent: IF IT'S YELLOW LET IT MELLOW. IF IT'S BROWN FLUSH IT DOWN. It wasn't amusing now. Over three days and nights the stench became nauseating. I stank too. You wouldn't have thought that just three days and nights without electricity, soap or sanitation would be so difficult to endure, but we've all become so molly-coddled by our twenty-first century civilization that within a day or two you can be reduced to pathetic helplessness. Golding was right in *The Lord of the Flies*: a week or two of living like this and most of us would lose all sense of decency and morality. On the second night I even contemplated screwing Suzy, if only for the brief release.

In the middle of the second day the wind and rain suddenly stopped and the sun came out. We opened all the doors and shutters to breathe some fresh air, and we walked outside and marvelled at the calm and sunshine. The cloudless sky blazed blue and gold.

'Thank god,' I said. 'It's over.'

'No way,' said Suzy. 'This is just the eye of the storm. In an hour or two it'll all be back again.'

I couldn't believe it: the day was perfect, the air still, the sun blazing. The storm had evaporated miraculously, the birds were singing again, tree frogs croaking, insects jabbering in the bush.

How had they all survived? Why had such fragile creatures not been blown away a hundred miles across the ocean? Maybe they're tougher than we are. And Suzy was right: by the late afternoon the storm had returned, if anything more ferocious than before. For two more nights and another day we endured the awesome might of Nature, huddled, frightened, filthy, hungry, living in the dark like animals. The next time I find myself in the path of a hurricane I'm getting the hell out.

Early on the fourth day the wind and rain abated at last, the sun came out, and we emerged to survey the damage. The wreckage was devastating: trees uprooted, shrubs and flowers flattened, soil washed away, smashed planks and sheets of metal from other houses strewn across the garden, gutters ripped apart, Suzy's TV satellite dish straddling the rockery, the swimming pool deep with vegetation and a child's bicycle, the pool deck thick with soil and plants, rivers of water running everywhere. We drove into town to buy fresh food and water but the ten-minute journey took three hours. Trees lay across the main island road, parts of it had been completely washed away, water cascaded in powerful torrents down the ghauts, huge potholes had appeared, and cars lay smashed on their sides and roofs. Electricity and telephone poles and cables lay drunkenly across the road. Some houses had lost their roofs, doors and shutters, dozens of windows had been smashed, and one tiny old wood and corrugated iron chattel house had been reduced to a pile of rust and kindling. Its owner sat weeping outside. In Columbus many of the shops were smashed and the streets were filled with debris. People wandered dazed through the wreckage, rescuing occasional objects from the mess. In the central square a body lay dead, an emaciated middle-aged man, a ragged, wild-eyed tramp whom I had seen several times sprawled on the pavement in Main Street, shouting abuse and swearing at passers-by. Our quest for fresh food was hopeless: most of the shops were still closed and most of their shelves had in any case been cleared before the hurricane had arrived; but we did manage to buy bottled water at the Innocent Pure Spring Water Company, which had somehow miraculously escaped all damage.

It took several days for the full scale of the damage to be assessed and several more for the worst of the mess to be cleared up and repairs begun. The hurricane had moved up north along the chain of islands to devastate the Grenadines, St Lucia, Dominica, Guadeloupe and Antigua before heading back into the Atlantic and eventually wearing itself out somewhere east of the Bahamas. But then we heard that Peregrine Featherstonehaugh had died during the storm.

'Poor old Fanshaw,' I said. 'What a way to die.'

And Nikita Malenkov was missing after stupidly going up the mountain a day before the hurricane arrived and not giving himself enough time to get back before it broke.

Featherstonehaugh had apparently died of a heart attack while struggling to close a door that had burst open at his Sugarmill Estate. He had always expressed a wish to be buried at sea, so the ice-making factory just outside Columbus agreed to keep his corpse chilled for a couple of days while a coffin was built by Moses Liburd, the carpenter whose wife, Hyacinth, ran the funeral parlour in Galleon Street as well as a thriving little business that sold second-hand buttons, bows, lace and frills that were rumoured to have come from the funeral garments of her corpses.

'Why not?' said Suzy. 'The stiffs aren't going to want them again.'

Washington Dempster assembled a small posse to search the mountain for Malenkov. Baby Dempster gazed at her husband with adoration. 'Isn't Washington just *wunnerful*?' she quacked. 'So strong, so manly, so public spirited.'

'Such a prat,' said one of the younger English expats.

276

'It is incumbent upon us to exhibit compassion for our fellow human creatures,' droned Dempster in his rumbling voice, 'to offer succour to our fellows in their times of tribulation, even if the guy *is* a lousy commie.' The posse was led by a lean, rugged Rasta who was said to know the mountain so well that he could climb it in the dark, and it consisted of three of Dempster's American cronies, the young Englishman, two reluctant policemen, Smartly's only male reporter, and a warder and six convicts from the prison farm. Dempster also bullied Alex McDowall into joining them in case Malenkov needed medical attention when they found him, but Anna Litvinova seemed to be quite unconcerned about her lover's disappearance. 'My Nikita he know how he look after heself,' she announced.

Already I'd wasted five days of my three-week holiday but it would have been churlish to refuse to join the search party, so I bought a stout pair of boots, smothered myself in Kill-Em-All anti-mosquito spray, and trudged unwillingly up the jungly mountain with the others, leaving Suzy to start clearing up the mess at her house and expecting to find Malenkov's body sprawled beneath a cliff or at the bottom of some steep ravine. At first it was not such hard going. We tramped through scrubland and higher up the mountain discovered hidden plots of land that had been cleared to plant illegal marijuana, which the two policemen hacked down with their machetes. But then it became much more difficult. Much of the undergrowth in the rain forest was impenetrable and the rough paths were often too narrow for even two to walk abreast. The hurricane had brought down several trees which obstructed the paths, and long vines, which Dempster called monkey ropes, trailed from the roof of the jungle and clutched at us as we passed. Thank god Innocent has no snakes, but high up the mountain there are colonies of scorpions and battalions of poisonous centipedes and spiders. We peered cautiously into caves, nervously skirted sudden holes in the ground, scrutinised the depths of dark ravines, and I carried a thick stick to beat back some of the vegetation. But we made slow progress. Sweat poured off my forehead, stinging my eyes, and my chest and back were lakes of perspiration. Sharp branches and thorns scratched my arms and legs and giant mosquitoes cruised the humid air, ignoring the Kill-Em-All and savaging everyone except the Rasta, who seemed to be inexplicably immune. Maybe it was the ganja flooding through his bloodstream that deterred the mozzies. Twice we found ourselves suddenly on the edge of a steep precipice, and at one stage the path became an alarmingly narrow, rocky ledge no more than a foot wide, perched above a thousand terrifying feet of space. What on earth had Malenkov been thinking of, to come up here alone, without a guide, without any food or water, just before the arrival of a hurricane? It was sheer madness. No wonder he'd gone missing. He *deserved* to go missing. And if he wasn't dead by now he was probably seriously dehydrated after five days on the mountainside.

I gave up the search after a day. Dempster berated me for backing out but I'd wasted nearly a week by now and I was determined to find Shermelle before I had to fly back to London.

'He's dead,' I said.

'We don't know that,' rumbled Dempster.

'After a week lost in this jungle? Of course he's dead, and I've got better things to do than to waste my life looking for a bloody stupid Russian.'

'That's typical of you Brits,' he sneered. 'No stamina. No backbone. No wonder you needed us to win all your wars for you.'

'You never won any of our wars,' I said. 'According to your precious Hollywood they were won by an Australian, Errol Flynn; an Englishman, David Niven; a Welshman, Stanley Baker; and an Irishman, Richard Harris. The only wars you ever won were against primitive Red Indians armed with bows and arrows.'

'I'll thank you to call them Native Americans,' he growled.

'That's shamefully racist,' I said. 'We don't call anyone *natives* any more: you might as well call them niggers.'

I did enjoy baiting Washington Dempster.

I spent a day helping Suzy to clean up the mess in her garden and two days talking to everyone who might know where Shermelle might be: the head of the customs department, her colleagues, parents, friends, relatives, neighbours, bank manager, pretending that I wanted to offer her a highly paid job in England, but without any luck. Even her parents, a charming, worried couple, said they'd heard nothing from her. I came to believe that the only person who knew her whereabouts was Suzy. One night we both drank too much and had a furious row about it. I called her a lying bitch, she called me a whingeing aarsehole, and in the morning I packed my case and moved to a cheap, decidedly seedy boarding house on the outskirts of Columbus.

'Don't be so childish,' said Suzy. 'Come on, Dave. Accept it. She doesn't want you to know where she is.'

'Who says?'

'She does.'

'You've spoken to her?'

She nodded.

'Recently?'

'Yesterday.'

'So tell me where she is.'

'I *caan't*. I promised her. I'd tell you if I could.'

'I don't believe you. She loves me.'

'I caan't imagine why.'

'You really are a devious, lying bitch.'

Her eyes blazed. 'OK, you wanker,' she said. 'That does it. I'll tell you why she doesn't want you sniffing around her, whimpering after her like some lovesick adolescent. She's living with another guy. OK? She's fucking someone else. *That's* why she doesn't want you any more. *She's fucking someone else!* And he's young and fit and bloody good looking, and stinking rich – and he's *black*. Why would she want to come back to a middle-aged loser like you?'

Something broke inside me, then. Shermelle with another man? Living with my darling, sleeping with her, making love with her, time and time again?

'Loser!' said Suzy, 'No wonder she doesn't want you any more.'

# CHAPTER 17

# A BURIAL AT SEA

Peregrine Featherstonehaugh's burial at sea took place at Hangman's Cove that afternoon. To try to take my mind off what the Australian bitch had said I joined a crowd of locals and a handful of tourists to watch the funeral on the beach near the Columbus jetty, where the hurricane had hurled ashore a thick tidemark of flotsam, jetsam, stones, and other dreck that it had dredged up from some distant ocean floor. It had also felled a dozen palm trees, tossing them across the sand to expose their tight, absurdly small roots.

The priest was the small, bald Rev Henry Stapleton, the fire-and-brimstone 'back up de chat' preacher who ran the Bethlehem Word of the Lord Tabernacle on the other side of the island. He was dressed in a flowing, colourful African robe and a neat little embroidered cap. I was surprised to see that Featherstonehaugh was being despatched to his watery grave in a beautiful, polished mahogany coffin with bright brass handles: it seems that no one in Innocent had ever been buried at sea and no one knew that the correct procedure is to sew the corpse into a weighted canvas bag.

It was still stiflingly hot but the sea had already recovered from the hurricane and the huge waves of a couple of days ago had calmed to a gentle swell. The coffin was perched in the bow of a small rowing boat that was somewhat irreligiously called PUSSY GALORE and lay alarmingly low in the water at an angle of thirty degrees. It carried the priest, the boatman, the corpse, and the undertaker, Hyacinth Liburd, a tiny, ancient, bony black woman who looked just like Popeye's spindly, bandy-legged, cartoon girlfriend Olive Oyl. She was dressed as if for a Buckingham Palace garden party: fancy straw hat decorated with little false rosebuds, flimsy veil, short pink cocktail dress, red high-heeled shoes. There was no sign of the grieving widow, Venetia Featherstonehaugh, who was still under restraint at her Rest Home for the Bewildered in Barbados, and only three whites had bothered to turn up – a sad indication of the affection that the Featherstonehaughs had failed to arouse in the expat community despite living on the island for several decades. The crowd wore a festive air, and laughter and calypso rhythms drifted across the bay. At the far end of the beach an enterprising caterer was selling hot dogs and hamburgers.

The Rev Stapleton stood unsteadily in the stern of the rowing boat and nearly fell overboard. The crowd cheered. He raised both hands high, calling in vain for silence, chanted a couple of long-winded prayers, and delivered a terrifying ten-minute sermon about the wages of sin that was punctuated regularly by cries from the congregation of 'Yes, Lord!', 'Hallelujah!' and 'Dat right!' Now and then he would slip in an advertisement for a local shop or business. He recommended the fine workmanship of Moses Liburd, who'd made the coffin, and praised the quality of its brass handles: 'ask Moses to build your own chariot to take you to Heaven and pay in easy instalments'. He lauded Olive Oyl's skill at prettifying a corpse ('your loved one might just as well be asleep') and the excellent value of her recycled buttons, ribbons and bows ('only one previous owner'). He enthused about Thrifty car hire ('Jesus urged us to be thrifty'), Columbus Dairies' ice-cream ('six heavenly flavours') and Carib Airlines' flights to Barbados ('they carry you closer to God'). This blatant marriage of God and Mammon, for which I discovered later he was paid handsome retainers, was refreshingly honest, an alfresco substitute for the collection plate during a church service. The crowd soon became as restless as a TV audience subjected to an endless stream of commercials, but it perked up when Stapleton jabbed a sharp finger at the coffin and denounced its contents as having been an outrageous lifelong sinner who was undoubtedly destined for the fires of Hell.

'Dat right!'

'Sure t'ing!'

''e gonna burn, oh yes!'

A joker in the crowd chortled. ''e not gonna burn too good, Reverend, if you be soakin' 'im in de ocean!'

'Shame on you!'

'Blasphemer!'

'Shut up you mouf!'

A strong whiff of grilled meat wafted from the barbecue.

'De Devil am cookin' 'im already!' cackled the wag.

The Rev Stapleton ranted on for another ten minutes about the frightening punishments in store for unrepentant liars, cheats, frauds and godless fornicators such as Peregrine Featherstonehaugh, who he claimed had been a notorious satyr, adulterer and philanderer who had once taken his startled wife from behind as she knelt unsuspectingly in a flower bed. Poor old Venetia Featherstonehaugh: perhaps she'd been driven doolally by her husband's incessant sexual demands, many (according to the reverend gent) of a dubious nature.

Eventually the Rev Stapleton raised his hands to heaven, made an extravagant sign of the cross, and gestured at the boatman, who began to row out to sea so suddenly that Olive Oyl sprawled face down across the coffin with her hat askew and pink knickers on display. The boatman struggled to row against the tide with a heavy coffin on board but after fifteen minutes, by which time the nautical hearse was no more than thirty yards from the shore, he shook his head hopelessly at the priest and dropped anchor. Their voices carried across the sea as they argued over where they should dump the coffin.

'We are too close to the beach, Hezekiah,' said the Reverend.

'Me cumpletely shagged,' protested the boatman.

'But I am paying you twenty-five dollars! U.S.!'

'You can stick you twenny-five dollar!'

The crowd cheered.

'We droppin' de old honky here,' said Hezekiah.

'But it is only six feet deep.'

'Dat just right, den: 'e gonna be six feets under, just like all de rest o' de stiffs in de cementary.'

'But…'

'We droppin' de old honky here!'

He shipped his oars and joined Olive Oyl in the bows, where they performed a gawky dance as the boat rocked and they struggled to push the coffin over the side.

'Oh Lord!' warbled Stapleton, gazing piously at the sky. 'In Thy Great Wisdom and Boundless Mercy accept, we beseech Thee, this our Humble, Worthless Offering, and receive into Thy Gracious and Bounteous Care this filthy old sinner Pair-o-green Feed-a-stone-hog here present. Notwithstanding, O Lord, that should the said foul sinner be totally unacceptable in Thy Sight then just chuck him down below into the furnace to be scourged by Satan and his Torments Eternal.'

'Ay-men!' bellowed the congregation.

'Ashes to ashes, dust to dust, semen to seawater,' chanted Stapleton.

The crowd groaned.

'Mercy!'

'Spare us, Lord!'

'Thus we commit the mortal remains of Pair-o-green Feed-a-stone-hog to the vasty deep,' intoned Stapleton, 'to be consumed by the denizens of the ocean, the whale and the shark, the barracuda and the dolphin, the wahoo and the mahi-mahi, just as the said Pair-o-green Feet-a-stone-hog often sampled the wahoo and mahi-mahi with French fries, salad and garlic mayonnaise like they serve at the two-star Blue Galleon restaurant in Prince William Street. *Justice is mine*, saith the Lord. *I shall not be mocked.*'

'Ay-men,' bellowed the congregation.

'Get un wid it, maan!' growled Hezekiah. 'We nut gut ull day.'

'OK,' said Stapleton. 'Drop the dead honky.'

Grunting and cursing, Hezekiah and Olive Oyl slid the coffin over the side. It landed with an impressive splash, drenching Olive Oyl, saturating the rosebuds on her straw hat, and rocking the boat so violently that she lost her balance again and Hezekiah had to grab her bony elbow to stop her falling overboard.

'Dey doin' de waltz!' cried the joker in the crowd.

'Dat de quickstep!'

'Never! It de foxtrot!'

'Dey jivin'!'

'For man that is born of woman hath but a short time to live,' warbled Stapleton, 'and then is snuffed out as quick as the perfume candles that you can buy cheap at the Cost-Me-Less Calypso Superette for just two dollar each or ten dollar for six in this week's special offer.'

An expectant silence crept along the shore as the crowd and the funeral party watched the coffin settle in the water. It bobbed on the surface, caressed by gentle wavelets, the polished mahogany lid glistening with water, the brass handles glinting cheerfully in the afternoon sun, and then it started to float gently back towards the beach.

'Oh, *Jesus*!' cried Stapleton.

'Yea, Jesus!' bellowed the crowd.

A couple of hundred people gazed at the runaway coffin as it headed for the shore.

'It not sinkin'!'

'It floatin'!'

'De coffin am comin' back!'

'De *body* am comin' back!'

'Back from de dead!'

'Risin' again!'

'De resurrection!'

'Praise de Lard!'

'Glory!'

'Hallelujah!'

The boatman rowed urgently back towards the shore in pursuit of the coffin, which beached itself daintily on the sand. Some of the onlookers shrank back but a couple of bold youths grabbed the handles and hauled the coffin onto the shore, breaking two of the handles, which snapped like twigs.

'So much for de quality of Mr Liburd's cuffins!' chortled the joker.

The funeral party splashed ashore, Hezekiah dragging the boat up the beach, Olive Oyl soaked and squeaking, the Rev Stapleton damp in his nether regions.

'De Reverend done wet 'eself!' hooted the joker.

'Moses!' cried Stapleton. 'Moses! Where's Moses?'

''e comin' down de mountain,' cackled the joker, 'wid de Ten Commandment.'

The carpenter stepped forward, a bent, gnarled old fellow as massive as his wife was minuscule. 'Moses Liburd present an' correct,' he boomed.

'Thank God!' said Stapleton.

'Ay-men!' chorused the crowd.

'Moses: you'll have to make some holes in the bottom of the coffin,' said Stapleton. 'Otherwise it won't sink.'

'Dat de finest mahogany in de world,' protested Moses. 'De

best.'

'That's the problem: it floats too well. You got a drill?'

'Not here. Back in de workshop.'

'Ah, *shit*!' said the priest.

The crowd hollered.

'Wash you mouf out, you darty ol' priest!' cried a woman.

'We got to get it back to de workshop,' said Moses.

'Jesus was a carpenter,' said the joker, 'but de handles on *he* cuffins did not break.'

Moses said something violent in an incomprehensible dialect that sounded nothing like English. The crowd roared. He rounded up six volunteers to lift the coffin and carry it back along the beach to his big, ramshackle old jeep, where it was joined in the boot by Olive Oyl and driven a hundred yards to the premises of Moses Isaac Liburd Symphonies in Wood (1972) Ltd.

A small crowd followed, excited at the prospect of glimpsing the corpse when the coffin lid was unscrewed. I joined them reluctantly, unenthusiastic about seeing poor old Fanshaw again. Moses raised the lid, Stapleton muttered an incantation, and the spectators jostled at the door of the workshop and gasped when the lid of the coffin was raised because the corpse suddenly sat up and farted. The late Peregrine Featherstonehaugh was wearing rouge, lipstick, mascara, a garish red and green Caribbean shirt, and an expression of surprise.

The spectators fell back in alarm.

'Holy Jesus!' cried Stapleton, turning as pale as his dark skin would allow.

'Jesus!'

'Jesus!'

'Oh my Lord!'

''e be resurrect!'

'De Second Comin'!'

'Praise de Lard!'

'A miracle!'

'Don't be pig ignorant,' snapped Moses. 'Dat breakin' wind was only de gas in de body. It make he sit up.'

'Dat happen all de time,' squeaked Olive Oyl, nodding wisely, 'because of de heat.'

I tried to imagine her wrestling regularly with huge, farting, jack-in-the-box corpses and trying to pin them down while she applied the makeup and struggled to make them look serene.

Moses plugged his electric drill into a power point, chose the largest drill-bit that he could find, and elbowed the sitting corpse so that it slumped forward with its head between its knees in the recommended Carib Airlines '*brace! brace!*' position. Poor old Fanshaw: the indignity of it all. Liburd began to drill into the bottom of the coffin. The tough mahogany resisted valiantly and it took him at least five minutes to drill the first hole, constantly nudging the corpse forward to discourage it from flopping back on top of him. After watching for several minutes I realised it was going to be a long job and drifted back to the beach, where I bumped into Miz Quaintance. She seemed bigger than ever, wearing what appeared to be a striped blue-and-white circus tent, a stylish yellow turban and scuffed old hiking boots.

'Lard David!' she shrieked, folding me in her massive arms in a crippling embrace, crushing me to her massive bosom and kissing me wetly on both cheeks. The rich smell of her perfume almost knocked me over. 'You Lardship! Me not seed you for mumfs an' mumfs an' mumfs! When you done return?'

'A few days ago,' I gasped.

'Why you not tellin' me you comin'?'

'Well, I…'

'By where you stayin'?'

'Nickeisha's Guest House.'

'What? Dat shit-hole? Never! Nut you! Dat shit-hole not good for fine gen'leman like You' Lardship. You come stay by 'umminbird 'ouse again.'

'Well, I…'

'You come by dere dis very day. Me got no guests. De tourists no come in September, so de 'ouse am empty.'

'Well, I…'

'No problem.'

'To be honest, Miz Quaintance…'

'Dat always de best policy.'

'… I'm afraid I really can't afford to pay the rent at Hummingbird House. It's a bit too expensive.'

She made an indecent sound with her lips. 'Bugger de rent,' she said. 'What rent? Me not charge you rent: you stay for free.'

'Oh, I couldn't do that.'

'Why not?'

'Well, what about the landlord?'

She made another rude noise. ''im? Dat skinflint? We don't bother 'bout 'im. Me not tell 'im, 'e never know. Anyways, 'e be off-island: 'e gone Trinidad, not back for two mumf.'

Her offer was tempting. Extremely tempting. The guesthouse was decidedly basic and uncomfortable, it had no garden or swimming pool, and I still had nearly two weeks of my holiday to go. It was *seriously* tempting: Hummingbird House had been a delight. Would it be wrong to stay there without the landlord's permission? Or even illegal? Yes, probably: I'd be no better than a squatter. But what the hell? Bollocks to the landlord.

'Well, that's really kind of you,' I said. 'I'd love to come.'

She was delighted. 'Excellent!' she said. 'You come dis evenin'. Me go now prepare an' buy food for you supper.'

'Please don't go to too much trouble.'

'Is not trouble at all, You Lardship, but mayhap you be givin' me some money for buyin' you food.'

'Of course. Would fifty US be enough?'

'Dat plenty.'

I handed her the cash and she tucked the notes between her vast breasts. When she came to spend them in the supermarket the check-out girl would probably keel over with the scent.

'What time you come dis evenin'?'

'As soon as the funeral is over, if that's OK. But don't you want to see the end of it too?'

She grimaced. 'Nah,' she said. ''e been a dirty ol' bugger, dat Fatter-stun-hag. 'e always been after de black girls. When me been young an' purty 'e done try lots o' times puttin' 'e big stick in me front bottom. 'e like puttin' 'e big stick in de black girls' bottoms, but me never permit 'im, not me.'

So Stapleton was right: the late lamented Peregrine had indeed enjoyed an insatiable taste for the local girls. You would never have guessed it: he'd looked like a dessicated old tosser. Perhaps that was the real reason he'd come to Innocent in the first place, for the free and easy chocolate totty. Obviously not all Old Etonians were poofs.

'You can't really blame him,' I lied. 'I'm sure you were very beautiful. You must have been very difficult to resist.'

I never realised that black people can blush.

'You just foolin',' she said coyly.

'Not at all.'

'I go now.'

'Fine. See you later.'

She wobbled off the beach and into town. What a result: Hummingbird House again; a lovely house for two weeks, a pool, a comfortable bed and her delicious dinners. And maybe she could help me find Shermelle. Oh God: Shermelle; with another man.

I tried to bury my misery again by returning to Moses Liburd's workshop to gawp at poor old Fanshaw. It was like an oven in the shop and most of the crowd had drifted away, bored by the lack of excitement despite the novel sight of a painted corpse bobbing up and down like a Japanese geisha. By now Liburd had drilled about ten holes in the bottom of the coffin and sweat was dripping from him. He stepped back, exhausted.

'I t'ink dat maybe sufficient,' he said.

Olive Oyl pushed Peregrine Featherstonehaugh less than reverently onto his back. His head bounced and a pair of discoloured false teeth shot out of his mouth. Olive Oyl scrabbled in the coffin, retrieved the teeth and slipped them into her pocket, no doubt to sell them in her second-hand shop ('only one careful owner'). Fanshaw looked thoroughly fed up, Moses replaced the broken handles, screwed the lid back on again, the Rev Stapleton mumbled a hurried prayer, and six volunteers hefted the coffin into the back of the jeep.

Word of the afternoon's events had spread quickly through Columbus, and back at Hangman's Cove the crowd on the beach had swollen to several hundred. The hot dog vendor had been joined by an ice-cream van that was playing over and over again a tinkly version of *How Much is That Doggie in the Window, the One With the Waggly Tail?* A stall had been set up nearby to sell beers, soft drinks 'an' somet'in' for de brain,' and a saucy young Guyanese woman wearing a tight tee-shirt and a tiny skirt had pitched a small tent further along the beach and was offering 'Authentic Ethnic Massages' for fifty dollars a go. The crowd cheered loudly when the cortège reappeared and the coffin was carried to the edge of the sea and loaded again into PUSSY GALORE, which now seemed to have a highly appropriate name, considering the corpse's reputation as an insatiable shagger. The priest and Olive Oyl clambered aboard again and Hezekiah called for a strong volunteer to help him row the boat out into deeper water. 'Me needin' a strong, voluntary parson for 'elpin' take de boat more farther to put dis ol' honky feller in de sea,' he cried.

Girls giggled, poked their boyfriends in their reluctant ribs, and called out their names until a tall young giant stepped forward. 'Me voluntary,' he said.

The crowd whooped.

'Cialis!' said the boatman happily.

''tis me,' said the giant.

'You good feller.'

'OK.'

I nudged a guy who was standing beside me. 'He's called *Cialis*?'

'Dat so.'

'*Really*?'

'On me life.'

'That's his street name?'

'Not so. He street name be Heart Attack. Cialis he real name. Cialis Pilkin'ton.'

'Amazing! Why Cialis?'

The fellow grinned. 'He daddy was an old guy what had to swallow lots o' de pills before he could get him born.'

The giant clambered into the boat, making it lurch violently. Olive Oyl clutched the coffin. Cialis grabbed one of the oars, and he and Hezekiah sat side by side and began to row towards the horizon.

'Praise the Lord!' cried Stapleton.

'Praise Cialis!' said Hezekiah.

Cialis grinned. 'Dat just what me Daddy say.'

When they reached a spot about a hundred yards from the shore Hezekiah dropped anchor and he and Cialis prepared to consign the coffin to the deep.

The Rev Stapleton raised his voice so that he could be heard by the crowd on the beach. 'O Lord of Hosts!' he cried. 'O God of our Fathers!'

'Get on wid it!' growled Hezekiah. 'We done all dat religion stuff.'

He and Cialis tipped the coffin into the sea. A cheer went up on the shore.

'O God, who knoweth all things,' chanted Stapleton. 'Pray, we beseech Thee…'

The coffin floated serenely on the surface of the sea. It seemed to smile at them.

'It goin' down soon soon,' squeaked Olive Oyl.

It did not go down soon. For more than ten minutes the coffin bobbed on the surface. The crowd grew restless. 'Push 'im under!' cried one.

''e don' wanna go down!'

''Cos he goin' to Hell, dat why.'

Hezekiah docked the boat beside the coffin. Olive Oyl removed her high heels and nudged the coffin with her bony feet, her scrawny legs flailing in the air. The coffin teased her, dancing away from the boat and chuckling playfully in the water. Hezekiah docked against it again and Cialis jumped onto it, bobbing away from the boat as he rode it like a rocking horse.

'*Fuck*!' said the priest.

The crowd hollered.

'Dat word wicked!' said Cialis. He began to bounce up and down on the coffin, as if he were competing in a rodeo, to try to make it sink. The coffin floated on serenely.

'Dem 'oles not big enough,' said Hezekiah.

'Oh, God!' said Stapleton.

Hezekiah grunted. ''e not gonna 'elp you, Reverend. Met'inks de Good Lard don' want de ol' honky after all! Met'inks dat Jesus don' want 'im for a sunbeam.'

They towed the coffin back to the shore. Hezekiah called for a machete. A small Rasta produced a large axe. Ten men turned the coffin over and I could imagine poor old Peregrine Featherstonehaugh's toothless face smashing into the underside of the lid. At Eton, had he thought of death at all, he'd probably imagined that one day, after a long, distinguished career, he'd have a dignified state funeral at Westminster Abbey, not *this*. Cialis set about the bottom of the coffin with the axe, splintering the wood in several places, and sent half a dozen volunteers alone the shore to find some heavy boulders. The coffin was turned face-up again and Moses unscrewed the lid, exposing the corpse to public view again and releasing a dreadful stench. Fanshaw's nose appeared to be broken. He looked thoroughly pissed off. The boulders were dropped heavily into the coffin, one of them smashing his left kneecap with a loud crunch. Poor old Peregrine: no one deserved to end up like this, not even an Old Etonian.

Moses screwed the lid on again, the coffin was loaded back onto the PUSSY GALORE, Cialis and Hezekiah rowed it out into deep water, the Rev Stapleton mumbled a quick prayer, and they pushed the coffin overboard. For a dreadful minute it looked as if the coffin still refused to sink, but suddenly it gurgled, belched, and disappeared beneath the waves. Third time lucky.

The crowd whooped.

'Dust to dust, ashes to ashes,' intoned the Rev Stapleton.

'Ah, shut up you mouf, you ol' jackanapes,' said Hezekiah.

# CHAPTER 18

# TWO BACK FROM THE DEAD

I rented a cheap soft-top jeep from Thrifty and moved into Hummingbird House that afternoon. It was a joy to be back. The hurricane had brought down a couple of trees beside the driveway and a part of the corrugated iron garage roof had been hurled against the garden fence, but the yellow bungalow still smiled in the twilight and its garden was as lush as ever, bright green splashed with red and orange flamboyants, pink and crimson frangipani, the swimming pool glinting a blue and gold reflection of the sunset, hummingbirds shimmering iridescent as they sipped at the flowers. The old gardener hobbled towards the jeep, snapped to attention, and gave me a wobbly salute.

'Good morrow, gentle sir,' he said. 'Forsooth, 'tis verily an honour to welcome you hither betimes and privily.'

'Hello, Grandad. It's good to be back. How are you? Keeping well?'

He smiled wanly. 'Forsooth, my master, methinks 'twould be churlish folly to rail against the frailties of mine three score years and twelve.'

'I saw you playing in the carnival procession last week.' I said. 'I never realised that you're a musician. You played beautifully.'

He smiled shyly. 'Prithee, noble sir, thou art most kind, but mine is but a poor talent learned at my dam's knee, though it hath in truth vouchsafed me sundry pleasures these many years.'

Despite his age he insisted on carrying my suitcase.

'No, really,' I protested. 'Please. I can manage,' but he brushed me aside and staggered towards the house with it.

Miz Quaintance emerged onto the verandah, drying her hands. 'Goodnight, Lard David!' she bellowed.

'It's great to be back.'

I thanked Grandad and carried the suitcase into the bedroom, pulled on my swimming trunks and dived into the pool, relishing the cool caress of fresh water after the heat of the day. I was back again: home; and for one giddy moment I wondered how much it would cost to buy a small house like this, and what it would take to find Shermelle and persuade her to share it with me for the rest of my life.

Afterwards, as I sat on the verandah and sank a large, icy vodka and tonic, Miz Quaintance emerged from the house with my stolen laptop. She handed it to me. 'You computer,' she said.

'Miz Quaintance! Where did you find that?'

She smirked. ''e done come back all by 'eself. Not long after you gone off-island 'e done come back.'

'Really?'

'Sure t'ing. Me telled you dat you computer be comin' back all by 'eself.'

I shivered. Could it really be possible? Windy Billington and his chauffeur, both struck down by this simple, mountainous woman and a slaughtered chicken?

'I can't believe it,' I said. 'You're a marvel. Thank you so much.'

She smiled benignly. 'No problem. Nobody mess wit' me.'

I could well believe it. I took the laptop into the second bedroom, switched it on, and checked my files. They all seemed to be there, but why had Billington stolen it? What had he been looking for? Evidence that I was not who I'd pretended to be?

Miz Quaintance served a delicious dish of 'goat-water', a rich, spicy, marinated stew that justified at last the existence of all the dozy, bleating beasts that ambled gormlessly along every road on the island. I opened a bottle of Argentine red, enjoyed a wickedly creamy banana dessert that she'd made, and she even insisted on doing the washing up before she left.

'You're a marvel, Miz Quaintance,' I said. 'Thank you so much.'

'No problem,' she said. 'Is me job. Me you arse-keeper.'

'And a fantastic arse-keeper you are, too.'

After she'd gone I tried to forget Shermelle and Billington briefly by watching the TV news on BBC World but it was as dreary as ever. I put the TV out of its misery and spent an hour listening to my iPod and puzzling over the mystery of Windy Billington and Shermelle's disappearance. Could she really be living with another man? Could she really have forgotten me so soon?

I felt nervous and jumpy that night and double-locked all the doors, but still I slept badly and wrestled with unpleasant dreams. The sounds of the night seemed louder than ever and unusually unfriendly: the sinister whistling and croaking of frogs, the threatening mutter of insects, the ominous braying of a distant donkey, the sudden alarming crack of the roof as it cooled. I tossed and turned and stared for hours into the darkness, imagining shapes, and twice I twitched suddenly out of a doze with my heart pounding. The luminous clock beside the bed seemed to move from minute to minute with agonising slowness, and as soon as the dawn began to finger the eastern sky just before six o'clock I could stand it no longer, got up, made a mug of tea, dived into the pool and washed my unhappiness away. Where the hell was Shermelle?

I asked Miz Quaintance about her when she arrived for work.

'Shermelle Donal'son? De girl what work in de customs at de airport?'

'Yes.'

'You sweet on her?'

'Ah… well, yes.'

She wagged a chunky forefinger at me. 'Dat not good, You Lardship. Smart English wristy-cat gen'lemans like you should not be sexin' no black girl like dat, no sah. She got de Hiv.'

'Hiv?'

'De Aids.'

So the rumour had reached her, too. I was angry. 'That's not true!'

'Yus. Dat de troof.'

'No! I *know* it's untrue. She did have an Aids test but it was negative.'

She screwed up her face. 'Pooh! Dey doctors don' know nuttin'. Me brung you two nice, clean girls wid nice big tops an' nice big bottoms but you not want nuttin' to do wid dem. No, sir: you want to be sexin' dorty girl wid de Hiv instead.'

'SHE HAS NOT GOT AIDS!' I said. I hesitated. 'And I love her,' I said defiantly.

She laughed, incredulous. '*Love*, You Lardship? *Love*? Mercy, maan! What dis "love"? You jus' like fuckin' her, dat all.'

My face was tight. 'No, Miz Quaintance, that's not all. I want to be with her all the time. I want to care for her, look after her. I want to live with her. I want to marry her.'

I thought her eyes would explode. '*Marry* her? Lard save us! You want *marry* some no-good nigger girl jus' 'cos she got nice quim? You gonna 'ave liddle brown childrens wid her, den, yes, dat it?'

'Yes, if that's what she wants.'

She looked appalled. 'You gone *mad*, Lard David. You needs you 'ead examine. Smart Englishmens like you must 'ave *white* chillens wid white wifes, not brown chillens wid dorty nigger girls. Lardy me, maan, de t'ings you stupid mens t'ink when you finds a nice bottom. You brain drop straight down into you big stick.'

'Shut your gob!' I said.

She was so surprised by my rudeness that she was stunned into silence and eventually agreed reluctantly to phone a few of her friends to see if anyone might know where Shermelle might be.

I drove into town and found Smartly alone in his office, trapped at his desk behind piles of paper, reports and photographs.

'Busy?' I said.

'Dreadfully.' He waved me to sit down opposite him. 'We're producing a special issue of the paper to preview the CARICOM conference here next week.'

'CARICOM?'

'Caribbean community. Most of the West Indian Prime Ministers are coming to Columbus on Monday for three days for one of their regular regional meetings. It gives them a chance to get away from their wives.'

'In that case I won't keep you, but...'

He looked at his watch and stood up. 'To hell with it,' he said. 'I've got time for a quick lunch at Sweetman's. Let's go.'

Sweetman's beach bar was deserted and had been badly damaged by the hurricane. The main bar area had been battered, uprooted trees and piles of debris lay scattered around the site, and the little thatched umbrellas shading the tables had been blown away. Sweetman emerged from the kitchen looking weary. 'It ain't possible to give you a proper lunch,' he said. 'The hurricane mashed me up proper. But I can give you a hot dog or hamburger and I got plenty o' rum an' beer.'

'What bad luck,' said Smartly. 'How's your house?'

Sweetman chuckled. 'That's fine,' he said. 'I made a heavy swing, tied it to the rafters, and when the hurricane came Mutryce sat on the swing for three days and stopped the roof from blowin' away. Yes, sir! Mutryce's one hell of a big girl. She weigh three hundred pound. No itsy-bitsy hurricane gonna blow Mutryce away.'

'Brilliant!' said Smartly.

Sweetman grinned and went to fetch us a couple of beers.

'I need to get into Angela Fellowes's house while she's away in England,' I said. 'I'm convinced she's up to no good. Can you still get me a key from her maid?'

'Sure.'

'That'd be great.'

By now the heat was stifling, the glare off the sea unmerciful, the horizon veiled by an impenetrable haze. We sat on the open verandah under one of Sweetman's ceiling fans, which succeeded in moving a patch of hot air from one end of the verandah to the other and then back again. We ordered two more beers and a couple of hot dogs and I asked Smartly about the CARICOM conference.

'Shouldn't your father be here to welcome them? Instead he's in Japan?'

Smartly shrugged. 'Of course he should, but he loathes these conferences. He says most of the Caribbean Prime Ministers are a bunch of wankers, and he's told Shefton Molloy to chair the meetings.'

'That sounds risky. Does he trust him?'

'Of course not, but then he doesn't trust anyone. By the way, I've just heard that they've found Malenkov: the idiot who went missing on the mountain.'

'Dead?'

'Not at all. He's fine. Not a scratch.'

'After nearly a *week*?'

'Amazing, isn't it? A Rasta was riding his donkey up the mountain yesterday afternoon and he found Malenkov sauntering down the road as though he was returning from a gentle stroll. Malenkov told the cops that he'd fallen into a deep hole on the mountain and that he'd survived all through the hurricane by drinking rainwater and his own urine.'

'He survived a *hurricane* for several days *sitting in a hole*?'

'That's his story.'

'Drinking *piss*? I don't believe it for one minute.'

'Neither do I.'

'So how does he say he got out of this hole?'

'He says that eventually he climbed out by clinging onto roots and hauling himself to the top.'

'What bullshit!'

'Yes, but I'd like to know what else was he doing for all that time if he wasn't on the mountain.'

'Maybe you should buy up his story for the *Gazette*.'

'Hey, that's not a bad idea at all. Ever thought of becoming a journalist?'

'Sod off, Smartly! But I wouldn't put anything past those two. They're seriously sinister. Maybe Malenkov wasn't even in Innocent at all during the hurricane. Maybe he's a KGB hitman and flew secretly off-island to kill one of Putin's enemies.'

Smartly nodded. 'That's not impossible. A lot of Russian expats and crooks have recently been buying land in the Caribbean. Maybe one of them was on the run from Putin.' He grinned. 'Or maybe Malenkov was just screwing some other woman, got caught in the hurricane, couldn't get home, and had to come up with some excuse for his wife.'

We chatted on for half an hour until Smartly announced that he really ought to be getting back to work. As we left Sweetman's bar I glanced out to sea and spotted some way out a large piece of driftwood floating towards the beach.

'More hurricane damage,' I said.

We both squinted at it, shading our eyes with our hands.

'It's a pretty big piece of driftwood,' said Smartly.

I stared at it again, trying to focus against the glare. 'It's dark, polished wood.'

We squinted at it again. 'Somebody's dining table?' he said, 'or maybe a bed headboard?'

We watched it for a couple of minutes as it approached the shore, bobbing gently on the waves, growing larger by the minute.

I stood up, staring out to sea, still shading my eyes with my hand. 'Bloody hell!' I said. 'It's not a piece of driftwood at all. It's Peregrine Fanshaw's coffin!'

We buried the poor old bugger hurriedly that evening, properly this time, in the ground, in the cemetery, where the hurricane had uprooted some trees and blown several headstones over. The funeral party was small: the Rev Henry Stapleton, Moses Liburd, Olive Oyl, a couple of gravediggers and me. We buried him beside the fancy grave with the wrought-iron railings, which was still decorated with the wrinkled little balloons and crimson ribbons that I'd first spotted there back in February, and the banner with pink hearts and the slogan that wished the dead of the neighbourhood a Very Happy Valentine's Day. Poor old Fanshaw, a flower of Eton, a pioneer of the late British Empire: that he should have ended up like this. I was glad to be there, if only as a small gesture of respect for a fellow Englishman. At least he deserved that. He deserved something.

# CHAPTER 19

## A NIGHT AT THE OLD MANOR

Miz Quaintance turned up for work in the morning sulking and reported belligerently that none of her friends had any idea where Shermelle might be. She refused to use her name, calling her 'she,' 'her' or 'dat girl', and she went about the housework in a sullen silence except for the banging of doors. To escape the sultry atmosphere I wandered into the garden, where Grandad snapped to attention as soon as he saw me and saluted like a boy scout, touching two fingers to the brim of his battered Paddington Bear hat.

'Morning, Grandad,' I said.

'Marnin', marnin', my master.'

'Were you ever in the Scouts?'

He grinned and saluted again. 'Dyb dyb dyb, dob dob dob.'

'You were!'

'In my tender years all youths of this blesséd isle owed obeisance unto Lord Booden-Pole and paid homage unto him.'

How times have changed: if Baden-Powell published his book *Scouting for Boys* today he'd be arrested for the title alone.

'Well, at least the hurricane didn't do too much damage, did it?' I said.

'We hath perchance been mighty fortunate. The Lord hath spared us.'

'The garden's looking very pretty. You do a wonderful job.'

303

His ancient face lit up and his tired old eyes glistened. 'Thank much, noble sire. Thou art most gracious in thy commendation,' and I wondered how often the owner of Hummingbird House bothered to thank him for his hard work.

'Tell me,' I said, 'what's that?' I pointed at a tree about forty feet high with long, shiny, oval leaves, drooping greeny-yellow flowers, and clusters of black fruit.

''Tis yclept ylang-ylang,' he said, 'and it bestoweth after nightfall a fragrance so beauteous that wenches come hither from far and wide to anoint themselves with its gracious odour.' He chuckled, wheezing. 'It hath also been rumoured abroad to strengthen men's members.'

'Does it work?'

He grinned. 'Forsooth, milord, I never had cause for it myself, but I hazard that it be sorely needed by the West Indies cricket team, a sorry crew of anti-men and pissabeds. In bygone times they bestrode the globe without pareil, smiting every enemy from Albion to Antipodes, surrendering to none. In those times mighty Carib warriors ruled the greensward – Worrell, Weeks and Walcott, Ramadhin and Valentine, Sobers and Richards – but their successors are become mere weaklings, capering fools and simpering knaves.'

I laughed at his passion. 'Hang on, Grandad. You've still got some great cricketers in these islands: Gayle, Chanderpaul, Bravo, Powell.'

He snorted. 'They hath their sundry merits, I do allow, but by compare with the giants of yore our current gladiators be-sport themselves as maidens do in petticoats, and poppinjays with crimson upon their cheeks and scarlet upon their lips. Gadzooks, master, they be too soft and cosseted and deem of value only gold and silver, wenches and swiving, above their duty, pride and honour. They have no *hunger*. A pox upon them all!'

I grinned, patted him on the shoulder, told him not to be too hard on the modern West Indies team, and left him to his plants and cricket memories.

I drove to Smartly's office and picked up the keys for Angela Fellowes' Old Manor House.

'The maid says the control for the security alarm is in a box on the right just inside the front door,' said Smartly. 'The code to deactivate it is 1, 7, 1, 8, and you have thirty seconds to punch it in before the alarm goes off. It's connected to the Hopetown police but they're hopeless...' He grinned. '... and notoriously lazy, and in any case they'd probably take half an hour to get there. Here: I've written it down.'

'1, 7, 1, 8,' I said. 'The date the house was built. Neat.'

'The year that the pirate Blackbeard was killed.'

I drove out beyond Hopetown to case the joint. There was no sign of the guard just inside the gates: his hutch was empty. I suppose some of Angela Fellowes' staff didn't bother to turn up for work when she was away. How would she know? *No problem, maan. Don' worry. Be happy.* The wrought-iron gates were protected by vicious spikes, a heavy padlock and a thick chain. I peered through the gates and up the gravel driveway between the long avenue of elegant Royal Palms and Victorian street lamps. Two of the palms had been felled by the hurricane and dragged to the side, onto the grass, leaving the driveway looking bereft. A couple of gardeners were working in the distance, one mowing a lawn, one weeding a flowerbed, and a distant strimmer whined like a mosquito on the far side of the lake. I could hardly break into the house while they were there. I'd have to return after dark.

I drove up into the hills to Aberdeen to question Shermelle's neighbours and I was startled just outside Jericho to pass three teenagers who yelled at me and threw stones at the jeep.

'Go home, honky!'

'Go back you own country!'

'We not want white parsons here!'

I was saddened and depressed. Until now I'd never encountered any racism here. What was happening to Innocent? Gangs, drugs, guns, knives, murders: the invisible snake slithering in paradise.

Nothing stirred in Aberdeen, in the silence of its ramshackle little wood and corrugated iron chattel houses. The hurricane had blown the roof off one of the shacks and had twisted the iron cross above the porch of the chapel, but the tiny settlement was so well sheltered by the looming forest that the houses were hardly damaged. The garden of Shermelle's little bungalow was shaggy and the hurricane had brought down two trees that had just missed smashing into her roof. The house looked lonely, its doors locked, its shutters bolted. Three small children aged five or six emerged from one of the shacks and stood a few yards away, staring at me: a pretty little girl with red ribbons in her plaited hair, another whose frizzy head was adorned with blue plastic hairgrips, a boy wearing shiny new green trainers and a solemn expression.

I smiled at them. 'Hello.'

If you say 'hello' to a child in England nowadays you'll be arrested on the spot but Innocent, thank God, is steeped still in a more innocent age.

The children gazed at me.

'My name's David,' I said. 'What's yours?'

They stared.

'Come on,' I said. 'I've told you my name, now you have to tell me yours. That's the rule. Fair swap.'

The boy bit his lip. 'Me Oriol,' he said in a shrill little voice. 'Her Zahvelisia, an' her Lyndeta.'

'Pretty names.'

He frowned. 'Me not pretty,' he piped. 'Me boy.'

'Of course you are.' I smiled, and nodded at the bungalow. 'Do you know the lady who lives here? Shermelle?'

They nodded.

'Does she still live here?'

They shook their heads.

'Do you know where she lives now?'

Zahvelisia looked coy. 'Her gone Barbados wid her sweetman,' she said, and they all giggled.

I felt a dull ache in my heart.

'Do you know where she is in Barbados?'

They shook their heads.

'Mebbe me granny know,' trilled the boy. 'You come talk me granny. Her very old.'

They led me towards the shack out of which they'd emerged. 'Granny!' yelled the boy. 'Me got white fellah want talk wid you.'

A remarkably attractive young woman, who looked as if she were little more than thirty, appeared at the door. How could she be a grandmother? She must have been pregnant at fourteen and probably was.

'Good morning,' I said.

'Marnin', marnin'.'

I shook her hand. It was rough from overwork. 'I'm David Barron, from London.'

Her eyes widened. 'London? Oh, Lordy!'

'I'm sorry to bother you, but…'

''e want Shermelle,' said the boy.

The woman smiled, as if to say 'join de queue, maan.'

'She gone Barbados wid her feller,' she said.

The children shrieked with laughter.

'She gotta sweetman!'

'He name be Stedroy!'

A pain twinged in my heart. Stedroy! How could she be living with a man called Stedroy?

'Do you know where she is?'

'No, maan,' said the woman. 'Sorry. She not done tell me nuttin'.'

'When did she leave?'

She thought about it. 'Mayhap four, five month.'

I looked at her hopelessly. Another blind alley.

'Thanks for your help,' I said. 'I'm sorry to bother you.'

'No bother.'

I fished three coins out of my pocket and gave the children a dollar each. The younger girl gazed at hers in wonder, turning it over slowly in her fingers.

'A dullar!' shrilled the boy. 'Look, granny, me gotta dullar!'

'An' what you say?'

'T'ank you.'

'T'ank you, sir.'

'T'ank much,' said the boy. 'Me gotta dullar!'

I bent down towards him in avuncular fashion. 'So what do you want to be when you grow up?' I said.

He looked me boldly in the eye. 'Retired,' he said.

The woman smiled at me. Her teeth were blindingly white. She was very pretty. There must be something special in the air at Aberdeen.


I left it until 10pm before I drove back to Hopetown and the Old Manor House, wearing dark clothes and rubber-soled Docksides, smothered with mosquito repellent, carrying a small holdall, a computer memory stick, a notebook, a couple of biros, a safebreaker's jemmy, and the torch that I'd bought for the hurricane. I had no idea what I was looking for but I guessed that somewhere in Angela Fellowes' files there must be evidence that she was dodging tax, committing fraud or worse.

The night was so calm that when I switched the engine off I could hear the Atlantic pounding against the shore three hundred feet below and almost a mile away, and the darkness was lit only by a million pinprick stars and the thin silver sliver of a hammock moon. I parked the jeep in a little clearing in the woods at the side of the road a hundred yards from the house and approached it quietly on foot. The security hut at the gates was shut and the street lamps along the driveway were dark. I stood by the gates and listened for a minute, straining to catch the slightest sound of voices, a generator, maybe music, but there was only the distant susurration of the ocean far down on the coast. I slid the smaller key into the padlock, opened it, and started to unwind the chain, which clanked against the gates. I heard a car approaching along the main island road and shrank into the shadows as it swept by, its windows wide open, its radio blaring some thunderous rap 'music' that shook the entire vehicle. When it had passed I unwrapped the chain, opened one of the gates, slipped into the driveway, rewound the chain, and locked the padlock behind me. As I walked up the drive my footsteps crunched so loudly on the gravel that I moved onto the grass beside it even though there was obviously no one around: it made sense not to take any risks by making a noise. The Royal Palms loomed above me, grey giants in the dark, and the old Victorian street lamps formed a rigid guard of honour, tall black ghosts, all the way up to the manor, a massive, brooding silhouette against the sky, where the moon glinted on the lake and reflections winked from the high windows. I stood motionless again and listened for a couple of minutes but the only sound was the slight breeze that ruffled the trees. Even the frogs and insects had fallen silent, as if they were watching me. The night seemed alive with a thousand eyes.

I crunched across the gravel apron in front of the house, mounted the steps to the broad terrace with its vast stone jars and cascading flowers, and used the big iron key to unlock the huge front door. It slid open smoothly without a sound. My heart started hammering as I stepped into the hall and closed the door quietly behind me. What was there to fear? The house was obviously empty and Angela Fellowes five thousand miles away in England. Moonlight gleamed on the old Spanish tiles. I switched the torch on and opened the alarm control box just to the right of the door. A red light was blinking and a small electronic screen was counting down the seconds: 21, 20, 19, 18. I shone the torch into the box, punched in the numbers 1718, the screen flickered CODE OK, and the winking red light turned a solid green. I began to walk across the hall towards the broad staircase to look for her office, which I knew was somewhere on the top floor.

'Bollocks!'

I jumped. Mother Teresa! I'd forgotten the bloody parrot! My heart was thundering. 'Jesus!' I said.

'Arsehole!' squawked the parrot.

I froze. If the parrot was here then so must be someone to feed and water it and clean its cage. Gascoigne, the butler? Was he somewhere in the house?

I stood still for two or three minutes, listening. The floorboards on the upper landing creaked and somewhere deep in the bowels of the house something was humming: a fridge, perhaps, or a freezer, or an air conditioning unit in the wine cellar. But otherwise the house was dark and silent. My heart began to slow down and I breathed deeply. I shone the torch onto the parrot's cage.

'Fuck off!' said Mother Teresa, her beady little eyes glittering in the torchlight.

I tiptoed across the hall, my rubber-soled shoes squeaking against the tiles, and started to mount the stairs. They creaked at every step. I ignored the first floor, which I knew consisted entirely of bedrooms and bathrooms, climbed to the second floor, and went from room to room flashing the torch into every doorway. Two of the rooms were furnished with massive four-poster beds, heavy dark-wood tables and chairs, thick carpets and curtains. They smelt of England – dusty, musty, claustrophobic – and they might have come from the long-forgotten wing of some stuffy, crumbling old stately home in the depths of the English countryside.

Her office was the last room on the right-hand side of the house.

I thought of drawing the curtains and turning the lights on but decided against it: some neighbour might spot the light and become suspicious if he knew that she was away. I looked out of one of the huge windows. The moonlight flickered on the lake, the trees dancing gently in the breeze. A mongoose darted across the lawn and in the shadows of the undergrowth some small creature screamed. I flashed the torch around the room: a big desk, up against the wall, a gigantic computer screen; a couple of squashy sofas; a filing cabinet; oil paintings on the wall, one of them an amazingly honest, unflattering likeness of Angela Fellowes herself. The filing cabinet was locked. I rummaged around in the desk drawers, looking for keys, but a woman like Angela Fellowes would never be that careless. Still, I've broken into several houses and quite a few filing cabinets in my time – it's one of a taxman's essential skills – and I dug the jemmy out of the suitcase and set to work.

It wasn't easy. The filing cabinet was sturdy and had two different types of lock. I struggled with it for more than ten minutes before one of the locks gave a loud crack, the other a sharp click, and the top drawer slid open. I riffled through dozens of files: bank statements, savings accounts, company records, company accounts, private accounts, business letters, contracts, old tax returns going back for ten years. *Yes*! This was how we'd nail the bitch. London would love to see these. Hare would wet himself with excitement. I bundled them into the holdall and searched through the second, third and fourth drawers, discovering dozens of share certificates, personal letters, printed emails, records of loans, mortgages, property deals. I tucked them all into the holdall to photocopy in the morning and I'd probably be able to return them within twenty-four hours. She'd never know I'd seen them. She'd be suspicious about the broken lock, of course, but there was no way she could put the finger on me.

I sat at the desk and switched her computer on. It whirred,

hummed, flickered, winked, and asked for a password. I thought about it. What sort of password would Angela Fellowes choose? The most modern computers allow you to enter the wrong password only three times before they lock themselves and deny access, but this one looked several years old and I was able doggedly to try nearly fifty possibilities, from *gasc0lgne* to *1nn0cent*, before I struck lucky and found the right one. I typed *m0thertere5a* and suddenly I was logged on. I scanned the names of the files in her documents folder but nothing obvious jumped out at me, so I opened her Google Desktop, typed *Barron* into the search box, hit the return key, and the titles of ten files cascaded down the screen. My name was everywhere. I was the ghost in her machine. I haunted her computer.

She'd named the files BACKGROUND, CONTACTS, DONALDSON, EVIDENCE, FAMILY, FINANCIAL, PHOTOS, TARGETS, THEORIES, TRAVELS. Some of the information had obviously been taken from my laptop after Billington or his chauffeur had stolen it, but there was plenty that hadn't. She knew the name of Barbara's lesbian lover, the details of our divorce settlement, the children's schools, the exams they were taking. She had copies of my bank and credit card statements, and the photographs included snaps of me with Shermelle, me with Smartly, me and Miz Quaintance. There was even a picture of my grotty block of flats in Battersea. Someone had been spying on me, possibly for months both here and in England. It had to be Billington. He'd never believed my story that I was a *Sunday Times* reporter and he'd obviously decided to have me investigated, and Suzy had told me that Fellowes and Billington had been friends.

I opened her email and there too was a folder entitled BARRON. I opened it to find several emails to and from Billington back in February as well as reports from a private detective in London. The private eye had dug deep into my life and had confirmed that I worked for HMRC, but Billington had refused to believe it and insisted in his final email, sent just before I left the island in February, that I was probably working for Interpol and was bent on arresting him for several unsolved murders. Most alarming of all he asked Fellowes whether he should have me murdered or arrested and hanged for spying.

Suddenly I was extremely nervous, even though Billington was safely dead. The old house creaked again, as if footsteps were approaching along the corridor. The roof groaned, and suddenly I was in a hurry to get out. I downloaded all her email folders onto my memory stick, switched the computer off, shut the filing cabinet, picked up the holdall, and hurried downstairs towards the front hall, eager now to escape as quickly as possible.

'Hello,' squawked the parrot. 'I'm David Barron.'

'Shut up!' I hissed.

'Thank you,' said Mother Teresa. 'That's very kind of you.'

'Shut *up*!'

'I'm sorry? Come again? Bollocks!'

In a heavy moment of silence I heard a faint sound from somewhere down in the basement. I switched the torch off. Mother Teresa and I both listened intently, the bird cocking its head in the moonlight, and we heard it again: a very faint cry, a woman in pain, maybe crying for help.

Mother Teresa scratched her ear, produced a series of clicks and whistled loudly.

I hesitated, torn between helping the woman or getting the hell out. Gallantry won. I left the holdall by the front door and moved softly towards the cry, through the darkened drawing room, the moonlight gleaming on the huge polished table in the dining room, towards the kitchen and the stairs down to the basement. The cry came again, louder: a woman moaning, pleading.

I shone the torch down the stairs into the darkness and was ambushed by a moment of shameful cowardice. I backed away from the top of the stairs. This was none of my business. This had nothing to do with me. Why should I get involved in something like this? If some woman was locked in the basement that was hardly my problem. I should turn back, go home, phone the police, give them an anonymous tip-off.

My courage was dented even more by a memory that shivered down my spine. Could the whimpering woman be the ghost of one of the slave women who had been chained and raped in the dungeon by the eighteenth century plantation owner? The hairs stood up on the back of my neck. Then she gasped and moaned, and I thought 'that's no ghost', and I knew that I could never face myself again if I ran away.

I crept down the stone stairs, following the torch beam. It was unexpectedly cold at the bottom of the stairs and I thought nervously again of ghosts. I stole along the corridor towards the dungeon and came to a heavy wooden door. Beyond it the woman was still whimpering. My heart was pounding. I was breathing heavily, afraid of what I might see. I peered through the huge old keyhole. The dungeon was lit by several tall, chunky candles on iron stands, each as fat as a wrestler's forearm. In the flickering candlelight I could see that Angela Fellowes was chained to one of the stone walls. She was naked and being ravished vigorously by Gascoigne, who was also naked. 'More!' she grunted. 'More, you big black bastard!'

I turned away in a panic and moved as fast and silently as I could back along the corridor, up the stairs to the kitchen as she shouted 'Yes! Yes! Yes!', through the dining room and across the hall.

'Fuck off!' squawked Mother Teresa.

Excellent advice. I grabbed the holdall, slipped out of the door, locked it behind me, and ran along the grass to the front gates. My heart was thundering. I was sweating profusely and gasping for breath. I could barely believe what I'd seen, yet why not? There had always been a hint of something secret and obscene about

314

Fellowes and Gascoigne. Yet who were they hurting? No one, and it's not illegal to have a taste for kinky sex. Millions do.

I drove back to Hummingbird House in a daze and sat up for several hours, until three in the morning, poring over her files, scanning them for even a hint of anything incriminating. I found nothing. She'd kept all her airline tickets for several years, proof that she'd never spent more than four or five weeks a year in the UK, well within the time limit allowed by HMRC. I found nothing suspicious in any of her letters, emails, old tax returns, bank statements or company records. For a multi-millionaire she seemed to have been amazingly honest. How had she become so rich and successful by being honest? Even her emails to Billington about me were utterly innocuous: while he had ranted about me she had tried again and again to calm him down. Yes, she'd had me investigated by a private eye, but why not? I'd behaved suspiciously and until the detective confirmed that I was a taxman she'd suspected that I might be from MI6, perhaps, or some other murky outfit. She had every right to check me out. Angela Fellowes was clean. I'd broken into an innocent woman's house, damaged her property and stolen her private papers. For that I could go to prison, maybe for years.

Soon after three I went to bed but I couldn't sleep. I tossed and turned for an hour and eventually fell into a light doze, but I was soon jolted awake by the sound of glass smashing. Someone was breaking into the house. I jumped out of bed, switched the lights on, pulled on a pair of shorts, and headed barefoot towards the noise. The intruder was reaching in through a broken window in the living room, lifting the latch, opening the window and climbing in. I switched more lights on.

'Get out!' I yelled. 'What the hell do you think you're doing? Get out or I'll call the police.'

'Oh, I don't think you will, sir,' said Gascoigne smoothly. Gascoigne?

'Gascoigne!'

I stammered.

'How dare you break into my house? What the hell do you want at this time of night? How *dare* you?'

He smiled politely. 'I have been instructed by Mistress Fellowes to retrieve the documents that you purloined from her study tonight,' he said. 'And then, Mr Barron, I intend to teach you some manners.'

# CHAPTER 20

# A MONKEY'S WEDDING

'What the hell are you talking about?' I said. 'What documents? I've stolen nothing from Angela. I haven't been anywhere near her house ever since I came for dinner months ago.'

He gave me a mocking grin. 'Dear, dear, Mr Barron,' he said. 'You have a shocking memory. You broke into Mistress Fellowes's house this evening, you smashed the lock of her filing cabinet, and you stole several dozen of her private files.'

'What the hell are you talking about? Now get out or I'll call the police.'

He chuckled. 'I don't think you will do that, Mr Barron. Should you be foolish enough to do so Mistress Fellowes would ensure that you were arrested for breaking, entering, trespass, damaging private property and burglary – an impressive catalogue of crimes that would earn you several years in prison with hard labour, and I can assure you that even a month in Columbus prison is not to be recommended.'

'This is absurd,' I blustered. 'I'm sorry if someone has stolen Angela's files but how could you possibly imagine it was me?'

He smirked. 'The parrot told us.'

'The parrot?

'Yes. Mother Teresa. That scrofulous beast.'

'Don't be ridiculous.'

He chortled. 'When Mistress Fellowes discovered that her files were missing she suspected you immediately. She has always been suspicious of your presence in Innocent and never believed that you were a journalist, and after making enquiries she discovered that you are a British tax inspector, which would explain your interest in stealing her confidential files. And her suspicion was amply confirmed tonight by the parrot, which kept squawking over and over again: "Hello. My name's David Barron. That's very kind of you. Sorry? Hello. My name's David Barron." The creature has not mentioned you for months, so why would it suddenly start repeating your name *ad nauseam*? The answer is patently obvious: it had just observed you sneaking into and out of the house.'

Shopped by a parrot! *Bloody* bird!

'That's just ridiculous,' I said with a horribly unconvincing laugh.

Gascoigne chuckled. 'But only for you, Mr Barron.'

He licked his lips and flexed his muscles. He grinned again, and I realised with alarm that he probably much enjoyed inflicting pain.

'So,' he said, 'are you going to give me Mistress Fellowes's files voluntarily or am I going to have to beat the shit out of you?'

I've always been a coward and he was lean, fit and much stronger and younger than I. What was the point of resisting? Once he'd beaten me up he'd search the house, find the holdall and files in the guest bedroom, and in any case I no longer needed them. I'd skimmed them all and there was nothing in them that was of any use to me at all, so why would I need to keep them? If Gascogine took them back it would save me the bother of having to return them surreptitiously the next day.

I shrugged. 'I was only doing my job,' I said pathetically.

'Of *course* you were, Mr Barron. Most commendable. Just doing your job, as I am.'

'They're in a holdall in the guest bedroom.'

'Get them.'

I sighed. 'Oh, all right.' It sounded sulky and peevish.

He followed me into the second bedroom and I handed him the holdall.

'These are all the files you took?' he said. 'Every one of them?'

I nodded.

'Should any be missing, Mr Barron, I shall return and you would regret it. Do you understand?'

I nodded.

'Excellent.'

He lifted the holdall and carried it towards the front door. I followed close behind, eager to see him out of the house and the door locked behind him. He put the holdall down on the floor, turned suddenly, grasped my arm, and twisted it agonisingly behind my back in a half-Nelson.

'Hey!' I yelped.

He smiled broadly. He was really enjoying himself. 'And now, Mr Barron,' he said. 'It is time to teach you some respect for other people's property. It is time to teach you some manners.'

He punched me on the nose and I heard the bone crack. Pain pierced my brain, blood spurted from my nostrils and I nearly fainted.

'That is lesson number one,' he said.

I have never endured as much pain as I did in the next minute. That's all it was, no more than a minute, but it seemed to go on for ever. I tried at first to restrain him, to fend off his blows, hold his arms, briefly to fight back, but he was far too powerful for me, and he was having so much fun that he was smiling broadly all the time. He boxed my ears, leaving one of them buzzing and the other deaf.

'That's lesson number two,' he said.

He fisted me twice in the right eye and thrice in the left.

'Lesson three,' he said.

He smacked me in the mouth, breaking two teeth, and then on

the chin, dislodging my jaw.

'Number four.'

He punched me in the ribs and kicked me in the stomach.

'Five.'

He kneed me viciously in the groin.

'Six.'

He picked up a dining chair and smashed the legs against my kneecaps and then my shins, smiling vacantly all the time.

'Seven.'

I thought I heard the shin-bone crack. Even the thought of a breaking bone makes me feel nauseous. I staggered and vomited on the mat by the front door.

He loosened his shoulders and dangled his arms. He was not even out of breath. 'Seven lessons,' he said, 'and that is just the short course. The full-length course is longer and much more effective, Mr Barron, and I would not recommend you to sign up for it. Not many of my pupils have ever graduated.'

I fainted.


I came round a couple of minutes later. He had gone. I looked at my watch: 3.35. My entire body shrieked with pain. Every bone and organ was screaming. I crawled to the telephone and dialled 911. It rang for far too long.

'OK,' said a lazy woman's voice eventually. 'You want police, fire or ambulance?'

'Ambulance,' I croaked.

'Say again?'

'Ambulance.'

'Me no hear you.'

'AMBULANCE!' I yelled.

'No need to shout,' she said.

I gave her my name and address, having to spell both slowly

more than once, and then crawled onto the sofa. The pain was indescribable. I wept, sobbed and howled.

It took more than twenty minutes for the ambulance to arrive, its siren wailing unnecessarily into the empty and deserted night from miles away. I crawled to the front door and onto the verandah, and when the ambulance came keening up the drive I passed out again.

They told me later that I drifted in and out of consciousness for nearly two days as I lay in the little Princess Diana Cottage Hospital in Columbus. At times, they said, I'd fought with the bedclothes.

I surfaced slowly into a fog of pain. Every bone, muscle and organ tormented me and my eyes were blurred. I dared not move. A fat young nurse was standing over me. 'Welcome back, darlin','' she said. 'You been gone a long time.'

I tried to speak. My jaw refused to move, my lips were numb, my tongue paralysed.

'Don't vex yourself, darlin',' she said. 'You just rest. Just sleep.'

I groaned.

'You gonna be better soon,' she said, smoothing the sheets. 'You'll see.'

She was wrong. It was four days before I could turn over in bed or sit up without flinching, even though they pumped me full of painkillers, and when eventually I saw my reflection I was horrified to see my cut, bruised and battered face. My eyes, ears and lips were monstrously swollen, my nose jagged, my body a kaleidoscope of crusty wounds and black, purple and yellow bruises. But the hospital's two doctors and four nurses were wonderfully gentle, cheerful and unexpectedly professional.

'World-class nurses are among our few exports,' said Smartly when he came to see me on the third day. 'We have a superb medical school over at Jericho and there are Innocentian nurses in hospitals all over Britain, the US and Canada. We're famous for them. They have a wonderful bedside manner.'

One of the doctors kept apologising because he had to disappear regularly to see to his own one-year-old daughter, who was ill with some gastric infection in the small children's ward. The hospital's medical equipment was hopelessly out of date, its supplies inadequate, its operations regularly threatened by sudden power cuts, but the staff managed somehow to infect their patients with affection, confidence and optimism. One day, when a pretty young nurse came to give me an ECG, dabbed blobs of jelly on my chest and limbs, and attached the leads and electrodes, I noticed that the machine was not connected to any power point. 'It's not plugged in,' I mumbled.

She laughed deliciously. 'You right!' she said happily, 'but dat no matter. De machine she don't work nohow no way!'

'So why do you pretend it does?'

She beamed. ''Cos it make de patients feel better. It give dem cunfidence. Dey t'ink dey gettin' de best treatment an' de latest technology.'

Sergeant Pomeroy turned up to question me on the third day, this time in uniform. He looked admiringly at my wounds. 'My, my!' he said with awe. 'You sure been mighty mash up, maan!' He sat on the chair beside the bed. 'Why done dis to you?'

I couldn't finger Gascoigne: if I did I'd be arrested too.

'Burglars,' I muttered.

'How many?'

I couldn't say just one: that would be too humiliating. 'Three,' I croaked.

'What dey take?'

I had trouble shaping my swollen lips to form the words. 'I don't know.' I winced. 'They wanted money. I told them I had only fifty dollars and I gave it to them, but they didn't believe me. They said I must have much more, and when I told them I didn't they started beating me up. Every time I said I didn't have any more they hit me again.'

'What dey look like?'

'Young, I think. I don't know. It was dark.'

'What dey sound like?'

Desperately I improvised. 'One had a very deep voice and one had a shrill, high-pitched voice and kept threatening to kill me. At first I thought he was a woman, but then he hit me.'

'Dey. gut weapons?'

Christ! How much longer could I lie? 'One had a gun.'

He shook his head sadly. 'De crime on dis islan' getting' worse and worse,' he said. 'De kids am runnin' riot wit' de guns an' knives an' drugs. Dey gotta do somet'in' about it. Someone gotta do somet'in' about it.'

'Isn't that what *you're* supposed to do?' I said sourly – and unfairly, since this was a crime that had never happened.

'Me?'

'The police. Aren't you meant to prevent crime and arrest criminals?'

'Nah. Us not got de 'quipment an' felicities. Me blames de parents.'

He promised half-heartedly to make enquiries and let me know if he came up with any leads or suspects but it was obvious that he thought it a hopeless task.

Smartly brought me fruit, chocolates and wine gums that afternoon and proceeded to eat most of them. He also brought the latest issue of the *Innocent Gazette*. 'I told you I'd get you onto the front page one day,' he said. The splash news story was a report of the CARICOM Prime Ministers' conference but under that a headline shrieked **FAMOUS BRIT WRITER IN BRUTAL MUGGING** beside a particularly sinister photograph of me.

'Where'd you get that dreadful photo?' I croaked.

'Your passport,' said Smartly, chewing a banana. 'I found it in your desk drawer.'

'Thieving bastard! It makes me look like a paedophile.'

'That's true: it's an excellent likeness.'

'Bastard!'

'So who attacked you?'

'Burglars. Three of them.'

'Could you identify them?'

'No. It was much too dark.'

'This is getting beyond a joke,' he said. 'The level of crime has become unacceptable. I'm going to launch a campaign to mobilize the public against the criminals. We'll start with a petition and a march through town. We can't go on like this. If this sort of violence continues to escalate some holidaymaker will be murdered one day, the tourists will stop coming, the expats will leave and the island will go bust.'

It was ironic that it had taken a crime that had never happened to inspire him to try to do something about it.

Suzy came to see me too on the third evening, smuggling in a bottle of vodka and a couple of cans of tonic. She was wearing a tiny pair of white shorts and a tight black tee-shirt with white lettering that said DON'T MESS WITH ME, BUSTER. I'd forgotten how good she could look.

'Jeez, mite, you look crook,' she said. 'Completely fucked.'

'Thanks for nothing,' I croaked.

'No, I mean... you poor old baastard. Strewth, they did you over good and proper, didn't they? You look like a Technicolor map of the Himalayas.'

'Sod off, Suzy,' I grunted.

'Come on, mite. You're not still angry with me, aare ya?'

'Too right I am.'

'In that case, you miserable old wowser, I'll cheer you up by telling you a story I heard the other day about another grumpy old baastard.'

'Do me a favour. Don't bother.'

'Come on, you miserable sod. You heard of Ethel Merman, the American singer?'

'Of course.'

'Well, she took a break from the stage when she was in her fifties, but a few years later she made a fantastic comeback in *Hello, Dolly!* that turned out to be a triumph of applause, encores, standing ovations, the works. Her boyfriend at the time was a grumpy old baastard just like you who couldn't be bothered to go and see the show, and he wasn't impressed when she got back home over the moon about her success. "They *loved* me!' she said. 'They *adored* me! I may be sixty-two but they loved everything about me! They loved my sixty-two-year-old *voice*, my sixty-two-year-old *dancing*, my sixty-two-year-old *legs*..."

'"Oh yeah?" he sneered. "An' whaddabout your sixty-two-year-old cunt?"

'"Oh, no," she said brightly. "Nobody mentioned *you*."'

I laughed. I couldn't help it. She was impossible: coarse, filthy, but *funny*. My lips cracked, my jaw ached, my throat throbbed, but I laughed.

'That's more like it,' she said. 'By the way, you know your friend Smartly: he's getting divorced. Apparently he's been shagging Ponsonby's secretary for months and his wife found out and she's chucked him out.'

'I can't believe it,' I said. 'He's just been to see me but he didn't mention it.'

'Well, he wouldn't would he? Pride.'

'I thought West Indian women didn't mind their men having girlfriends.'

'This one did. She says she's going to screw him for everything he's got.'

On the fourth day Miz Quaintance and Grandad both came to see me. She was distraught. He was wearing his soft felt hat pulled well down over his ears. 'Oh, *maan*!' she wailed, kissing my hand. 'You poor Lardship! You is all mash up! What dey done to you? What dey *done*?'

'*Rapscallions*!' fumed Grandad. 'A pox upon them! Verily, I would fain chastise such knaves anon with a sound whippin'.'

Eventually I got around to reading the paper that Smartly had left for me. There'd been another murder, a double shooting, a rape, a knife battle between two gangs of young men, and a racist incident in Cotton Beach, where a group of unemployed men had set fire to a house belonging to a family of Guyanese immigrants, yelling at them to go back to Guyana. The serpent was stirring in paradise.

On the fourth day there was a timid knock at the door. I croaked 'come in', and Shermelle poked her head hesitantly around the door.

Shermelle.

Oh, God!

Shermelle!

'Shermelle,' I croaked.

She was as lovely as ever. Oh God, she was lovely. I trembled. My heart pounded. My mouth was dry. For a moment I couldn't speak. She looked radiantly beautiful, and she was pregnant.

She looked at my battered face and wept. 'Oh, David!' she said. 'Oh, David!'

She sat on the bed, tears sliding down her cheeks, and held my hand.

'Oh, my darling man,' she said. 'My dear, dear man. Who did this to you? How could they even think of it?'

Hope leapt in my heart. She was back. She still loved me.

We sat like that for several minutes. I didn't dare to speak. I gazed at her through damp eyes, putting the pieces back together again, remembering. She stroked the back of my hand. She was mine again, after all. She had come back.

'I came as soon as Suzy told me you'd been attacked,' she said. 'But I never thought you'd be like *this*…,' and she wept again.

When I trusted my voice I asked all the obvious questions and she answered in a fragile little voice that made me want to protect her for the rest of my life.

'I was so ashamed that day at the racecourse when you saw me talking to my ex-husband,' she said. 'He told me that he'd got Aids and I was terrified that I might have got it from him and infected you. I had to drive you away, to protect you.'

'I thought he'd gone to Trinidad.'

'He was back for a week on holiday. I had an Aids test the next day but by the time I found it was negative it was too late: you'd gone back to England. Suzy told me that you were a tax inspector so I phoned every British tax office I could find but no one had heard of you. I wrote letters. Oh, God! I missed you so much, and all the time people here were horrible. They spread disgusting rumours about me and whispered behind my back, even people I thought were my friends. Tourists who come here think that Innocentians are so jolly, relaxed and friendly, and so they are – to the tourists. But they can be so cruel to each other. There's so much envy, gossip and malice. I had to get away, so I went to Barbados and found a job as a maid in one of the big hotels.'

Oh, my poor darling. A *maid*? I couldn't say anything. There was a lump in my throat.

She bit her lip, looked away and twisted her fingers. 'And then I ran into Stedroy again.'

I squeezed her hand.

She seemed to be dragging her words slowly and reluctantly from some deep well. 'We were at school together and by sheer chance I bumped into him in the hotel where I was working in Barbados. He was attending some business conference, and he couldn't believe that I was working in a lowly job like that. He was so kind to me. I was so unhappy, so lonely, and the manager of the hotel kept hitting on me, and Stedroy protected me and made me feel better. He made me laugh again, and he didn't hurry me. I began to see a lot of him and he was so patient with me…' She looked distraught, as if she were in pain. 'And so… you know… we…'

I tried to smile reassuringly. 'So he's the father?'

She looked down at her hands. They were trembling. She nodded.

'When's the baby due?'

'In four months.'

'So you're five months gone?'

She looked down and nodded again. I patted her hand.

'So there's plenty of time,' I said. 'We can get married tomorrow and I don't care where we live. We could go to England, or stay here, or one of the other islands. I don't care, so long as we're together. I love you so much, my darling.'

She looked up at me. Her eyes were haunted, her face stained. She shook her head. 'We can't,' she whispered.

I held her hand. 'Of course we can.'

'No.' She shook her head again. 'I can't leave Stedroy now. Not now.'

A chill fingered my heart.

'Why not? Do you love him? More than me?''

She shook her head. Her tears were running free now. 'He's my baby's father, and he's asked me to marry him, and I've said yes. I can't go back on that. It wouldn't be fair to him, or to you.'

'Of course it would. I love you so much and I know you love me.'

'Yes, I do. Oh God, I do. But Stedroy's a good man, a kind man, and my baby deserves to know his real father, and you shouldn't have to raise another man's son.'

'I wouldn't mind at all. I'd love him. I'd love him because he's yours.'

'No. After a while you'd resent us both.'

'Never!'

'You'd see Stedroy in him all the time. You'd hate it. You'd hate him, and eventually you'd hate me.'

'No, no. How can you say that? He'd be *my* son, *our* son. Trust me. I'd love him just as if he were my own.'

She started sobbing and shaking her head and I knew that I'd lost her. She was going to marry another man and I'd never see her again. They'd have more children and make a loving home together, and she'd forget me. For one wild moment I thought of suggesting an abortion but that would have been unforgivable. That would have been callous and selfish, and *she'd* have hated *me*.

She pulled a couple of tissues out of her handbag, blew her nose, wiped her eyes and dabbed her cheeks. She sat up straight and looked directly at me. I'd lost her. She was not coming back.

'God, I must look a terrible mess,' she said firmly. 'I must go.'

Why are women so much stronger than men? I grabbed her hand. 'Don't leave me,' I said.

She looked at me with such tenderness.

'Please, darling. Don't leave me. I couldn't bear it. Marry me.'

'I can't,' she said. 'I mustn't. That would be unfair to everyone. You'll find another girl. Of course you will: you're a lovely man.'

She stood up, bent over the bed, and kissed me on my raw, stinging lips.

'Just remember what we had,' she said. 'It was beautiful.'

She loosened my fingers and stood. 'I'll never forget you,' she said. 'I'll always love you. Always.'

She turned and walked away, out of the door and out of my life.

For days afterwards I lived like a zombie, sleep-walking through life, stunned and battered, the living dead. To find her and lose her again was the ultimate cruelty. The days were long and empty, the nights endless. I could think no further than an hour or two ahead. I made no plans. My life was over. I was forty-five but I might as well be dead.

On the day that I left the hospital, still bruised and battered but healing at last, I thanked all the nurses for their wonderful tenderness and concern, and I thanked the doctor.

'How's your little girl?' I said.

He smiled sadly. 'She died. I couldn't save her.'

Oh, God. Perhaps if he'd spent more time with her and less with me... How did I dare to feel sorry for myself?

'I'm so sorry. So very sorry.'

He smiled. 'It was God's will,' he said. 'I will see her again.'

As I waited for a taxi at the hospital entrance I spotted a large sign on the wall beside the front door. 'FAMILY PLANNING ADVICE,' it said. 'USE REAR ENTRANCE.'


I returned to Hummingbird House but the magic had gone. It had been violated, and Innocent was no longer paradise. Perhaps it had never been.

I said goodbye to the kingbird, which was sitting alone on a pillar on the edge of the pool deck. 'Where's your mate?' I said and was suddenly overcome by a moment of weakness. I said goodbye to Miz Quaintance, who insisted on packing my suitcase for me, fussed over me as if I were a cripple, cried when I left and squeezed me to her massive bosom so tightly that I was nearly asphyxiated. I said goodbye to Grandad, who gave me his Boy Scout salute. I shook his rough old hand and he said in a wavering voice: 'Godspeed, good sir, and thank thee for thy loveship.'

On the way to the airport I stopped at Smartly's office. He

looked unusually harassed, and more reporters than usual seemed to be working in a frenzy.

'You're very busy,' I said.

'Yes, frantically.'

'Then I'll just say goodbye.'

'They've just arrested Malenkov and Litvinova.'

'The police?'

'The CIA.'

'*What*?'

'They discovered that the Malenkovs came here to recruit and train a few young Muslim suicide bombers and to start a campaign of terror on several Caribbean islands, and they were going to start with a huge explosion at the CARICOM conference that could have killed all the West Indian Prime Ministers.'

'Christ!'

'Exactly. That's why they're here: they hate Christians. They're both fanatical, radical Muslims.'

'*What*?'

'The Malenkovs aren't Russian at all: they're Kazakhstanis, and they're Muslims.'

'*Muslims*? But they're white!'

Smartly shrugged. 'Clever, eh? Who would ever suspect a white couple of being Muslim terrorists? But there are millions of white Muslims in Bosnia, Croatia, all the old Central Asian ex-Soviet republics like Chechnya, Azerbaijan, Turkmenistan, Kyrgyzstan, Uzbekistan. And where better for Islamic terrorists to slaughter Christians than here in the islands of the Caribbean, where Christianity is rooted deeper than anywhere except the Vatican? This is their *jihad*. This is their crusade.'

So that was why they wouldn't drink alcohol at Angela Fellowes's dinner party all those months ago: they were Muslims.

'A couple of suicide bombers at the CARICOM conference would not only have killed a dozen West Indian Prime Ministers and scores of officials and onlookers, the terrorists would also have exploded bombs on other islands and a widespread terror campaign would destroy every Caribbean economy, every one of which depends almost entirely on tourism. Thousands of tourists would cancel their bookings, none would return for several years, and the Caribbean would quickly collapse into a ghetto of hungry, hopeless, murderous, crime-ridden, poverty-stricken Fourth World slums. What a triumph for Islam over the infidels!'

'Dear God!' I said. I was stunned. It all made perfect sense. 'How did the CIA catch up with them?'

Smartly shook his head. 'Washington Dempster and Don Rogers,' he said.

My brain clouded. I couldn't think straight.

Dempster? *Rogers*?

'Dempster's CIA,' said Smartly, 'and Rogers is MI6.'

My brain refused to function. It felt like cottonwool.

'They've both been watching Malenkov and Litvinova independently for several months until they each began to suspect that the other was also a western agent, and they joined forces. They knew that the Malenkovs must be up to something dodgy, and they knew that they were flying their plane secretly from the racecourse at night to land at remote airstrips on other islands and contact their suicide cells. At first they suspected them of drug smuggling but when Malenkov went missing, allegedly on the mountain, Dempster alerted the CIA that maybe he'd gone off-island secretly and was up to no good, and the CIA discovered airline records showing that he'd flown to Miami, then Moscow, then Turkmenistan, where one of their agents found him a couple of days later trying to buy a small nuclear bomb.'

'Fucking hell!'

'Apparently there are still a few old Soviet nuclear bombs tucked away secretly in some of the ex-Soviet republics and enough disgruntled, hard-up Soviet scientists to make them work.

Malenkov was planning to fly over Mount Innocent, drop the bomb into the volcano, blow the island sky high, and set off massive volcanic eruptions along the chain of volcanic Caribbean islands, many of which are connected by deep underground tunnels of boiling lava. The eruptions would cause huge earthquakes and tsunamis and reduce the West Indies to rubble, but thank God Malenkov found it more difficult to buy a bomb than he'd expected.'

I stared in silence at Smartly for a minute or two like a zombie, my mind a sieve, unable to take it all in, unable to think or speak, but eventually I pulled myself together.

'*Dempster*!' I said. '*CIA*! Bloody hell! I always thought he was a complete arsehole.'

'Didn't we all?'

'And *Rogers*!'

Smartly nodded. 'Yes, and listen to this: Baby Dempster is CIA too.'

'Never!'

'They say she's a brilliant linguist, speaks Russian fluently. In fact she's not his wife at all: they're just CIA colleagues working together. Nice touch: who would expect a bumbling married couple of being secret agents?'

I was stunned. 'Baby Dempster is a CIA *agent*?'

Smartly shrugged. 'So they say. And this'll amuse you: Tracy Rogers is not just a gormless trophy wife; she's an accomplished actress who specialises in playing drunks. She gives Rogers camouflage to work for MI6 without arousing suspicion: people assume that they're just a pair of drunken yobs, which makes everyone underrate him.'

Including me. My brain went into neutral.

'By the way,' said Smartly, 'remember all those silent phone calls you were getting back in February? The red jeep that kept shadowing you? The broken locks? The gunshots at night? The monkey crucified on your front door? That was Malenkov.'

'Come again?'

'Malenkov. He reckoned you were so obviously not a journalist and became convinced that you were a British or Interpol agent intent on arresting him, so he tried to frighten you away. Oh yes, and you remember Rupert Williams, the guy who runs the Judas Iscariot fan club?'

'Jesus! Don't tell me he's from Mossad.'

Smartly chuckled. 'Hey, that would be fun, wouldn't it? No such luck. He's suddenly disappeared and the police are searching for him. He's probably done a runner off the island. Baby Dempster discovered that he's been smuggling drugs. All those bibles and prayer books that he sent out by post were hollowed out and packed with cocaine.'

Dear God! And I'd thought he was just a cheeky conman with a taste for underage black totty.

Smartly looked at his watch. 'I'd better get back to work,' he said, 'there's a hell of a lot to do and we go to press tomorrow. You wouldn't care to lend a hand, would you? Write a leader for me?'

'I'm sorry,' I said. 'I've got a plane to catch.'

He shrugged. 'Sure. Of course.' He shook my hand. 'It's been good knowing you, Dave.'

'You too.'

'Come back one day, and don't forget: you still owe me that article you promised to write. About being an undercover taxman investigating British expats in Innocent would do nicely.'

I found Suzy at her beach bar and told her about Malenkov and Litvinova. She was stunned into silence for several seconds. Then 'Jesus wept!' she said. 'Shit a brick! What *baastards*! So they were going to blow us all up, were they? What *fucking* baastards! I hope they lock them up for a hundred years. Hang them. No, hanging would be too good for them. Lock them up for ever. Christ, I hope they suffer.'

When she'd calmed down I told her that I was flying back to London.

'Bloody hell, mite!' she said. 'You a sucker for punishment? You must be mad. How can you bear to live in that climate? Why not stay here? You love it here.'

'I did, but not any more. Not now.'

'Too many memories.'

'Yes.'

'Shermelle.'

'Yes.'

'You'll forget her one day.'

'Never.'

She hesitated. Suddenly she looked shy and unsure of herself. I'd never seen her looking shy or uncertain. 'I'd look aafter you, Dave,' she said awkwardly. 'I'm very fond of you, you know. Christ knows why, but we'd be good together. I know it. We could have a great life.'

I looked at her sadly. I'd never really understood the depth of her loneliness and vulnerability. It would have been easy to say 'yes... maybe... let's see how it goes.' She was good looking, sexy, and fun. For all her Australian vulgarity she was honest and she made me laugh. But she wasn't Shermelle.

'That's very sweet of you, Suzy, and I'm very fond of you too. But it wouldn't work.'

'You'd be thinking of her all the time.'

'Yes.'

'That'd wear off. Eventually.'

'I don't think so.'

She looked at me sadly. 'What a lucky girl she is, to have had a man who loves her so much.'

I kissed her goodbye, a proper kiss on the lips, not a peck on the cheek, and I drove to the airport just as the sun was going down.

Along the coast more palm trees than ever were dying of the Lethal Yellow Disease. It was so sad to see: dozens of them were bald, leaving only stark, dead trunks pointing accusingly at the sky like corpses' fingers. On an impulse I stopped for a final walk along the beach. The sun was flirting with the horizon and in the final second before it sank beneath the sea I saw it clearly for the first time: the Green Flash; a brilliantly verdant stab of light along the horizon. So it did exist, after all, even though I'd refused to believe in it. Like God. I still didn't believe in God but I'd come to believe in the Devil.

I checked in at the airport and picked up the latest issue of a government free sheet called the *Innocent Informer*. The lead story reported that the Sunshine Resort had at last been granted permission to open a casino and construct two hundred luxurious houses along Casuarina Beach, and by coincidence Shefton Molloy, the Deputy Prime Minister, had decided to build himself an $8million, eight-bedroom mansion high on a hill with a huge infinity pool and a stunning view across the Caribbean.

When the incoming flight from Barbados landed a crowd of officials besieged the hall outside the VIP lounge to welcome some important passenger. He strode through the doors onto the concourse: a handsome, light-skinned, well-built, middle-aged man, upright, confident and charismatic, exquisitely dressed in an expensive Savile Row suit, MCC tie, diamond tie-pin and gleaming shoes. I was sure I'd seen him somewhere before.

'Who's that?' I asked one of the porters.

'Dat am de Prime Minister,' he said, 'de Hon'able Eustace Q. Ponsonby.'

I laughed sourly. Of course. Who else?

As I sat in the departure lounge, waiting for my flight to be called, the sound of a lazy, lilting guitar caressed the loudspeakers, James Blunt singing his gentle, melancholy lament to lost love, *Carry You Home*.

When we landed at Gatwick the next morning it was raining as usual, but a weak sun was glinting through the drizzle.

# THE END

# ACKNOWLEDGEMENTS

After thirteen years of living in the Caribbean, and eight years of research for this book, I have learned a great deal about those wonderful islands from extensive travel to most of them and from dozens of local people, but for special help I am particularly indebted to Alastair Yearwood and the late Major Nigel Frazer, both of whom gave me long, fascinating interviews about the history, customs, beliefs, superstitions, folklore, characters and everyday life of the West Indies.

I must thank Brian Dyde, author of *Caribbean Companion* (Macmillan, 1992), which taught me a huge amount about West Indian flora and fauna, and I am also extremely grateful to Father George Agger, Pam Barry, Vince Hubbard, Nikka von Liemandt-Ketlerov, Sheila Williams, and Mavis Yearwood, all of whom told me wonderful tales of the Caribbean, both old and new. My old Rhodesian school friend Kit Cumings, who now lives in Australia, enlightened me often about the weird and wonderful ways of Australian slang and humour. And as always I must thank Juliet Lewis for putting up with me for twenty-three years and for designing and painting the cover of this book.

None of the characters in this novel bears any resemblance to any of them, of course, nor to any other living person, though the dead have crept in here and there, grinning like jumbies.

# REVIEWS OF GRAHAM LORD'S LAST TWO NOVELS

## *SORRY, WE'RE GOING TO HAVE TO LET YOU GO*

* This marvellous satirical tale of our materialistic times. In Jason Skudder... Lord has produced a magnificent villain... and Peter's mother-in-law, Monica, always ready with a cheering dirty limerick, is a glorious creation – *Sunday Times*

* A brilliantly cynical look at modern corporate Britain. I enjoyed it thoroughly – *Manchester Evening News*

* This satire on office life [is] very funny – *Mail on Sunday*

* Hilarious and exceptional black comedy – *Amazon.co.uk*

## *A PARTY TO DIE FOR*

* Lord produces some splendid characters to slither across his story... The cyberspeak is wonderful... In many ways a black book, it damns late 20th-century mores to face the wrath of the gods – *Richard Stott, The Times*

* Laugh? I burst the buttons off my bodystocking. Graham Lord's rollicking swipe at the lunatic preoccupations of the late twentieth century is a work of wild and dazzling satire... the novel is a riot – *Val Hennessy, Literary Review*

* A vicious satire of media life... the most cynical, scabrous and entirely accurate account of life among shiny sheets that I have ever encountered – *David Thomas, Mail on Sunday*

* Lord's engaging wit results in a terrific media farce – *Daily Mail*

# BOOKS BY POTBAKE PRODUCTIONS

*90 Days of Violence* by Lyndon Baptiste. When 1 tonne of cocaine goes missing, Trinidad and Tobago is thrown into a state of disarray. A string of bombings and kidnapping sprees occur, and Prime Minister Ambrose Taylor and his team must plan and respond to the security threats through conventional and unconventional means. The race is on for the drugs and not only the government, the Syrians, East Indians and Africans find themselves involved, but also members of the Irish Republican Army. **US $9.99**

*oOH My Testicles!: A tale of entanglement* by Lyndon Baptiste. A true funny story of one man's journey through private and public healthcare in Trinidad and Tobago. **US $9.99**

*Across The Caribbean.* In 2009 Potbake Productions hosted a short story competition for aspiring Caribbean writers which resulted in sixteen finalists. Read stories from authors living in Barbados, Trinidad and other islands. The winning story, *The Only Man*, was written by Raymond Yusuf of Guyana. Today, you too can become a judge, for this book, perhaps the first of its kind, is an eclectic snapshot of Caribbean literature. **US $14.99**

*Boy Days: Short stories about Trini Men* by Lyndon Baptiste. This collection, unique to contemporary Trinidad and Tobago, shows Lyndon Baptiste equally adept at the short story as with the novel. Stories range from the love song of *Samo and his dulahins* to a ghetto youth in *Simon and The Babylon* to the acid vision of arranged marriages reflected in *Her Bitter Life*. **US $14.99**